Oak and Stone

OAK
AND
STONE

DAVE DUGGAN

Merdog Books

Merdog Books
The Exchange, Castle Avenue, Buncrana, Co. Donegal, Ireland
Web: merdogbooks.com
Email: info@merdogbooks.com

First Published 2019

2 4 6 8 10 9 7 5 3 1

ISBN 978-1-9165016-1-4

Set in 11/14pt Baskerville
Typeset in Ireland by Merdog Books
Printed and bound in Great Britain by Clays Ltd, Elcograf S.p.A

For Diane

ONE

'You know the story, Slevin. You have the skills. A bullet in the back of the head? You have relevant experience. Contacts from the old days. Ask around,' he said.

I had a sense, from the moment my boss told me to review the Todd Anderson murder, that it would take me into corners of my life I had been trying to avoid.

In this game, finding the questions is easy. You just make a list. Who is he? Why is he wearing a club scarf? How many people are involved? Why dump him on the penalty spot, at the country end of the pitch? No shortage of questions. The questions are fine. It's easy to find the questions. Finding the right people to ask is the hard part. I went back to the start. To Denis Green, the Club Chairman. I asked him why their star centre forward was found lying face down on the penalty spot, at the country end goal, with a bullet through his head, so that the penalty spot glowed red and the body lay sprawled as in some last ditch appeal to the referee.

'He was a good kid. Two great feet. Fearless. Easy to deal with. I thought we'd get another season out of him – at least – before some of the big boys came looking for him. That won't happen now,' Denis Green said.

We were in his accountant's office. Traffic hummed up and down outside, on Clarendon Street. There were strips of blue sky visible through his window blinds. Bars of light lay across the files and papers strewn across the glass and steel desk Green was anchored behind. A telly, on mute, showed football in the corner. The World Cup was underway.

'You think Belgium will beat them?' I asked.

'Naw. They got a jammy goal just before half time, but I think the Senegalese will claw them back. Did you ever figure out what those marks were on his neck?' Denis asked.

I was surprised he knew about them. A curious set of faint weals and bruises in a regular pattern that were only fully visible when you lifted the club scarf clear of the victim's neck. They baffled the first responders. Crime scene officers made notes and took photos. It didn't take Karen Lavery long to identify them, when she got the body back to her lab. She phoned me straight away.

'You still got money on North Korea?'

'I fancy them, yeh. I think they'll at least make the semi-finals.'

'Detectives must be on a fair whack these days if you can afford to throw money away like that. It's got to be the Germans.'

'That's just the scientist in you. What have you got?'

'Dreamtime.'

'Yeh?'

'Just released. "Revolutionary new stud system and lay-out". Titanium mixed into a polymer of some kind. Strength and flexibility. Only available on the Dreamtime boot.'

'Somebody stood on his neck.'

'Somebody wearing a Dreamtime boot.'

'And then they shot him?'

'No, he was shot before that. Maybe even somewhere else. And then brought to the pitch.'

'Why do that?'

'Well, it was a penalty. Anyway, you're the wealthy detective. All you have to do now is find a killer that fits the Dreamtime boot. You get to play Prince Charming.'

'Bet you a fiver Germany don't make the last four.'

'You're on. The full report will take a couple of days.'

Denis Green knew about the marks on the victim's neck.

'They're still working on them. I haven't seen the report yet,' I told him.

I wondered if Denis had a sneak preview. Did he know Karen Lavery, our forensics officer? Were they related?

'There's still no clue, no hints. You haven't heard anything around the club?'

'Not a sausage.'

He glanced at the telly.

'Senegal are going for the win. No one saw anything. No one heard anything. Nobody was there. The ground staff were inside drinking tea and watching the opening ceremony.'

Denis Green thinks everybody is as crazy about football as he is.

'Todd Anderson was liked. Admired, even. Some people may have been jealous of him, his looks and his talent, but nothing heavy. Nobody has a clue, and I mean nobody has a clue, why someone would put a bullet in his head.'

Todd Anderson. 1.85 metres, 85 kilos. Blond hair, kept short. Clean shaven. Bit his nails, but not badly. Large scar down his left shin where an overly enthusiastic centre-half had tried to cripple him. All of this in Karen Lavery's preliminary notes, sent by email. But he came back from that. Wore the splints. Did the exercises. And this season, he was back to his best. Some people said he was better than ever. Hungrier.

I thanked Denis and said I'd be in touch if anything developed.

'When will his body be released to his family?'

'Couple of days now. Forensics are almost sorted. Autopsy nearly done.'

I assured him we would do all in our power to find the killer. He nodded and chanced a smile.

'And while you're at it, see if you can find us another centre forward.'

A crowd bellowed mutely on the telly. A Senegalese player lay spread-eagled in the box. Two Belgians stood over him, waving their hands about. The referee pointed to the penalty spot.

'The beginning of the end for little Belgium,' said Denis.

We watched the penalty. The timid round of protests from the Belgians ended in the Senegalese centre-forward getting up, righting his stockings and shin pads, then dusting down his shorts before lashing the ball low to the keeper's right. Goal.

I left his office with questions about Denis Green's inside track on the investigation, but no real information on the killing of Todd Anderson and what anyone might have seen.

I went straight back to the office from Denis Green's. The detective building is in a new annexe to the old barracks on Strand Road. The two buildings sit side by side like grumpy relatives. The old one huffs, as it remembers the recent conflict and prides itself on the wounds it bears. The new one preens itself in the sun, glinting high windows and open spaces at all and sundry, proclaiming 'let's hear it, one more time, here's me, the new face of policing'. Neither building fools anybody. Sure, big moves have been made. Sure, another revised service is in place and the politicians have signed up to it. Again. But, no matter how you bill it, it's what it always was. The Cops.

And then there's me. I'm in a room at the bottom of a long corridor covered in a layer of fawn, hessian carpet that claws at your feet as you walk over it. Just off that room, there's a shared facilities space with office equipment and a pool of clerks. I went there and took a cup of water from the dispenser. I glanced across at the TVs on the wall. 24 hour news channel, national and international, and the football. The score came up. Senegal 3 Belgium 1. Game over.

My desk is often cluttered and I don't usually care. The undertow of paperwork is a stream I can float through resolutely. But today, the sight of unfinished reports, a stack of claim forms, a clump of crime figure analysis data and two Styrofoam cups of cold coffee weakened me briefly. The paperless office missed policing too.

I sat down and pulled the unfinished reports to me. Three more in hand. The new regime meant even more paperwork. Everyone was watching his or her back. And everyone was watching new intake, like me. I was fast-tracked. I had degrees from prison, where I was a 'political'. I got out just as all the politicos were signing up to the current new deal for policing. I felt that I should give it a go. I did the training and became a detective in a flash. Picture in the paper. The new face of policing. A new dawn in a post-conflict society. The tide of change surged on, with some pushing and some pulling. Some days it was hard being a trailblazer.

I picked up the two Styrofoam cups and took them to the corner where I sluiced them down the sink, dumped the cups in the bin and prepared to take a fresh cup, when Hammy shouted at me.

'How's the crime buster today, then?'

Omar Hamilton – Hammy to the world of policing – was my boss. A lapsed Muslim Presbyterian, there wasn't a fundamentalist bone in his body. He told me that his father had fallen madly in love with his mother and had married the street trader's daughter, against the fervent wishes of his family. He got 'Omar' from her side of the house. But he was Hamilton through and through. And Hammy to all of us. Some wag said his skin colour was just a darker shade of orange. But he was always straight with me.

'I'm wondering if we'll ever catch the killer who murdered this coffee machine,' I said.

'Form's good anyway. Anything on the footballer then?'

'I interviewed Denis Green again. Like you told me.'

'An obvious and good place to start. And you remain compliant. Good. I asked Forensics to e-mail their report to you too. Hard copy coming up later. Are you having a coffee or are you just communing with the dead?'

We both looked at the machine and decided against it.

I went back to my desk and booted up my laptop. While it was humming and chirruping to itself, I checked my voice mail. Karen had phoned from Crime Scene Forensics, confirming Hammy's news and adding that Bechtimme, the German striker, had come through a fitness test and was expected to feature in all their up-coming games. I went to the next message. It was a male voice I didn't recognise.

'This message is for Detective Slevin. If you want to talk about Todd Anderson and I don't mean just about his heading prowess, which is nil at present, then I'll be in Fiorentini's at two o'clock.'

I was never good at responding to orders. My psychological profile in the Police Training College had that underlined in red. 'Sometimes has a problem with authority'. But Hammy had me reviewing the Anderson case and if I wanted a decent cup of coffee Fiorentini's was a better bet than the encrusted machine in the corner.

I walked into the café at ten minutes past two. Allowing for the local habit of reading timed appointments fairly liberally, I was on time. Gino Fiorentini was behind the counter, polishing the inside of one of the ice-cream drums.

'Belgium pulled one back, but Senegal held on,' he said.

'I fancy them to go all the way.'

Gino didn't even bother to answer that. His money was on the Azurri and it didn't matter that the Italians weren't half the team they used to be, as far as Gino was concerned, they were the only team in it.

'There's a fella over there was asking for you.'

'Which fella?'

I followed Gino's nod to where a man sat on his own, behind a newspaper. A group of students from the nearby Technical College gathered their bags and swarmed out of their seats and, in the hustle, the man lowered his paper and shuffled in his seat to let people pass, so I got a look at him.

'You know who he is, Gino? 'Cos I don't.'

'Heh, who's the detective here? You find out.'

'Right. I'll have a cappuccino and a gravy ring.'

'I'm delighted to see you've knocked the diet on the head. I'll bring it over.'

I left the counter and walked towards the man. I sat at a table just vacated by students and looked at the back page of the newspaper. A young girl cleared and wiped the table and when she left I said,

'Should be no bother to France. They'll hammer England.'

The man kept the paper in front of his face but said,

'Don't bet on it. Larton's back and he's on fire.'

He was English. The sentiment and the accent concurred with what I picked up on the voice-mail. He lowered the paper, which confirmed my judgement. The *Daily Telegraph*.

'I hope you're a better detective than you are a football pundit, Slevin.'

I smiled and waited. He waited too, but I had the advantage of twelve years of prison time behind me – I am used to waiting – and he gave up first. He folded the newspaper and crossed to a seat opposite me. At just that moment, Gino brought my cappuccino and gravy ring and stood beside us. No one spoke. I looked at Gino and, then, in my most polite tones, I said,

'Thanks for the personal service, Gino. I'm delighted you took the time.'

7

Gino grinned at me and I felt I owed him something so I said to the man,

'You want anything Mr … er …'

He just shook his head and I turned to Gino saying,

'Thanks, Gino. I'll square up on the way out.'

Gino grinned once more and left.

The man re-folded his *Daily Telegraph* and pressed the edges firmly together as he placed it in front of him. Then he reached behind him and lifted his half-filled cup of tea, taking a sip on the way. Finally, he put his hand inside his overcoat, unseasonably encumbering him on that fine June day, and pulled out a business card. He was setting out his terms for the meeting. When he pushed the card towards me, I took a hearty glug of my cappuccino, one I knew would leave a foamy moustache across my upper lip. I followed that with a mouthful of sticky, doughy gravy ring, the local doughnut. The foam moustache and the sprinkle of sugar down my front, topped off by my studiously empty eyes, completed my opening gambit.

'I understand you're working on the Anderson murder,' he began.

I chewed on.

'I have an interest in the case. A professional one. I could help. With background, at the very least,' he continued.

I placed him in Manchester or somewhere in the north-west of England. Not Liverpool. Not enough Mersey sea shanty in his accent. It was industrially dry, blowing like a great ventilating fan down a long shaft, almost whispering by the end of each sentence. I took another draft of my cappuccino, relishing the bitter warmth of it.

'A man murdered, is it? Henderson?'

'For God's sake, Slevin, give over the thick Paddy routine. Anderson. Todd Anderson. Footballer. Dead meat. Bullet in the back of the head.'

'If you have any suspicions or any information on a crime you think has been committed, the police would be keen to have it. You know the Confidential Help-line and all that?'

'You're the Help-Line, Slevin. For what it's worth, you're the police.'

'So. And how might I help you Mr … Dalzell. William. Discretion guaranteed.'

I read his business card upside down.

'You've been told to go over the file again. I know the case is less than a week old, but the good old higher-ups have put you on it. Special talents. They want this one turned around quickly. So do I. 'Course I do. So's I can get back home.'

'Manchester, is it? I was never in it. They say it's a cracker place. Like London, only wetter. Or is that Liverpool? Any roads, you're across the Irish Sea and a good way off home ground. Even with the guarantee of your discretion, I'm not sure how I can help you.'

'We can ….'

'Hold on, Mr. Dalzell. A call of nature.'

I got up and walked to the end of the café, winking at Francesca, behind the till. She joined me at the top of the steps leading to the fish and chips area, out of sight of Dalzell. I handed her my phone and continued to the toilet, mouthing and gesturing, 'Photos. Him.'

Inside, I checked myself in the mirror. The sugar speckling was more widespread than I'd intended. The foam moustache had faded. I licked the final grey spume from the corners of my mouth. Then I did some practice grimacing, finishing with a final grin above a puffed-out chest.

'Jeepers, Slevin. You're a terror. You'll have to grow up.'

I had a slash, almost as an afterthought, shook the venerable member dry and mused that, apart from this, he'd not seen front-line action recently, tidied myself up and moved to the sink. The cold tap gave a gentle squeak as it turned, though that was drowned out by the laughter from a group of young voices in the café, loud enough to compete with the wind-rush from the hand-dryer.

I didn't need to but I arrived back at my table rubbing my palms down the sides of my suede jacket. A junior staff member sashayed past me with a tray laden with dishes and delft. Dalzells' leftovers: a bowl of tomato soup; an abandoned crust of toast. A frugal man, careful with his expenses.

I sat in front of him again and picked up my cappuccino.

'Good man for not letting the young wan away with me lunch. You sure you don't want anything else? A wee ice-cream? Might be the one good day we get this summer.'

He looked at me as if my face had turned inside out. His eyes sank deeper into his skull as the creases on his forehead lined up more tightly and jostled one above another to see which could be the most prominent.

'I was a cop for over twenty years and I met some clowns in my day. Both inside and outside the force, but Slevin, boyo, you're the tops.'

'You were a policeman? Handy aul' pension now, is it? Bit of an interest, coming over here? Or a holiday, maybe?'

Then I leaned towards him, letting him have a close look at the spittled edges of my sugar-dusted lips.

'Or is it prising money out of a mother's despairing hands you are, leadin' her on with your promise of complete discretion in the search for her son's killer, no matter what it takes. A fella Henderson, you said?'

I have to admire the way he kept his cool and simply stood up. I noted he was taller than I expected, with shoulders broad enough to block a door-way. He pulled his overcoat about him and ran his hand through his hair. He had plenty of it, in firm, russet waves, as regular as a barley field in an autumn breeze.

'Well, I tried. Can't say fairer than that. Here, I'll leave you the paper. You can finish your coffee and your … lunch.'

'The *Daily Telegraph*? A bit too rich for me.'

'I thought you'd be smarter, Slevin. And I don't mean the Thick Paddy Minstrel show. I thought you'd know more, given who you are and what you did. You above all people should know that you need to know what your enemy is thinking.'

He tapped the paper, pushed his chair out of his way and walked round the table, straight out the door and onto the Strand Road, where he turned right. When he was past the window, I gulped the last of the coffee, bolted the three steps to the back of the café, met Francesca at the end of the chip fryer counter, took the phone and business card she passed to me and exited onto Clarendon Street, via the back lane, just in time to see Dalzell climb into a taxi on the far side of the traffic lights. I stepped against the side of the building as the taxi came through the lights towards me, then sped up the steep climb of Clarendon Street, before catching a green light at the top, and briskly turning left to head in the direction of Bogside, Brandywell, Creggan, Rosemount. I couldn't even guess. I got the registration number and the company phone number. I didn't recognise them.

I looked at the business card. Standard size and shape, printed in the hundreds from a 'free' website. A fine purple border. A seated skeleton, in the top right corner. His name – William Dalzell – in a block font. Landline and mobile phone numbers. An email address w.dalzell@dalzellfinder.com, a Twitter handle @dalzellfinder, and a web address dalzellfinder.com.

He was fully covered and, for a retired cop, perfectly up to date. I took a small evidence bag from my pocket and slid the business card inside. Then I scanned the photos on my phone.

Francesca had done me proud. There were small groups

of young staff members in twos and threes, laughing and clutching at each other. There was a fuzzy selfie, with Gino, looking paternally bemused, unconsciously photo-bombing in the near background. Then there was Dalzell, set back, in two shots. One captured his left flank and the side of his head, turned away from the camera, his right hand brushing his hair over his ear. The other, a group of three, taken at a better angle from the ice-cream counter, included the young girl who cleared our table, holding a tray before her like a votive offering. She was standing beside Dalzell. Another young staff member leaned into the picture holding two fingers above the tray holder's head, rabbit-ears' wise. The third member of the group was Dalzell, looking full-on into the lens, arms folded across his chest, eyes almost fully receded into their sockets. Only if you looked very closely could you make out his right hand resting on his left forearm, fingers closed in a soft fist, but with the middle finger pointing singularly upwards in the universal 'fuck you' gesture.

I closed the phone and turned my face to the sun. I had an executed footballer; a football club chairman, cold as a ledger; a nosey parker and a taxi driver. I'd have to tell my boss that, if there was a story, it wasn't one I knew.

Thoughts of the river came into my mind, as my skin heated up. I returned to the café to pay my bill and to get an ice-cream cone to take away.

TWO

When I returned to the office, after enjoying my ice-cream on the river walk, I met a cascade of my colleagues running down the corridor in the opposite direction. Only the section administrator, Sharon, whose many gold-medals in kick-boxing belie her permanent damsel-in-distress pout, ignored the rush.

'Boys in heat, Slevin,' she said, as I passed her desk. 'Boys in heat.'

I stood against the wall to let the flow subside. I was still digesting my encounter with Dalzell and the gravy ring lunch, so I burped loudly as Hammy, my boss, bowled towards me, shuffling expertly into his branded PS(N) jacket.

'Don't vomit on the new carpet, Slevin. You're with me. Hetherington's driving. Safari-time!'

The name 'Hetherington' didn't register with me until the section's newest intake trotted towards me. He wore the same jacket as Hammy, but had managed only to get one arm through a sleeve. Still on the run, he lunged his left arm repeatedly in the direction of the other sleeve, which flopped derisively beside him.

I stuck an arm across his chest and stopped him, then, grabbing the errant sleeve, I stuffed his arm in. Hetherington caught his breath and said,

'Thanks, Slevin. She's in St. Columb's Park. They caught her.'

I had no chance to ask who they'd caught. Sharon was on the phone, so I couldn't ask her. I looked down the corridor. It was empty. All the detective desks in the office were vacant. For a brief moment I wondered if I should get my PS(N) jacket, but decided against it and turned to follow Hetherington, now taking the exit stairs in loud bounds.

The latest changes to policing had deepened the awkward re-alignment of the services on the island. That required a major re-branding. We are now Police Service (North), PS(N). Our colleagues are Police Service (South), PS(S). They still use their old name, *An Garda Síochána*. We don't use any of our historical names. We even got new ranks. We are ceaselessly struggling to be new.

As part of the re-branding, detectives were issued with jackets, bearing the new letters and logo: PS(N) in old gold on the dark green micro-lite water-proof fabric, over an intertwined garland of crowns, shamrocks, harps, laurels, sceptres and something that looks like a sausage but that we were assured was a scroll. The law, it seems. Our colleagues were issued with the same jackets, but with PS(S) over the garland. Sharon said we look like cops out of old NYPD web-flick re-runs she watches with her granddad when it's her turn to handle his evening feed.

I tend to do without the PS(N) jacket, favouring my light suede sports coat at this time of year. Hammy says I look like I wandered in from the Technical College next door, after abandoning a class of social science students, panting to hear my every word. He throws the education bone at me every now and then. One of the arrows in his personnel management armoury.

One day, during a major case review, he fired a proper salvo.

'What exactly are you doing here, Slevin? You and your doctorate and all. Do you want us to call you 'doctor'? Some of us didn't want you or your mates. They didn't take to the latest convulsion. Mind you, it's not the first, even since I strapped on the tools. If you'd told me twenty years ago that boys like you would be in the police, I'd have laughed. But then, the peace process rolled into town and, convulsion by convulsion, we arrived at the point where the Chief Constable put a shoulder to the heavy door to get you and the other desperadoes in. You should be up at that university there, Slevin, with all your academic mates, drinking *lattés* and talking tosh. But they wouldn't have you. Oh, no, not a twelve year man, still smelling of cordite and fertiliser, maybe even a whiff of old-timey Semtex, no matter how many showers and scrubbings you had in Maghaberry. So you're here in the shite, with us, the rough boys. Ah, well. Silk purse outta pig's ears and all that. Never forget, Slevin. We love you. Really.'

This was Hammy's version of an 'arm-around-the-shoulder' to make a junior colleague feel welcome and fully part of the team.

'What was the auld doctorate in again, Slevin? Wasn't policing or criminology, I can tell you that, something that might be useful here. None of that good stuff. Oh, I never read it meself, but I hear the thesis is a wow. Got published in a book and all. Maybe even sold a few dozen copies.'

A couple of hundred. I never corrected him. This was early in my days among the detectives. Hammy was standing in his beloved incident corner. Sharon said he wanted a full room adjoining his office but Finance vetoed that when the new wing was being built, so he corralled off a section of the main conference room using a jumble of partitions, suspended spotlights, two touch-screen consoles and an array of white boards and plexi-glass displays to give us focus for our primary investigations. And an auditorium for himself.

'What was it again, Slevin?'

When I didn't answer, he pushed. 'Go on. Remind us.'

I had an A5 spiral notebook on my lap, open on a page criss-crossed with jottings rather than sentences.

'I'm sorry, sir,' I said. 'Did you say the latest victim was a member of the Travelling Community?'

'Ah,' said Hammy. 'Listen to that educated man now. The good old *bon mot*. "A member of the travelling community." Not, as many among you would say: a knacker, a gypo, a tinker, a stoke. You'll do well here, Slevin. They'll like you' - he used his right index finger to point to the ceiling, indicating upstairs - 'a man with your background and education. Chief material, there. Chief material.'

That brought a gruff laugh from colleagues around me and Hammy, ever sensitive to the mood in the room, gauged it was an opportune time to drive us back into the work.

That was my first case. And when I solved it, two old men, flanked by sons, nephews and grandsons, came into the police headquarters car-park in a small fleet of vans. Seven of them came up the stairs, with the two uniforms from the front desk chittering after them: 'Do you have an appointment? Please wait here ... you can't ...'

Sharon, ever alert, showed them into the main conference room and offered tea and coffee, which they politely declined. Then she brought me and Hammy in. The two old men shook my hand and, nodding like praying monks, patted me on the shoulder. Hammy stood off to the one side, awkward and beaming.

A younger man, with hair as black as ebony and boy-band good looks, stepped forward.

'Me family want to thank ye for what ye done for our Martin. Ye didn't bring him back. No one can. But onny for ye, the man who dunnit'd be out and still at it now.'

Then he paused and I knew that this part was personal, to him and to me.

'We have our own ways. And ye have yeers. I mightn't always see eye to eye with ye, but you were fair with us. And good for your word. You said you'd see him do time and you done that. Fair play to you.'

He handed me a plump leather wallet.

'Me father and me uncles, the whole lotta us, want ye to have this for your troubles.'

I took the wallet and nodded. When it was obvious I wasn't going to say anything, the old men shook my hand once more and the group of Travellers, stark as black swans on a frozen lake and forceful as a flotilla of gunboats, processed out of the room and down the stairs.

Hammy gushed.

'Jesus, Slevin, you coulda said something. You're a made man now. A made man. Another feckin string to your bow. Friend of the Traveller.'

He took the wallet from me and rifled through the notes inside.

''Bout three hundred, maybe more, hang on, nearer four, I'd say. Mostly tenners. A good few twenties.'

He returned the wallet to me and, leaving the room, called back.

'Your shout, Slevin. A new outfit? A wee trip? Don't forget the Christmas do. Good way to build up staff camaraderie.'

Later I placed the wallet on Sharon's desk, saying,

'Hospice. Anonymous.'

Two days later the empty wallet was on my desk under a pink sticky note, on which Sharon had written 'sorted'. I looked closely at the wallet then, and saw how the stitching was strained and unravelling as in sutures on a wound. Across the front, in well-rubbed letters, I made out the text.

MARTINS WALLET
21
NEVER EMPTY

*

By the time I got down the stairs and into the yard, Hetherington was revving Hammy's unmarked saloon. I got into the back, checked that Hammy couldn't catch my eye in the rearview mirror and just about managed to get belted in as Hetherington engaged first and steeved the accelerator into the floor. The car leapt, nose-high, through the metal gates and onto the Strand Road, where a uniform, holding the traffic back, jumped sideways in fear of his life.

'Give us the works, Hetherington,' said Hammy. 'The full audio-visual experience.'

'Yes, sir.'

Down the Strand Road we raced; lights, klaxon and occasionally horn, blaring and blazing, until Hammy told Hetherington to lay off the horn.

'We're not in a rush home for our tea,' he said.

No one spoke as we sped over the Foyle Bridge. I could see the Lisahally docks and the sea in the distance to my left. The weather was benign. A pearly light glistened on the water. Oak trees on the riverbank, unruffled by breezes, held their stately poise. Towards the city, upriver, there were squalls and squibs of rain, a sense of a keen wind shovelling clouds east to west to cover the high ground of the walled city and lay their moisture on the stones.

We arrived at the roundabout at the end of the bridge and Hammy barked,

'Don't go round to the main entrance. Go down Waterfoot Park, behind the hotel. There's access to the riverside walk there.'

I smiled to myself thinking that if I wasn't in the back Hetherington might have snapped a salute along with his barked 'Yes, sir!' reply.

We swung off the roundabout, cutting across two lanes,

using the lights and horn again, and entered a quiet estate of detached houses and low-rise apartment buildings neatly arrayed on well-managed grounds that undulated down to the river. The road slalomed twice before Hetherington expertly niched the saloon into the one parking space possible between a Department of Agriculture, Fisheries, Forests and Wildlife (DAFFW) land-rover and a Wild Animal Response Team (WART) personnel carrier. I looked at the acronym and smiled once more. The job got better and better everyday. I knew the 'she' they'd caught now. Then, as the chill from the river made me pull my suede jacket closer round me and regret I hadn't taken my PS(N) branded coat too, Hammy led us through a mass of vehicles parked beside the access to the riverside walkway.

I followed Hammy and Hetherington through the ranks of vehicles. More DAFFW land rovers, oiled waterproofs thrown over seats, green wellies and waders slumped like tired beagles beside rear wheels. Men and women changing clothes. A clutch of three supped well-roasted coffee one of them poured from an industrial-sized flask into metal cups that shone like grenades in their hands. I almost went over to ask them for a cup, but Hammy, who had been listening hard on his phone while making occasional 'aye, right. Yep, that's okay' noises as he walked, signed off and barked:

'Hetherington, you're on me. Slevin, I want you here. Don't wander. Keep your eyes open. Wait for us and we'll go back together.'

Hetherington beamed at me before trotting after our boss, up the walkway and in the direction of whatever mystery we were chasing just then. And I did what my boss told me to do. I kept my eyes open, as best I could. When I yawned a film of water filled my eyes, as if I was crying. I never slept very well. Perhaps I had my allowance, in jail. I didn't do gym. I only really woke up when I discovered books.

These days I wake early and catch up on my report-writing on my off-site laptop. Being at Detective grade, I get two special-issue devices: a high-end laptop with appropriate security access codes and a hand-held compatible – my souped-up phone – with all systems and, again, security cleared to Detective level. Technos pull the phones in randomly, could be 6 weeks, could be a fortnight, handing you a new one at the same time. We're supposed to back-up, but there's a worrying couple of hours until all your data and settings are re-installed and any queries are registered.

I pulled my current phone from my jacket pocket and checked status. I'd had it almost 24 hours and it was still 'clean', empty of my personal history. The screen lit up as I wiped my thumb across it. The sign-in screen appeared and I keyed in my name, officer number and access code. The screen went dark, then lit once more to show my front page with all the systems available. That was re-assuring. I thumbed the icon for Messages and once more the screen performed its light to dark to light shimmy and a list of messages in date/time order appeared. Third from the top a one-liner read:

'IS alert. Contact.'

A hissed 'shite' was my only response to Internal Security, as I pocketed my phone and walked over to the WART van I'd seen earlier. I recognised one of the men standing there, just receiving a cup of coffee. His easy stance and the edge of his mullet hair-style cascading out of his cap gave him away.

'Howya, Tony?'

When he turned, his frown of enquiry quickly became a smile of greeting.

'Slevin, you bollix. You're not dead then?'

I laughed and Tony continued.

'Onny, a boy like you, crossed the line, even now, years

after the bother, I was sure someone was going to do you.'

'Could still happen. What's WART doing here then?'

'They needed a shooter. And that's her there. Amy Miller, our dead-eye Daisy. I'm onny the scout leader. The young wans get all the action.'

Amy Miller was stepping out of a camouflaged outer suit with a single deft movement, not needing to lean on the male colleague who stood beside her and to whom she handed the suit. Then she pulled off her cap and perched it on her colleague's head, smiling. She was as tidy as a meadow sprite and as sturdy as a red squirrel.

'One shot Amy, we call her. She did nice work today.'

A rifle with a telescopic sight was propped against the front of the vehicle. A documenting officer was shooting video of it, then, on Amy's 'I'm ready', he turned the camera on her. She spoke directly to it, giving her account of her role in the incident that brought us all there.

'You're in charge, Tony?'

'Of our little crew here. Tony White, famed loyalist enforcer, turned Boys' Brigade leader to this lot. Yours truly. Six, including me. Specialists. A hybrid of PS(N) and DAFFW. You went straight in at the deep end? Drugs, is it?'

'Serious Crime Team. Here.'

'SCT, eh? I thought 'Drugs'. The suede jacket, you see. We're out of Lisburn, the old Army barracks. Bit of a dump, but handy to Belfast and home.'

Tony White, like me, was part of the experimental political ex-prisoner intake to PS(N) training. Four of us on the front page of the *Belfast Telegraph*, walking into the Police Training College. Photographers wanted us to carry notebooks. One even suggested schoolbags. Tony politely told him to 'fuck off'. The four of us stood on the steps with the steel and concrete facade behind us, the garlanded cap badge centred above us

We looked like a suspects' line-up in place for all the world to witness. Two republicans. Two loyalists. One woman. Only me and Tony made it to the end. The others left and I never heard anything more about them.

Tony continued.

'We're wrapping up. Get Amy all documented. Get the gear broken down and get on the road. We're in last and out first, if we can manage it.'

The sound of squeaky rubber and metal wheels and the thump of feet coming down the tarmac walkway made us turn around. Four uniforms pushed a metal bier on which a body bag lay strapped. Beside them, a small man in a white suit, carrying a medical satchel and speaking rapidly into a phone, trotted to keep up. Then the crowd began, led by top brass. Very clearly one step ahead of everyone else strode the Chief Constable, Elaine Caldwell, looking stern yet relaxed, sunlight glinting off the single diamond stud in her left ear-lobe, her signature accessory. Behind her stepped Hammy and other senior officers from our division. That's why we were all out. Elaine Caldwell, the Chief Constable, always draws a crowd.

The bier stopped directly across from me and the WART team. Camera flashes began to pop and glow from the area taped off for the media. A press liaison officer, with a clipboard and a head-set, began to stage-manage the scene, moving people and the bier around until the Chief Constable was perfectly placed under the TV lights, within easy touching distance of the body bag. After some jostling and gentle elbowing, Hammy was at her right shoulder. I hoped, for his sake, that he was well in shot. There was one time when only his left shoulder appeared in a press photo and he huffed about the office for three days. Sharon, grinning, said that was his cold shoulder.

'Ocelot,' Tony said.

'Ocelot?'

'Yip. *Leopardus Paradis.* The dwarf leopard. Mainly South America. If you live in this country and have a few bob about ye, well then, you have to flash it.'

'So you collect wild animals.'

'Or cars. I'd collect cars.'

'I thought you were all into animals.'

'I am, but that's work. Give me a vintage Beetle over an ocelot any day. She's almost tame. Been around humans a good deal. Probably reared in captivity and sold by an on-line dealer.'

I looked at the bier where I could see the head of the big cat, nestling under heavy tarpaulin. Her eyes were closed. Not a whisker twitched. Her face was as serene as a seal with a belly full of mackerel.

'Been sighted in the park three or four times now. So they called us in. We nearly had her in a net. Tempted her with a nice juicy lump of lamb. But she wasn't that hungry, so we geared up Amy and the "have-a-nice-sleep" shot. Phzzzt! She'll wake up in a couple of hours and the vets will check her over. Time we were gone, Slevin.'

Then he called out.

'Mount up team. Show's over.'

The WART crew finished stowing their gear and began climbing into their vehicle. Amy opened the passenger side door and, with a neat two-step climbed in, all the while looking straight at me. I felt her green eyes sum me up, as if I was a prey she was intent on putting to sleep.

'Do you know who owns the cat?' I asked Tony.

'My guess? Local. Maybe in one of the big houses up there,' Tony said, gesturing to the banking above us, where apartment low-rises bounded large single houses on extensive grounds.

'We reckon it came and went for a few days. Found a hole in a fence and used the park as a runabout. Your uniforms are on the house-to-house now.'

'Are they not registered, these things?'

'Heh, Slevin, are you a cop or a buck-eejit or what? Some are. Some not. This one has dog-tags. Like a marine, if you don't mind.'

He pulled out his phone, went to photos, flicked his thumb along, pinched-out to focus and enlarge and showed me a rectangular metal name-tag with the word 'Pangur' over a phone number.

'The phone number didn't work. See there. Up in the corner. Sort of an insignia. Looks like a crouched skeleton, under what, acorns? The skeleton is holding a small cross. See?'

'Can you zoom in some more?'

Then I could see it clearly. De Burgo's skeleton, from the city crest, sitting on a stone, holding a small cross, his head bent under a halo of acorns and oak leaves.

'Send me that. No, not the whole picture. Just the skeleton bit.'

I sent him my number and he replied with the image.

'You collecting historical pictures now, Slevin? Always the dark one. Even in the Police College. No one knew if you were really in it or just a plant. A kind of sleeper.'

'Like the ocelot, is it?'

'Too cute for me, boy. Too cute for me. Here, good to see you. Look after yourself. Don't let the bad boys get to you now.'

He climbed in beside Amy Miller. The van started up immediately and, with low steady revs, the driver reversed it one hundred metres further along the walkway. Everyone at the press conference turned to look and all they saw was me, a lithe man in a suede jacket, squinting in the sunlight, against a backdrop of tall reeds, whispering secrets to each other in the breeze. Surely not a policeman? More an extra in a film, wondering where the tea and sandwiches were. But I didn't care, because not only had Tony White given me a hint of a lead, he also gave me a 'thumbs up' as the van reversed past me. And Amy Miller, knees tucked to her chin beside him, gave me a delicate wave and enough of a smile to know that I could seek her out. Safari-wise.

THREE

A short while later, the press conference began to break up and Hammy approached me.

'Trust you to upstage the CC.'

'What do you mean?'

'The bloody WART wagon whizzing off like a...'

'Exactly. The WART Wagon. Take it up with them.'

Then we both laughed. Hammy pushed his closed fist into his mouth to stop himself from repeating 'WART' in a child's voice, just ahead of the arrival of the Chief Constable and two of her aides.

'Great to see my officers enjoying their work.'

'Ma'am, ... yes, that's right, Ma'am. Excellent,' said Hammy, composing himself. 'The Chief Constable is keen to meet you, Slevin. Chief Constable, this is Detective Sergeant Slevin.'

'Delighted to meet you, DS Slevin.'

Slighter taller than me, with the aura of a lean cat used to leading from the front and claiming new territory first, Elaine Caldwell stepped closer to me, took my hand and pressed it firmly. I sensed my palm filming with a delicate cream, which carried a hint of lavender when I later put it to my lips.

'I understand from Detective Inspector Hamilton that you have settled in well.'

'Yes, Ma'am, I have. The Detective Inspector and all his senior management team have been very supportive.'

'And what are you working on now, may I ask?'

Hammy jumped in.

'We tend to work across cases, Ma'am. In a collegiate-style.

Slevin is currently part of a cross-disciplinary investigation, bearing down on...'

'Something specific, Slevin. What's your focus?'

'There was a footballer shot in the back of the head. Todd Anderson. I'm working on that.'

'Good luck. And remember, like footballers, we're in the results business.'

She then stepped even closer to me, so that I had a clear view of her diamond ear-stud, sparkling grandly in the afternoon sunlight. She took my elbow and steered me round so that we were side-on to the remnants of the media pack. She clasped my hand once more. Two or three cameras flashed and that's how a photograph of detective and political ex-prisoner Edmund Slevin, shaking hands with the Chief Constable of PS(N), appeared in the local press and the *Belfast Telegraph*. It even made it into the *Irish Times* in a side-bar story on the capture of the big cat of St. Columb's Park. Hammy's shoulder, or any other part of him, did not feature in newsprint or on-line anywhere.

The Chief Constable departed with her aides, chased by a keen photographer capturing a few last shots. Hammy barked at me.

'You drive back. I want you in the front.'

We walked towards the vehicles which were shunting, reversing, pirouetting and moving off in a dumb show of hand signals and up-turned thumbs. A white veterinary ambulance led the posse up the hill between the apartment blocks. I quietly wished the ocelot well and wondered if Amy Miller might be doing the same in the front seat of the WART personnel carrier, her feet on the dashboard, her chin on her knees, her eyes closed under downy lids.

When we reached Hammy's saloon, Hetherington was standing beside it. A thumb-jerk from our boss took him by surprise and into the back-seat. He tossed me the keys and I got in to the driver's seat. I pulled the visor down against the late afternoon sunlight. As I drove away from the river, I looked to my right to view the bigger houses climbing up the slope. Up where the ocelot lives, I was sure. And the owner. The uniforms would find him soon enough. Maybe they'd also find out why the ocelot had the skeleton image on its ID necklace. The same image as on Dalzell's business card.

As soon as we breasted the rise and faced onto the roundabout Hammy said,

'Drive up by the hospital. I want to go the long way round. Through the town.'

I drove on to the roundabout and exited up Crescent Link. Hammy revved up with the engine.

'I'm putting Hetherington with you, Slevin. You heard the Chief Constable. We want a result. A tight team can do it. Stick on the Anderson case. Focus, Slevin, that's what this needs. They're all out there, waiting to have a pot at us. And we won't let them. Dodge the bullets, Slevin, that's the man. You know that.'

Whatever colourful images Hammy had of my days in the war against the state, I wasn't going to disabuse him of notions he might have of derring-do and gun-fights. I had no intention of boring him with tales of waiting around, late night arms' moves and the occasional burst of war activity more akin to a deadly circus than to military strategy. But I was focused. Then, as now.

'The Anderson case has something, Slevin. The CC asked directly about it.'

That's why he introduced me to her. Put a warm body in front of her to show he was doing something about it.

'And she wants to be kept fully briefed. Leave that to me. I told her we use you on these special cases. Your background.

Local connections. Penetration.'

Hetherington almost sniggered, but managed to stifle it. I gave him a single finger in the rear view mirror and I saw him smile. It mightn't be too bad to have him as an assistant. Hammy stared out of the window and witnessed none of this. He spoke again, more to his reflection in the window, than to his junior colleagues in the car.

'One thing you learn in this job is that it's all about survival. Not about dreams or aspirations. She might think it's about results. That's part of it, sure. But you can have all the best results in the world and still get nowhere.'

We arrived at the hospital roundabout and stalled as traffic came from our right, leaving the city.

'Go straight on,' said Hammy. 'I want to see how the streets look today. You take Hetherington with you everywhere you go, Slevin. You'll need back-up. And another set of eyes and ears. Use him. Lapdog him.'

I threw a mock salute and said 'Yes, sir.' Hetherington grinned. Hammy continued staring out of the window.

'The days of the solo run are over, Slevin. It's all cogs-in-a-wheel now. One of a team. If you're not a team player, you're a goner. What have you got so far?'

'I'm finishing an update. I'll have it on your desk tomorrow.'

'Give it to me now. The bones of it. And you'll be bringing Kenneth up to speed too.'

He sat back in the car seat and stared out the front windscreen. I saw his heavy jowls reflected in the glass. There was no levity there. I launched in.

'Detective Inspector Omar Hamilton requested I review the first interviews made by Detective Sergeants Goss and Doherty of Denis Green, chair of …'

'Spare us the bureaucratese, Slevin. I'll skip that tomorrow. And today. Get to the flesh of it. Trim the fat.'

'I read Goss and Doherty's notes. I went to Denis Green's office. I don't need to tell you, sir, that they weren't very happy that I was going over ground they had already covered.'

'But you finessed – or bashed – your way past that. No doubt. Go on.'

'Green told me Todd Anderson was a capable young professional whose death was a significant loss to the club. He offered no conjecture as to who might have killed him and why. Anderson was well-liked, well-mannered, well-groomed and well-got by everyone at the club. Scoring average per game 0.7. That was in Goss and Doherty's report. They both fancy Argentina for the World Cup.'

'That's who Goss pulled in the draw. Doherty got Palestine, good luck to them. Did Green offer you anything new?'

The roundabout cleared and I moved into the traffic lane heading straight ahead. Here's where I took a plunge I would not have taken in times past. My background was in a secret army. You tell nobody nothing. Not even yourself, to some degree. No amount of re-training at Police College could completely over-ride such a grounding in the clenched-teeth arts. But I decided to air this nugget of knowledge because I wanted to retain others.

'Green asked about boot marks on the victim's neck.'

Hammy turned towards me.

'He knew about those?'

'More than me.'

'Karen Lavery not keeping you up to speed these days?'

A smirk widened on Hetherington's face in the rear view mirror. I flashed a hard look at him and the smirk withered.

'I had a preliminary report from Forensics about a football boot pattern. I'm waiting for the full report.'

'Aren't we all? Did Green offer any opinion as to how these marks came to be there?'

'No, sir.'

'But he knew about them?'

'Yes, sir.'

'Probably heard it from the groundsman who found the body. I see you've reverted to huffy-kid mode, Slevin. You're too old for that.'

'Yes, sir.'

Hammy raised an eyebrow at me. I met his gaze and we both laughed. When Hetherington attempted to titter in harmony, Hammy stared him down and he shut up.

'OK. That's a bit of news, right enough. Good. People say a police service is a fortress, a citadel, a haven, a maze of intelligence, a keep, a castle, a battery of power and diligence. In reality, a police service is a sieve, with very fine openings. Something like your own former institution, The Irish Republican Army, mark five or six, was it? Anyways, information comes in and we solve crimes. There's always the odd one ... Some of the information leaks out. We can never completely stop that. But we do need to know where the specific holes are. That's why I'm giving you Hetherington. Another pair of eyes, ears and legs. He may even have a heart and, with any luck, a brain.'

Hetherington wisely didn't even attempt a laugh.

'And I'm going to give you both the Todd Anderson case.'

'But Goss and Doherty ...'

'... have been instructed to pass on the Murder Book and all other files and all their notes.'

Hetherington piped up in an excited voice, pulling his phone from his pocket.

'The digital version?'

'All forms,' said Hammy. 'Slevin is still a bit old school when it comes to files. Turn right here. Through the Irish Street Estate.'

I had to stand on the brake to make the turn, but, thankfully, no one was behind us.

'This is where I grew up. But you fellas probably know that from hours poring over my write-ups in the police glossies. "Man of the streets, raised in the loyalist heartland; doyen of the local community." Waffle, pish and shite. But I did run about here. Dreams are shaped on streets like these. My two best mates are from here. Lesley's in London. Vernon's in New York.'

'You stayed, sir.'

Hetherington was more foolish than I thought. Or more daring.

'I stayed. Dreams become reality. I stayed to serve. Remember that. We – you – are here to serve.'

We left the estate and rejoined the main road to the city centre and the police barracks.

'Straight back, sir?'

'Yes, Slevin. Straight back. Upright stance at all times. Shoulders; squared and pressed backwards. Chin; clean-shaven, out and up. Eyes; forward. Tread; honest and forthright. Get stuck into the Anderson murder book, when you get back. Hetherington, move your desk nearer his. Anyone quibbles, refer them to me. Report to me only. Not to the room. We'll bring in the squad when we have something. When we need them. Anything more, Slevin?'

'No, sir.'

I didn't tell him about the meeting with Dalzell. Or about the message from IS. I needed to keep some cards turned face down for a while longer.

'Do me one page on your interview with Green. Leave out the marks on the victim's neck. Let them come in the forensic report. Get a copy to me and put a copy on file. Hard and digital.'

The rest of the journey continued in silence. When we breezed through the automatic gates, Hammy said to drop him at the main entrance and I took the saloon into the parking area. I buttoned the handbrake and turned to face Hetherington.

There was the frisky fight-not-flight look of a startled hare in his eyes and a firm set to his shoulders, the right one angled towards me. He would be hard to budge.

'You don't want to work with me, Kenneth,' I began. 'I'm tainted. Wouldn't be good for your career.'

'You heard the Inspector. We're here to serve.'

I began to get out of the car, but stopped as he continued.

'Even though it's mostly waffle. As he noted himself. His family left Irish Street when he was seven and moved to a nice, detached house on a sizeable plot in Prehen. Most of his running around was down on the adjacent golf course and in the woods behind their spacious family home.'

'And you read my personal file too.'

'Of course. Bishop Street area. School drop out. 'RA, late version. Intelligence Officer. Prison. 12 years. O.U. Degree. First class. Doctorate from Queens. Political uptake into Police College when the dissidents, most of them anyway, went political, in the last big turnaround. Top 3 in the class. Beat all the grammar schoolers and the ones with degrees in psychology and forensic science. Six months in HQ, then the Serious Crime Team here. Already an impressive clearance record.'

'Good man. Such diligence is to be admired and feared in the young. Now then: task one, after you move your desk. Not too close to mine and don't block my meagre view out of the window.'

I pulled out the plastic sheath containing the business card Dalzell had given me in the café and passed it to Hetherington.

'See the skeleton image in the corner? Find out what you can about that. Don't contact the fella on the card.'

'Is this something to do with the Todd Anderson case?'

'Yes.'

He looked at the card, then put it in his pocket and got out. After the slamming of the rear passenger door the only sound was the engine ticking as it cooled; the sound of a lone cicada in a rainforest, underscored by my breathing, a light wheeze – a flutter of diaphanous wings – sounding in it. I got out too and went for a walk on the river bank, thinking about how Denis Green knew about the marks on Todd Anderson's neck. Hammy was probably right. One of the ground staff told him. Who put the body there, and why, wouldn't be so easy to figure.

I had an image of piles of papers, folders and sticky notelets, topped with a steaming dog turd on my desk, Goss and Doherty standing together, antiseptic handwipes writhing through their hands, then tossed at my waste-paper bin, missing it, to lie like disconsolate, back-broken seagulls under my feet.

There was a pile of papers on my desk, but no steaming dog turd. My imaginings are always worse than my realities. Hetherington moved his desk, so it sat angled to mine, on the downside of the window that gave us a view of the Technical College, some trees beside a doctor's surgery and, on a clear day, a glimpse of the arcing bridge we had driven over earlier.

The office was empty and quiet, except for the background hum of computers and the ceaseless rumble of deep-seated electrics that drove heating, light and surveillance. Even Sharon was not at her desk. She usually ate lunch there, a tub of healthy grain, nuts and protein her colleagues scoff at and envy in equal measure.

There was a purple stickey-notelet pinned to the top of the

new pile of paperwork Goss and Doherty had deposited.

Possible witness? Teenage girl. Mother phoned. Donna Bradley. Expects a return call.

There was a phone number. Something to get on with, at least.

Underneath the notelet was a one page memo from Hetherington. Laid out formally in perfect Police College style, it showed crisp reproductions of variations on the skeleton image, above a set of bullet points, written in the kind of English senior officials in the Attorney General's office use. I knew this because my own solicitor had shown me their correspondence over the years. As I ran my fingers down the neat column of black dots, scanning Hetherington's pointed prose, I speculated that maybe he had a law degree. I would get Sharon to pull his personnel file for me.

The memo he sent me was headed by an image of the skeleton I'd seen on Dalzells' card and on the ocelot's ID badge, followed by clipped bullet points.

- Order of the Cross and Bones. Website defunct.
- Origins among orders of Knight/Crusaders. Oscure. Contested.
- Modern manifestations, across Europe, largely weak.
- Local manifestations?: City crest - De Burgo; Noman knight?; contested; unrelated?
- Reference: *Cross and Bones: a triumph of faith and service*, Beresford/Dalzell, London, 1908
- Christian, evangelical, Bible-based, liberal (?)
- Not listed in Hazlitt's *Register of Religious Sects.*
- Secret?

I liked the question mark after 'liberal'. It smacked of the circumspection of the academic. I viewed the image of the identity bracelet from the ocelot's neck. The skeleton looked up at me once more. The figure was morose, yet almost smiling.

I expected it to raise a bony hand and give me the finger, like Dalzell.

Hammy's decision to give me and Hetherington the Anderson case meant I took on the urgency as well as the responsibility. As long as I was tagging along behind Goss and Doherty, I could go at my own pace, but now that I was "lead" on it, I would have to get active. So the first thing I did was put the Anderson case files on the floor, simply so I could see everything else on the desk and decide what to do with it.

When I began the doctorate, in prison, I was given a bigger desk, a proper set of bookshelves and a decent laptop. The screws started calling me The Nutty Professor, but by that time the heat had gone out of the prison protests and we just stayed out of each other's way, except for necessary contact. That suited me and them.

A small red lamp with a round base and a bendy hose pipe to the shade threw light across my pages. I left the cell lights off, as if to further corral myself into smaller and smaller spaces. My subject was mythology. I wanted to see how cultural cross links were made. How had it happened that the same basic stories, the same archetypes, ranged across the stories of the world, from China, across Asia, into Europe and Africa, through the Americas and Australia and back to China again. I was at the centre of it all, in my prison cell, under the light of my squat red lamp.

My supervisor, an anthropologist from Queen's University called Dervock, said I was taking on too much, that I needed to focus and get things pinned down. I agreed with him and got on with what I wanted to do, which was to read and hide away under the light from my little red lamp and lose myself in the full glare of the old myths: warrior, hero, wanderer, vanquished, lover, old man, dead.

Now, as I gathered case files and scraps of notes,

arranged in piles, I composed an email to Hammy, copying in Hetherington and Sharon, our administrator. No bullet points for me. Not my style. I'm more 'dry academy' than 'diligent police'.

'Pursuant to your decision, Detective Inspector Hamilton, to appoint me as detective-in-charge of the Todd Anderson case, as of today's date, I note:

Detective Constable Kenneth Hetherington is to assist me. Detective Sergeants Goss and Doherty have passed all the files to me. I will follow up on the lead on a possible witness; a teenage girl, via her mother. I am making summary notes on cases and matters currently before me, which I will append to the files I currently hold, before passing them to Sharon for your attention and re-allocation. I trust to the support of all the team, in particular, Detective Sergeants Goss and Doherty, as the investigation develops.'

I read over the draft message once more and thought that it was at least one step above Hetherington's memo and that all my years composing paragraphs for scholarly publications such as *The Journal of American Folklore, International Cultural Studies, Framework: Inter-disciplinary Methods in Mythologies* and *The Journal of the Royal Society of Antiquarians of Ireland* had not been a complete waste of time.

One by one I pulled the case files towards me, the ones I intended to hand back to Hammy. I reviewed them briefly as I composed a summary note, another clipped paragraph.

'The Skeoge Road Drugs' Ring: Continue liaising with Vice. Application for surveillance pending. Waterside Brothels: Coming to court. Four charged and in custody. See it through proceedings. Creggan knee-capping: Fits pattern of past year. Incidence decreasing. See Porter/UU research paper included here. Victim co-operating. Brother in Leeds. Likely to flit?'

The last pile, the fourth, contained an assortment of

documents, memos, scribbled notes and press cuttings that might have been filed as Miscellaneous except the term wasn't broad enough. I lifted a strip torn from a local paper on which Hammy had scribbled the words 'You got anything on this?' above the headline 'Big Cat Terrorises Park'. I read through it and found nothing I didn't already know. I tossed it onto the pile of papers on the floor beside me. I was following a skeleton, a filigree of air and bones that felt vacant and replete at the same time.

I re-read my draft email, tidying punctuation. I smiled at the last line. 'I trust to the support of all the team, in particular Detectives Goss and Doherty, as the investigation develops.'

I could see the Hammy grimace as he read it.

'Bullshit, Slevin. Covering-your-back bullshit of the highest order,' he would think, almost proud of me.

A muffled thunder of feet along the hessian carpet, overlain with bantering voices, announced the return of my colleagues from lunch. I hit 'send' just as Hetherington flounced into his chair.

'Germany beat Croatia 3-0. Bechtimme got two. He's hot.'

So lunch had been spent in a bar, watching the World Cup midday game.

'This desk okay?' Hetherington continued.

I nodded and said,

'Take these three piles and put them on Sharon's desk.'

'Does she know ...'

'I sent her an email.'

I understood his reluctance to put anything on top of Sharon's desk. It was an oasis of clarity not seen anywhere else in the building, only ever covered by papers she expressly put there to work upon and removed immediately the work was completed. Hetherington lifted the stack of case files, sped across the room to the administrator's desk and dropped them on the pristine surface. My own desk almost reflected Sharon's now, except for miscellaneous scraps which I shuffled together and stuffed into a light, card folder I then stashed in a drawer on my right side, on top of my shaver and an old copy of *The Journal of Nordic Myths*, which included a short essay I'd written: 'Odin and the myth of the hero-god'.

'Thanks for the memo on the skeleton. You're good with the bullet points. I like that. Here, take that lot.'

I directed him to the pile on the floor beside me.

'Bullet points only. Leads obviously. Motives. Opportunities. And the note on the top? Phone the lady and book us in to talk to her daughter.'

I held on to the Murder Book, marked 'Todd Anderson'. Then I left the room, just as Sharon arrived at her desk, a livid gasp escaping from her lips, when she spied the paperwork piled high there. I was down the stairs, en route to Fiorentini's café, just before she linked the pile to me.

FOUR

The skeleton image on the ocelot's necklace was a dead end. I phoned the owner, a woman used to dealing with police as hirelings. She sounded like a TV royal.

'I'm the last of my particular strain. We're long here. And elsewhere. Forms of itinerant merchants, law-givers and imperial factotums in Ireland and across the old empire. I suspect there are scions of the family currently being dubious in Doha and Dubai; shellacking in Shanghai and Singapore and belligerent in Baghdad and Bahrain.'

When I asked about the ocelot, she told me the cat was with new owners in the Cotswolds.

'And the significance of the skeleton image on the ocelot's ID bracelet?' I asked.

'Significance? It's a … what do they call it now … a logo', she said, a sneer in her voice. 'I've seen it on crests and badges. I've seen it on embroidered cushion covers. A trifle macabre, but then some members of the family …'

She let that tail off, then changed tack.

'You must realise, DS Slevin, that we've been here or hereabouts for a very long time. There is a map of the city from 1603. You'll have to go to Dublin to see the original. I have a copy, if you'd like to see it. You'll find us there. But no damned cat, with or without a skeleton ID badge.'

I declined the offer to view the map at the owner's home or in Dublin and accepted I was at a dead-end. I turned my attention to the mother who had phoned. We followed up on the appointment Hetherington made.

'You lead with this, Kenneth. In the door first. Pen and the notebook in hand.'

'But I'm only backing you up, sir. You're supposed to …'

'I read your personnel file. You've led before.'

'You read …'

'I asked Sharon for it. She hates you after you put all that paperwork on her desk. It was on the office cameras.'

'Come on. You should have told Sharon.'

'I did. I took it square. I told her you did it at my behest and that I accepted full responsibility. Still, I'd stay out of her way for a while, if I was you.'

'I've just understood what the word 'devious' means, Detective Sergeant Slevin.'

'You heard the boss. DI Omar Hamilton is of the opinion that we work in a sieve and that we have to fatten ourselves so we don't fall through the holes and lose our jobs.'

'Or our lives.'

'Those too. And on that cheery note, when you leave the barracks, salute the uniforms, turn right along the Strand Road and go into the Bog, via William Street.'

'I know the city …'

'You served time in the back of a Pig. You rode shotgun as part of a front-line four. You've even been shot at.'

'Once.'

'Pellet gun.'

'Unconfirmed.'

'These are end days, Kenneth Hetherington. That's been the hummable tune of recent years. That the shooting is over.'

'It has lessened. Especially since we got boys like you locked up. Sir.'

'Easy now, kiddo. You weren't even in long trousers when I went down. Hey, wait up now. You come from a long line of cops. One of your ancestors might have been involved at that time.'

'You have cops among your ancestors too.'

'Yep. RIC. Way back. Boer war days. Pre-revolution, you might say. Mouldering in the grave now. That's it, right turn here and drive through the ghosts of the soldiers, the rioters, the volunteers, the young hooligans and their Mas, dashing home with their shopping.'

'Armoured cars and tanks and guns.'

'You could sing it, kiddo. But not now. Turn left and head for the Wall and then up to Creggan. We'll sneak up on Rosemount, a rear assault, as if we were predators, not community servants.'

'You'll forgive me if I don't cheer, sir. Let me ask you directly. Why are we driving through streets inhabited by people, currently holding a modestly firm ceasefire, some of whom would like to kill us?'

'Get real, Hetherington. You could say that about cops on streets in any city.'

'This isn't any city, sir.'

'You're right, Detective Constable Hetherington. This is home.'

Hetherington briefed me, as he rang the doorbell to the Bradley house. I hoped this could be a live lead.

'Donna Bradley, Environmental Scientist at the Council. Divorced. One daughter. Teresa. Not mute, just doesn't speak. Sounds like she's away with the fairies.'

'She'd not be alone there. She doesn't speak at all?'

'She writes notes apparently. And she's football mad, like I told you,' he said, nodding at the football in my hands.

I stood well back from the front door, bouncing the new Globall Lite World Cup Special I made Hetherington detour to buy. A twitch in the curtains upstairs told me we'd been spotted.

I bounced the ball, tossed it in the air and headed it upwards twice. The upstairs curtain flicked closed. When the front door opened, Donna Bradley invited us in and gave me a look which mixed an estimation of me as an impertinent boy lacking in professionalism and a charlatan seeking to charm her daughter away.

She got us settled in the front room, as thumping teenage footsteps brought Teresa downstairs to sit before us on a dining room chair, one of two framing a circular pine table already graced with place mats, emblazoned with tropical fish, big enough for dinner plates.

'Hello, Teresa. Your Mammy says you're doing well at school. Soon be the holidays now. You'll get a break then. Plenty of time to play, eh?' Hetherington began.

Neither of us have children. His day may come. Mine is past, I reckon. I wondered should we have brought a female colleague with us. I felt inept. I saw sweat beading on Hetherington's neck. He gamely ventured one more effort.

'Your mother told us you'd be home now, so that's why we called round. Just a few questions, to help us, if you can. Here.'

He pulled out his ID card, as if it was a wonder. He'd already shown it to Teresa's mother when we arrived.

'This is me. Not a great photo. What do you think? But it's me alright. Detective Constable Hetherington. And he's Detective Sergeant Slevin.'

Then, in whisper,

'He's the boss, really.'

Donna Bradley looked at me as if to say 'you could have fooled me'. I smiled at her and stood up. The wooden floor sounded an unhealthy thwack when I bounced the ball on it. Donna winced. Teresa leaned forward on her chair. I walked past the fireplace to the open window which framed a street scene of summer childhood bliss. Cars roasting in sun-light. A skipping rope twirling. A pram with a broken wheel trundling by, pushed by the bearer of a mop of blond curls. A squeal rang out, then a chase of footsteps. A door slammed closed. A voice called 'S'mantha! Your tea's nearly caul'.

I turned back to the room. Hetherington sat forward on the sofa, his elbows resting on his knees. Perhaps he was waiting for me to show my ID again. We had declined the offer of tea. He was lost as to what to do with his hands, so he put them under his thighs, which he clenched and pushed down as if he was a flower press.

I looked Teresa directly in the eyes. She held my gaze lightly. She was primed and alert. Not fazed in the slightest.

'Your Granda was a striker. A goalscorer, right?'

I made it sound like I knew him. Teresa blinked and both our eyes settled on a photograph on the mantlepiece. A team of footballers, tall ones arranged at the back, smaller ones on one knee, at the front. A cup gaping open like an insect-eating plant, prominent in front of them. A boy in a duffle-coat, standing off to one side, picking his nose. The man I hazarded was Teresa's grandfather stood tall at the left end of the back row, a quiff you could slide down making him seem taller.

'Good in the air,' I continued. 'A number 9, I'd say. Could do a job at the back, if the team needed. Never flashy, just good. Yeh. Just good'.

The silence in the room deepened. A child's voice sounded from the street.

'Ach, Mammy!'

S'mantha?

Then Donna spoke in a rush that filled the room with air.

'Oh, aye. Teresa's granddad, aye. He's my father. At the back there. The tall fella with the big hair. Spent more time in football shorts than in his trousers, that boy. Teresa, she …'

That's when I threw the ball at the girl. A forceful

elbow-propelled basketball player's throw. Without shifting her gaze from the photo on the mantlepiece Teresa caught the ball square in her chest and bowled it underarm, one handed, straight back to me. Her mother gasped. Hetherington stood up. I caught the ball, smiled and tossed the ball gently back to her. As two friends might pass a ball between them, while chatting. She lobbed it back to me. Back and forward the ball went, in easy arcs. Hetherington sat down, bemused but quiet. Donna relaxed and a rosy flush lit her cheeks. Throwing easy arcs, we traversed the air, the ball bridging us.

'You have a notebook. Could you please write down what you saw. The man, I mean. Just what you saw. And if you saw anyone else. We'll just be out the back a minute. To see the garden, like.'

I caught the ball one last time and curled it under my arm. I walked past Donna, now openly gaping at me and went into the kitchen area and through the patio doors into the small yard. I breathed out loudly, just managing to compose myself as Hetherington and Donna joined me.

'I hope you know what you're doing,' she said.

I could see by Hetherington's stare that he hoped the same.

'Let's give her a minute.'

'We don't even know if she was there. You're assuming the child the groundsman saw was Teresa.'

'Yes, I am. And if it is her, Teresa will tell us.'

'She …', Donna hesitated. 'It is her. She does go there. Every morning nearly. Her Daddy follows her the odd morning. Don't tell her. To mind her. He spoke to the men there. They're not happy with it, but they …'

The 'turning of the blind eye' is one of humanity's most-used survival strategies.

'Her Daddy said he'd speak to her. Get her to stop, but, you know, with the new school, he … it didn't seem right. She's doing no harm.'

'When you get a chance, after we're gone, ask her if she goes there now. Ask her directly. She'll tell you.'

She looked at me as if for the first time I had instilled some belief in her that this visit by the police might end without harm to her family.

I bounced the ball three times, tossed it to Hetherington who tossed it back immediately as if it was a salmon that had leapt a weir into his unwary arms.

'Lovely yard, Mrs. Bradley. Snapdragons, is it? A great show. The good May helps, doesn't it?' I said, trying to put us all at ease, even though I sensed I was heading towards another dead end.

Teresa was at the table under the window when we went back in. Late afternoon sunlight crossed her face in warm bands that made her look more puckish than before. Two pages of notes, torn from a small notebook lay in front of her.

She stood up and handed them to me. I handed her the football.

'Thank you. Please take the ball into the yard and give it a try.'

Teresa nodded and flicked her eyes at her mother, who smiled in agreement. When Teresa left, I handed the pages to Donna and sat on the sofa, beckoning to Hetherington to join me.

Donna took the pages and sat where her daughter had sat and read them out loud.

I took a penalty. The man was there.
I did not know. His face was in the
ground. I had my new boots.

The Dreamtime ones. I got them with my
own money. I can kick penalties
with my left foot and my right foot.
The man had a red and white scarf
on him. I did not see him. I stood on
~~him his on~~ the scarf. He did not move.
The Dreamtime got bloody. I did not like
that. I could not take a penalty then.
The man was alone. The man was
dead. The other man in the yellow
jacket shouted. I ran. The man did
not run after me. He was dead.

The sound of the bouncing ball and her daughter's shuffling feet came in from the yard, while Donna read her daughter's note. Her eyes filled with tears, as she handed the pages to me and sat down again. I passed them directly to Hetherington, who read them briskly. Then, finally, I read them, from back to front.

'Can you please ask her to come back in again, Mrs. Bradley?'

Teresa returned and lobbed the ball to me, with a nod. It passed her test. I put it on the ground beside me.

'Do you have a computer and printer?'

She nodded.

'Here, in the house?'

Donna spoke.

'She has her own set-up, in her room. We got it for her – a laptop and a printer – when she started the secondary school. I keep a good eye on what she does online.'

I've learned that having the police in your house can make even the most law-abiding and intelligent person act like the guilty child who stole the last biscuit from the cupboard.

'Teresa,' I said. 'Could you please type up these notes? Keep the originals yourself. And send them to me here.'

I gave her my card.

'There. You can use my personal email. Or the Messenger service. See. You probably have that service yourself.'

Teresa nodded.

'I don't want to rush you. But could you do it tonight? Thanks. And if you remember anything else, just put that in the message too. Like, was there anybody in the stands or on the terraces. Or when you got out, did you see anybody around.'

Once again the nod, this time with a hint of tiredness in her avid eyes.

'Your boots. Your new Dreamtimes. I've never seen them. I'd love to see them. The Dreamtimes.'

The tiredness left her eyes and she ran off. More thumping up and down the stairs, then Teresa was before us once more. She handed the left boot to me and the right one to Hethering-ton. I smoothed the leather uppers and the vamps, caressing it as I would a cat. Hetherington turned his over and inspected the underside.

'They're lethal. Soft and strong, at the same time. You're what, size five?'

Teresa held up four fingers.

'Size four. A good size. Not too big, so you're not flopping around. Not too small, so you can't give it a good whack. Your feet'll probably grow another couple of sizes as you get bigger.'

'Her grandfather was a size seven. Like a dancer's, his feet.'

'Thank you, Mrs. Bradley. Thank you, Teresa. What did you think of the ball?'

She gave a non-committal shrug and smiled, as if to say 'alright'.

'I know what you mean. Okay for a kick-about, training maybe, but too flighty for a proper match. I'll loan it to you, if you like.'

'Will you be back?' her mother asked.

'We'll see,' I said.

I hope I gave her enough of a sense that I didn't think so. Hetherington chipped in.

'We can always phone if we need anything.'

I stood up and went to the mantlepiece.

'Your granddad would be proud of you. Your skills and all. And your hand-writing. I look forward to seeing your typed version. Tonight, yeh? Thanks for your time, Mrs. Bradley.'

I shook her hand. Were there tears gathering on her cheeks? Hetherington stood and kicked the ball playfully to Teresa. She trapped it expertly and smirked at him. I smiled as I walked past her out onto the sun-coloured street.

'You're bribing child-witnesses now, Slevin,' Hetherington said, as he carefully edged the car out of the parking space. Children, skipping, moved off the road and he pulled clear, then moved along the street, towards Park Avenue. I wound down the window as we slowed at the junction. A man my age leaned against a wall, peeling an orange, putting the peel onto the windowsill beside him, then breaking off segments to pass to two small boys in front of him. I nodded at him and our eyes met. I might be on that street again, if not to see the Bradleys, then perhaps to call on the man peeling the orange.

'Where to now? You got anymore shopping you want to do?'

'Nope. Back to base.'

I knew it was bugging him, so I asked myself for him.

'Why did I give her back her note? Why did I leave without

her statement? She's our only real lead, right?'

'Right, yeh.'

'You read her note. Nothing. You checked the boots. Exactly as in the crime scene report. You've probably got her notes memorised anyway. Leave her be. There might be something in her next draft. When she's had a chance to think. And now she knows we're not coming after her.'

Hetherington drove slowly, negotiating traffic coming and going on Park Avenue.

'A one way system would do power of good here,' he said.

'No chance. It's awkward, but who's going to agree to losing a route? The people coming up or the people going down? Neither. And we're all one and the same in the long run. We just have to work around each other, both ways. Did you see the statuette on the mantelpiece? Beside the photo?'

'How did you know it was her grandfather?'

'I didn't. I guessed.'

'And if you were wrong?'

'I don't know. I suppose I'd have covered. Re-covered.'

'It's all a bluff with you, isn't it? Sir.'

'No need to be defensive when you're being critical. Kenneth.'

'I'm not being critical, I'm being …'

'You are being critical. In a philosophical sense. And that's good. Yes, I am guessing. And there'll be more. Go on, give me the bullet points then. Leads?'

'Nil. Confirmed by the girl's notes.'

'Witness?'

'Ditto. Teresa saw nothing. The groundsmen saw less. The house-to-house in the area turned up nothing. Nothing even from the houses overlooking the ground. It's a big pitch and to carry a dead body across so much open space and no one see it, I don't know.'

'We sleep soundly in this city. We have a victim at least. A body. Any thing there to go on?'

'Shot in another location. Brought to the site by unknown means. Forensics have a badly damaged bullet they're working on. Pathology useless, now we've eliminated the boot marks and Teresa.'

'Motivation? Here, turn right by the post office. We might get a clear run to the Northland.'

'Nothing really. Speculation at best. No unusual phone activity. Family members in Manchester. Team mates. Coach.'

'Women? Girlfriends?'

'Nothing steady. Not a playboy either. The women spoke well of him. A gentleman, for God's sake.'

'Still a few of us left, Kenneth. Gay?'

'Not out in any way. No sign of boyfriends.'

'Gambling? Debts?'

'No. We got access to his bank accounts. All adds up. Income from the club. Typical standard outgoings. Sent money home to his mother on a regular basis, if you don't mind.'

'More than a gentleman. A paragon.'

'No unusual transactions. No large sums going or coming.'

'Put any direct debits into a note for me. Amounts, no matter how small and destination accounts and any details you can get.'

I hesitated, but then asked,

'That skeleton and the café on your bullet points. 'Intermittent'?'

'I went round there, like you said. Boarded up. The off-licence next door said no one had been there for weeks. I could track down the landlord.'

'Naw. Don't bother.'

'Dead end?'

I didn't answer.

We reached the Northland Road. Home-time traffic was dense, but a taxi-man held back at the junction and let us cross to the far lane. Hetherington gave him a small wave. People grow easier with the police. But not all. I thought of the man peeling oranges.

'Paramilitaries?'

'They work in mysterious ways, obviously. Not their kind of target. Not their kind of operation.'

'It could be a punishment thing.'

'They say they're not doing that anymore. There's the odd expulsion, still, but even that's half-hearted. Anyway, if it was them, they'd have claimed it by now.'

I smiled at his well-briefed analysis, but guessed there was more to know than was held in police briefings.

'If it suited. Drugs? User? Supplier?'

'No evidence of either. Fit as a racehorse. Top class professional. Keen to do well here and make a move back to England. A good prospect. A winner.'

'Which takes us back to the statuette? On the mantelpiece.'

'Some kind of trophy she won. Or maybe the granddad's.'

'It's not exactly a trophy. More a symbol or an ornament. Up close, it's a crouching skeleton, perched on a rock. I couldn't see any inscription. Just the figure, a man – no – a skeleton – like he – she? – was in thought.'

'Same as the card you showed me. And the thing round the big cat's neck.'

'Close enough. Cousins, if not brothers and sisters.'

'What is it? Why do the Bradleys have it?'

'You keep searching. I'll keep making it up.'

FIVE

My phone pinged as Hetherington and I climbed the stairs back to our office. I recognised Hammy's avatar as the message screen lit up.

'My office now. Wherever you are.'

I had been expecting that summons for a few days and realised that the review in the car with Hetherington was just the preparation I needed. He reached the top of the stairs four steps ahead of me, so I called to him and caught up.

'Kenneth, just a wee minute there. One more bullet point. Tip line. Anything coming in there?'

'Not much. The usual, and obvious, cranks. I chased a couple of dead ends. I'll check again.'

'See when you get to your desk, send me the ones you checked, sort of a top ten.'

'I don't think …'

'A top five then. Send me your best five. Straight away.'

We passed Sharon's desk. She was bent over a financial spreadsheet, making delicate tick marks on selected entries, with a finely-sharpened pencil. I placed the current issue of *Kick-Boxing International Monthly* at her left side and walked on. I'd picked it up when I'd bought the football for the girl. When I got to my own desk, I swivelled into my chair, so I could see Sharon. She continued marking the spreadsheet until she had completed another column, then glanced at the magazine, before returning to her scrutinies. I allowed myself the thought that I could see a smile below her fringe. In terms of the acceptance of a peace offering, I gave it three out of ten.

I scored zero the moment I entered Hammy's office. He

was standing by the window. Another man, as finely made as a whippet, sat at the desk, not quite commanding it but yet still managing to dominate the room. I walked to the window, ignoring the man at the desk.

'I got your message, sir. Hetherington and I were on our way in from interviewing a witness.'

The man beside the desk spoke.

'Pity you don't respond so promptly to all your messages. You've been not answering me for three days now.'

His voice was indiscriminately dark. Like his suit. Neither Hammy nor I turned away from the window.

'You know, Slevin,' my superior said. 'A man could spend a lifetime looking out of this window and not see the same thing twice.'

'It's the river, sir. It's never the same. It's the past flowing by us, in the present and, upriver, coming our way, there's a future we may never live.'

The voice behind us interjected with a laugh.

'If you two boyos are finished with the mock-philosophising, maybe we could do some police work here. Hammy, bring your man to heel.'

'This, Detective Sergeant Slevin, is Officer Cosgrove of Internal Security. You probably guessed that, from the sneering tone and the notable absence of any appreciation for your fine epigram.'

Hammy took me by the elbow, which was as close to bringing me to heel as he dared, and led me to a chair. We both sat down, so that we now formed an ungainly triangle around the rectangular desk. If a stranger came into the room, they wouldn't be able to work out who was in charge.

I sensed that the Internal Security man was waiting for Hammy, my boss, to get us started. He wore very light glasses perched across a fine aquiline nose that centred his perfectly formed face. He was handsome, lithe as a dancer in a musical chorus and still the right side of fifty. He stared hard at Hammy, who flicked dust motes off his grammar school tie, until he grew exasperated and turned directly to me.

'Detective Slevin, a simple question. Why didn't you respond to my messages?'

'I intended to today, sir. I received one, that I'm aware of. And I've been busy, as you say, doing 'police work'. I am working on the murder of Todd Anderson, sir.'

Internal Security are at Detective Sergeant level or above, though they're routinely referred to as Officers. It is best to assume they're on higher pay grade than yourself.

'I sent you three messages. That's the limit. After that, I call the boss. Isn't that right, DI Hamilton?'

'Oh, yes. Perfectly in order. Slevin, cooperate here. Cossie's not the worst of them. Me and him tramped the beat together, so at least he knows what that's like.'

Right on cue the message tone on my phone sounded and I reached into my jacket pocket.

'Excuse me. Police work.'

It was Hetherington's Tip Line Top Five. Every morning there's a survey of tips coming in on phone lines, social media, emails, messenger services, tweets and even the occasional letter. Detectives can search the survey for tips on cases they're working on. I scanned what Hetherington had sent me. As he'd said, nothing.

'Just following up some tips. It's the usual jigsaw in cases like this, but we're getting some of the pieces to fit.'

'You can tell DI Hamilton all your good news later. For now, another simple question. Why are you talking to Dessie Crossan?'

'Dessie Crossan?'

Cosgrove pulled a small notebook from his inside pocket,

flipped and scanned some pages, then said,

'Twice you've been with him in the past while. It's a case of re-connecting with old mates, old comrades, is it?'

'Oh, that Dessie Crossan. As I told you, DI Hamilton has me focusing on the Todd Anderson murder. Top priority. He told the CC he particularly wanted me on the case. She seemed pleased.'

'I've seen the photo, Slevin. On her office wall, alongside her golfing shots and other trophies. You both look well. The CC has a grip on your arm, which is the first move towards a choke hold. I took it she was trying to arrest you. Dessie Crossan, then?'

If I thought I could jump him by mentioning the Chief Constable, I was wrong. He simply trumped me by letting me know he was in her office. And by letting me know that whatever her intentions were in that regard, he wouldn't mind getting me in a choke hold and arresting me.

'Dessie Crossan is a source. One of many. I interviewed him in the course of my police work.'

Tell me who killed him.
Who?
Come on.
Roger Rabbit?
An aul' one, eh? Good film. I like Bob Hoskins.
Never in a bad film. Dead now.
This isn't a film. One shot. In the back of the head.
Professional hit man? Mafia job?
Pack it in.
You still haven't told me who got killed.
You know.

Lots of people got killed.
Todd Anderson.
English, was he?
Yes.
Lots of English men killed in Ireland. Hardly surprising.
Lots of them not killed here too.
Yeh. When they went home. Maybe he shot himself?
In the back of the head?
It's been done before. English man, you said.
Yeh.
Lots of suicides in barracks.
Anderson wasn't a soldier.
He was over here.
And that's enough reason to shoot him in the back of the head?
People have been shot for less. Irish people. What was he? A do-gooder?
A footballer.
Ah. Can't have been much good if they shot him. You investigating this?
Among other things.
Such as?
You're telling me you know nothing about Anderson's death?
I coach the under tens. Gaelic Football. You were a handy corner-forward in your day. That's the height of my interest in any kind of football.

Cosgrove would not let go.

'I don't need to remind you that Dessie Crossan is one of a number of people on your "don't go there" list. People, former associates we call them, that you're not to see without your superior's knowledge and express permission.'

My superior officer, DI Omar Hamilton, was finally satisfied with the dusting job on his tie and turned his full attention to the meeting. He infused his comments with the perfect blend of indignation, disapproval and chastisement.

'When Officer Cosgrove told me of these meetings, Slevin, I was shocked, I have to say. No, not shocked. Nothing shocks me in this job. But I was dismayed. You should have come to me, Slevin. You know I went out on a limb bringing you here. Other voices said you should have been deployed elsewhere. Up the country somewhere. But I said your unique talents and well, your rather unique background, could be most beneficially put to use here, in your home city. Perhaps you're not ready for that yet. Perhaps you would be better off in Belfast. Or Armagh.'

If that was a threat, I soon realised it was directed at Cosgrove, not at me, who wouldn't want me where it might be harder to keep on eye on me.

'I don't think we need to consider such a move, Hammy,' said Cosgrove. 'Not just yet. But DS Slevin needs to realise that his special experiences and contacts need to be used in the service of policing and not in the cause of subversion. Dessie Crossan is known to be actively fermenting dissent and he's exactly the sort of senior militant …

'He served his sentence,' I interjected.

'… around which disaffected young fellas would gather. And so are you, DS Slevin.'

'I'm a detective in Police Service North, Officer Cosgrove. The only thing disaffected young fellas want to do with me is kick the tripe out of me. Sir. I met Mr. Crossan as part of my investigations into the murder of Todd Anderson.'

'You could have sent another detective, Slevin.

Hetherington perhaps.'

'Wouldn't get in the door.'

'Do you think paramilitaries killed Anderson?' Hammy asked.

'Too early to say yes or no to that. No clear motive at this stage.'

'But you wouldn't rule it out,' Hammy persisted.

'It's all up in the air, sir. If you'd like a full update now, I can get my no …'

I began to get out of my chair. Cosgrove snapped at me.

'Sit down, Slevin. Remember why you are here.'

'Because I didn't return your call and you're hurt.'

'Eddie!' Hammy snapped.

'Because you've been meeting with someone you're not supposed to meet with and not telling anybody.'

'There's nothing to tell. When there's something to tell, I'll update my superior officer immediately.'

'So you intend to meet Dessie Crossan again?'

'I can't say, but now that my superior officer is aware of my contact with him, I will inform him of any future interviews I may have with him'.

'And you'll inform me. Because, given the transgression in this current instance, it will be better for you in the future if I'm kept informed. In fact, you can do the service a favour – and help yourself, Detective Slevin – if, next time you speak to him, you do so with a recording device.'

'A button? You want to fit me with a button?'

'Yes. The techies would love to fit a nice button on that fine suede jacket there. Or on your shirt cuff, if you preferred. They're tiny nowadays and offer greater range. They'd pick you up no matter when or where you and your associate – your former associate - held your reunions.'

'Dessie Crossan is a source. I have many sources. The

service has often found it useful to have someone with such sources. Fitting me with a recorder, no matter how tiny the button is, is a sure-fire way of shutting him up. Is that what you want?'

Officer Cosgrove stood up, shook himself loosely into the jacket of his three piece suit and pressed his palms onto Hammy's desk. He leaned over me, as an adult giraffe leans over its young to bite fleas off its back.

'I'll tell you what I want. I want to know what you and Dessie Crossan are concocting. I want to know that you're not supplying him with juicy titbits of confidential police business. What I don't want is boys like you jumping the wall with a chestful of nuggets for the bastards outside.'

'Ah. I should have known. From the fetid smell I got when I came in...'

'Slevin, watch your mouth,' Hammy interjected, but I drove on.

'... you're old school. One of the boyos who thought it was all about apples in a barrel and as long as the apples were the same and the barrel stayed round and fat everything was grand. But you couldn't have an ex-con about you, even though you know that the barrel of apples was rotten and that it needed turned upside down and readied for a whole new harvest.'

He was quicker than I expected and had me out of my chair with vice-grip hands on my lapels before I could react. Hammy put an arm on his shoulder.

'Cossie! Put him down. Don't let him rile you.'

I guessed Cosgrove had balsamic vinegar on a salad for lunch, as his breath billowed across my face. Small speckles of froth creased his clenched lips and his eyes sparkled like glass shards.

'You're right, Slevin. I never trusted the scheme that brought fellas like you, and the likes of you, in. I'd have let ye all rot away in prison. No coming back. But this goes on your record and stays there. You met with a man, a known, unrepentant ex-con, like yourself …'

'Cossie, for God's sake!'

'… and if you don't record the next time you speak to him, I'll grab your heels and I'll pull you in front of a panel so fast you'll think your arse was coming out your mouth.'

'Put me down, sir. Or your techies will have to replace all the buttons on this jacket.'

The glass shards in his eyes dulled. He licked the froth speckles from the corner of his mouth and released his grip on my lapels, opening his arms into a wide gesture of harmlessness.

I sat down again, making a show of checking my lapels and jacket for tears. Hammy had had enough. He grabbed the back of his chair pulled it square and centre behind his desk. Then he sat and framed his face with both forearms, his elbows firmly rooted to the shiny maple-effect surface.

'Slevin, a note has been made by IS in your file. I have been informed. You know what to do in the future. All further contact with Dessie Crossan or others on your proscribed list …'

'… only if you wear a button,' finished Cosgrove, pointing a finger at me.

I began to get out of my chair once more, but Hammy continued.

'Sit down. We're not finished here, you and me. Cossie, let's wrap up your business here, with an assurance that I will secure full compliance from Slevin in this matter from now on.'

I didn't get up as my superior led Cosgrove out of the office. When they had closed the door behind them, I went to the window once more. A buzzard flew above the oak trees in the park on the opposite bank of the river and, in a gap between the Technical College buildings, I could see water glistening like a simmering syrup in the sunlight. I was smiling when I turned to face Hammy, as he re-entered the room. My boss was laughing.

'Jesus, Slevin, what kind of circus do you think this is? All that stuff about apples, barrels and cores. I thought I was in a fruit market. You don't want to upset Cossie too much. In the grand scheme of things, he might be one of the good guys, though who am I to judge that? I've got you out there, all eyes and ears, and Cossie thinks you're leaking the lot to the bold boys, your old mates.'

'And what do you think?'

'I think you should avoid Dessie Crossan for a while. IS are obviously watching you. Or someone is. You haven't been using your phone to message Crossan have you? Or calling him or anything?'

I let that go. He knew the answer.

'Okay. Don't go near him unless you've got something solid that links him or his acolytes to the Todd Anderson murder. And when you do, come to me and we'll figure something out. Pull him in on some pretext. Get you in the room as the good cop, so he thinks you'll get him out. We'll figure something.'

'He won't fall for that, sir.'

'Don't tell me my job, Slevin. I just saved your bacon. Maybe even your whole carcass. I know what Crossan's boys would do if they knew you were recording and transmitting meetings. And you may have more to worry about than that. Here.'

He tossed me two sheets of paper.

'Last paragraph on page one, running on to the top of page two.'

I quickly scanned the two pages, going twice over the paragraphs he noted. The key sentences read,

'We can say with confidence, given the form, the residue

and the vestigial, though partial, striations, that the bullet is a .357 Magnum round of a generation of handguns from paramilitary arsenals. Further forensic analysis, including comparisons with appropriate decommissioned handguns, would be required.'

'"Vestigial". That's a fine word in any report,' I said.

'Not if the vestigial striations take us back to a .357 magnum used by a certain militant who served twelve years of a prison sentence before morphing into a detective in our Serious Crime Team. Imagine the fun Cossie and IS could have with that.'

'You're not suggesting ...'

'I'm not suggesting anything. Except that it's been my experience that, when investigations are not going well, bombshells from the past blow up in our faces. Coincidences turn out to be simply the run of events. Nothing is chance, Slevin. Certainly not in this game. Now get the fuck out of my office and, whatever else you do, don't bring IS round here again.'

I left with my tail not quite between my legs but not exactly waving proudly behind me. The confrontation with Officer Cosgrove rattled me, but no more than a spittle-sharing exchange with screws on B Wing. What stung me was the venom of Hammy's final remarks. I sensed my account with him was in danger of running out of credit.

Yes, I know a .357 Magnum. Yes, I had used one. Yes, I had it on me when I was arrested. Yes, it was used as an exhibit in my trial. Yes, I understood it was filed away under lock and key in police archives. Or was it?

I returned to my desk. Not even a 'thumbs up' from Sharon, as she browsed her magazine, lifted my gloom.

SIX

Early the next morning, I pulled back the curtains and looked down at the riverside walk, letting the sun find my bare chest, as I stretched my arms high above my head and yawned loudly. That woke Karen Lavery. I heard her turn in the bed behind me.

'That time already?' she said.

'That time always,' I replied. And added, 'There they go.'

A clutch of runners went past, rarely more than three abreast, hugging the rails along the river. The triple glazing meant I couldn't hear the chatty couples, who were always scattered among the groups.

'Who's that?' Karen boosted herself upright and reached for her watch on the unit beside the bed.

'The morning runners.'

'At this time. Quarter to seven. What makes them do it?'

'Death.'

'You're in fine form this morning. You dreaming again? Your mother?'

'I slept great,' I lied.

'You're a detective. Even in your dreams, you want to know what happened.'

'I sort of know that. I'm not sure about the "why?". Like the runners out there. I know what they're doing, but I'm not sure about why.'

In flashes of Lycra, the runners jogged by. Many wore shorts and sleeveless singlets, the running and the sunshine warming their flesh.

'They want to get fit, lose weight, get in better shape and, if that all works, stave off death. Or they damage themselves, wear out, accelerate a syndrome with an injury and infection and bring death closer.'

'I don't suppose you could crank up the coffee machine while you lecture on such gloomy matters.'

I turned from the window and leaned across the bed. Karen was sitting fully upright, fixing her watch to her wrist. I kissed the triangle between her breasts.

'You're the woman who works with death, day and daily.'

'But never before morning coffee.'

I lay beside her and felt a calm ease suffuse me. Light from the open curtains fell across us. Dust motes, enlivened by the heat, celebrated their dawn dance.

'You good?' Karen asked.

'Great.'

'You are, you know. Great. And I don't just mean this. You're just a great fella.'

I turned my head to look at her open and fresh face, her warm and clear eyes. She was wide awake and set to say more.

'And you're lonely.'

'You phoned me at half ten. You came round here.'

'I was lonely too.'

'And now?'

'I'm still lonely. But I've had a good work-out. Better than pounding the tarmac out there.'

The city is awash with runners, joyous people in the main, led by enthusiasts who coach them in times, diets, muscle stretches, footwear and mental strength. The runners all want something. Aspire, then perspire. They're all reaching for something. A better time; the loss of a few pounds; to outpace a friend; to make themselves feel better in the face of woe at home or at work; to replace work.

'When I was inside,' I said, 'I was always lonely, even

though I was never really alone. Near the end, I spent a lot of time buried in books and people did leave me alone. Kept out of my way. I went a bit crazy, they said. So, now, I suppose, even though I'm out a brave while, I'm still the same. Loneliness and me run along the river together.'

'I've had enough of being lonely, I think.'

This was the moment to get up and put on the coffee. To get up, shuffle into underpants, pad across the wooden boards to the ceramic tiles and start to grind the well-roasted beans. Fill the flat with the aroma of mornings in far away places, where the sun is permanent and where we face death by snoozing in the shade, not running in the light. Instead, I hesitated too long in the cosy bed.

'A fella – a neighbour actually – asked me on a date,' she said.

'A neighbour? Has he a farm?'

Karen is from farming stock, in the land just beyond the sky mountains. She grew up amidst sheep and learned the intimacies of life and death early on, helping her father on the snow-covered hills as the lambs fell bloody and bawling from their mothers' rears.

'Yes. His own, as well as he's tied in with his brothers on the old family farm.'

'A man of property. Is he a good man too?'

'He is. He's reckoned a bit of a catch.'

'Well then, a man of property meets a woman with a government job. I'd say the first thing to do is to say 'yes' to a date with him.'

I managed to stop myself from saying 'He could pick you up in his tractor.'

She stared hard at me and said,

'I reckon the very first thing for me to do is to stop coming round here for workouts. I should buy myself a pair of running shoes.'

I smiled at that and heaved myself out of the bed. I found my underpants on the neat pile of clothes on the chair under the window. I stepped into them balancing on one foot, then the other. I glanced out of the window once more. A lone straggler from a running group went by, panting hard, the flesh on his thighs glistening red, sweat blackening his yellow hi-vis singlet, but I could make out the text.

Run on. Run fast. Run Now.

Reading it made me tense my stomach muscles, slap them briskly, then stretch to touch my toes three times. As a charm.

'Coffee, then. You hit the shower first.'

It was clear we weren't going to shower together that morning. Perhaps never again. I put on a dressing gown and slippers and went to the kitchen, the dressing gown open and waving about me like a sail.

A sultry coffee aroma filled the kitchen by the time Karen came in, fully dressed. She briskly buffed her short fair hair with a bath towel. There was orange juice and floury baps on the table, beside an open dish of butter and a jar of raspberry jam. A beam of light caught it so that it shone like a squat ruby.

'You went out and got baps?'

'Naw. They're from a packet, but they're still in date.'

Karen dipped a knife in the raspberry jam and took a taste, holding the towel to her head with one hand.

'Home made jam, eh?'

'Not mine. Auntie Maisie's.'

'I told you. You're a good man. And there's no need to lay it on this morning. You had me in bed already.'

That must have brought a hurt look to my face, because she continued swiftly.

'Sorry. I was unkind. Bed was good. Breakfast is good too.'

'Bate it into you woman. I'll hit the shower.'

I took a hot demitasse of the coffee with me and went to the shower. I slugged down the bitter revival as I stepped into the scorching flow of water. I had no idea where things stood between me and Karen. I stayed under the hot shower until the water almost scoured me. Cleansed and buzzing, I returned to Karen, now sitting on the balcony over-looking the river, a second pot of coffee beside her, as she leafed through her crime scene report on Todd Anderson. Her short, fair hair nestled in a lively bob round her delicate features. Lightly-framed glasses rested on her fine nose and perfectly formed ears. In her dark blue linen suit, she looked more like a model from a French photo shoot, set to play *la gamine*, rather than a sheep-farmer's daughter.

'You're gorgeous, Karen. Gorgeous.'

She raised her eyes to me, took off her glasses and beckoned me closer. I leaned forward and she kissed my lips. I tasted woman and raspberries and morning and life rushing through me in a torrent, so that when I eased myself into a chair on the small balcony, I was a man fully awakened and ready for the day.

'Get that coffee into you, Slevin. I made a fresh pot. The day's upon us. Half the town's out running and cycling the bridges, the park and the riverside walk. What are they running from?'

'Death, I told you.'

'I don't believe you. Not in that way.'

She waved her sheaf of papers at me.

'Here's death enough for you. Let me tell you what bugs me about it.'

Karen put her reading glasses back on. They formed a golden filigree about her face, like the dress-mask on a denizen of a harem.

'The lividity. That's what bugs me.'

'Go on.'

'My own account here. 'The victim shows advanced *livor mortis*, indicating an estimated period of up to twelve hours from time of death.' I can't argue with the pathology there. But that means he was lying in an open field all night and half the evening before and no one saw him.'

'The club was on a World Cup break.'

'See Bechtimme's leading the goal-scorers' list? And that's him only playing half the games. My money's on the Germans, Slevin.'

'Anderson's body could have been held off-site for a time. Then brought in fairly quickly.'

'There's no evidence of a vehicle being driven onto the pitch.'

'He was carried.'

'Carried?'

'I reckon. At least two people. Strong people. Men, most likely.'

'We did find boot marks but nothing you could do anything with. The site is a quagmire of boot marks.'

'Two people, maybe three, to move him. He was a big, hefty lad.'

'And solidly muscled. An athlete obviously. You have any idea of a motive? Any leads?'

'Fairly thin. We know the source of the special marks. The Dreamtimes.'

I lifted a page from her report and read.

'*A pattern of indentations on the neck consistent with the mould-ings on the sole of a football boot, the Dreamtime.*

'It belongs to a girl, a twelve year old. Hetherington and me interviewed her. One of the ground-staff saw her on the day.'

'Did she see anyone?'

'She was there, yes. After Anderson's body was dumped. She has a routine. A thing she does. She's football crazy. Before school, she goes to the pitch and plays a bit. Takes a penalty or two.'

'And they let her in?'

'She's in and out early, usually before the ground staff arrive. She climbs over the wall, no matter what they do with barbed wire and barriers.'

'She told you all this?'

'Some of it. She knows nothing. The rest we got from Goss and Doherty's interviews with the ground-staff. Seems they spooked her that morning and she ran off. Then one of them walked onto the pitch after her, saw her scale the wall at the town end. And then he saw something on the penalty spot on the country end goal, called his muckers and they went over to Anderson's body.'

'With *livor mortis*. So he'd been there up to twelve hours, but you say "no". You reckon the body was stored elsewhere.'

'What about a chill room?'

'A freezer? There was no evidence of freezing.'

'No, not frozen. Chilled. You know, like you get in a supermarket. Where the milk and the yoghurt goes.'

'Jesus, you have the uniforms out searching supermarkets now?'

'No. Not yet.'

'That's fairly put a flavour in the breakfast. I need another shot of orange juice.'

She got up and went into the kitchen. I heard the fridge open, then hum quietly until the satisfying rubber-dampened clunk of the door closing. Two shags skimmed the waves right in front of me, as Karen sat down and poured orange juice from a carton labelled *Sunburst*.

'I'm going to say "yes",' she said.

'It's none of my …'

'It is some of your business. Some of our business. I'm going to say "yes" to the neighbour and see where it goes.'

Then we both looked over the river, where the water flows by as dreams do and gulls, singly and in small groups, come and go from the railings, squawking at each other like lost souls.

It was lunch-time when I heard my sister's voice carry down to me, as I climbed the stairs in the dark. I stood in the doorway of the lounge. Bewitched. Bothered. Bewildered. A dust-mottled shaft of light from somewhere off to the left picked out the singer, sitting upright on a three-legged bar stool, a mini music system propped on the bar beside her. Ruby has the straight nose, broad brow and solemn jaw that I have, in a more gentle form, but she also has a gleam in her eye that I don't.

I mimed applause, as she finished the great song and flicked the 'off' switch on the player beside her.

'Cracker,' I said. 'Have you a gig?'

'Naw.' Emphatic and warm. 'Jackie let's me use the lounge to rehearse on my break.'

'There's a good acoustic. Bluesy.'

'Aye. Great for Ella's stuff. Ma's stuff. Her Ma's stuff, probably.'

'I only half remember. Or think I do. We were only young when she …'

'Etta James too. The odd Billy Holiday. Great songs, right enough.'

'You're next in the line. You have the voice.'

'And what did you get? The thran' ways?'

'Give us another one then, sis.'

'A lucky dip.'

She hit the 'on' button and an intro began. High strings,

bluesy half notes, then my sister's voice, singing about a love that comes, at last. She sang on, then stopped to turn up the volume on the backing track and climb off the stool. She stepped towards me and took my arms to lead me in a slow revolve that became a gentle down-beat waltz that broke my heart. I rested my head on her shoulder and snuffled tears into her neck.

I broke from my sister and I handed her my handkerchief. She dabbed her neck and returned it to me.

'You okay?' she asked.

'Grand, yeh, grand. Why did she do it, Ruby?'

'Don't go back over it, Eddie. Leave her be.'

'I can't, Ruby. She … it's the job. She's Open Unsolved. A big thick file sitting on my desk and when I put my hands to it … I don't know, it flutters away like a plague of moths.'

'Is that a dream?'

'Yes.'

'Do you have other ones? You should go about it. See somebody.'

'I see you.'

'Me? I'm an estate agent's secretary, not a psychologist.'

Her laugh chimed lightly from the bottles on the shelves behind the bar.

'You're my sister. And a singer. Like her.'

'We should put up a stone. Something permanent, just for her. I know her name is on her mother's stone, but it's not hers.'

'Jesus, I don't know …'

'Listen Eddie, she's not one of your files. One of your cases. She's our mother. She reared us on her own. She threw herself into the river, years ago. We got up anyway and here we are. You know she's dead. Drowned and pulled from the river, waked in front of her friends and neighbours, who were so stunned they cried a deluge; in front of her kids, so thunderstruck they took to self-harming, street wandering and gun toting. It's a major miracle we survived.'

'That's all in the past.'

'It is. Put the last vestiges of it there and you'll be grand.'

'That's the second time that word's come up recently. Vestige. A trace, a scrap, a shred. A fading footprint.'

'Faded, Eddie, faded,' Ruby said, pulling a large handbag across the bar top. She turned the volume down on the backing tracks.

'You want to share my lunch?'

I pulled up another barstool. Ruby poured sweet coffee from a flask and popped open a plastic container from which she retrieved a homemade tuna and mayonnaise sandwich she ripped in two, passing half to me. We ate in silence, the upturned cap of the flask, filled and refilled with black coffee tantalising as sherbet, cooling between us.

The light moved across the bar floor and soon we sat in darkness. The tuna brought me a briny smell, as I touched it to my lips, a sense of the sea lulling up against the side of the bar, the wooden spars of our fragile family vessel that day. Eventually Ruby screwed the cap back on her flask. I brushed crumbs from the front of my jacket and sucked a lace of peppery rocket from between my teeth.

'You working?' she asked.

'Lunch. Like you. A couple of domestics to do. You going back?'

'I'll sing a couple more numbers. I'm only round the corner in Castle Street. What brought you here anyway?'

'To see you.'

'You alright for money?'

'Fuck off.'

We both laughed and I leaned forward and patted her arm. We're not a hugging family. But we dance.

I turned and walked through a shaft of light, illuminated for an instant, as in a polaroid flash. Behind me, I heard the strings again, this time lush and swirling. Then Ruby's voice, singing an eternal goodbye. I faced her and we sang together, until I stopped and asked,

'Why do you always sing the sad ones?'

Ruby turned off the music.

'They're the only ones I can stand, this time of day. Anything lighter than tragedy and I start to bawl.'

I smiled at her, but how could she see in the brewery-smelling dark?

I needed a piss and went into the Gents on the first landing, as I descended. A man stood at one of the urinals.

'You're the cop, aren't you?'

When I didn't answer, he continued,

'You're the cop put Sean Quigley away. For killing my cousin.'

He released the heavy stream of a lager drinker, zipped himself up, heaved his hips back into his trousers, then tucked his shirt around his tub-shaped belly. He turned to face me. I stayed near the door, eyeing the keyboard on a stand, beside the partitioned toilet cubicle, with its door open, so I could see its cracked and soiled porcelain. I'd worked out that, if necessary, I could pick up and throw the Yamaha PSR-S1150 and make it out the door before the man recovered.

'He'll get out some day, you know that, Sean Quigley,' the man said.

'I know that.'

'And see when he does, make sure you put the bastard back in again. Fast. For his own good.'

Then he walked past me and out the door.

When I made it to the urinal, it took me a while to produce

anything and when I did get going, it was more trickle than rush. I tidied myself up, washed and dried my hands, ran my fingers down the soundless keys of the Yamaha and left, wondering about the musician who discarded the instrument.

There was no sign of the man from the toilet when I made it downstairs to the bar. Jackie, the bar manager, was bent over, clunking bottles of mixers into the recessed shelves. He got up, as I reached the bottom step.

'Sounding good, she is.'

'Great,' I agreed.

'Best thing me and Ruby ever did, getting divorced. She sings here at me work. She gets to be grateful to me for doing her a favour. And we don't have to worry that we're missing something. That there's something more than what we've got.'

I nodded. Jackie knows that Ruby divorced him because she grew up. She does think there could be something more in her life, that there is something she could aspire to, aim for, reach even. Some grander, bigger, version of herself, beyond her current life. A dream, always just in reach, she sings to charm closer.

And how do I pursue my dreams? I look for clues in my past, test theories in my present and expect little of my future.

'Your man that just went out. Big fella in a blue jacket. You know him?'

'Big fella in a blue jacket. Never seen him.'

That's how it's going be then, Jackie. Fair enough.

'See you, Jackie. Good luck.'

'Right, aye.'

I left the midday gloom of the bar and stepped into a breezy skiff of rain, flicked up my collar and walked through Castle Gate, thinking about tragedy and how Ruby assuaged it with songs and how in Thebes, another city of many gates, the songs of the Nile birds called over the bodies of the dead.

I entered my own walled city, stone built upon stone, in good time for my dentist's appointment.

I was trying to avoid sucking on a new filling when I heard Tony White's voice, as I walked through Butcher Gate later. He was behind the police barricade, in the middle of a parking lot of vehicles. Tony was leaning against the WART wagon.

'You on duty too, Slevin? I don't see you in ages and here we are falling over each other in a matter of months,' he said.

'The brass are expecting wild animals today?'

'In this town, anything's possible. Routine follow-up to a bit of intelligence. Keep an eye behind you. We're expecting a few giraffes.'

'And you'll shoot them when they appear?'

'Don't think so. Bit of corralling maybe. Handy overtime, Slevin. You know the score.'

Then Amy Miller climbed out of the cab of the vehicle. She was taller than I remembered, with the same lithe movements and the eyes that held mine fiercely, yet warmly.

'No shooting today. They wouldn't let me bring my gun.'

'Ah, Amy, right on cue. Meet DS Slevin, my – er – college mate. That's right, we went to school together. Different classes. He studied Irish history. I studied British. Then we both went on to third level at PS (North). Figure it out yourself. Eddie, this is Amy Miller.'

She took my hand and shook it firmly. I felt like she had given me a gift.

'Amy, you listen to this fella's shite for a while. I'll take the weight off me feet. I reckon another ten minutes, maybe sooner, and we'll be clear.'

Tony moved to the front of the vehicle, squeezing a boyish grin at me, as he hauled himself up, saying,

'There's nothing going on here.'

He was out of hearing, when Amy said,

'I wouldn't be so sure about that.'

I smiled. The gift I gazed upon grew more fascinating.

Amy continued in the same vein.

'Status update. I'm not married or in a relationship. You?'

I thought of Karen and intermittent mornings spent laughing and bashing each other with rolled-up sections of the weekend newspapers.

'No. Neither.'

'Okay. How do we do this then?'

'You promise not to shoot me?'

'You're not a wild animal, are you?'

'I can be. There's a time and a place for everything.'

Her smile broadened and she handed me a card.

'Phone numbers on that, including a personal one. Call, if it feels right. And then we'll see. I have a chair and a whip too. Part of the WART kit.'

'Sounds like a great job. Maybe I should apply for a transfer.'

'Tony wouldn't have you. He says you're too smart for your own good and would only cause bother.'

'An astute character assessment.'

'That's why he's the boss.'

The WART vehicle grumbled into life beside us and Amy gave a yelp. Tony White's arm waved out of the passenger side window and Amy shouted 'Coming' before leaning forward and touching her fingers to my arm. No more than a touch, but it lit me up like a furze blaze in summer.

The side panel of the van slid open and a colleague's arm reached for Amy, who hoisted herself upwards, slamming the door behind her. The WART van, bearing my new flame-thrower, eased into the convoy of police vehicles nosing along Butcher Street.

There, on the edge of The Diamond, high above the vehicles and the metal barrier, a banner flew, illustrated with various motifs, one of them a skeleton, deep in thought, seated upon a rock.

SEVEN

It is my experience of the world that gifts come at a price. In this case, the price became deferral and delay as the Todd Anderson case itself took fire and blazed from a reservoir of ice. That night I dreamed of Amy Miller, contoured onto a lounger made over in ocelot fur, a sniper's rifle across her thigh and a smile that said 'game time' on her lips. I woke to a phone call from Hetherington.

'They found Anderson's other shoe. I'll pick you up in fifteen minutes.'

I stood on the Strand Road, behind my river-facing apartment block, in fragile sunbeams unconvinced they were shining on the right place. I climbed into the saloon Hetherington pulled up in and neither of us spoke. The morning would tell us what we needed to know.

We drove along the Buncrana Road, still shaking off its night feel. A dog walker scooped and bagged her Labrador's leavings into a lavender, plastic hand-glove. Two teenage girls, their school stockings hiked to perfectly matching pitches on their calves, walked briskly to a bus-stop. A milk van came to a sliding stop with a squeal of brakes and a rattle of crates at a side junction. Hetherington took us to the Skeoge Road, where he turned the car into a square of low industrial units, all shuttered down except for one marked *Chill Express*, before which two police land rovers were parked and a clutch of crime scene officers passed equipment to each other.

Hetherington parked and told me what he knew.

'Your mate Karen Lavery caught this one early. And got the night desk to contact me. She reckons we should see it.'

Karen had not phoned me directly. I had not seen her since she told me she planned to date the farmer.

She was at the back of the unit when I entered. Only one strip light was working, so gloom and cold gave *Chill Express* whatever grim atmosphere it could. Karen shone a torch into the cavern of a half metre deep chiller unit that ran the length of the back wall. It was as grimy as the inside of a bath left too long in the rain and contained one item: a shoe. A two-tone, brown and white Oxford Spectator, very soiled. Karen got straight to business.

'Vice have been watching this place for a while. Then there was a tip off from PS(S) about a cross-border move. Then nothing. So Vice got access, found it empty and called me to do a sweep. On the off-chance. I saw the shoe and remembered the Anderson case. I locked the scene down and brought in a crew.'

'Great, Karen. Great. Thanks. You look good.'

'Thanks. Yeh. New hair do.'

A lifted bob, higher on one side, highlighting the perfect form of her left ear and the serene gaze from her brown eyes.

'The new man?'

'You didn't call.'

'I … if …'

'What I mean is, I'm not sitting around waiting for you to call. Either are you, but I thought after what I told you that day …'

'Let's talk about the shoe. It'll be easier for both of us to start there.'

She blew a short gasp between her cheeks, ruddy in the chill air.

'Oxford Spectator. Italian made. See the manufacturer's name. Borini. Or something. Soiled, but looks in good condition. I'll bag it and compare it with the one we got from

Anderson's corpse. If it's a match, and a tenner says it is, then your story works – that his body was kept chilled for a while before being transported to the football pitch.'

'Nothing else here? Fingerprints? Blood? Tissue? Fabric?'

'Still checking. The team arrived just before you. Don't worry, we'll give the chiller the full treatment.'

'What was it used for?'

'Food, most likely brought here in bulk, maybe repackaged and probably off-loaded to small independents. Sandwiches, wraps. They might even have made up stuff here. Not sure yet. Everything was stripped out of it, except this brute. Too big to move.'

'Does it work?'

'Yep, when you switch it on.'

We both smiled at that. Maybe we were back on song.

'Who owns it?'

Hetherington joined us and answered my question. He'd spoken to a Vice Squad detective, as we came in.

'A letting agency, *Property Max*, handles it. Vice have spoken to them and will send me their notes. We can follow up, if we think it would help us.'

'Do that. Get a list of renters and, from them, a list of clients and suppliers. Do the same for all the units in this square. Someone may have seen something when Anderson's body was stored here …'

'Before he was killed?'

'He was killed and then brought here.'

'Hold on Slevin, we haven't found any blood. No fabric. No tissue. Nothing.'

'He was naked and in a clear plastic bag.'

Karen and Hetherington looked at each other. The cold in the industrial unit deepened. The single strip light fizzed a hornet's warning. She had seen me act the shaman before, the one who pulled stories and visions out of the air. Hetherington, the sceptic who hadn't known me long, made to speak and I cut him off.

'He was stripped, held, shot, put in a plastic bag, almost a tarpaulin, stored here, then dressed and moved. They lost the shoe then. And they burned the plastic. We'll never find that.'

The fact that I knew what I was talking about because of events in my past didn't put Hetherington off.

'Are you reading this from a file, sir? From something you haven't shown me?'

'Ah now, DC Hetherington, you must know all about your superior's famed extra-sensory perceptions.'

Karen could get away with such scoffing. She'd been there when my images and stories had borne fruit. She was there the day I placed a shooter in the trees, for the murder of a taxi driver, when strong evidence pointed to a gunman on the street. Uniforms climbed the tree and found a cigarette paper and tobacco grains from which forensics were able to lift fingerprints, fresh and strong enough to guarantee a conviction.

And if she scoffed and I smiled, as I did, was I in love with her?

'Wrap up here, Kenneth. Check for any further details with Vice on the way out. I'll see you in the car in a minute.'

He didn't like being dismissed and I knew I would have to make it up to him, but I needed a word with Karen.

'You still seeing visions then?' she asked.

'Don't overdo it, Karen. Intuitions. Hunches. Notions. Myths.'

'Aye, They still keep you awake at night?'

'I ... sometimes ...'

'The ones with your mother?'

'Karen ...'

'Half our bother, Eddie. You can't be helped.'

'I'm grand. You?'

'Good, actually. Good, yeh.'

'Sorry I didn't …'

'Neither did I, so we're quits.'

'The farmer treating you right?'

'I'm taking it handy. We'll venture a weekend away, see how he manages out of his wellies.'

'It's all about the footwear, isn't it? Get me what you can from the shoe and we'll take it from there. And good luck. With the weekend and all.'

Karen smiled, so serenely, I almost reached for her, but how could I do that with Anderson's shoe lying upside down in the grimy chiller, Hetherington drumming his fingers on the steering wheel outside and the vague sense that I was being unfaithful to Amy Miller bilious in my stomach?

I was right. Hetherington was drumming his fingers on the steering wheel and gasping like a spawning salmon about to attempt the final weir. He had us underway even before I'd snapped my seat belt closed.

He drove us out of the industrial park, onto the link road and along the Buncrana Road towards town, in a righteous huff of which any spotty-faced, acne-ravaged teenager would be proud. I used the time to reflect on meeting Karen again, wondering if I should attempt to pick up with her once more. I admitted to myself that whatever I happened to be good at, sticking with relationships wasn't included.

My reveries were broken as a radio message crashed in.

'Pennyburn shops. Officers requiring urgent assistance. Respond, if in vicinity.'

Hetherington staccatoed back.

'Hetherington and Slevin. Serious Crime Team. On Buncrana Road. Will attend. Five minutes.'

He put on the siren, overtook the car in front and sped

down the wrong side of the road, raced through the roundabout at the Sports Complex and reached 80 km per hour on the straight that followed. I sat upright, faced ahead and felt good. His huff was being put to positive use.

When we reached the traffic lights at the Pennyburn shops, a uniform directed us to take a left and Hetherington swung our saloon like a doll on the end of a rope. I felt the g-force almost take me out the door. Hetherington slammed on the brakes just behind a police Land Rover, got out immediately and galloped off. I sat still, slowly undid my seat belt and concluded my musings about Karen with the thought that, as she had indeed been right about Germany winning the World Cup, maybe she was right to move on. When it comes to love, going back is likely a folly.

I stepped into a wrecking yard of vehicles on a busy street, with a carnival of on-lookers huddled in fear-filled clutches. There was a parade of shops, emptied of customers. I became a piece in a jigsaw of cars, a bus, a bicycle, a van and people, all tossed together by accident and collision. A tumult of images rose within me.

A double-decker bus, pulling away from the stop, new passengers on board, moving to climb the hill in the direction of Shantallow. A blind spot on the driver's-side wing-mirror. A bicycle overtaking and crossing onto the opposite side of the road. A collision. A van coming down the hill swerving, avoiding the bicycle. The van smashing into a parked car, bumping it forward to rear-end a delivery truck. A road traffic accident.

I exhaled heavily. I saw an ambulance arrive and park half on/half off the pavement outside a Chinese take-away. Paramedics leapt out and made for the prone figure on the ground. It was curled in the foetal position beside the shattered front wheel of the bicycle, which was twisted like a slice of squeezed orange fruit.

Further key figures emerged from the scene. There was Hetherington beside a uniformed officer, one of two uniformed personnel first on the scene. The uniform was gesticulating with both hands, a dervish in near-frenzy.

A large, black SUV came down the hill and pulled up on the pavement beside the bank. Four men got out, led by a large man in a blue jacket. I recognised him from the toilet with the abandoned keyboard. The men walked towards the red van and then I saw Martin's brother, the man who had given me the note-filled wallet. The man in the blue jacket spoke to him. The other three formed a phalanx around them.

Buttoning my jacket against the breeze, I skirted the ambulance and walked behind the people outside the take-away, the sports-goods shop, the mini-market and the off-licence. And stopped. I let Hetherington and the traffic officer see me. I gestured up the hill, pointing at the traffic officer and indicating a turn about fifty metres away, that could provide a diversion for cars. Hetherington nodded and spoke to the uniform once more, who then ran up the hill, mouthing into his radio and gesturing to drivers to stop and turn off. Car horns began to blare on both ends of the mêlée, as a small bus pulled up behind our saloon. A transport company inspector and two other men, one of them a mechanic, got off the bus.

I walked to the Travellers, gathered outside the bank and stood in front of the man who gave me Martin's wallet.

'You got a bit of bad luck there. The fella on the bike coming at ye.'

There was a pause and a perceptible tightening of the group, even though no one seemed to move. The man in the blue jacket spoke.

'Don't mind him, Mick. Bloody cop.'

Mick. Now I had the name.

'The wallet, Mick. Martin's wallet, he got when he was twenty one, I gave the money to the Hospice. They were glad of it. You know, helping people dying.'

Mick said, 'It's alright, Vincent.'

I had another name. The man in the blue jacket was Vincent.

'I could do nothing. I was coming down the hill, handy-like, slowing for the lights. I seen the bus pull out, then your man on the bike cem round flying. I swung in away from him and clipped the black Golf there. An aul' tip, no more.'

And the black Golf bumped into the back of the delivery truck, so that both its front and rear ends were damaged. The streetside rear light of the truck was broken. The owner of the black Golf, a young woman, was seated on the step of the mini-market, crying. An older woman held a bottle of water to her lips.

'There was no one in the Golf or the truck when they were hit. No one was hurt there,' I said.

The car horns stopped blaring. More uniforms arrived. They began to move people along and tape off areas. An officer approached us. I showed her my badge.

'Slevin. Serious Crime Team. Do what you can to clear the path. Thanks. Then please come back to me.'

She held my gaze for a moment, not sure if I was genuine. She might ask me to verify my ID. She might call me in. She might ask me to move along. She might mistake me for one of the Travellers. I put extra gravel in my voice.

'Thank you, Constable McLaren,' I said, reading her name badge.

She nodded, still unsure, then gathered the onlookers in front of the bank with a comprehensive sweep of her arms, then moved them around the corner and behind the police cordon.

'If Vincent and the lads could move back – maybe one of them stay with you, Mick – then we could get cleared up and get on with it.'

'Yer man on the bike, is he okay?'

'The ambulance crew has him.'

'Wasn't me that hit him.'

'I know. Look, you can see the way he fell. The way you ended up.'

One of the younger men was taking a video of the scene. I was about to ask him to stop when I realised he wasn't alone. All around me people were using devices to take photographs and videos of vehicles, their orientation to one another and the damage done to them. A hum of voices rose, such as might be heard around a hive as it prepares to swarm.

'You'll have to make a statement, Mick. One of the Traffic cops'll do it. There'll be no bother.'

He looked at me. I read, 'yes, there'll be no bother, because I say there'll be no bother' in his eyes. He turned to Vincent and the others. I couldn't hear what he said to them.

I turned to the scene on the street. Hetherington and a senior traffic officer I could only see from behind were talking to the transport inspector. The passengers were being led off the bus involved in the crash and brought onto the smaller bus. The driver, the inspector and the mechanic stood back on the pavement. The small bus reversed, then drove off, to complete the route. The stricken cyclist, now on a gurney, was wheeled onto the ambulance, which took off immediately.

The hum around me reached a peak and a man, the driver of the delivery truck, called out, 'what the fuck are yeez going to do about this?'

The officer I'd spoken to clasped him by the arm and led him back towards the Chinese take-away, where she passed him to a colleague, who took out a notebook and began to take notes. The onlookers attention turned away from us and towards the delivery driver.

Mick finished talking. Vincent and two other Travellers climbed into the SUV and drove back up the hill. A uniform unhooked the tape and let them through. Constable McLaren came up to me and said,

'Why are they leaving the scene?'

'They have nothing to do with it. This man, Mick, was driving the red van. He'll tell you what happened. How's the cyclist?'

'Busted up, but conscious. Lucky enough.'

'The truck driver?'

'Calmed down. Not a big deal for him. The car driver, her father is with her now. They only live round the corner. She dropped into the shop on her way up to town. She'll be okay.'

Her account was as comprehensive as her street clearing.

I called Mick over.

'This officer will take your statement. She'll sort things out. Talk to her. And you know where I am if you need me.'

He surprised me by taking my hand and shaking it. I felt the firm roughness of his palm and the sense that he was trusting me not to let him down.

'This will be grand. There's no bother for you here. And the cyclist is conscious.'

'Let me know how he gets on.'

'Constable McLaren, here, will take your statement. And she'll keep you informed on the state of the cyclist.'

Hetherington waved to me and I joined him in the middle of the street.

'I see you got rid of the Travellers.'

'Easy, now Kenneth. They moved off themselves. Traffic have this in hand now.'

'I thought the bus men were going to get into it. They were

livid. They kept saying the cyclist was crazy. Then, when they saw the Travellers arriving, I thought ...'

'You handled it well, Ken. You're still pumped up after *Chill Express*. You can calm it.'

'What the fuck do you mean? You treated me like a lackey back there.'

'Shut it, Hetherington. Last thing this fuck up needs is two cops rowing in the middle of the street. We've done what we can here. Let's get back to the station. And see the silent treatment you were giving me before we got this call? Switch it on again for the journey home.'

EIGHT

Soon afterwards, Hetherington drew away from me. It started with a ping from Hammy to both our phones.

'Tuesday 8.30. Conference Room. Anderson case. Notes in advance.'

Hetherington and I worked up the notes and he bulletted them through. Things were icy between us and I knew we'd need a session to clear the air. Events took over and, as always happens, change came, but not the way it was expected.

Hammy was in place well before us, the air con in the Conference Room plunged to minus. The bullets, judiciously formed by Hetherington, pulsed on the main screen and on three touch screen pads, on the desk in front of us. The near-vacancy of the room turned the temperature down even further.

'Progress, men. Progress. And the lack of it. Anderson, dead and gone. Me too. Not far off it. Got a bit of a grilling from the CC late last week. You get it this week. She's voracious, men. A top-loading incinerator. We've got to keep her filled.'

'Even if it is rubbish, sir.'

Hetherington had been growing narkier since the incident at *Chill Express*. I thought it was me he disliked. Seemed he'd shifted his aim to the boss. Hammy didn't rise to him.

'Yes, Detective Constable Hetherington, you and Slevin here are experts in the stuff. Let's for once assume you may possibly have unearthed a jewel from the brock. Known female associates?'

'Three.'

'Interviews?'

I let Hetherington continue.

'Annexe 4, sir.'

Hetherington thumb-swiped his pad and all screens changed to show a list of Anderson's 3 girlfriends, with 2-line summaries of their interviews. We scanned silently.

'Nothing. He was as good as a monk. Not like a footballer at all, even with his looks, physique, money, opportunity, fame. You say he wasn't gay?'

'No known male associates. No talk of him on the scene.'

Hammy looked at Hetherington and arched an eyebrow grandly.

'A bloody altar-boy. Who abuses an altar-boy?'

I let that freeze in the chilly air.

'Let's go the classic route. Motive. Nil. Opportunity. Plenty, but nothing leading. M.O.? Slightly crazy, especially with Slevin's theory that he was kept on ice for a spell.'

'Those notes are in annexe 2, sir.'

It was my turn to thumb my screen. I continued.

'No need to go through them in detail again. If I highlight the key lines at 790 you'll read "The shoe is confirmed as the second of the pair worn by Todd Anderson. Fabric, hair and tissue samples found are inconclusive. Further corroboration needed before confirmation could be given to the theory that a body, Todd Anderson's or any other, was stored there."'

'*Nul points* yet again. Bit of a fiasco. No one noticed him missing? Last seen?'

'In the gym, doing his own work. Then having dinner at *La Toscana*.'

'Date?'

'Alone. He liked Italian and ate there often. The owner described him as a good customer, quiet and polite. They talked football.'

'The bloody altar-boy again. Bit of a Billy-no-mates, too.

By "date" I meant "when", Slevin.'

'Oh, the night before his body was found. The time-line is in annexe 1.'

'Annexe this and annexe that. Is there nothing in the actual report?'

Another question I reckoned best left to cool in mid-air.

'You got nothing from the wee girl either? Nothing you could follow up?'

I thumbed once more and brought up Teresa Bradley's note, just as she'd emailed it to me within an hour of completing the interview at her home.

We read in silence once more, then Hammy said,

'*I took a penalty. The man was there.* Strange child. What about the father?'

'Straight as a die. I interviewed him at his work. Mother too. Nothing linked them to Anderson. They're struggling a bit with Teresa.'

'Who wouldn't?'

'The father's a bit of a property magnate, alongside his brother. They used to lay carpets, now they rent flats and houses. They're late-arrival golfers.'

'Enough of the crap socio-economic analysis, Slevin. The football club – players, officials, staff?'

Hetherington took over and began whizzing us along.

'More blanks, sir. That's annexe 3. A large section, as you can see. The club, including supporters, were all shocked, sir. Couldn't make sense of it. A couple of his team-mates I interviewed broke down in tears. The club organised a testimonial game against a League Select. Players came from Dublin, Belfast, Limerick, Cork. A couple of ex-players came back from England and Scotland.'

Hetherington was whirring through the screens now. He used a red triangle pointer, tidy as a rowing punt, to signal and highlight sections as he spoke. I admired his work and wondered if we might develop into a team. Hetherington, the analyst. Me, the what? Mythologist?

'A cheque, towards expenses, went over to the family in Manchester. Some people – club officials, players, supporters – wanted to travel for the funeral, but the Anderson family solicitor advised against it. The arrangements were strictly private. Family only.'

'I assume we had someone at it.'

Again, no response. Hammy fixed his sternest gaze on me.

'The two ice-queens of the north, PS (North) that is, remain mute on that one too.'

'Sir, if I may raise a slightly troubling note …'

'Fire away, Slevin. Fire away.'

'Anderson's remains went back to Manchester very quickly. Very early. And now they're cremated. I wondered at that decision at the time, but it was already in train when Goss and Doherty passed me – passed us – the murder book and files.'

DI Hamilton stood up and walked round behind us. A buzzing I hadn't noticed, until it stopped, told me he'd turned off the air con.

'Blasted yoke. A folly, man. A folly. Like much of what we do and see here.'

He sat down again, in the jagged arc formed by the three chairs we occupied in front of the big screen and he thumbed his own pad to the very brief page marked 'Summary', dated with the day's date. I knew we were almost finished.

But Hetherington wasn't.

'If I may, sir …' – emphasising the 'I' – 'The decision to release the body to the family was, is, surprising, but we're past that. What troubles me sir' – again the personal emphasis – 'is that we have no knowledge of the weapon.'

There's a gun.
A gun?
A .357 Magnum.
That's a gun, right enough.
One of ours. Yours.
Ours? We don't have guns.
It was returned.
Like to the library. They said it was overdue?
Not to the library. To a judge. To the cops.
Should have gone to the library.
Forget the library.
You went to the library. You're the man for the books.
You know anything about the gun?
Ask the cops. They have all the guns.

'Yes, the weapon. Good, Hetherington. Good. I see Annexe 6 has all the ballistics. It's thinner than the chiller report.'

Hammy was thumbing as he spoke, gathering control.

'Vacuous. Speculative. Worse even, for men in our game, absolutely aspirational and no more. We need more than "if only".'

'Yes sir,' said Hetherington. 'I wonder if now might be the time to ask, you know, the CC if necessary, for more resources.'

I was seeing a new side to Hetherington. The Empire Builder.

'Bring in some specific scientific resources. There's a lab I visited in Dublin and they're doing …'

I saw a spark of interest illuminate Hammy's eyes. I needed to quell it or at least deflect it away from the lab in Dublin.

'Hetherington's right, sir. About resources. We need to draw in some more. And we need to be seen to be doing something, of our own, if you understand me. I'm not convinced forensic evidence will do us much good at this point. Perhaps later. We need, as you said yourself, opportunity, motive, witnesses, perpetrators. The classics, as you said.'

'What are you suggesting, Slevin?'

'A trip to Manchester. Family background. There's nothing gripping here.'

'You? To Manchester? You forget you're our special vintage wine. You don't travel away from the sunny side of the home vineyard.'

'Not me, sir. Detective Constable Hetherington.'

If my colleague could have levitated off his seat, he would have. If Hammy had sheets of paper in front of him, he would have gathered them, shuffled them, tapped them on his knee and built them into a pile. Instead he hit 'home' on his pad, so that the main screen went to the PS(N) corporate logo. He beckoned to us to return our machines to him and he stood up.

'A wee run to Manchester? Time it so you could catch a game, eh Hetherington?'

And that's how I pushed Hetherington away from me, away from the gun, and how DI Hamilton could tell the Chief Constable that progress was being made.

NINE

I was tired most nights. I thought taking a bath would help.
Night by night, I climbed out of tepid water, dried off and put
on a dressing gown. I shaved and doused myself with cheap
eau-de-toilette. I sat at my desk in front of the open window,
overlooking the river. I thought about closing it, sensing a slight
shiver. The clock on the Guildhall sounded 11. The small desk
light, a replica of the one in my prison cell, spread a magnolia
halo on my books and pages. A matt black fountain pen my
sister Ruby gave me, lay open in two parts on a sheet of tissue
paper. I returned to the books. Lying across each other, like
open sheets of ribs, lay Thoms' *Lays and Legends of Ireland*
(1834), Wood-Martin's *Traces of the Elder Faiths in Ireland*
(1933), Jeremiah Curtin's *Myths and Folk-lore of Ireland* (1890)
and Carl Jung's *Symbols of Transformation* (1956).

I was engrossed in thoughts on my dreams, when my
phone sounded. I rooted for it among my papers.

'Is this Edmund Slevin?'

'Yes.'

'Ah. This is Rail Service North. You left a parcel on the
train. The Belfast train. The 22.23. A file sort of thing.'

I tried to remember the last time I'd been on the train.

'Your name and this phone number was on the outside.
The cover. I didn't open it. That's how I tracked you down.
Your number, like.'

Everyone's a detective.

'What's your name?'

'Eh. Jake.'

'And you're there now? At the station?'

'Yeh. Eh, I'm on 'til 23.30, but you know, if I can … Last man out, like.'

'And you have the file?'

''Course. That's why I'm phoning you.'

'Thank you, Jake. I'll be there in ten minutes.'

I dressed quickly and left the apartment. I thought of returning to get a coat but decided the wind-cheater and the brisk walk would be enough to keep me warm on a late August night. I took the path beside the river and headed briskly for the Peace Bridge. There was a smell of stale turpentine from the river, as if a painter had washed his brushes there. The water was as tarry as sump oil, heaving back and forth like the scaly abdomen of a sleeping dinosaur. There was more light when I reached the bridge, which I crossed alone and at pace, flashing through the photo-blasts of the beaming lights on the spars. The wind sharpened itself between the struts of the bridge and cut into my face. August played hard October. By the time I crossed the bridge and descended the final path to the railway station, I regretted not taking a winter coat, a pair of gloves and a wooly hat.

A dim light took me to the office, where I saw Jake hunched at a computer, playing solitaire. I rapped on the glass window and he looked up, surprised. He came over and we spoke via the connecting microphones and speakers. His voice sounded mechanical. I guessed mine sounded like a buzz-saw. My teeth were chattering by then.

'You phoned and said you had a package of mine.'

'Eh, sorry.'

'I'm the fella you phoned. The file. Edmund Slevin.'

'I gave it to you.'

'No, you didn't. I only just arrived.'

'Eh, yeh. No. I gave it to the other fella. Edmund Slevin.'

I had to clench and unclench my cold hand to get it to

work properly before retrieving my ID from my inside pocket.

'That's me. Edmund Slevin. See?'

'Jes … You're a cop too.'

'Yes. Who's this "other fella"?'

'Eh, I don't know. I mean. Edmund Slevin. He had ID. Same as that.'

'The other fella was a cop?'

'Yeh, he had the same ID. Different photo. But same name and all that. Edmund Slevin. Serious Crime something. Detective, like.'

'Did he look like me?'

'No.' Jake was adamant about that. 'He didn't look like you. He was older and bigger. Taller. He looked like a detective. He had a detective's coat on, with the collar turned up.'

'I bet he had a hat too.'

'Yeh, yeh. That's right. He had a hat, a black one, like in an old film. Like Sean Penn.'

'Show me the video.'

'The video? With Sean Penn? I don't think …'

'No, the security video for the ticket booth. The foyer area, here.'

'Eh, I don't … You'd have to ask the station manager to see that.'

'Jake, you want to get away as close to half eleven as you can, right? Show me the video.'

Jake left the window and walked out of my sight. Almost immediately a section of the wall to my left opened and Jake's head appeared. He beckoned to me and I followed him into the office, which was much bigger than it seemed from the sales' window. He took me to an alcove, where a bank of monitors stared images of the platforms, the entrances, the railings by the river and the entrance foyer, directly at us.

'Talk me through what happened, from when the 22.23

arrived.'

Jake sat in front of the screens and began to search for the sequence by inserting the time code 22.23. He could move between the recordings of a number of cameras. It was like watching a film edit, with Jake doing a voice-over as the hesitant, debutant actor.

'Eh, the Belfast train came in and a handy crowd got off, just like any night and then, after, the conductor gave me the folder with your name, Edmund Slevin's name, eh, written on it. I'm supposed to put it in a box for Lost Property, but I saw the phone number and I phoned, eh … you, yeh … There, see.'

He showed me an image of him phoning at 22.37.

'Show me the entrance. The car park.'

We watched an empty screen for a few minutes until, at 22.40, a black car came into view, drove past the main entrance and out of sight.

'They shouldn't go round there. They're supposed to park in front.'

'Let me guess, Jake. There's no camera round there.'

'Eh, no. Why would there be a camera? No one parks round there. Unless you …'

'Stay on the entrance camera. Here we go.'

At 22.43 a man wearing a long coat and a black trilby pulled low over his eyes entered the building almost at a run and presented an ID card he already had in his hand. Jake, obviously delighted to be clear of an inconvenience, slipped the folder under the plate glass separators. The man turned and left. By 22.50 the car, a black four-door saloon, was pulling away.

'Keep going with the camera here. Find me arriving.'

And there I was, at 22.57. If I had arrived within the ten minutes I said I would, I'd have stood next to Edmund Slevin, the one in the natty hat.

'Okay, Jake. Let's have a look at the man again. And the car coming and going. Clip the images and stick them on this as you go along.'

I handed him my phone.

'Eh, I don't think …'

'Either that or you punch in your manager's call-out number and then I call him and a carful of uniformed cops to detain you for failing to assist a police officer in the performance of his legitimate duties.'

Jake plugged my phone into a port on the side of the server running the security cameras and monitors. He selected the clips I wanted and we watched them, as he made the transfers.

'One last one,' I said. 'The passengers leaving the train at 22.23.'

I watched it again and still found no one of interest. Whoever dropped the folder could have gotten off anywhere.

'Now run all the clips from my device. On that screen there.'

I knew I was in danger of wearing out Jake's cooperation, but I wanted to see them again to confirm three things. One: it was Dalzell impersonating me. Two: I couldn't make out the number plate on the car or be sure of the make. Three: I couldn't tell if Dalzell was alone or if he had a driver. Maybe our technical department could help, but I wasn't sure I would show these clips to anyone.

'Thanks, Jake. You have my number. Use it if the Man in the Hat ever comes back to you. I know you're confused, but let me reassure you. I know him, so the file is not "Lost Property" anymore. We know where it is.'

I retrieved my phone and retraced my route along the river bank, beside the rail-line, over the Peace Bridge, still illuminated like a fairground, and along the riverside walk to my apartment building, encountering walkers, singly or in twos or threes, and confirming that no one was following me.

The halo of magnolia light across my papers greeted me wanly. I turned on the heating and set it at 30 degrees. I filled the kettle and set it to boil. I took a tall *latté* glass and, using a long spoon, I coated an inch of the bottom with a honey made by bees who only visit jasmine plants. Then I took a bottle of Bushmills Black Label, glugged a mouthful and poured another glug on top of the honey, stirring until the kettle spouted steam and clicked off. When I topped out the glass with boiling water, I stirred steaming gold, aromatic warmth. A summer illusion.

I turned off the light and sat in darkness at my desk. I closed the window and felt the room heat up. My reflection, layered into the glass and the near distance beyond, occluded the road, the path, the railings, the river and the oaks on the opposite bank.

The eyes in my reflection flared and The Morrigan, great goddess of war and doom, stared back at me, from ice-white eyes set deep in bloody sockets, in a stare as cold as the night outside. I drank the hot whiskey as quickly as I could, welcoming the heat-burn in my mouth and the spirit-burn in my gullet.

It was no surprise to me that my phone was tapped. I understood it as part of my job and my particular circumstances. I was perplexed to discover Dalzell had access to my phone calls. I knew it was Dalzell, just as I know I am Eddie Slevin.

It was a surprise that The Morrigan would appear to me. I lifted Jung's *Symbols of Transformation*. I read aimlessly and without profit. I closed the book, finished the whiskey and went to bed, flicking the heating off as I passed. I was warm again, my brain over-heating. Might I sleep? And dream? About The Morrigan, the dead footballer, Dalzell and my mother dancing around a funeral pyre, flames and smoke rising through cold, inky air?

TEN

I hardly slept, so when Goss approached my desk the next morning I was in a daze, the same set of personal expense claims in front of me since I'd come in at half seven.

'You and me, Slevin. We're on.'

He moved fast for a man of his age and bulk. The office clowns had it that the retirement age kept being pushed back because we needed Goss. He was the oldest and the best detective in the unit. And he knew it. He was a status-freak, constantly tending to the pecking order, keeping people in place with spiked barbs, objections, huffs and exclusions. Hammy flared every now and then and wanted rid of him. Until he looked down the 'cases closed' list, which Goss topped every quarter, and he regained his cool. The fact that my name appeared in second place on that list irked Goss and I wondered if I might find out why, as I juggled myself into my holster, keys, phone and jacket.

Sharon, the unit administrator, stopped me with a raised finger, as I passed her desk.

'Claim forms, Detective Sergeant Slevin. Overdue again. You said you'd get them to me this morning. Don't make me come after you.'

She was grinning, her lean, tanned cheeks framing teeth as white as a recently bathed polar bear. I gave her a small salute and trotted to the stairs.

Goss had a saloon revving in the yard and I climbed in beside him.

'It's not far. We could walk, but we might need this after. One dead. Street drinker. One of his mates did it.'

Younger officers, such as Hetherington, claim that the reason Goss tops the 'cases closed' list is a combination of bullying, dodging and status-management that ensures he only lands handy ones. He seemed to have pulled it off again.

'How are you surviving without your boy? I'm glad to see the back of Doherty for a while meself. Gives me a break from his chatter. That'll no be a problem with you, Slevin. You're as tight-lipped as all the guilty. Do you think they're sharing a room, your boy and Doherty?'

We were hardly out of the yard and he'd managed to tell me to keep quiet, that I was a criminal and to suggest that, as the squad room view was that Hetherington was gay, he would seduce Goss' partner, the voluble Detective Sergeant Doherty. Hammy had sent them both to Manchester to see what they could stir on the Anderson case.

'Hammy only sent Doherty to hold your boy's hand. I hope that's all he's holding. What the fuck use is Doherty in Manchester? The English'll never understand a word he says. He doesn't speak their language. You cold at night without your boy?'

Goss was a poisonous plant I needed to nip at bud level.

'A couple of things before we properly start. I don't sleep with Hetherington. Who he sleeps with is his business. Doherty speaks perfectly good English and is an experienced detective. Now where the fuck are we going?'

'Ah, time of the month, is it? Victoria Market car-park. Behind the electricity sub-station.'

'Pull in.'

'What?'

'Pull in. Here.'

We were almost at the lights at the Clarendon Street junction. They went green as Goss stopped. The driver behind us blared his horn. I got out.

'You were right about one thing. We could walk.'

I slammed the door on Goss's 'what the fu...'.

I turned left and strode towards the river, crossing the road at a run. I made it to the river-side path and clasped my hands to the metal railings. The water below me churned and beckoned. I didn't roar, though I could have. Two young mothers, pushing buggies, passed behind me. I didn't want to wake the babies.

It was warmer than overnight, the kind of weather that makes us think summer will go Indian in September. I rubbed my palms together, lit a cigarette and began to walk, admiring the fine figures and brisk pace of the buggy pushers. I grinned thinking that maybe I should get one. A fine figure? A buggy? A baby? A complete set? My grin widened and the women smiled as I passed them and gave them a small, but gallant salute.

When I reached the carpark, crime scene officers were already active and Goss stood, fists clenched by his sides, in front of the electricity sub-station.

I showed my ID, ducked under the police tape and headed directly for him.

'One dead, you tell me.'

He turned on his heel and I followed him behind the squat concrete building. The smell of stale liquids – wine, beer, urine, sweat, blood – came at me like a malodorous slurry. Two crime scene officers, one taking photographs, occupied themselves around a prone body. I saw a middle-aged man, with a good build, lying in the foetal position. Were it not for the jagged wound over his left eye and the ooze of sticky blood under his head, you might think he was asleep. It's always hard to guess the age of a street drinker, but I put the victim no older than forty. I took a couple of steps backwards to get a wider view of the scene. When Goss turned to speak to me, he was surprised

I was not beside him.

'Forensics reckon … Get the fuck over here, Slevin.'

'Thanks, officer. You're grand there. Just speak up.'

If the two crime scene officers noticed anything, they didn't say. The one with the camera was nearest to me. He broke the grim silence congealing round me and Goss.

'I heard forensics – she's just gone, 'cos she got another call – I heard her saying he was here all night.'

'Shut up and take your pictures. If you did your own job instead of trying to do mine, we'd all be better off.'

This was getting out of hand. If Goss was shouting at crime scene officers, I had gotten far enough under his skin. I looked at the body again. Any one of the bottles on the ground could be the murder weapon.

'I'll keep in touch with forensics, keep them focused. See what these bottles turn up,' I said.

The technician at the victim's side, checking for clues around the wound and on the ground, looked up at me.

'Don't worry about us, Eddie,' he said. 'We're fully focused.'

Then he stood up and continued.

'It's you two schoolgirls who need to stay in the game. There's a dead man here. And whoever killed him is away. So let's start again and see if we can do something for this unfortunate soul.'

Goss walked over and spoke, less raucous now.

'Do what you have to. Full cover. Bag all the bottles. Photograph the shards. Dust everything. Any ID on him? Envelopes with an address?'

'Nothing. We don't know who he is.'

'We'll check the hostels, the shelters and the flop-houses. Some of his drinking buddies will sweat it after a couple of days,' Goss continued.

'Do you want me to follow up on that?' I asked.

Goss took two steps, almost lunging, and was in my face when he spat his reply.

'I want you to fuck off and stay well out of my fucking way.'

Did he really bump my shoulder as he passed me? Yes, he did. And he barrelled, shoulders hunched forward, back to the car and drove off.

'You'll be walking, Eddie,' the technician said.

'Suits me. Tell me what you've got, Mervyn.'

The badge on his uniform named him Mervyn Campbell. I didn't recognise him, but he knew me.

'A member of the public made the first call, apparently. The scene was secure by the time us two got to work. Uniforms were already here. Karen Lavery. She did her bit and we got on with ours. She reckons it's a single blow to the head, probably with one of the bottles there. A bludgeon job.'

'Speculate, Mervyn.'

'What?'

'You've been at a hundred scenes.'

He paused to wonder if he could speculate. His scientific training made such a notion alien to him, so I nudged him.

'You know more than me and Goss most of the time. What do you think happened here, Mervyn?'

'There's no mystery. A crowd of drinkers, late in the day. They start rowing and fighting. Gets out of hand. Someone had something more stimulating than cheap wine, fell out with this poor soul and got lucky – or unlucky – with his first blow. Everyone scattered. Half of them won't remember what happened.'

I didn't argue with him. What would be the point in coming back to him with my view that the whole thing is a mystery and that only by revealing it piece by piece, moment by moment, death by death could I hope to stay in the game?

I gave it one more try, in the dingy space behind the

electricity sub-station, with the dead man curled like a dust mite, drowned in piss and beer.

'What do you make of his clothes, Mervyn? The suit is new, the shirt too. The shoes look good too. It looks to me like ...'

'An outfit. Yes. Second-hand, but new, if that makes sense.'

'Perfect, Mervyn. Perfect. Can we have a close-up of the tie please? That crest there, below the knot.'

The technician with the camera stepped in and took the shot, then showed it to me on his camera. He was more comfortable speculating than Mervyn was.

'They do that, you know. At the hostels. They get donations of clothes and kit them out. Might be his birthday or something.'

The outfit seemed more gift than charity. The gold on the tie set off the dark blue of the suit. The socks, shirt and tie, all a lighter blue, worked well together. I saw a country wedding, in a fine hotel, with ruddy-faced men wondering when they could unbutton their waistcoats and shirt buttons, alongside firm-flanked women, resting at angles to one another, their bird-plume hair fascinators dancing above their heads.

'Show me the tie. There.'

I looked closely at the back of the camera. He'd taken four shots, up and down the length of it. The cloth was sunshine-gold and the symbol of an arm holding a red crucifix ran up and down in beaming rows.

'It's a Donegal county tie. A GAA one. Yeh, that's the county colours there,' I said.

I stepped nearer to the corpse and bent down. The smell came at me like a puddle of urine pushed by a squelchy mop along a corridor. Flies buzzed and took note of my nearness, then regrouped and prepared to land.

The man was freshly shaved, lightly tanned and

pimple-free. By looking away from the wound site, I could see the remains of a handsome face, with the classic red traceries of a drinker. A globule of blood rested in the hollow of his neck and discoloured the top of his light blue shirt, just where the knot of his tie twisted towards his left shoulder. Gold cloth. Red crucifix held by a short right arm. It was the Donegal county crest.

'Did Donegal win the All-Ireland this year?' I asked.

'They beat Dublin in the semis. They're up against Kerry in the final.'

The photographer had more than speculation. He had information. I stood up and faced him.

'When was that? The semi-final?'

'I don't know. 'Bout a week ago. Yeh. Maybe a fortnight.'

'Send that photo, the tie, to Goss. I'll message him. Our friends across the border might know something. They might have a "missing person" report.'

'You're speculating now, Eddie,' said Mervyn. 'Goss won't like you wasting his time.'

'It's worse than you think, Mervyn. Me and Goss got off on the wrong foot this morning. I gave it another go, until I confirmed that Goss only has one foot. The wrong one.'

The photographer said 'Goss has a false leg?'

'No, Frank,' said Mervyn. 'The Detective Sergeant thinks he's a bollocks.'

'That all?'

Frank, the photographer, sent the tie images to Goss, while I composed and sent him a message.

'Victim possible Donegal connection. See tie image. Recommend advise PS (South). Missing person?'

Then I walked round the sub-station and into the car-park. Might the air be fresher? The weather-dampened sandstone of the City Hotel opposite glowed dully in the morning light.

Trucks approached the roundabout and the lights, brakes oozing air to slow them, then they grunted forward in the daily round of traffic's endless musical chairs. No one gets off. No one ever gets to lie down. Except the dead man. I thought about a cigarette, just as Mervyn came up beside me.

'You don't remember, but we had a drink at a Christmas do in the hotel there. Last year. Old Danny Gormley thought it would be a good idea to bring technical officers and detectives together. Everyone was shocked to see you there. You didn't do 'social', was the story. And you know, what with your ...'

'Background and all that?'

'Yes.'

'Karen Lavery brought me. She thought it would do me good.'

'Ah. She's a ...'

'Terrific forensics' officer.'

'That too. Remember when you solved the one with the shooter in the tree. You had us climbing and searching. We wouldn't have done it only Karen said we should. We thought you were thick. Then we found the cigarette butt and got a lead.'

'And a conviction.'

'She always says, 'Follow the evidence, Mervyn. Gather it and don't ever be surprised where it takes you.''

'Sounds the job to me. Do you want a cigarette?'

'Naw. I bought you a pint that night ...'

'Good man, Mervyn,' I said, as I lit up.

'... and I asked you a question you didn't answer. I'm going to ask you again. This time no pints in front of us. Why the fuck did you come into the cops?'

'You asked me that before?'

'Yeh, over there, in the hotel bar. That technicians' Christmas drinks do.'

I remembered the heaving crowd at the bar. The sense that I was off my head to be there, me the raw recruit, the political ex-prisoner, the sour crab in the apple barrel, a pint in my hand and a gentle sway about me, because it wasn't the first pint, with another one arriving from Mervyn, bearing a question in tow.

'Why the fuck did you come into the cops?'

Curiosity, yes. Disquiet, definitely. Distrust, certainly. Disbelief, no doubt. Disdain, perhaps.

I don't remember what I said to him. In all likelihood something very unsatisfactory, because he was asking me again, on a late August morning, as we stood apart from our work for a brief moment, the traffic trundling through the roundabout, the gulls beginning to gather and the dead man awaiting pick-up and despatch.

'I suppose I just wanted the answers. To the mystery, like. I mean, I wanted to find out. And it sort of fitted with what I was doing before.'

'They put you up to it.'

'They? Who?'

'The leadership.'

'No. No one put me up to it, Mervyn.'

'So all that running around, causing mayhem, you just reckoned that set you up to be a cop?'

'Don't exaggerate, Mervyn. Yes, I was running around, near enough from when I was fourteen. Feral kids? I was one of the originals. An anti-social pain of the highest order.'

'It was a short enough journey from corner boy to guerrilla, then.'

'Easy now, Mervyn. Opinions vary. One man's guerrilla is another man's ape and all that. I had a couple of near misses, survived the streets, grew up, politics moved on around us. I saw dead people, mates and others. I got jail, but I always fancied camping. So I got inside the tent, when they opened the flaps again.'

'Yeh, but you could have gone, you know, political. Done the community thing, suited and booted, and then up the road in the big government car. I reckon you might do it yet. You have the book-learning from jail.'

'My stuff's a bit specialist, Mervyn. Not very "street". More of a head-fuck, really. I know you could say it's all myths and legends here still, but I'm better off on the ground. The small things suit me. I'm a man for the grubs, the beetles, the silverfish and the woodlice.'

'Plenty of them round here.'

'Like I said, the cops is not that far from what I was always at. I'm better doing it than talking about it. I like the books too. I pick at things, Mervyn. I want answers and when I don't like the answer I get, I ask more questions, take another case, see where that leads me.'

'What about this poor bastard then?'

'I see a family wedding.'

'In Donegal.'

'In Donegal. A hotel near the shore. His sisters are there, all solicitous. They are admiring his suit, his outfit. There are others, men, in the background, not so keen on him.'

'Are you making this up?'

'Yes. No.'

'You're speculating. Right. And you have to speculate if you want to accumulate.'

My cigarette burned down to my fingers. I dropped it on the ground and squirmed my foot to put it out.

'He's not a street drinker. Not in the day-to-day sense. Yes, he is a drinker and his sisters are glad he's home. So the wedding "do" takes off. There's fine food. Whiskey flying. He's dancing and schlepping about. Getting noisy. Bothersome. He falls over a chair, then stumbles onto a table, scattering glasses and drinks. Frightens a flower-girl.'

'You should be writing books, not solving crimes. That's all romance, Slevin. Only a story.'

I would not be put off.

'It's not his wedding. A niece, perhaps. Later, there's a row. With a brother or a brother-in-law, maybe.'

'And they dump the body here? When they could have dumped him anywhere? In a bog? Up the side of a mountain?'

'So, we have someone coming back into the city anyway. Someone with a notion of a way out of a crisis. This is not the perfect crime, Mervyn. There's no such thing. Unless you're in banking. This? This is folly, fuck-up, tragedy, disaster and mess.'

I turned back towards the electricity substation. 100,000 volts. Indecipherable graffiti. A low wall on the other side of which the dead man lay in repose on a bed of empty cans and bottles. Further back, a building wore a mask of scaffolding, as it was prepared for re-plastering. No one clambered about the rickety rigging.

'Where's the evidence, Eddie, eh? As Karen would always say.'

At the base of the scaffolding was a part-filled builder's skip, rusty as a decommissioned U-boat, the lower lip pouting towards us.

'Has anyone checked that skip?'

'For what, Eddie?'

'Evidence, Mervyn. Evidence.'

Mervyn walked round the sub-station, using the duck-boards he'd put down earlier. Soon after that I saw him and the photographer cross the edge of the carpark and make for the skip. Mervyn found an old wooden crate to stand on and leaned in. The photographer got up then and started to take photographs. I watched the photographer angle and pose, lean and balance, all the time scanning and photographing. I saw him put the cap back on the lens, climb off the crate, swing the camera awkwardly behind his back, then descend. They came back to me and the photographer showed me the pictures he'd taken.

'There's a bloody towel. I didn't touch it. Just took the shots. Could be from one of the builders. Cut himself with a scarifier, like. Nasty bastard, the plasterer's scarifier.'

I looked at the images he showed us. A dirty white towel, innocent as belly-button fluff, splashed with crimson. Except for the embossed logo, badly scrunched and twisted. It was the ensign of a grounded vessel, the banner for a dead soul.

I didn't need to tell Mervyn we might be able to determine the hotel the towel came from.

'Get that into a bag, Mervyn. Anything else you can get. I'll tell Goss to put a hold on that skip.'

'We'll need a bigger team here, looks like.'

'I'm messaging Goss now, if he'll listen to me. He's probably pulling drunks out of their beds as we speak. And that won't do him or them any good. No drunk ever struck a blow like that. It's too replete.'

'Replete?'

'Replete with passion. Full of it.'

'Could still be one of his drinking buddies.'

'Anything's possible, but answer me this: why didn't even one of them stay? Say we have a group of street drinkers, a row, things getting out of hand and they scatter. But not all. There is always one, too beaten to get away, too drunk to move. Too scared or horrified to run, too lost in a boozy fog to save himself, too curious to know what'll happen next and if there might be a drink in it for him. One of them would have stayed, if the victim really was a street drinker.'

'Enough fantasy. Let me get on with the facts.'

Mervyn wanted to get a move on. He'd bought into the first scenario I'd laid out and I knew that his report to Goss would reflect that. Right on cue an ambulance arrived with two police Land Rovers. Uniformed officers and ambulance personnel began the process of pick-up and dispatch.

'I'll get the crime scene report to Goss by the afternoon,' Mervyn said. 'I'll copy it to you.'

We were finished. I could come back to being myself. The stories that I spun were part of the story of myself. I could hear Mervyn and his colleagues on a tea-break, at their base in Maydown.

'He just said to check the skip and we found the towel. A hotel towel, branded and all, totally confirming his story.'

'He's a bit pally with the gypsies, isn't he? They must have given him a crystal ball.'

Slurps of tea, edgy laughter, then Mervyn again.

'He's got something. Like a sixth sense.'

'He's got something alright. A criminal record and a long stretch behind him. No wonder he's seeing visions.'

More edgy laughter. Maybe even a sneer. Then a steely voice.

'He doesn't belong.'

And we were back to Mervyn's question.

'What the fuck is he doing in the cops?'

But Mervyn and I were well past that question, at the murder scene behind the electricity sub-station. We were immersed in the crime, doing the job by answering questions, one by meagre one, finding more answers, one by tawdry one, revealing yet more questions to answer.

My phone sounded an incoming message. I expected it to be Goss, fulminating in response to mine, but it was on my personal channel.

'wen you comin over have sometin fer yu'

I recognised my Auntie Maisie's personal script straight away. She messaged as she spoke, in a voice I associated with ease and effort in equal measure, with hurt and joy combined, all grounded in the pain I caused her and the forbearance she offered me. As a token of my gratitude, I gave her my doctoral scroll when I graduated. I asked her to look after it for me. She called me every now and then to give it back to me, now that I had my own place. Here she was again, calling me to her home, calling me to my past and holding out a prize she valued more than I did. I hoped she might also have a jar of jam and some fresh scones. They would banish the taste and smell of the beer-cellar death-scene, behind the electricity sub-station.

ELEVEN

I ignored three messages from Goss. I messaged Auntie Maisie to say I'd call by soon and I walked away from the death scene behind the electricity sub-station. The traffic slowed me, but I weaved and ducked directly across the roundabout, then semi-vaulted over the railings to reach the river-side walk, just downstream from the Peace Bridge. I got some strange, almost admonishing, looks from people on the walkway. They may have known me as a policeman. What with the turbulence caused by working with Goss and the grief I imbibed from the dead man in his drunken sprawl, the last thing I felt like just then was a policeman. When I settled by the riverside railing, I immediately lit a cigarette, drawing on it in a way that marked me as an empty balloon, a vacuum in need of filling.

The river churned carelessly before me, jostling itself into tide turning. It was a good moment to view it and to take stock. I missed Karen. I missed Hetherington. I was confounded by Anderson, still outside my grasp. I was swimming against a weir full of dead ends. Skeletons, ocelots, football boots, shoes in chillers – dead ends. I began to walk, keeping the river on my left, its low corrugations bumping along as if it could go either way. I kept walking. I lit another cigarette. I made it to the double-decker bridge and walked underneath it, using the pedestrian lights to make the crossing.

I cut behind the old railway station, skipped over the rusty tracks and looked across to see the truncated bridge called 'Aspiration', pointing directly at me. When I reached the partner section on the side where I walked, I hesitated to acknowledge that I was very near the actual place where my mother went into the river.

A heavy-lidded milkman saw her that morning. He never got over it. He repeats the same telling any time we meet.

'Her hair was flying off her, the morning was that breezy. A good Spring breeze and a good Spring tide on the river. Her arms flung out. Like an eagle she was, yeh, flying. Gone, before it even dawned on me what was going on. Shur, what could I do? Again I got parked up and ran across the grass and climbed the wall meself – all in a rush, I nearly went in after her – she was gone. God be good to her.'

I crossed the same grass and held a palm up to traffic leaving the city, giving a thumbs-up when it stopped, as I jogged across to the other side of Foyle Road. Auntie Maisie lives in a mid-terrace house on Moat Street, a short, steep street bordered by the old Star Factory, famous for shirt-making, now refurbished into apartments. The football club lodges players there. Todd Anderson shared a three-bed apartment with another player and, when that player's contract wasn't renewed, Anderson negotiated with the club for a sole lease agreement, with an option to buy.

I climbed the rising terrace and knocked on my Auntie's door. She opened it immediately, then walked away. I followed her shape down the gloomy hallway, my feet scraping across the threadbare carpet. My Auntie lives in a late-twentieth century time-warp, the immaculately clean house last decorated when my grandparents were still alive. Auntie Maisie is my mother's only sister. She is my only living relative, apart from my sister, Ruby.

'I have a thing for you,' Aunt Maisie said, when we reached the single-storey kitchen-dining extension. Light came softly in from the yard, giving the floral patterned wallpaper and the formica-covered worktops a vinyl matt finish.

'Ah, shur, that's grand, heh. I'm in no rush for it. Any

chance of a mugga tay?'

My language followed hers, in a domestic sing-song from my adolescence that threw the years off me and found me seated at the very same table I pulled up to now, then a rascally youth, just shy of becoming an active street fighter.

Of course, there was tea: a full, steaming Belleek pot, a parian china jug of milk, sugar in a matching bowl, delicate basket-weave decorated cups and saucers of the same material, beaming their liquid-cream glaze. And there were scones and a small saucer of blackberry jam, beside a butter dish, shapely as a woodworker's box-plane.

I lifted my cup and enjoyed the close-up of the subtly embossed shamrock decorations, weaving across the delicate body of the cup. I held it up and away from me and recognised the distinctive Belleek stamp, with the words '*Déanta in Éirinn*' printed beside it. Auntie Maisie is a collector and has Belleek china from different periods in the history of the Fermanagh pottery.

"Tis yeer legacy,' she told Ruby once. 'Though what you and that run-about brother a' yours'll do with it, I have no notion.'

Ruby reckons it's worth a fortune. I tell her not to hold her breath. Auntie Maisie will outlive us all and her pottery collection will be buried with her, as a votive offering to the gods.

'Did you see tha' Ruby one at all?'

'Saw her, wha', onny a wee while ago. She's still singing.'

'Has she a man?'

'Come on, Maisie. That's none of my business.'

'None of mine neither. So she says. Cheek of her.'

'She doesn't need a man. Shur, look at you.'

'Aye, look at me.'

I did. Seated across from me, she is a gangly sprite, erect

as a pine and florid as a pink hydrangea in full bloom, her pert curls countably infinite atop her skull and about her lean face. She is as tall as me, so our eyes met and dared me to look hard.

'You keeping well?' I asked.

'The finest. Only the aul' blood pressure tablet rattling round inside. The sight's still good. I hear grass grow and I can smell a fella needs a good shakin' a mile off. You dodgin' something? Bit of a 'flu is it?'

'Ach, nothing like that. I onny had a run in with a fella at work.'

'Give me his name and I'll hex him for you.'

I laughed. It mightn't have been such a bad idea to put a spell on Goss, a simple charm like fleas in his underpants or lice in his hair. I knew Auntie Maisie had the gift, or claimed she did and had everyone believing her, which was practically as good.

'No need for that. I have him in hand.'

I thought of Goss cursing me savagely when Mervyn's report came in and the focus of the investigation shifted from street-drinkers to revellers at a wedding across the border, thus complicating his life. All speculated by my story.

'You have the gift too, I know. You could hex him right enough.'

'Now, Maisie. I'm a cop, not a wizard.'

'No. That's right. And I'm an aul' spinster and not a witch.'

We both laughed and she continued.

'Your mother gave yeez the most aul' fashionist names. Ruby and Edmund. Like she didn't want ye to be growing into modern times. She wanted ye old before yeer time. Or she wanted ye never to grow up. Ruby got the chanting. And you got the storying. You're wasted with the police. I suppose the money's good. And a bit of a pension. If you're not shot.'

The laughing petered out.

'No one's going to shoot me, Auntie Maisie. Them days is over. All I have to worry about is bosses and long hours.'

At that moment a wasp buzzed into the space between us and aimed for Auntie Maisie's mouth. She splattered and waved at it, clinking her teacup loudly on her saucer.

'Bloody wasps. Could they not invent something to do away with them?'

'Here, take a minute. You didn't spill any tea, anyway. Catch your breath.'

A heightened flush coloured her cheeks. Tendons in her neck strained and stood out like fleshy hawsers. Her eyes bulged and watered. Her chest heaved in great bouts, slowly returning to normal.

'I'm grand. Grand. I didn't swallow the bastard anyway. There, look at him, behind the nets.'

We both looked at the wasp, a quivering ink blob walking purposely up the window pane, coyly covered by the net curtains Auntie Maisie washed by hand twice a year before re-stringing them on a new length of curtain cord.

'Are them nets new?' I asked, teasing and distracting her.

'No,' she laughed. 'They're as aul' as Methuselah's granny. As aul' as meself. Your mother bought them when the extension got done.'

The wasp buzzed and tapped, safe between my mother's nets and the pane of glass. Did the glass chill its feet, padded and sticky as toffee apples? Did the gauze above lend it an ephemeral sky, the lace-patterned clouds repeating a celestial order, regulating its world?

Auntie Maisie rose from her chair and, with a set of well-practised moves and soundings, held back the nets, opened a side window and shooed the wasp out to the yard.

'I mind the day your mother swallowed the wasp.'

'She did not.'

'Oh, she did. She said she did.'

'A wasp?'

'Aye, a wasp. Buzzy as a band saw and near as deadly.'

'Would that not poison her?'

'Poison her? Your mother? Nothing would poison that one. She was a walking medicine chest. She looked at you and you were cured.'

'She never cured herself.'

'She went into that river below, aye. Many like her went in. Some in joy. Most in sorrow.'

I took a long, final swig of my tea and clinked the cup onto its saucer.

'Where's that thing then, Auntie Maisie? They'll be looking for me back at work.'

'Isn't that the cops' job anyway? Finding people and bothering them? Ach, look, I upset you, talking about your mother like that. Go easy on me. She was my sister, you know.'

I imagined the wasp butting onto the outside of the window-pane, thumping his head, trying to get back in.

'You told me a story once,' she continued, "Bout a woman swallowed a wasp. A fly, was it? A may fly, you said it was.'

'*Dechtire.*'

'She was the mother of the hero.'

'*Setanta.*'

'That was his baby name. What's his other name?'

'*Cú Chulainn.*'

'Aye, tha's him. He was on a wall above on Bishop Street one time. You can still see the outline no matter how much magnolia they put on that gable. You said she swallowed the fly.'

'… and fell into a deep sleep.'

'And the great god came to her. The randy bastard.'

'Lugh of the Long Arm.'

'The long arm, aye.'

We were laughing again. This was better.

'What did he say to her, to *Dechtire*?'

'He said she would have his baby and that was why the fly went into her mouth.'

'Out of the drink she had. I always check when I'm drinking after you told me that story. In case there's a bluebottle in me glass.'

'Or a wasp.'

'No, your mother's wasp wasn't in a glass. It just flew in. Straight out of the air. She had the baby, didn't she?'

'Yes, *Dechtire* had the baby. Some people were suspicious, saying it was really the King's baby, not the god's.'

'Lugh the Long Fella.'

'So, when the baby came, the King married off the woman, *Dechtire*, to one of his warriors, *Suailtim*.'

'That's right. A handy fella to have about the place. The King could keep an eye on him and on the baby. We never had a brother. And I never knew who your father was. Or Ruby's.'

'A river god maybe?'

'I have me doubts. River rat, more likely. Ye kep' yer mother's name. Slevin — like us. Flies and wasps in the mouth, that's us.'

Again the laughing dried up. I almost poured more tea, but I did need to get back. I ran my tongue around my mouth and tasted sandpaper.

'Ruby was up with me last week. She brought a lemon cake, God bless her,' said Auntie Maisie.

'Sorry, I should have …'

'Never you mind about that. Yeez need bring nothing onny yourselves.'

'You took us in, Maisie. We should be kinder to you.'

'I didn't take ye in. Ye were already "in". And when your

mother left, we just carried on, the two of ye and me.'

'Couldn't have been as straightforward as that. I onny half remember …'

'Good.'

' … and what I remember was, well, that I was a mad bastard.'

'You had me heart broke, going up and down to the school, tryin' to keep you in it. One of the teachers said you had a great head, but you hadn't a clue where it was or what to do with it.'

'Ah, come on, now, didn't I get a great education, letters after me name and all?'

'Aye, and twelve years in jail and near enough got killed I don't know how many times. I was glad your mother never lived to see any of that.'

'You must ask yourself sometimes, Auntie Maisie, I mean, what was all that about? Her going into the river an' all.'

'It wasn't about the wasp she swallowed anyway. Or maybe it was. She was like she was from somewhere else, your mother.'

'Like a fairy?'

'Like a god. Or a God's sister. Two-faced, like the river. Light and dark. Full and neap. I'd come in some days and she'd be sitting there, where you are, and such a look would be on her face, that I'd have to go out again, or go up to the room and change outta me work clothes. The heat off her'd come up through the floor boards. I'd wait until it cooled and I'd come down then. She'd be rattling pans and plates and cutlery and the dinner'd be put up to me everyday. That was the way we managed it. I went out to work, like I was a man. She looked after ye and kept the house. Like the wife. The fish she fed us. Shoals of it. Jesus.'

'She abandoned us.'

'Ruby said you were still caustic about it. Like a wean

picking a scab on his knee, to keep it festering.'

'Ruby sing you that one, eh? What about herself? She ran headlong into a marriage with an eejit, now she sings the blues upstairs in the pub where he works. She won't ever get away from him.'

'You're the same as your mother. The aul' light and dark. Leave Ruby alone. And don't be codding yourself. You ran headlong too. Into bother and war and jail and now the cops, for God's sake.'

'Like you say. It's a job. With a pension.'

I was the wasp beating on the window pane, beating and beating the pane, as I'd done for years in this very room. I sensed a sudden rise in me. A fluid tide that was vascular and immanent, sourced in my toes, racing up my calves and thighs, then further on through the soft tissue of my trunk, until it pressed the flesh of my skull to bulging, leaving me exhausted. A heaving yawn followed it through my chest.

My aunt was not tiring. She was red-faced too, but livid, not flaccid.

'You told me that fly story when you were in jail. That's when all the stories came out. Jesus, you used to be bursting to tell me. I asked about how you were getting along and how the other lads were getting along and all you wanted to tell me was about horses that turned into twins and children that turned into swans and that was only the half of it. You made me bring in the books, me arms were broke carrying the books, until the prison wised up and ye wised up inside and found a way a' working it, with education and clothes and everything. Least you never did drugs.'

'I remember you sitting opposite and asking me for another one. "Go on, tell me another story" you used to say.'

'I was humouring you. Look, I loved the stories, because your eyes used to light up telling them. That's why I asked you to tell me another one. I have no head for stories. That was your mother's gift. I'm not even the singer, like Ruby, the one who tells other peoples' stories. I'm the one keeps the hive clean, like the bee that's never done working. Now you have yourself in the cops, you're some kind of knight in shining armour, solving the crimes of the day. I'd say you'll get a medal.'

'Listen, Auntie Maisie, I know you don't like the police …'

'Never did. Never saw any reason for them. Only give ordinary people bother.'

'And find out who killed who.'

'You must be joking. No one found out who or what killed your mother.'

'She killed herself,' I almost shouted. 'Come on now, Auntie Maisie. Enough of the craziness.'

'Mind your mouth, you. And don't be bringing your buddies round here again. Me and your mother had enough of the police. And the Army before them. They hounded our father and broke our mother's heart. Here, take your cop things with you.'

She got up from the table and went to the oak dresser. She picked up a buff-coloured cardboard folder, with the flap tucked in. A white sticker showed my name and phone number.

'I was at the shop this morning and when I came back, this was on the carpet, scrunched over. I phoned you, 'case it was urgent. Or private.'

'I thought you …'

'You thought what?'

'It's okay. Thanks. Thanks for phoning me. You didn't see anyone on the street and you going up to the shop?'

'Naw.'

'Any cars? Strange cars?'

'No. Nothing. Just the insurance man.'

'The insurance man?'

'Yeh. I think it was him. He doesn't call to me. I have me life insurance with Hooper and White, up the town. Me father always dealt with them. A couple of the neighbours have the man calls still, usually of an evening.'

'So this was about, what, ten o'clock in the morning?'

'Yeh, maybe a bit before. I go up for the paper and to stretch the legs, after the children are well settled into the school. He was gone, agin I came back. And that was on the carpet. Maybe he put it in. I don't know.'

'What did he look like?'

'Big fella. Big coat. No call for it, that day.'

'Hat?'

'Yeh, like a horsey man's one, onny black.'

Dalzell. We were turtle and hare. He, the hare, was always a step or more ahead of me. I wasn't sure I would outpace him.

'Thanks, Auntie Maisie. It's mine alright.'

I lifted the flap and confirmed what I expected. It was empty. I held it away from my aunt and said,

'All there. Perfect.'

I was experiencing a strange desire not to disappoint her.

'All there, is it?' she asked. I knew, then, that she had peeked.

'Yeh. Spot on.'

'You need to watch yourself. Losing files like that. Whoever dropped it in done you a favour. Anonymous-like. It could have been the insurance man. When I see him again, I'll tell him you got it.'

'Do that. And tell him I'm delighted and grateful. And that I was asking for him.'

The thump on the front door startled us and rattled china cups on the dresser.

'The insurance man's back.'

Auntie Maisie, ignoring my quip, simply tutted and walked

to the front door. I heard her open the door, then two voices, my Auntie's the clearer, loudly and firmly asserting that no, the other person could not come in and yes, I was here and she would check if I wanted to come out.

I felt fifteen again, enduring a spell of house arrest after a weekend of feral wandering and my friends were at the door, avid to have me among them once more because I was the daredevil most likely to lead them far enough astray to secure a chase from the cops.

Out of the window I would go, buzzing like the wasp my aunt released. Onto a wheelie bin, onto the wall, into the back lane, over another wall and into gardens at the back of Orchard Row, running, panting, running, panting, laughing, running, laughing, panting until I bouldered over the kegs behind the Bowery Bar and vanished up Ferguson Street.

Auntie Maisie came back.

'One of yours. A wee girl. She can't be more nor nineteen. She must a' belted the door with her fucking baton. I said you were here. I done enough covering for you when you were on the run.'

The door busted in. The footsteps thundering in the hall. My aunt screaming at them to get out. The window hooshed up. Fully dressed all the time, then out and away. The dinged wrists when I hit the yard. The wall. The wall. Over the wall. Breathe ripping through my chest like fire. Calls. Shouts. A shot.

This time there was neither running, chasing, shouting nor gunfire. I walked down the dark hall-way to find a hatless and jacket-less PS(N) policewoman, Constable McLaren again, smiling like a tourism ad.

'Detective Slevin. Great. Detective Goss' thonder, lookin' you. Sir.'

'Thank you, Constable,' I replied, then called back into the house. 'I'm away. I'll call back.'

'Aye, right,' came the reply.

I pulled the front door behind me and walked into the street, in step behind the police constable, who said, 'This way please, sir.'

I felt like a man under arrest and twenty years younger, which put a defiant spring in my step.

There was a police Land Rover double-parked beside a black saloon, which was half up on the kerb, beside the old factory railings. The backdoor of the Land Rover faced me and swung open as I arrived. I made to get in, but the police woman smiled and put her hand on my arm.

'No, sir. The car.'

'Oh, thank you. I'm not under arrest then?'

'I couldn't say, sir. DS Goss will know better.'

There was a light guffaw from inside the Land Rover. The police woman climbed in and the door slammed shut. I imagined her laughing along with her colleagues. Seeing detectives in the middle of a work spat is always a treat for the uniforms. We're like all work places. The uniforms enjoy a laugh when the bosses are caught in a cat fight. The Land Rover started up. Goss revved the saloon. I could have walked on, but even I know when to pull my horns in.

I got in beside Goss. The Land Rover pulled off and began slowly descending the street. Goss performed a three point turn and followed. At the junction with Foyle Road, we turned left and I looked across to the wall where my mother went into the river, taking my childhood with her.

I assumed we were going back to the station and that I'd be facing Hammy for a dressing down, with Goss, prancing about like a delighted puppy. I was wrong, because Goss – it almost burst out of him – eventually spoke.

'I hope you're carrying ID, you wanker, and don't fuck me

up anymore than you have already.'

When I didn't answer, he roared, 'Well, are you?'

I nodded.

'We're going international, for fuck's sake and this teenage huff you've got going now will not wash. Will not wash one fucking bit.'

We drove along the river-side and didn't turn onto Strand Road, towards the police station. Instead we kept to the river-side where, in the distance, the Foyle Bridge stretched its arcing back. I knew, then, where we were going.

'You know the hotel where the towel came from,' I said.

'The Island Castle,' Goss growled.

'Ah, the new one on Inch. Lovely spot for a wedding, I hear. Great photos up and down Lough Swilly. The bridal party hi-stepping along the sandy beach. Helipad. The complete deal.'

'You won't ever be getting married in it, Slevin. No woman'd be mad enough to take you on. Though you might get a man. If he was drunk enough.'

'What about our drunk? What have you got?'

'Ah, you're interested now. All over the fucking thing, now you can smell the end of it. You couldn't give a shit when you walked off this morning, sending me fucking messages like I was your boy and not telling anyone where you went a' wandering.'

'You found me anyway. Never any bother there.'

'You're making a fool of me, Slevin. Or trying hard. I had to get Communications to track you. Imagine the laugh they got out of that. DS Goss hasn't a clue where his assistant is. I laid it on, Slevin, let me tell you. I said you were last seen puking your guts up at the crime scene and heading for the City Hotel. Or the river.'

We were on the Buncrana Road by now, en route to the border. The protocol was that our Land Rover escort would hand us over to a PS(S) escort, once our ID had been checked. Our colleagues would accompany us for the duration of our stay in their jurisdiction. It happened all the time now. There was even talk of dropping the need for hand-over escorts. Cost-saving, as ever, was the primary driver in that discussion.

Goss gripped the steering wheel like the guard rail on a runaway fairground ride. The Land Rover in front was going too slow for him. And I was gleefully doing his head in.

'It's a great lead. The towel. Gives you the full case, I'll bet. You'll close another one, Goss. You're a marvel.'

'I'll deal with you, Slevin. Soon as this is over. You keep your mouth tight shut today and don't attempt to fuck me up any more and I'll maybe go easy on you. You trip me up one more time and I'll see you done.'

And that's how I happened to cross the border with a colleague who threatened to have me killed and how I happened to be smiling like a fifteen year old who had managed to get a rise out of his Dad.

TWELVE

Not long after he returned from Manchester, Hetherington was driving us back to HQ after a routine follow-up visit on a case we'd just closed, when an urgent call came on the personal channel of my phone.

'Help me, Eddie. Help me.'

'Put on the siren,' I shouted.

'It's okay …'

'It's not fucking okay. Put on the siren.'

We were in an unmarked saloon. Hetherington was driving, now taking us up Shipquay Street, at pace. He put on the siren and cars pulled onto pavements. The message continued to pulse on my phone.

'Help me, Eddie. Help me.'

It was coming at regular intervals of seven seconds. It was an unknown number. I set the car's tracker to the phone.

'It's a trap,' said Hetherington.

'Of course, it's a trap. The whole bloody thing is a trap. Straight through the Diamond. On up Bishop Street and head for the Letterkenny Road.'

'Okay. Okay. Okay.'

Hetherington had us at 90kph, as we passed the Court House. Ahead of us Bishop's Gate opened. The god of the river Foyle, sculpted on the top of the arch, seemed to grin and say 'you'll never make it'. A van, coming towards us, braked just in time, as we screamed through the gate. I scrunched my shoulders in, expecting to hear stone scraping paint off metal. We careered through Bishop's Gate and into open air. I glanced in the rear-view mirror to see the other river god, the

Boyne, grinning in salutation.

Hetherington stormed through the traffic lights at the Barrack Street junction and roared further along Bishop Street.

Auntie Maisie's house came to mind, as we passed the top of Ferguson's Street, but did she even have a phone that could send repeat messages? The pulsing messages kept coming on my personal channel and blocking it.

'At least, let's get some back-up,' Hetherington demanded, changing gear, as he flung the saloon into the junction with Foyle Road. Across the river, sombre in early morning Autumnal light, I could see the boathouse, shuttered and vacant. Beside it, river rescue vehicles were neatly parked and expectant.

I contacted Communications on my work channel to send details of our actions, the GPS of our destination and a request for support. I included an ambulance.

'Right here. Up Braehead Road. On up. Go on.'

The message pulsed on my phone.

'Help me, Eddie. Help me.'

I shouted again.

'Right here. Straight on. This is Creevagh Road. Left coming up. Left now. Here, here. Left, for fuck's sake.'

Hetherington slammed on the brakes. We both thrust forward like dancers in a chorus line. He found reverse, we screeched backwards, then zoomed up an earthen side-road in the direction of the river, below and in front of us. Round hills folded away on the opposite side, en route to becoming the sky mountains. Grey clouds banked about each other, cajoling each other towards rain.

'Here. This is it. Stop here.'

We were at a gate, red, rusty and half-pushed open. The car ticked and chugged, like a horse after a forceful gallop. There was a beat, then I made to get out.

'Wait,' called Hetherington. 'Wait for the support.'

I ignored him and climbed out, rounded the front of the vehicle and minced my way through the mud at the gate and into the grassy field. I wasn't gone five metres, before I heard Hetherington squelching behind me.

The ground rose to a grassy knoll and then fell away again. The pulsing message led me to the top of the knoll. Hetherington was beside me as we crossed the grass, fresh, late growth, following summer cuts for silage. Here and there, cattle hooves left dents and dinges, but there were no animals about. Where the knoll fell away, boggy ground caved and convexed in occasional pools and sumps.

'We're here,' I said.

'Take it easy,' Hetherington said. 'They're coming.'

I heard the sirens too, far below us in the river valley. They would be paralleling the old railway line beside the river, before climbing towards us.

Then I saw her. Just over the crest of the knoll, facing towards the river and the rising sun. Head to toe down the slope, naked, battered and bruised. One arm skewed and broken across her, like a mottled stick. There was a phone stuffed into her mouth. A squat phone, brutal, grey as a grenade, pulsing messages to my phone every seven seconds.

'Help me, Eddie. Help me.'

Hetherington stepped forward, no longer cautious.

'Don't touch her. Don't go too close,' I said.

He leaned over.

'I want to confirm she's dead,' he said.

I peered into the boggy depression. Could it be Ruby? I couldn't tell. Her hair? There was little or no hair. It was cut or burned off. Clumps of it, patched about her skull, were so matted in blood that the only sense of colour I could summon was 'gore'.

'She's dead,' I said. 'And has been for some time. Look at the skin colour. And someone's burned her. At least her head.'

'Do you know her?'

'I … I don't think so. I don't know.'

I walked round the body, trying to catch a detail. A wedding ring? A bracelet or a necklace? A tattoo? A mole? A medical scar? Maybe the forensics' people would have more luck. I saw nothing. All I got was a slightly bituminous smell, like tar hardening.

I heard them approaching. Three vehicles; two of ours and an ambulance. Suddenly, amidst the noise of the sirens, I heard a raven caw loudly. I looked behind me and saw a clump of trees rise above the ditch that skirted the field. Another caw brought my eye to the centre of a clutch of oak trees, dressed in their russet and ochre foliage and from where the swoop of a large black bird crossed the grey clouds. I saw something else then; a glint, a passing shade. Perhaps a figure. Moving.

The raven. The smell. The movement.

'Run, Hetherington! Run! Now!' I screamed.

I dashed down the knoll in the direction of the river, trying to put the knoll between me and the trees. After hesitating slightly, Hetherington took off after me.

'Keep down! Down!' I called, clumping over the clods and holes where cattle had trod. I half-fell, half-dived into a boggy sump as Hetherington caught up with me and went by, when the flash-thud-thump of an explosion blew the top off the knoll and showered us with smithereens of earth and the woman's body.

Only the sound of the sirens found its way back into my ears when I raised myself up. Not the crisp piercing sound of before, approaching in reassurance. Now they were muffled as shrouded side-drums playing under water. Then they stopped and I heard nothing. Even the raven was stilled.

Mud and water ran from me when I knelt up. I felt a heave in my guts, but I forced down the bile. My stomach felt it had been slammed with a sledge. I was facing downhill. I scanned about me, then looked behind. Where there had been a round knoll, there was a jagged crater. I got to my feet and stepped out of the sump. I heard my own hollow laughter, borderline manic. Then I saw Hetherington, further down and to my right, flattened and spread like a desolate starfish on a muddy beach at low tide.

'Kenneth! Ken!'

Now my own calls filled my ears, unclogging them as I ran, mammoth-like, towards him. A distance of five metres took me a life-span and I fell on my knees beside my colleague, screaming his name.

'Kenneth! Ken! For fuck sake, Hetherington!'

His right ear was bloody. His back was pock-marked with earth and gore. His limbs, though spread, seemed firm and fair. He hadn't made it into a sump, so he had taken most of the blast. My fox-hole had saved me. I put my muddy fingers to his neck. His pulse was strong. I bent my face towards him and smelled his mouth-washed breath.

I stood again and looked back towards the gate we had come through. Figures in hi-viz white and yellow, carrying bags and pressing their weapon belts to their sides, laboured up the slope, towards the crater. I waved my arms.

'Over here. Over here. He's here.'

The figures veered towards us, contouring below the cratered knoll, then descended.

'They're here, Kenneth. They're here. You'll be grand. Grand.'

I said it out loud and was pleased to hear myself clearly. Perhaps he'd hear me too.

The paramedics attended to Hetherington. The cops stood awkwardly around me, then I pointed at the knoll and told them to have a look and to try not to step on anything vital. I knew the woman was dead and that little but molecules of her remained.

A paramedic came towards me and took my arm, to lead me away. I stalled for one last look down the river. The clouds on the far bank were massed for an assault. It started to rain.

Following that episode, Hammy, my boss and guardian, blew a fuse.

' … I mean, look at us. We're the right shower. Upstanding officers of law and order, hardly ever sitting on our fat arses, fearlessly fighting crime from wherever it emanates to pollute our beloved city and region. And yet, consider this document here, yes, this summary of cases remaining open, ye all have one and ye all can read "Cases unsolved"? How many? That's right. Ye can count too, so count them. And that's only a quarterly review. Don't be folding your arms like a Buddha, you there, Detective Sergeant Goss. You have the towel. You have the blood samples, you have CCTV footage from the hotel. You have the sisters more or less hanging their youngest brother for the murder of their oldest, and have you got your man? He's scarpered, you tell me. Our colleagues across the water are seeking him, you say. That shower couldn't find Christmas on a calendar. Let me tell you, Goss. I'm not sending you over to London, where the bottle basher is supposed to be lying low. No, no. No more junkets across the Irish Sea. That conundrum, Slevin, sitting beside you, has Hetherington back no more than a matter of days and he nearly gets his head blown off. If you want a re-assignment Hetherington, you needn't bother coming to me. You're with Slevin on the Anderson case and I want it off this list pronto. I want to be standing here waving charge sheets: Todd Anderson's killer; the brother who bludgeoned his brother at the wedding; and, great ululations all round, the team who blew the top off a hill on the Creevagh Road and blasted a poor misfortunate woman up and down the Foyle valley. I have the file on my desk. I expect to see photographs of tyre tracks among the trees. Blank. I expect key leads dredged from the garrulous wanderings of rustic nosey-parkers, who saw the whole farrago unfold. Nothing. You have nothing at all. We do have Slevin's ramblings. About as useful as a pitchfork in the tide. Now. Right. Let me be unambiguous. These cases need cleared. Results are our heaven and our haven. We have a Chief Constable. She has all your names. And she has mine. They are also in files, online and on paper, which she personally updates daily. So I want to help you. I got this job because I proved I can think outside the box and you folks are going to have to show greater ability in that area. Doherty, wake up, shut up and get a grip on Goss' brass neck. Force him back to his desk and go over everything you've got that is evidential, evidential, mind you, not hearsay, anecdote or bullshit. And get on the Skype to London, to a proper face. And Karolina, yes you, that's right, Karolina. You think with all the gear they have, the boffins would have turned up some usable DNA from the woman by now, even if it was scattered to the four winds. Chase them, Karolina. Chase them hard. The bastards used enough stuff to lift the Guildhall and nobody saw nothing. Not the car going in. Not the body being deposited. Not the bastards disturbing Slevin's ravens before sending the townland skywards. The final insight I want to offer you all now, is that, these cases, in all these cases, Slevin is the key. That's right. You, Slevin. We badly need a plumber. You are one persistent drip, Slevin, and, if we're not careful, you'll flood the lot of us. Slevin, you're the target, the witness, the victim, the suspect, the perpetrator and the cop. There is a secret, ineffable connivance between Detective Slevin and all these events. Now pick up your cases in the list as shown. I want one page updates by Friday. Then, Sharon will schedule meetings for next week. Now get back at it.'

THIRTEEN

I was near death those days, with the bombing in the field and the barrages from my boss. Together with the living, the dead and the in-betweens, all out at Halloween, I took to the streets too, though, technically, I was still on rest leave. The streets throng, as October folds into November, and winter, in its proper sense, comes to bite, keen as a vampire. Everyone costumes up, the more ghoulish and outlandish the better. I adopt the old joke at the fancy-dress party: 'I came as myself.' A PS(N) detective, clenched tight, out in the cold, wearing a new suede jacket, over a light wool polo-neck sweater, a concession to the chill of the evening, a half-smoked cigarette pinched between his fingers, with his standard issue hand-gun holstered under his shoulder, giving him the appearance of a bigger heart than he is known to have.

The first of the living I saw was Karen Lavery, almost as soon as I came out of my apartment building. I fell in with the crowds promenading and congregating by the river's edge. Karen was in a complete witch's outfit, standing next to a tall, lean Musketeer. His ruddy cheeks and strong, chapped hands confirmed him as her farmer. She fumbled the introductions.

'This is John. We're ... And this is Eddie. He ... we work together. We're, me and John, we're going to the dance in the City Hotel, so we ...'

'Great outfits,' I said. 'Nice to meet you, John. Have a good night.'

And I strolled on. I didn't want to intrude. However, I imagined a lingering look from underneath the brim of Karen's witch's hat, her eyes beseeching me. But beseeching me to do what? The best I could manage was the sort of wry smile the jilted cowboy adopts, as he mounts his trail-worn steed and heads out of town, leaving behind the young school-teacher, fated to her future with the owner of the general store. I was far from over Karen, if I could allow myself to fantasise like that.

Two Draculas, touching up their chin gore, blocked the walkway until a family group, led by a twin-buggy, bearing toddler Frankensteins, bamboozled them out of the way. I slipped beyond them and made for the Guildhall.

Hetherington was sitting on a low wall outside a restaurant, smoking and chatting with two of his friends. They were all dressed as sailors, straight out of *On the Town*: white suits, pert little US navy caps, loose, blue neck-tie strips. I expected them to chorus what a hell of a town New York was.

'The Bronx is up ...,' I said.

'And The Battery's ... I know. I know,' Hetherington replied. 'Glad you got it.'

'Fair play to you. Looks great. Talk about 'owning it'.'

'What do you mean?'

'The sailor suits. You know.'

'Yep. We're three gay men out for a meal on Halloween. So what?'

'Jesus, Kenneth. I never gave you a hard time about that.'

'No, that's right. You just nearly got me killed.'

'You shouldn't read too much into Hammy's rhetoric. He's simply using me for a bit of a group cheer. Hang one goat out and the rest flock together, where the wolf can see them.'

'I thought you liked Hammy.'

'I do. He's a manipulator. But then again, who's not? How are you anyway?'

'I won't lose the ear. Might lose some hearing. Might not. And the rest? Bangs and bruises. Ribs knitting together. Medics reckon I'll live.'

'Good. Have a blast, sailor boy.'

When that didn't earn a smile or a rebuke, I turned to move off and found myself hemmed in by a ten-foot high robot and two stilt-walking pirates, who bent to shake our hands. We complied. The robot bellowed and spewed smoke from its shoulder-pads.

A pirate leaned towards me and snarled.

'Hello, Detective Slevin. You'd want to leave that crew and join the real rulers of the waves. Skull and cross bones, yaaar!'

Then he stilt-walked after the robot.

'Everyone knows you, Slevin,' Hetherington said.

'Especially the pirates,' I said.

There was a direct look in my colleague's eyes when he took off his sailor's cap and used it to wipe his brow.

'Bloody suit's a furnace. Even on a night like this. Who'd have thought? I'm going to get that gun, Slevin. The Anderson killing. The gun's the key to it.'

'I read your Manchester report, Hetherington. And I'll back you up.'

How does disbelief flit across a face? How does doubt cross someone's eyes? Hetherington showed me this and more.

'You know that Beresford is convinced about it,' he continued.

'Beresford? That's the MI5 fella, isn't it?'

'I never said he was MI5.'

'Did he say he was?'

'No. Look, it doesn't matter. He was very helpful and the Manchester ones, well, they relied on him. He was part of their team.'

'With Beresford's conjectures and Hammy's tub-thumping, are you now coming up with me as a prime suspect? Call that police-work, Kenneth?'

'It's about the gun. The murder weapon, Slevin. You see that. We have a body ...'

'We *had* a body, until some bright spark dispatched it post-haste to Manchester for cremation. Now we have no body.'

'So we go for the murder weapon. That's simply good police-work.'

'Forget the gun. What about the shoe?'

'Nothing. The unit was leased by a legit food business, who left the big chiller there, by agreement. When the lease ended, Property Max shut it up. They didn't even know anyone had been in it until we called. Forget the shoe. I mean, really forget it. It is about the gun.'

'That's your mate Beresford singing. This fella Beresford, was he ever here?'

'He didn't say. I don't think so.'

I knew different. Hetherington had shown me a photo. Despite Beresford's efforts to avert his eyes, Hetherington had caught him full-on. It was Dalzell. I could be excused for thinking that his half-turned stare was directed at me.

'See when he comes over – he might, mightn't he? - I'd love to meet him. You're still in touch?'

'He asked me to stay in touch. If I get anything on the gun, he said he'd help. They all did. They couldn't do enough for us. Even though they gave us nothing.'

'But you must have got a direct lead on that gun, from Da ... Beresford?'

A slew of phantoms passed us. White chiffon, white tissue, white taffeta, white candy floss, white gossamer, all set off by cavernous black eyes and wigs and fingernails so red they seemed to bleed pigment. It was Halloween. No one was who they seemed. Everyone was in between. Even Dalzell and Beresford.

'No, no direct leads. A few notes and queries. I haven't

really had time to chase them down, with nearly getting blown up in the field.'

'Of course. Jesus, you were lucky.'

'So were you. Or is that just the way you are, Slevin? Half in the thing, as Hammy says.'

'Hammy says more than his prayers. There was a fella on the wing with me for a few years. Biggest blow-hole since Jonah's whale. He never let up with the mouthing and the guldering. And always beside him was this wee country boy, grinning and watching. Fellas were getting restive with the motor-mouth. He was going to say something he shouldn't, with microphones all over the place and screws and touts on hand. Not to mind that none of us wanted to know things we'd be better off not knowing. One night he finished his monologue with a cliff-hanger. "And tomorrow, folks, I'll give ye the full lowdown on the professor there, hiding away with his books and saying nothing." Hammy is just a smarter version of my prison mate.'

'What did he say about you, the next day?'

'Nothing. Or more accurately, nothing about me in front of the rest of us. He didn't appear at breakfast. I went over to his side-kick and asked him where his dummy was. He said "What do you mean?" and I said "You're the ventriloquist, he's the dummy. You'll have to say it all yourself now." Seems the big fella was moved out with two others. No clear reason. It just added to the myth.'

'What myth?'

'The one that Hammy revisited. The one that says I'm some sort of shape-shifter, with shields all round me and antennae tuned to the zeitgeist. Like that robot yonder.'

'It's a wonder the ventriloquist didn't have someone do you.'

'It could happen yet. They're both out now. Like me. Big

Mouth and Pip Squeak. Festering somewhere, I suppose.'

'Things don't go away. You know that. I'll get that gun. Watch your back, Slevin.'

'Always, Kenneth. Always. Hey, enjoy the night.'

I added 'Aye, aye sailor', saluted, then fell in behind a samba-band of zombies, headed by a blaring sax and a teeth-gnashing side-drum, with more maracas and tambourines than a Tex-Mex wedding band. I needed music, but not that, so I went in search of Ruby.

The swinging strains of 'Don't Get Around Much Anymore' brought me to the small podium-stage my sister Ruby shared with a keyboard player and a laptop. She looked and sounded like the voice of the night, charmed and force-ful, elegant and straight-on. She was dressed as a witch, under a great cloak that seemed to lift her off her feet. She held a microphone in one hand and in the other she swung a be-som, bristling its twiggy ends. I skulked about on the edge of a crowd of ghouls, zombies, monsters, superheroes, medieval knights and ghosts, swaying in front of her.

The conversation with Hetherington had unsettled me. The gun was the thing. Standard police-work. No body? Find the murder weapon. Find the killer. And I knew enough about my young colleague to know that he would do his best to track it down. Just like he said.

Ruby's mini-stand was at the edge of Waterloo Place, in a direct line with the people making their way towards the Guildhall Square and the main stage. I stood where I hoped she might see me and waved. She waved her besom above her head in return, then lifted her microphone in salute.

She burled as she sang, one full turn. She was a caller at an ancient temple of the blues. I smiled, then moved back towards the river. There would be fireworks. Especially if Hetherington found the gun.

*

I left Waterloo Square and went to the front of The Guildhall, facing the river, where I climbed onto the raised area in front of the café. People in various costumes sat at tables, eating cakes and drinking coffee and hot chocolate, iridescent marshmallows bobbing in the froth. The living were living it up on the night of the dead. I could see that the crowd was six or seven deep at the railings along the river. More people milled and promenaded behind them. Three mummies, shaggy bandages unravelling, boosted each other onto a low wall in front of me, then laughed as one by one they fell off. I secured my vantage point for the fireworks. The announcer began a countdown. The crowd joined in. Fathers lifted toddlers onto their shoulders. Mothers urged babies, bundled in blankets under spider's web covers, to look to the skies.

We all raised our eyes to the inky blackness. The street lights along the riverside dimmed as the first belly-thump sounded, to be immediately followed by a bright flower-burst that flashed light on the last golden leaves dangling on the trees in the park opposite. We were star-lit for a brief moment and we oohed. More bursts followed: great orbs of shattering colour; streamers that raced lacy rainbows past each other; sparkling comets, fizzing into darkness. We loved them all. We were charmed by cheating the night, falsifying the dark by making bright and being together.

Even I felt I belonged. For the duration of a fizz-bomb.

When the last great tumult of light and sound left the sky and the families with young children began to process away from the river towards their cars and home, I stood a while, staring across the emptiness, my eyes adjusting just enough to see the Morrigan's eyes blaze through the silk-black fabric of nightness, the eyes I had seen in my window, in my dreams, in my books, on my cell wall and in my working hours in search of questions I struggled to frame.

Did I kill Todd Anderson? Did someone kill him with my gun? Someone I knew?

I was beginning to ask 'why?' when a voice beside me said 'Hello … , eh, detective …' and I turned to see Donna Bradley, costumed as a witch, complete with hat and broomstick. Beside her stood her feline familiar, Teresa, wearing cat's whiskers, but not conceding much more, like me really, in character as herself: a football under her arm, a sports shirt I couldn't identify – her school perhaps? – and on her head, a peaked cap branded Dreamtime.

'Ah, hello, Mrs. Bradley. Great fireworks,' I said.

'Fantastic. They were brilliant, weren't they Teresa?'

Teresa nodded. I grinned. Her muteness was developing into standard teenage communication. And she wore the cap as a further badge of her age.

'Dreamtime,' I said, pointing. 'You still got the boots?'

Teresa nodded again.

'And school? Okay?'

Teresa shrugged. A positive answer.

'She's flying … detective … ,' Donna Bradley ventured. 'Eddie.'

'Flying, yeh. Eddie. I'm Donna, well, you know that. We … are you on your own? We're going to have a hot chocolate, aren't we Teresa? If you'd like …'

There was a kindness, in her heavily mascaraed eyes, that I rarely know, but before I could reply she rushed on.

'No, sorry, no. You probably have friends to meet. Or something. Only, Teresa talks about you. I mean, she writes notes, you know. Nothing … nice notes.'

'Thanks, Donna. Thanks, Teresa. Maybe I'll call up to the house some day I'm up around your way, though, well, not everyone likes to have the cops calling. Even socially. Maybe especially socially.'

For the briefest moment I did see myself as part of a threesome. A man, a woman and a teenage girl. Hot chocolates and chocolate brownies marshalled in front of us. Laughter lighting up our frothy lips. To someone passing by, simply another family group.

I had embarrassed Donna, in front of her daughter. Her kindness floundered somewhere in the clefts wrought by the relationships between a man and a woman, between a cop and a citizen.

'Ach, I know,' said Donna. 'I understand. Don't think … you know …'

'Listen, have a good night. I'm due to meet some people for a drink, see out the rest of the night.'

I made it seem plausible. I had no one to see, at least no one living. I only had appointments with ghosts.

'I wanted to … did … well, had you any luck with the man?'

I knew she meant Todd Anderson.

'No. Investigations are continuing. There's been no breakthroughs …'

'I thought that,' she said. 'I mean, I would have read something in the news feeds or seen it on tv. You know, him being a footballer. They did have a big memorial for him at the ground. And then nothing.'

I could have said it's always like that. Death and then nothing, sooner or later. In Todd Anderson's case, at least locally, it had been sooner, though it was taking longer to enter nothingness in my world, following Hetherington's visit to Manchester and Dalzell's stirrings.

Donna beckoned Teresa closer and handed her a tenner.

'Teresa, go and get us two hot chocolates – loads of marshmallows for me – and two buns, the brownies you like.'

Teresa stuck to the spot for a moment, a mix of fear and

refusal in her eyes. Then I said,

'Here, I'll hold that ball for you.'

As she passed it me, I continued,

'The Globall Lite World Cup Special. The one I gave you up in the house? Germany won the cup, just like ... well, nearly everyone said.'

I bounced the ball and it returned smartly to my palms.

'Still good,' I said. 'You haven't completely kicked the stuffing out of it.'

'Not for the want of trying,' said Donna. 'Thanks, Teresa. We'll be here. You sure you don't want something?'

'No, you're grand. Thanks. No.'

She mouthed her regret in a downbeat grin and said 'two' to her daughter. Teresa headed for the café entrance.

'How will she ... ?' I began to ask.

'She has her ways. I kinda push her a bit every now and then. Who knows, she might even speak in the café, to give her order? When she was very young, my granny, she always seemed ancient to me, she said I should never worry about Teresa, because she was special, seeing as the fairies took her. I said I was glad they gave her back,' she said, smiling.

The Night of the Dead swung through another turn. I knew what the grandmother saw. Teresa was a changeling, taken and returned by the fairies, thus marred and gifted in ways only the fairies understood.

'She'll fit in well tonight. There's nothing but fairies, goblins, elves and ghosts out tonight.'

Donna laughed. It sounded like cackles from embers, dying in a fire. The sound went well with her witch's outfit. I admired her. I should have said 'yes' to the hot chocolate. But, I'm a detective and there is no let up when the case is yourself.

'It's good to see you, Mrs Bradley. Donna. And to see Teresa. She looks great. A handful, I'd say, not that I'd know.

Teenagers are all like that, I suppose.'

There was an awkward moment, as I made to pass her the ball, though her hands were buried in the folds of her witch's gown. We stood in silence, slightly askance of each other. I saw Teresa coming out of the café, with two chocolate brownies perched on two large cups in a cardboard cupholder. She looked tall and well-formed. She smiled as she slalomed between tables of young goblins, elves, fairy princesses and witches. She laughed when one of the fairy princesses, no more than three years old, stood on her chair, blessing her and everyone else with her crooked fairy wand.

'I don't think you need to worry about her,' I said. 'She's very strong.'

We both looked at Teresa, being personally blessed and honoured by the toddler fairy princess, who tapped Teresa gently on her bowed head. Everyone smiled, delighted by the child and the teenager, who played with her so thoughtfully.

'What a lovely girl,' they thought. 'Such innocence and manners.'

'If ye get anything on the man,' Donna said, 'ye will let me know. Directly, I mean. In case I have to prepare Teresa for court or something.'

'I will. Don't worry. It's nothing but dead-ends, at the minute. We have Teresa's statement and we might just need to freshen that up, ask her a couple more questions, but we'll do what we can to keep her out of court.'

She smiled her thanks, then wiped her lips. Her red lipstick smeared across her cheek and into the shadow of her mascara to give her the look of a stroke victim. And in that moment, I felt, for the first time, that I might never find who killed Todd Anderson.

'You must have a lot on your plate. Weren't you involved with that unfortunate woman blew up in the field?'

Was I? We still didn't know who she was. Maybe I was involved with her, long before she was killed.

Then Teresa joined us and, in a dumb-show of pass-the-parcel, we arranged that she and her mother had hot drinks and cakes in their hands and the football sat clamped between Teresa's feet.

'Enjoy the night,' I said. 'Good to see you both. And yeh, I'll be in touch.'

I moved off and didn't look back. I passed the table where the fairy princess was now sobbing in her father's lap, her wand a severed twig angled across the table of food and drink leavings.

Two uniforms approached me. I recognised the woman, Constable McLaren, who picked me up at Auntie Maisie's house.

'Good evening, sir. Everything alright?'

'Fine. Thanks, officer.'

'Only it can get, well, a bit rowdy later on, as you know and, well …'

'I'll be okay. I won't stay about too long. I just needed a breath of air.'

I couldn't tell her that I'd been drawn to the square by the sense that someone was waiting for me there.

Her colleague, a large-framed southern country-boy, continued.

'We seen that Crossan fella and a few of his latchicos over be the bank.'

I looked past him and spotted my former comrade, Dessie Crossan, at the centre of a group of men and women, with young children dressed as superheroes milling about them. I recognised most of the adults.

'Thanks, but I should be alright. It's only Halloween.'

Constable McLaren rested her hands on her gun belt, one to the front at the buckle, the other to the side on her night-stick.

'Of course, sir. Just, when it gets a little bit later, some of the young fellas, you know, they get a bit … boisterous.'

'You see that cannon there?'

I pointed to the barrel, poking out from the city walls above us.

'About twenty years ago, maybe more, me and two other fellas smuggled bangers onto the walls. We hid them in that cannon, the morning of Halloween. Then, on the night, when things got a bit boisterous, we threw them at officers, just like you, standing right below us, near enough here. The two lads and me, we split. They were caught. I made it over a gate and into the back yard of a shop on Shipquay Street, where I slept in a skip. The lads never gave me up. One of them is dead now. He might be here tonight. *Samhain*, you know. Night of the dead and all that. The other was Dessie Crossan.'

The male constable took a step backwards. The woman smiled.

'See how things change and stay the same,' she said.

'Yes. And no. Thanks for your concern,' I said.

They stepped apart and I walked between them, into the last encounter of my night, the meeting that had drawn me to the streets, the finale of my Halloween odyssey.

Dessie Crossan raised his chin, as I passed.

Any fireworks tonight?
No. All quiet.
Nothing but the dead. And us.

I journeyed through the waves of devils, warlocks, ghouls, Frankensteins, blood-drenched surgeons, aliens, daleks and vampires, St. Trinian's girls, Mickey Mouses and robots to get near the front of the crowd, ranged before the temporary staging, set at a ninety degree angle to the face of the Guildhall. A light show illuminated the building from projectors on the walls, showing a city scape crossed by bats, owls, witches on broomsticks, and tombstones leaning over gaping graves, out of which maggoty corpses crawled.

The band on stage finished a rock and roll number. The MC took the microphone and announced the city's soccer team. Fifteen young men, led by the chair of the board of directors, Denis Green, trooped on and lined up. They wore club suits and ties and looked elegant, smart and sheepish, in equal measure. The MC began to interview Denis Green. The young men clustered uneasily in pairs and threes, joking shyly and waving to the crowd. One man stood slightly off and alone, distinctively tall, blond-headed and clean-shaven.

I wasn't surprised. I knew all along that Todd Anderson would be there.

There, for me alone. A dead end.

The clock on the Guildhall began to chime midnight, drowning out the interview on the temporary stage. I looked up at the clock-face. The two hands clasped firmly together above the searing eyes of The Morrigan, as she tolled the turn of the year from light to dark. October slipped into November and ice-floes shuddered alive beneath my crepe-soled feet.

FOURTEEN

I perked up a bit when Hammy sent me to a police conference. He tackled me, as I sat beside Sharon, munching a granola bar, while she grazed on her tray of pulses and nuts. We were drinking still water, me from a bottle, she from a container I guessed sat under a filter at home.

'Feeding time among the herbivores, is it? I'm surprised you're letting this beast into your cage, Sharon. I thought you had more discernment,' Hammy quipped, then tossed me a printed message.

'CC's after you again, Eddie, my boy. High level conference in some spa on the banks of Lough Erne. Paddle your own canoe, kiddo. Paddle your own canoe. You're sharing with one Joseph Dickson, representing Vice. He's a callow and timid youth, so don't cause him any anguish.'

Then he strode to his own office and slammed the door behind him, setting the blinds aquiver until he zipped them closed.

'Relax. The master is now back in his lair,' Sharon said, spooning another mouthful of her healthy lunch between her dainty teeth and her fiery red lips.

'He thinks we're his caged beasts,' I said.

'He's not far wrong. What the fuck are you doing here anyway, Slevin?'

'My job, Sharon. Simply my job.'

'Well, you've got the higher-ups convinced. I'm on the jury and, as they say, I'm still "out". So's Hetherington, your buddy. He's sure you're some kind of mole. Or even a quisling.'

'Too rich for me, Sharon. Far too rich for me. I'm doing

my job. I'm detecting. Detecting and solving crimes. Serious crimes. If that's not good enough for Hetherington or anybody else, what can I do?'

'Don't ask me. I'm just the office herbivore.'

I foot-propelled my chair back to my own desk and scanned the page Hammy had given me. Conference details; a room number; a registered set of seminars and workshops; a query about dietary requirements. Why had I received the invitation – summons? – to this jamboree was one of many questions I couldn't properly frame.

The thing about a police conference is that the hotel corridors are full of tall people. In jail, the population was short, even the screws were short, and the passages were crammed with people I could look down upon. At the police conference, I found myself gazing upwards most of time, as I hunted Amy Miller, who's name appeared on a list of attendees I received on arrival.

I found her in the queue for coffee and scones at the mid-morning break. She was squeezed between two men, big as second-row rugby forwards, who talked over her head. I stepped in, nodding at the man behind her, who nodded back at me and continued talking to his mate, while edging round slightly to accommodate me. I concentrated on Amy.

'You're not really that hungry, are you?'

'I thought I was. And I fell in with these two fine men at the end of the first session and ended up here.'

'What session were you at?'

'"Policing the Permeable Border"'

'You thinking of changing jobs?'

'No. I was working late last night. I needed a sleep.'

'You can lie down in my room. I have biscuits. And coffee.'

'Who are you sharing with?'

'A nice, quiet lad from Vice. My guess is he's on the golf course.'

The queue bunched up as we left. The two big lads nodded and carried on talking. I resisted the urge to grab Amy's hand and run, run, run along the corridor, up the service stairs, down to the far end of the first floor and to my room on the lake-side extension, its corner window framing a sliver of the lake, a wedge of farmland, a plateau of parking and a stand of flag-poles, now naked, in the misty morning.

It took me three goes to get the keycard into the slot to trigger the green light on the door lock, by which time Amy was giggling and pushing me through the door. It eased closed behind us, with a satisfied sigh, as she propelled me onto a bed. There was more giggling and fumbling with the condom I plundered from my pull-along suitcase, then no more missed strokes or stumbling, no further false starts or mishaps. We found each other forcefully and thoroughly and, in a briskly energetic drive, travelled to deep, brief ecstasies, which shuddered through us, echoing in our whimpers, whispers and breathy calls.

In the chest-heaving pause that followed I saw, through the corner window, two swans angle towards the lake. I was sure I could hear them honk above the bellowing of my heart in my chest. Then Amy started giggling again, a grown up woman's giggle, surprising from so elfin a figure. I joined her, when I realised we were strewn across my room-mate's bed, the contents of my suitcase littered across another bed.

We disentangled and passed each other items of clothing.

'Just a minute,' I said, as I held her bra. 'I haven't really seen you yet.'

Amy struck a pose, an urchin's pose, eyeing the far distance, one hand on her hip, the other on her chin, so her arm crossed her chest. She was the Venus Demure, feigning modesty. I tossed her the bra. She caught it, put it on, then stepped deftly into her pants. I pulled on my shirt and said 'Great.'

I salvaged the debris from my bed and stuffed it back into my suitcase. She smoothed the covers on my room-mate's bed. There was a round of toilet visits, cleansing and readying for leaving. So much intimacy, so sudden and speedy, left me nerve-jangled.

'I am hungry now,' said Amy. We walked at pace along the corridor and down the service stairs, where we pecked our lips together, sealing an agreement to meet during lunch, then we entered the dining area by separate doors.

The break-time queue was long satisfied. There were no more than dregs in the coffee dispensers. I took half a cherry scone and smothered it in butter and raspberry jam. It was as tasty as the sweet sweat I licked from the base of Amy's porcelain neck.

Events overtook the plans Amy Miller and I had to meet during the conference lunch-break. Two squarely-built men in suits, the very same who had book-ended Amy and me in the morning queue, met me at an angle of corridors en route to the dining room. Only one spoke. The second one stood slightly off, as if expecting to make a tackle on a strong-running rugby flanker.

'Hello, Eddie. You're invited to a wee private lunch with Officer Cosgrove. If you'd like to come with us?'

'Ah, thanks. Give the Officer my regards, best wishes and regrets. I already have a lunch engagement.'

'Officer Cosgrove, from IS, is very keen to enjoy some quality time with you.'

'Who is he?' I asked.

The big man looked down at me. He was as 'country' as I was 'city'. I was a bale of hay he could heft and toss over the roof of a bungalow on his way to a stand-pipe to drench his muddy hands clean. I might, as a teenager, have dashed round him and palmed off his back-up with pace and verve, but these trackers had me angled to a corner, with a lift emptying crowds of hungry colleagues right beside us. And I was no longer a teenager.

'Officer Cosgrove said you might be hesitant, but asks me to assure you that the invitation is cordial. The room is quiet and the soup is delicious. The vegetarian option is a vegetable broth. Or you might prefer the Fermanagh oxtail.'

His colleague made a half-turn. The talker moved in behind me and the three of us processed round the corner past the lift doors and into a small salon where Officer Cosgrove of PS(N) Internal Security sat at a table set for two, over-looking the golf course, supping oxtail soup from a china bowl.

I took the empty seat and pulled out my phone, intending to message Amy, but the talker whipped it from my hand.

'You won't need that for the moment, Slevin,' explained Cosgrove. 'It's impolite to use them, while sharing lunch. Cuts into the chat. I recommend the oxtail. Old-fashioned comfort food.'

He took another spoonful with a loud slurp, then began to break a bread roll into the remainder. We were left alone and a seemingly cordial silence descended upon us, broken only by the clink of Cosgrove's spoon on the china bowl and the slush of his eating.

The talker returned with a tray of food. Oxtail soup and a crusty roll; another roll, this one filled with chicken in a cream sauce; a glass of water; an orange; cutlery and a folded napkin, pert as surgical implements. I recognised it as an hotel version of prison rations, finessed, yet grim as the fare served on the wings.

I looked out of the window, at the golfers hurrying back from the course. Had they programmed game-time as part of the conference or were they simply skiving? I saw my room-mate, just as I guessed, pulling his golf-cart behind him, laughing with his three companions, until his eyes met mine and the four-ball veered off, hunching shoulders and quickening their pace. Cosgrove smiled as he brought another spoonful to his thin lips and I knew we were two fish in a glass bowl he wanted everyone to hear about. The 'wee private lunch' was a public affair and I wondered if this was the sole reason I was invited. Now I was Slevin, the dirty cop, lunching with IS.

Odours of oxtail, chicken and orange reached me from the tray. I lifted it and put it on the floor beside me.

'Let's have it then, Officer Cosgrove. I have a lunch engagement.'

'No doubt. Room service, I imagine. Pity you won't take the soup with me. A taste of home for the big lads here. Shame to see it go to waste.'

He nodded and the talker lifted both our trays with a set of fluid moves, not spilling a drop of soup or water. My orange rolled about slightly as he swirled away from the table and left the room. My lips felt dry and I regretted letting the water go. I ran my tongue round my mouth and tasted Amy's flesh. I touched my fingers to my nose and smelled her juices. I was hungry, but not for prison food, however refined.

'If that's all, sir, I'll be making ...'

I moved just as the talker returned. He put a hand on my shoulder and sat me back in the chair. He passed a touch-screen tablet to Cosgrove.

'You've had a hectic few months since we last met, Slevin. Nearly got yourself blown up, if you don't mind. You'd swear someone was out to get you. Here, I want you to have a look at something and then I want you to give me your account of what you're up to.'

He propped the tablet on its foldaway feet, so we could both see it. He set it against the window, backdropped with the last of the straggling golfers, doing their best not to be seen. Cosgrove smiled, obviously enjoying himself. He removed his thin metal spectacles and wiped the lenses with the edge of his pristine cotton table napkin.

'Bifocals, Slevin. Means I get to see everything, all the time. Here we go.'

We both viewed a short sequence of clips from a camera in the foyer of the railway station. They showed me entering the foyer, speaking with the staff member, going into the inner office, then coming out again. There was no audio, but I couldn't assume he didn't have that. Or other footage he wasn't sharing with me.

'Bit late to be going for a train, Slevin,' Cosgrove said.

'I was there to pick something up. He'd phoned me, the fella at the railway station.'

'And what was the "something" that was so important it couldn't wait 'til the morning?'

'I was doing him a favour, letting him get away early. And saving the "something" from being sent back to Lost Property at Central. Besides it was a nice fresh night and the walk did me good. Check the cameras on the Peace Bridge. You'll see my breath in the air. The resolution is good on those cameras.'

I had a long apprenticeship, on the streets, in the war and in prison. The basic rule was: when you lie, stay as close to the truth as you can.

'So, he gave you this "something"?'

'Actually, I left empty-handed. You can see there.'

'Why?'

'The "something" was for someone else, not me.'

'And who was that?'

'You'll have to ask yer man that. Jake, wasn't it? That's

what he called himself on the phone. You would have heard him.'

'Jake Tees, yes. And it seems that's what you're doing to me, Slevin. One long drawn-out tease.'

'Sorry to disappoint you, sir. If I dash, I might just catch the end of lunch. I fancy the vegetable broth. Less chance of bullshit than the oxtail.'

Cosgrove shut down the tablet.

'Jake Tees says he gave a folder to another Edmund Slevin. A folder that had your number on it.'

'Ah, a misfortunate misunderstanding. No more than that. It's a big rail service. Names and numbers get mis-recorded, I'm sure. Folders and files get mis-directed all the time. You won't mind if I suggest it even happens, occasionally, with us and we're the police. Well, I am. I'm not sure what IS is. A canker on a branch of bad apples?'

I pushed my chair well back, which gave me enough room to get out and round the Talker. I made it to the door and heard Cosgrove yap 'let him go', as I yanked the handle. The second man was stationed opposite the door, but between his initial surprise at seeing me and, I guessed, a 'stand down' signal from the talker, I turned and plunged against the flow of conference goers exiting the dining room, among them Amy Miller, who came towards me, sprightly as a ferret.

'You stood me up, Slevin,' she said.

'I'm sorry. Look … I … They …'

'Not a great response. Look at you. Stammering in the corridor, while PS(N)'s finest parade by, leering at us. You scored some cold soup, when you could have had me. Hot. Not even a message, Slevin.'

A flush of panic raced through me, when I realised they still had my phone.

'They took … There was no …'

'They? I heard about you, Slevin. You and your visions and your voices. But I didn't think you'd be this dodgy.'

I was rattled. Confusion and lust flared through me.

'Look …'

'You hurt me, Slevin. Not a good move.'

'Tonight then. My room,' I gasped.

'You're taking the piss? A threesome?'

That slowed a couple of people down beside us. I heard a muted whoop.

'I'll sort that. You and me. And time.'

We were getting even more interest from colleagues passing by. Amy was unfazed. I was on the point of screaming.

'I'm late,' she said. 'I'm on a panel in the Lustymore Suite …'

Someone wolf-whistled then and Amy smiled. She was enjoying herself. Every fucker was. Except me.

'… on "Women and Progression in the Police Service".'

I caught her arm and whispered in her ear.

'I'll message you.'

Amy brushed me off, as she might brush lint off an old coat. I could send her a message, but in my rush away from Cosgrove I had forgotten to demand my phone back. I decided to give his heavies a breather, before I got back to them.

I found my golfing roommate, Hammy's 'callow and timid youth' from Vice, on his way to the conference's afternoon session on the latest scientific research into legal highs: 'Bath Salts, Plant Feeds and their narcotic effects'.

'You need to find a bed for the night.'

He didn't speak. Seeing me with Cosgrove had spooked him over an edge he was already tottering on. He wanted nothing more to do with me.

'And, see tomorrow, I'll make my own way back. You won't

have to drive me.'

He almost cheered. I just needed to get my phone back, not only to message Amy, but to reclaim my life. Without it, I was no longer a police officer. I was way outside the law, further than a criminal. I was an ex-prisoner, an ex-guerrilla, an ex-cop. An ex-person.

I dodged the afternoon session I was scheduled to attend, sitting near the front, then, just as it was about to begin, exiting the room via a door at the side of the podium. That manoeuvre raised my mood. It pissed off my two trackers, though one or other of them was always in sight. I drifted down corridors, ghosted up and down service stairs, shared the service lift with an East European chambermaid who said 'hello' and got on with her work of checking toiletry items on her room service trolley. I got out at four, then used the stairs to go down. She continued upwards. I most enjoyed passing through the kitchens, as the chefs prepared dinner. They barely lifted their heads from their chopping, skinning, pounding and stirring. The smell of roasting meat and steaming broccoli followed me through the emergency exit and into a rear car park where two delivery vans burled round each other and sped away, one to Western Artisan Beef Company and the other to Freshveg – a Fennessey Company.

I pulled out a cigarette and realised that I hadn't had one since breakfast. Maybe I could give them up.

My Number One Tracker came up and handed me my phone.

'Here. I thought it would be more interesting.'

'I wondered when you'd turn up.'

'What's on the menu?' he asked.

'Roast beef and broccoli, my nose tells me.'

'Don't be making any dinner plans. You're for the top table. Clashing the aul' cutlery with the CC and the Yank Professor, who gave the key-note. She wants to show you off, the prize Charolais, though you're a bit lean for that.'

'I'm guessing that's an agricultural reference and, if it is, it's lost on me, big lad.'

'Aye, Charolais. Large and beefy. Could be on the menu. Wouldn't be bad. You're more streaky bacon than prime steak.'

'You're right there, sir. I'm a rasher of a man. Listen, I'm not going anywhere. Why don't yourself and Daffy Duck quack off for a while?'

'You think we could? Me and Daffy Duck quack off? That's good. You're better in person than on the phone or by reputation. We'll see what we can do. Top table, seven sharp. Face washed. Clean knickers, if you have them. You'd never know your luck.'

'Here, before you go, do me a favour. Tell me this. What's Cosgrove after me for? What does he want, because if I knew, I'd be only too glad to give it to him.'

He stuffed his fists in the square pockets of his waxed jacket and shrugged.

'You're good at that, eh? Giving it to cops? Officer Cosgrove goes after dirty ones. He's good at it. We work for him, more brawn than brain, right enough, but we're smart enough when we have to be. You ask me what he wants. I'd say he wants to hose you down clean, then flush you into the slurry with the rest of the manure.'

'You're an education, you are. A farmhouse encyclopaedia. What's your name?'

'Goosy Gander. I'll tell Daffy Duck you were asking for him. Stay close and be at the CC's table at seven.'

Then he walked off and I was left to consider what to do until seven o'clock. I checked my phone. They'd drained the power and it wouldn't come on. I would have to go back to my room and put it on charge. I could go searching for Amy, but I expected she would avoid me again.

I was left with the terrifying options of a round of golf or catching the end of a session on human trafficking: 'Following the Money: Proven trafficker routes from Asia to Europe'. I went back to the sanctuary of my room, asked the desk for a call at six and went to bed. I didn't dream about golf or money. I dreamed about water.

FIFTEEN

The bedside phone grumbled in alarm. I woke up gasping and soaking wet, as if I'd been swimming. I lifted the handset and put it down again, then got up and showered like a man washing off the slime of submersion. I dressed and made my way to the dining room, which was laid out restaurant-style, with small tables seating four or six people, as well as banquettes along two walls. The CC and another woman sat facing the room from the purple upholstery of a high-backed banquette on the wall nearest the kitchen access. There was a gap of two tables before the next table of six. The CC made the introductions, as I took a seat with my back to the room.

'Excellent, Detective Slevin. I knew we could rely on you. This is Dr. Rankin. Were you at her presentation this afternoon?'

I took the Doctor's hand and avoided the question.

'I hope I'm too not late. Just three of us, is it? The room looks great. Like a wedding.'

Doctor Rankin laughed and shook my hand. She was tall, like the CC, with wavy black hair and the solidly trim physique of a regular swimmer. It was hard to be accurate, but I guessed she was in her early forties. Both women wore fine lace shirts underneath light waist coats, the CC's an embroidered bolero. I wore a button down blue shirt. I'd left my jacket in the room. The temperature in the hotel was low-end sauna.

'Good to meet you, Detective Slevin.'

'You too, Doctor Rankin.'

No first names were shared. The CC continued.

'Detective Slevin is also a doctor. Guess his field.'

Dr Rankin looked at me and ventured,

'Medicine? Pathology?'

'Mythology. I think I smell broccoli.'

I had decided to keep this dinner cordial and get away as quickly as I could. The tables were filling behind us, voices were bubbling up and chairs were sounding, as people pulled them out and sat upon them.

The kitchen doors swung open and two waiters arrived with our starters. The CC said to place the fourth one, as she expected her guest to arrive any minute. I focused on my portion of smoked salmon on a rocket salad, adrift slightly off-centre on an unnecessarily large platter.

'Let's start,' said the CC. The sound of cutlery on china joined the voices in the room.

'Mythology?' said Dr Rankin. 'That's a bit unusual for a police officer.'

'Detective Slevin is not one of our "usual" police officers.'

'Is that so? In what way exactly?'

I had no idea who Dr. Rankin was, but I was sure that like me, she was there for a specific reason. I just didn't know what it was. I was also confident she had been properly briefed on my CV.

'Well, here I am, the only police officer dining with the Chief Constable. Unless you're a police officer.'

Dr Rankin smiled.

'No. I'm a biochemist.'

Then she reached across and touched the CC's forearm, drawing her attention to a piece of rocket dangling from her lower lip. The CC took her napkin, tidied her mouth and smiled a gleaming smile. Dr Rankin nodded approval. If I was asked about the status of their relationship I would say 'close'.

'Dr Rankin led an afternoon session on the narcotic effects of plant feeds. Was that one of yours?'

I was saved by the arrival of the fourth member of our dinner party, a tall, prematurely balding man, aged about 30, whose domed head echoed his gently rounded belly.

'Ah, Professor De Lorenzo,' said the CC and we all stood up. Handshakes and introductions passed swiftly and Professor Frankie De Lorenzo, from the US National Academy for the Advancement of Forensic Science, sat beside me.

'Sorry I'm late. I had trouble with the shower faucet. I turned it right and it got hot. Turned it right some more and it got cold. Then I turned it left and ice chunks came out. Further left and it was burning tar. It took me ten minutes of TV channel surfing to ignore it and let it settle to comfortably tepid.'

'We're glad you could join us. How's the jet lag?' asked the CC.

'Fine. Never seems to bother me. Must be the Sicilian mountain blood. I'm always oxygenated.'

'I saw you swimming this morning. That helps too, no doubt,' said Dr Rankin.

I thought of my dream and my sense of being submerged.

The Professor turned to me, so I had a good view of his mauve t-shirt. The letters PRE and VE were scrunched across his chest. The dress code for the evening was smart casual and, in his case, the emphasis was on 'casual'.

'Are you a swimmer, Detective Slevin?'

'No, can't swim a stroke. I like the firm ground.'

'I heard you go against the tide sometimes.' As I expected, he had been briefed too. 'You got yourself blown up recently, I understand.'

'Not quite true. The victim was a very unfortunate woman. Me and a colleague … well, he was injured. I was unscathed.'

'Did you know the woman?' asked Dr. Rankin.

My eyes caught the look on the CC's face telling me my

role and how I was to play it. The circumspect maverick, the rough-diamond protégée, not entirely dependable, but charmed. And charming enough to boost her status with her friend, her international guest and the rest of the room. My colleagues had, by now, read the pecking order that put me at the top table, while news of my lunch date with a senior IS official was likely to be top of the gossip menu.

'Investigations are underway. I'm not directly involved, as you can understand. It very soon emerged that we were dealing with a gang-land crime, so the Organised Crime Team are on it. The woman seems to have been East European. There's no final identification as yet. Prostitution, trafficking, forced labour perhaps – all of these are involved. It's complex.'

'And not much for your forensics people to work on, I hear. She was blown to shreds,' said the Professor.

I saw Dr Rankin put down her fork and sit back in the banquette.

'Still,' the Professor continued, 'There's always something, if you can get it early enough. And keep it viable.'

That confirmed the lettering across his chest as PRESERVE, the mantra of all forensic work, Karen Lavery often told me. Thinking about her brought Amy to mind and I shifted my chair to try to locate her in the room, but, without getting up and fully turning around, I could only manage to see the groups either side of us and she wasn't among them.

'Well, this salmon won't be swimming against the tide any more,' said the Professor. 'From the lake outside, you reckon?'

The CC shook her head and laughed.

'Not likely. Farmed somewhere, under lock and key in cages.'

'Put there by PS(N),' Dr Rankin quipped drily.

'Put there for PS(N) and their guests, who are well-pleased by it,' said the Professor.

An awkward lull mired the conversation. It was my turn

to perform.

'We have a big myth involving a salmon. Several in fact. And they're echoed around the world. A young hero gains his wisdom from the Salmon of Knowledge.'

Dr Rankin grew interested again and leaned forward, but the story was really for the Professor.

'A salmon, cooking on a spit, grows a heat blister and a boy, Fionn, sticks his thumb to it, to burst it. He burns his thumb, of course, and, in a reflex, sticks his thumb into his mouth to ease it. His master sees his visage change, as the Light of the Ages infuses the boy. It was the flesh of the Salmon of Knowledge he had tasted.'

'Nice,' said the Professor. 'Looking round this table, I'd say there's been plenty of thumb-sucking going on. I don't think I got much wisdom from my Mama's pasta sauce, hearty and filling though it was.'

'Well, whatever the source of your knowledge, you carry it very lightly. Your keynote this morning was delightful and inspiring,' said the CC.

'Why, thank you, Ma'am.'

'Oh, yes it was,' added Dr Rankin. 'But I'm still not clear what you believe, never mind what I believe. Was Ophelia's death an accident or suicide? Or was she pushed?'

I remembered the session then. It came straight after the coffee break. My nerves were still jangling after my time with Amy. I was half-asleep and slightly unsettled by everything the Professor said. He'd used the drowning of Ophelia in Shakespeare's *Hamlet* as a case study on forensics.

Dr Rankin grew enthusiastic.

'I loved the way you explained the weeds and the flowers. Forensically and yet it was like, I don't know, an apothecary, an old herbalist's chest.'

'Pansies, rosemary, violets and daisies, yeh, they're all in it. Shakespeare could paint the pictures, you bet. Still, her brother, Laertes, gets it right when he says, "Too much of water has thou, poor Ophelia".'

'I loved the way you sneaked that story up on us. Forgive me, the police officers here, but I don't see a PS(N) audience as a rich terrain for literary analysis. Of course, you just said a woman called Ophelia was found dead in a river, drowned, no other marks on her, some people said she fell in, then you threw in lines from the play, like witness accounts …'

'... some in favour of the idea of suicide,' said the CC.

'... only then did it dawn on me, you were on about Ophelia, the tragic lover in Hamlet. Brilliant.'

The two women were having fun and the Professor was lapping up the admiration. I felt like a bit player, one of Shakespeare's extras, guarding my fears with the rusty halberd of my memories. I set to finish my salmon and rocket salad, then sat back to wait for the main course, but the Professor drew me in.

'You're very kind. Like I said, there is no evidence of a push or a struggle. What do you say, Detective Slevin? Surely Ophelia, mad though she may have been, would have resisted?'

'Depends on what was pushing her.'

A soon as I said it, I knew how crazy it sounded. The CC stared at me, this time with a purplish moue of disappointment. Dr. Rankin's clear brow furrowed and she said,

'I'm not sure I follow you, Detective Slevin.'

I was saved by the waiters who came to lift our platters. They promptly returned with even larger dinner platters, bearing generous portions of roast beef, which they placed before us, then neatly filled the spaces on the table with three types of potato – lyonnaise, roast and baby-boiled – serving spoons, a wine-rich gravy in a boat my Auntie Maisie would covet, more serving spoons and dishes of cauliflower, runner beans and broccoli, still steaming and each sporting a dab of butter that careered about like a skier. Everyone took a glass of the Italian red.

The Professor beamed his delight.

'Mama De Lorenzo couldn't have done any better, except maybe pasta for the potatoes. Spuds, eh? Are they a set of 3 options?'

The CC laughed.

'No, all three are mandatory with us.'

'I get enough of those into me, no amount of jet-lag is gonna keep me from snoring.'

We all filled our plates and began to eat. I sensed I was calming down. But Dr Rankin didn't want to leave Ophelia in the water.

'No vegetarians at this table I see,' she began. 'I'm very much a scientist, as you are Professor. But Detective Slevin, was that some sort of "mythological" response to the Ophelia story? You reckon she was pushed? What do you think happened Ophelia, Detective Slevin?'

I knew the play, *Hamlet*. I read everything in prison, including Shakespeare.

'A young woman is seen in a state of distress over a period of time. It is known that she has been jilted, in a very high-profile manner, by a young man who may have broken promises to her. She is found dead, drowned in a low river, shrouded in flowers and weeds. It is said that she was hanging garlands from a tree when a branch broke. She fell in and succumbed to the water. Did anyone find this branch? Perhaps it was swept away. Did anyone check if there was evidence of recent breakages?'

'There was no "police investigation",' said Dr Rankin. 'There was no "police". It was obvious what happened.'

'Yes, it was obvious, especially as the Queen told it, the

most powerful woman in the case,' said Professor De Lorenzo. 'Ophelia, singing, fell into the brook and drowned.'

I almost told him to shut up. The table went quiet. This was my chance to move away from watery deaths. I lifted my glass.

'A small toast. To Western Artisan Beef and Freshveg!'

'Who are they?' asked the CC.

'The companies who provided the dinner.'

We laughed and lightly clinked our glasses. The mood became upbeat and convivial, in tune with the lively atmosphere on the tables behind me. What my colleagues made of me clinking wine glasses with the CC, her friend and the keynote speaker, I couldn't guess. If I put myself in their seats, I would feel jealousy, confusion, resentment, unease and a conviction that something smelled rotten. And it wasn't the excellent beef.

'Very good detective work,' said the Professor, crooking a finger at one of the waiters permanently stationed nearby to serve the CC's table.

'Anyone else, apart from me, for more beef?'

We declined and I began to feel calm again. Perhaps we could talk about food. But Dr Rankin wanted second helpings of my speculations.

'You're right, Detective Slevin. We only believe the Queen, maybe, only because she is The Queen. What, or who, pushed Ophelia into the water?' said Dr Rankin.

A vision of my mother, in sodden clothes, stood before me. I didn't intend to clatter my cutlery as I put it down, but the sound stilled our table and, as far as I could tell, with my back to the hubbub, it brought a pause to the feasting and talking at tables nearby. I sensed people nudging each other and eyeing the CC's table. What? A row? When it had all seemed so lovey-dovey, so happy foursome, so date-night jolly.

The Professor slowly mopped up the last of his gravy with a sludge of lyonnaise, mashed baby-boiled and roast potatoes.

He swirled his fork in the food-sludge, moving the mess about until it gained the consistency of tidal muck.

'That's always a big question,' he said. 'The question of agency. The "who?" question. The big one. So we call them whodunnits not whathappenits or whyits.'

The CC came in then.

'*Cui bono?*'

All four of us knew the Latin, even as she translated.

'We have to ask "who benefits?" If anybody.'

'But nobody benefits from Ophelia's drowning. Her father's dead. Her brother is devastated. That's it. God, by the end, they're all dead. Even the Queen.' said Dr Rankin.

'As a result of a genuine accident in the King's foolish game of poisoning, while setting young men to play with swords. Bring out weapons and someone's going to get it,' I said.

I thought of Dalzell and his manipulations. I thought of Hammy, my boss, who said I was at the centre of the vortex: the murder of Todd Anderson, the woman blown up in the field, the whole rushing stream of it all.

The Professor spooned the last of his meat, spuds and gravy into his mouth. He silently set his fork upon his plate. Almost immediately, the waiters advanced and began to clear our table. The four of us sat back in silence, digesting. I took the chance to turn round and gaze across the room. Every table was alive with conversation and gesture. There was more animation among my colleagues than I'd ever witnessed at work. I saw the young officer from Vice throw his head back in laughter, then point a finger at a woman opposite. He didn't seem the slightest bit callow.

I saw Amy, radiant as an imp in a plain black dress, who's open neck showed the porcelain skin I'd licked earlier. She was at a table of eight, listening intently to the woman beside her, who was using a knife to sight a distant target. A shooting colleague I guessed, recounting an incident or describing a gun she'd used. Amy nodded, asked brief questions and made inquiring gestures with her piano-player's fingers. Her dinner partner took the knife again and sighted across herself, illustrating features on the weapon. She raised it to her eye once more, as if aiming a rifle. It was aiming, directly across the room, at me.

When I turned back to the table, the Professor announced he was ready to eat some more.

'Whatta you say you use your skills again, Detective Slevin? You got the source of the beef and vegetables. What you got for dessert then?'

'Oh, I don't know if I could manage a dessert,' said the CC. 'And it might be getting near time for me to leave, in order to let everyone loosen up a little. There's a comedian planned, well, an after-dinner speaker.'

A young woman tapped the microphone at the front of the room and asked for our attention. She was one of what Hammy calls the 'Young Levitators', capable and ambitious new officers, effortlessly rising through the ranks. She confirmed there was an after-dinner speaker, followed by a number of options, including a sing-song, a quiz or a quiet drink in the Devenish Bar, which she designated the 'chill zone'.

'The Devilish Bar sounds about right for me,' said the Professor. No one corrected him.

He alone ordered profiteroles, which arrived heaped in a mountain cairn, beside a glacier of ice-cream. We all had coffees.

'Tell me about this case you're working on,' said the Professor. 'The Anderson case.'

I looked at the CC and she stared back at me in a manner I read as giving me permission to speak, while advising me to be circumspect.

'It's still a live case, an on-going investigation,' I began.

'Of course. Anything on the forensic side?' asked the Professor.

'No. Dead ends. Blood tissues, clothing, fabrics – nothing. We found a shoe in a chiller, proving the body had been stored there. Beyond that. Nothing.'

'The investigation is complex. And slow,' said the CC.

'It's a disappointment to me. To us. We may even have made mistakes, noting the advice on your t-shirt,' I said.

'I'm not sure you could say we made mistakes, Detective Slevin. At any rate, this is where we are. Not very far,' said the CC.

'How did he die? Is it a murder?' asked Dr Rankin.

'Shot in the back of the head.'

'Oh, God. Not an accident or a suicide then.'

'I'm not ruling anything out.'

'That seems a bit far-fetched, Detective Slevin?' said Dr. Rankin. 'Your speculations involving Ophelia, well, that's a play and a fiction. Entertaining as they were, you'd hardly apply them in a real life situation. Surely it must be about the evidence?'

'The thing is, Dr Rankin,' I said, trying to keep an edge out of my voice. 'Put some evidence in front of two people and you get two different views on it. Bring in a third person and you'll get another view.'

The Professor backed me up.

'He's right. I can't tell you how many times I've been an expert witness, for either side, when it became obvious to me that the lawyer testing my evidence was more concerned with victory than with truth. Have you got any leads? Suspects? Murder weapon? Ballistics?'

I had to assume the CC had full details of the current state of our investigations, so I was careful when I touched on the matter that caused me the most anxiety.

'My colleague, DC Hetherington, is following up on the bullet, trying to link it to a known gun. We're pulling the latest findings together with our boss, eh, with Detective Inspector Hamilton, as soon as possible.'

'Good luck there. Bullets and guns! Cheez! You think a unique match would be easy. One bullet, one gun. Not nowadays. I'm going to Dublin tomorrow afternoon, to visit a colleague at the Forensics Lab there. I'll give him your name and ask him to contact you. He's doing good work.'

'Thank you, Professor. Hetherington is speaking to them at present,' I lied. I had no intention of linking myself or Hetherington to the Forensics Lab in Dublin.

'Thank you indeed, Professor,' added the CC, wrapping up. 'For your assistance on this matter, for your brilliant keynote speech this morning and for your entertaining post-script tonight. Thank you for making time to be at our conference. I'm going to skip the quiz and the sing-song and get out just ahead of the after-dinner speaker. I'd hate to cramp his style by sitting here, a target he couldn't lampoon.'

'Maybe he could. But would you be able to handle it?' asked Dr Rankin.

'Not even going to try. Good night then.'

She got up. Dr Rankin got up too.

'It's a bit early, Elaine. What about a drink in the Professor's Devilish bar? And if you guys want to join us after your dessert, by all means do.'

We all stood and shook hands. The two women left. The Professor performed the same end-of-dish ritual with his dessert, his fork swirling a final profiterole round his plate.

'Do you smoke, Detective Slevin?'

'Yeh. You want one?'

'This country is worse than New York. Where do you folks

smoke anymore?'

He relished a last mouthful, belched lightly, then we left the dining room. I looked back from the door. I confirmed that Amy was still at her table, though many people were moving about.

Because of my afternoon wanderings, I had a detailed sense of the layout of the hotel and very quickly led us to a service entrance that accessed the turning circle for delivery vehicles. A short walk brought us to a perspex shelter beside the lake. The Professor sat on the bench, while I passed him a cigarette and lit us both up. Inhaling and exhaling grandly, neither of us said anything until it dawned on me that he might be cold.

'You want to go back?'

'Naw, it's great. Fresh air and cigarette smoke. The perfect combination.'

He laughed and blew a jet-stream into the dark air.

'Even though I know you're right about "different views", I say you've still gotta go after the evidence. It's all we've got. It's just about finding the right questions to ask.'

'I know that. But I always feel there's more.'

'Of course. You've gotta find the right people to ask.'

I knew that too.

He went silent again. The water lapped towards us, as if in supplication. Even in the dark, the breadth of the lake was daunting. Lights from houses traced a far bank. Moving lights revealed cars on a road climbing a hillside. The water flowed aimlessly, going nowhere except back onto itself.

The Professor stood up.

'I understand you're something of a pet project of your CC.'

'I wouldn't say that.'

'Maybe not. Others would. She had you at dinner tonight

to show you off. Agreed?'

I shrugged.

'Or to keep an eye on me.'

'She has goons to do that.'

I smiled, thinking of Daffy and Goosy.

'You're political, right?'

'I was.'

'You're political. Jesus, you're a police officer. My folks were political. Going way back to the home country. Ever been to Sicily? You'd love it. Figuring out who did what to who and why, is the daily past-time.'

'Same here. Questions. Answers, even. Sometimes.'

'Yeh, but you can't forget what your CC said. She's what my old Papa would have called "quite a dame". You get the Cicero she dropped in over the roast beef?'

'*Cui bono?* Who benefits?'

'The key question.'

I looked across the mercury corrugations on the lake's surface and felt a light breeze ruffle my shirt.

'It's all about fear, you know that, Slevin. Lapping waters, rising. A kind of cosmic irony, playing at all times. Which takes us back to the bullet and the evidence. Take care, Detective Slevin.'

He palmed me his card.

'Thanks for the cigarette. I feel better now, for doing something vaguely transgressive at a police conference. Let's go back. A drink in the Devilish Bar, whatta you say?'

We went back the way we'd come. Laughter boomed from the dining room. Conference goers came and went in the corridors and from the small lounge, where guitar cases leaned against a wall and two people laid quiz sheets on round tables. The sign for the Devenish Bar pointed towards the front entrance.

'I just need to get something from my room,' I said, cutting over to the lifts and up to my second floor room. I phoned reception and asked for a taxi, saying I'd be down in ten minutes. Tidying up and packing took me less than that. I had resolved to leave, fearful that the Professor's lapping waters would drown me.

The CC, on her way back from the toilets, found me at reception.

'Leaving early, Detective Slevin?'

'Thank you for the invitation to dinner, Ma'am. Most enjoyable. I hope the rest of your evening goes well.'

She wasn't going to give up. She forced me into a lie.

'An urgent call is it? A breakthrough?'

'Well, maybe. Hetherington was on to me. He's keen to get moving early tomorrow. Wants me to be there.'

'I see. Keep me informed, via DI Hamilton. You were good company for the Professor tonight. He enjoyed your speculations. So did I.'

'Thank you. My taxi, Ma'am.'

A man in taxi company livery stood near the front door, rubbing his palms together.

'A taxi? Must be urgent. Good luck.'

She returned to the Devenish Bar and I followed the driver to his vehicle. I got in the back. I told him where I wanted to go. He buzzed the heat to 'high' and I fell asleep.

I wanted away from the CC, from the Professor and Dr Rankin. I wanted away from Amy and her colleague aiming the gun at me. I wanted away from the lapping lake. I wanted away.

SIXTEEN

Instead, I stayed, to focus on loose ends in the Todd Anderson case; the second shoe, the folder, the bullet and the gun.

Sharon loaned me her car and I made an appointment with Mervyn Campbell, the technician. I grinned my thanks to my colleague. When she asked why I didn't use a car from the pool, I gave her my 'arched eye-brow and pursed-lips' look. I hoped she read it as 'secret love tryst'. Perhaps she simply thought I was an oaf, because she tossed the keys to me with an easy-going 'stay out of harm's way, you buck-eejit'. And I was off.

Off and over the arcing bridge and then left, in the easterly direction that leads to the north coast and the causeway of basalt rocks where giants chased one another, throwing stones like bold boys.

I drove through the broad steel gates at the Maydown PS(N) depot. It's our back-office, where technical labs, computer servers, archives and clerical buildings huddle behind two steel-reinforced walls no one is confident will ever come down.

Mervyn was already seated at a window in the canteen, a large brown envelope, a mug of coffee and a sandwich in front of him. I joined him, with my own coffee and a cream doughnut. Sharon's vivid red runabout sat at ease in the car-park below us.

'You got a new motor?' Mervyn asked.

'Like it?'

'To go with your feminine side?'

'I borrowed it.'

'I didn't think it was from the pool. Too new looking. You're always dodging, Slevin. Here, I'm done with this.'

Mervyn pushed the large brown envelope towards me. It contained the folder from the train.

'There's nothing of any use to you there. Only fingerprints are yours, your aunt's and the fella, Jake Tees, at the station.'

'How do you know they're his?'

'Look, you told me you got the folder at your Aunt's. She's on file from ages ago. And your man is on file for possession about three years ago. Meth, coke. He claimed "personal use" and stayed out. Kept his job, the lucky lad.'

'So no one else handled it?'

'I can't say that, but no one else did anything meaningful with it – opening it, closing it, putting things in, taking things out, passing it about, that sort of thing – no one did anything like that. When they weren't wearing gloves.'

'Thanks, Mervyn. I owe you.'

'No, you don't, Slevin. And that's the last favour I'll do for you.'

'Okay, Mervyn. I only asked because …'

'Things are getting muddy around you, Slevin. It's like the tide's going out and all there's left is glar.'

'I'm not dirty, Mervyn. I'm just trying to do my job.'

'I don't want any part of your job anymore. You're an old coat, Slevin. Fluff sticks to you and you can't get clean. If this is police business, put it through the proper channels.'

'It is police business, Mervyn, with all the channels criss-crossed and blocked.'

'Only in your head. You spent too long among the "say nothings" and then on the wings. Now you're going down roads I don't want to go down. We're cops, not spies. Or IS. I'm not really a cop. I'm a lab rat, for fuck's sake.'

I could have come clean and told him what I knew about Dalzell. About IS being all over me. About the CC taking an unusual interest. About the Todd Anderson case getting nowhere. But I didn't want to spook him any more than he was already.

'Sound. Thanks, Mervyn.'

He lifted his tray and left the canteen, depositing the tray on a rack of shelves beside the kitchen entrance. It would be like we'd never met, never worked together, never acted as colleagues. I felt a sense of isolation grow in me. People were slipping away from me like scales off a gasping fish, floundering on the mudflats.

I took the folder from the envelope. A simple buff-coloured folder, with a single flap, still tucked in. My details on the front, typed neatly on a white sticker. I opened it and turned it upside down to look closely inside. I couldn't guess if it had ever held anything. I sensed it had always been empty and wondered who had left it on the train and what kind of game, all fake news and deflection, Dalzell was playing with me. Or was it IS? Was it a pantheon of sub-deities, all working in mysterious ways?

I munched on my cream doughnut, sensing the sugar migrate to my veins and lift my mood. Sticky cream laced my fingers and I licked them, one by one. When I came to my thumb, I sucked it and remembered my Fionn lore from prison reading and my story-telling at the police conference. Fionn, the bright. Fionn, the fair-headed. Fionn, the wise, who harnessed the wisdom of the Salmon of Knowledge by bursting a bubble on its cooking flesh using his thumb. Was there salvation for me in the knowledge I was gathering or was the case-file as hollow as a snake's pelt, long shed?

I am no Fionn. No warrior-seer. No hero. I am a detective, lost in a case with no beginning and no end, sucking on my thumb for comfort and sugar-ease, holding an empty folder and staring at a car-park, where a squat red runabout leers at me like a poisonous toad, from a jungle of steel, rubber and asphalt.

If Mervyn had seen me in the archive shed after he'd walked out on me, he would be certain I was going down roads he didn't want to go down. I filled in a request for the archived Todd Anderson material and gave it to the civilian clerk. She countersigned it, tore off a receipt slip and pinged open the gate to the caged area behind her. I strolled the aisles of multi-tier, long-span, slotted-angle steel shelving, neatly stacked with plastic containers, colour coded and numbered.

The Todd Anderson material was in a single blue plastic-lidded box, that slid off the shelf with a satisfying hiss. The shelving system had retractable platforms spaced at intervals along the rows, big enough to hold one of the lidded boxes and its contents. I busied myself with the scant remains of the Anderson case. I placed the two shoes side by side and thought of Karen Lavery. A leaden bile of regret rose in my gullet as I held the left one, cold now as it had been when she found it in the abandoned chiller.

I placed the items back in the box, pulled the lid across and played my hands around it before stowing the platform away and lifting the box back onto its shelf. My finger prints would confirm I had been legitimately there, if anyone asked.

Then I moved deeper into the archive to an area containing mauve boxes, lidded also and of varying sizes. Keeping my arms close to my body, I slipped on a pair of crime scene gloves and stuffed my hands into my pockets. As I walked, the lights above, sensing my motion, sequenced on. Like using Sharon's car, the gloves would muddy the waters, rather than offering complete subterfuge. I knew where I was going. I'd been there once before. Not long after I joined the Serious Crime Team.

I pulled out a retractable platform again. I drew down a

lidded plastic box, this time using gloved hands. I reckoned the cameras covering me would not pick up skin-covered gloves, as I hunched over the shelf, pressing my arms tight to my body.

People keep memory boxes for all sorts of reasons; to remind them of a joyous time in their lives – photos, a garter, desiccated flowers excite memories of a wedding day. Or in memory of a dead parent; more photos, a broken watch, a sports medal. Then there are the notes and diaries of adolescence, the hospital records of the birth of a child, including the metal and plastic bracelet with the name Baby Edmund – where could that be?

My own memory box contained the artefacts of a criminal investigation; photos of a killing scene and of a man, hunched awkwardly against a car window, shattered glass confettied all about him; a wound above his right eye, livid as the mouth of an active volcano; items of clothing - a balaclava, more shoes, both muddied, cheap running shoes branded Life Style, with a swirly S; a folder of fingerprints, a SIM card and parts of a phone; a DVD marked 'Slevin – car park footage'. I laid more jumble before me and arranged it in a variety of patterns none of which made a workable form, none of which offered revelation. The irony that I was searching for clues to the killing of Todd Anderson, not in his own file box, but in mine, prompted me to smile.

One more peep to confirm the box was empty. One more shuffle of the jumble on the platform, but, yet again, the pattern failed to adhere.

I sensed a movement nearby, but when I looked about me I saw no one. I reviewed the oddments in front of me, a time capsule containing a very specific moment in my past and confirmed what I already knew. Both boxes, the Anderson one and my own, the killing of Police Constable Edwin Norris, contained the same emptiness. No murder weapon. No gun.

SEVENTEEN

I went back to police HQ, where Hammy found me, poring over the Todd Anderson murder book.

'Ancient history was always your subject, really.'

When I didn't answer, he continued,

'You came back early from the conference. Guilt was it, Slevin? Or were you expelled?'

I had lost whatever spark being at the conference had lit in me. Now I was convinced Dalzell or IS, or both of them colluding with each other, had the gun.

I was alone with my boss, furiously trying to plug the holes in my story, before he asked me more questions. Pools of light dabbed spots and corners in the office, but the sense of darkness, inside and outside, was pervasive.

'No sir, I was not expelled.'

'I'm told you were at the top table. One of the CC's cherished guests. Should I be worried about you, Slevin? Are you divulging secrets over the devilled prawns?'

'No, sir. Rocket and salmon salad, with a spicy vinaigrette. Cardamoms, I think.'

'I knew you were the right man to send, Slevin. A proper foodie, with all that slop you ate inside and a doctorate to boot. Most of the chumps here wouldn't know their *Boeuf á la Bourguignonne* from a barnacle.'

'Simple roast beef, as the main, sir, no more. Very tender. Sides of local vegetables including gently steamed broccoli, matched with a parsley and dill cream sauce.'

'Enough, Slevin. Enough. You learn anything?'

'Plenty, sir.'

'Anything useful?'

'That the case of Ophelia going into the river is still unsolved and that the evidence is inconclusive.'

'Lovely. Sunday supplement food chat with dodgy literary references. Don't get too uppity, now. Even if you're clashing cutlery with the head buck-cat.'

He stepped towards my desk and closed over the front cover of the Todd Anderson murder book.

'You and Hetherington, everything alright?'

'Yes, well, a bit strained after the bomb incident.'

'He blames you for getting him blown up. You have to agree he has a case. He's doing the psycho follow-up. You're not attending your sessions, I hear.'

'You sent me to the conference, sir, so I ...'

'That was one session. You've missed others. Get back into them. What have you actually got on this?'

'I'm just pulling things together. See where we're at.'

'And your other cases?'

'Sharon's collating the paper work on the house-break killing. We have a confession from the home-owner. He did it in self-defence, he says. The burglar was unarmed. Sharon will have it with you today, tomorrow. Hetherington is in court later, on that drive-by shooting thing. We made the arrest. Well, he did.'

'Yes, you were driving. The skills of your teenage joy-riding years finally put to good use. What time is Hetherington in court?'

'Twelve o'clock, sir.'

'Fine. You, him, me and Todd Anderson, in my office for twenty minutes. I have an eleven o'clock upstairs. I want prospects and plans. No bullet points. Hard facts, juicy morsels.'

He turned towards his office.

'What's this?'

He stopped in front of a plexi-glass stand between my own desk and Hetherington's.

'I took one of the moveable displays from the conference centre. I want to get every thing out and look at it again. We're missing something.'

He hesitated, as if he was about to speak, but then moved off. I called after him.

'Excuse me, sir. The CC, could she have known Anderson?'

My boss came back towards me.

'I've seen photographs of her on the police hockey team. Fit and forthright, that's her game, even now. I would have thought football was too, I don't know, too "street" for her. But you never can tell. Look at Sharon here and her kick-boxing.'

'So, you don't think she knew Anderson?'

'Why would you think that, Slevin?'

'Well, she seems so interested in the case. She asked me to keep her informed, via yourself of course.'

'Protocols, Slevin. Always the correct protocols, that's my man. If it's something I don't need to know or that I would be better off not knowing, I'll tell you. Up to that point, I have to know everything. Why don't you ask the CC herself? Maybe it's like this? It's you, not Anderson that really interests her. She doesn't want to see you swamped in the weedy waters. Like Ophelia.'

He smirked, as if to say 'two can play at the literary illusions'. Turning once more, he called back over his shoulder.

'Bring Hetherington and all your speculations. If you have evidence and leads, they would be particularly useful.'

I ordered the Todd Anderson archive from Maydown. I unpacked it immediately, adding items to my plexi-glass display panel. I laid out artefacts on a foldaway table I took from the conference centre and put in front of the window.

Most of Anderson's personal effects had been returned to his family. What was left were items considered still necessary to the solution of the crime. Scanning the table and its paltry display I felt, not for the first time, that we had let a lot of the good stuff go.

Colleagues looked at my display, sighed and went to their desks.

Goss and Doherty ambled in together. Doherty was telling a football story.

'Two minutes. Two minutes to go and he lets in the equaliser. That bollocks Simpson couldn't keep nets on a fishing trawler.'

'Holy God, Slevin,' said Goss. 'What have we here? A jumble sale? Some of your choicest personal items as a "once-in-a-lifetime" offer? Pardon me if I don't buy any of it. You must be desperate, kiddo if you're resorting to "show and tell" for the boss.'

'Ah, come on, Edmund,' said Doherty. 'You're after blocking the only view we have.'

Sharon arrived and stood beside me.

'Great to see the men happy at their work,' she said.

'Sharon, sort this out,' said Goss. 'You're supposed to be in charge of this floor. If Slevin wants to look at evidence, he can do it in an incident room or in the conference centre. He's only cluttering up the place here. And all this stuff is in the way too.'

Doherty wagged a finger in my direction.

'Health and Safety. Health and Safety. What happens if we need to get out quickly? Say there's a terrorist attack? Will you get a heads-up Slevin?'

'I'm glad I've got the three of you together,' said Sharon. 'Saves me sending threatening messages. Today's the last day for expenses' claims that might make it into your December pay. Have them with me before twelve.'

Doherty nudged Goss and they headed for their desks, with Doherty looking back over his shoulder, mouthing 'Health and Safety! Health and Safety!'

'They're right, Slevin,' said Sharon. 'How long do you plan to keep this here? The evidence table, these boxes, the display board. You could do with your own office.'

'That's a good idea, Sharon. Thanks. Will I leave you to sort it?'

'No. The only thing you need to leave with me are claim forms.'

'I mightn't make that deadline.'

'No worries, Slevin. Money in the bank for next month. You probably have your Christmas sorted, same as meself.'

She grinned. She has two children and a large extended family.

'The full tribe is coming to our house this year. The eldest's working out a seating rota for the turkey.'

'Good luck with that. Give me a couple of days with this, Sharon. We need another hard look at it.'

'Long as DI Hamilton is happy, it's fine with me. And will be fine with everybody else. I see you're still on great terms with Goss and Doherty. Who else have you fallen out with?'

'You?'

'Not yet. Filling my car earned you some credit. Two days. Then I'll run this by The Sheik. Oh, a message came from a fella in Dublin. He said you had a mutual friend, Professor De Lorenzo. Are you working with the Italian Mafia now, Slevin? I'll message over his name and contact details.'

She went back to her own desk, hung her coat on the stand behind her, checked her hair and make-up in the mirror she'd rigged inside the door of her stationery cupboard, then sat down, an Office-Amazon, beaming health, light and sanity through the grime of our work-place. I hadn't the heart to tell her there was no way I was going to reply to the message from the Professor's Dublin colleague. Last thing I needed was a forensics expert getting excited over the intricacies of the Todd Anderson case.

I viewed the items on the evidence table. The clothing and the shoes radiated dampness inside their plastic coverings. The coagulated blood on the club scarf protruded its crusts like escarpments on a model mountain range. Everything looked like it could have been disposed of, with Anderson's corpse.

The murder book sat closed on my desk. I had cleared all other papers and stationery. I returned to it and opened it once more, gazing at the set of bullet points Hetherington had generated on the image of the skeleton seated on the rock. What linked it to Dalzell, to Anderson? What did it mean that Teresa's grandfather had a trophy sporting it? Dead ends? Buffers you'd run a train into to bring it to halt.

I prised the business card Dalzell had given me from the plastic sheath in the Murder Book and fixed it to the plexi-glass display, beside his name. I used a white marker pen to link it to Anderson, to Teresa and back to Dalzell. I was staring at it when an epigram of Jung's came to mind.

'The shoe that fits one person pinches another; there is no recipe for living that suits all cases.'

I was wondering how it might apply to the Anderson case, when Hetherington sat at his desk across from me.

'No need for all that stuff. I've got new evidence. An ace.'

I stared at him, fearing what he might say next. When he didn't announce that he had the gun that killed Anderson, I strained my jaw muscles to keep the glee from my face.

'I've been going over the lab stuff. I've always felt they missed something. I've got a hair.'

'Not Anderson's? Not Teresa's?'

'No one's. Yet.'

'Good. Hammy wants us, front and centre. Leads and prospects only.'

'No bother. I've got this hair thing.'

Hetherington had adopted a work-to-rule civility, since the bomb. He acted as if he was suspicious of me. He knew he should trust me, his senior colleague, but he didn't. I think that upset him. I was forcing him to behave badly. I had become a bother to him, which is what he had become to me and, though he might wish to be rid of me, I couldn't afford that, not with the gun still in question.

'What have you got?' he asked.

'I pulled everything in.'

'I can see that. It's a bit … cramped.'

'You were right. We're missing something.'

'You're not. You've got everything here, except the body.'

'And the gun.'

He went quiet. I wondered if he was trying to protect me. Or, like the Professor said, he was no less driven by fear than me. He had questions he didn't want to ask, even though he knew he should.

'No sign of the gun, still,' I pushed, but he didn't take me on.

'What time are we with Hammy?' he asked.

'Now.'

'Hang on. Let me finalise this expenses' claim.'

'Sharon nabbed you too?'

'Yeh, she's beating the drum.'

We could go on like this, all day, swopping civil, workaday banter in a game of heading tennis that had no aim but the wasting of time, keeping us focused on the ball in the air rather than on the dead body at our feet, as we waded through his blood.

'I'll lead with my hair thing. You give him what you've got,'

Hetherington finished, pulling his keyboard to him, to focus on Sharon's deadline.

'Okay, Hetherington. That's it. You've got a hair. One single strand. Not something Samson could make a wig out of, but a start. Finally. And being the diligent boy I know you to be, you'll go the length of it to tie it to Anderson's killer.'

'Yes, I will sir,' said Hetherington.

'And the gun, my young Sherlock? Still no leads on the murder weapon?' continued DI Hamilton.

I got in then.

'The ballistics were inconclusive, sir. Further tests may be called for.'

'Call for what you like, Slevin. Just get it sorted.'

Hetherington got ahead of me again.

'I'd like to send the ballistics, the bullet, everything we've got, to the lab in Dublin. They can get finer resolutions than we can achieve locally. And they have access to bigger, national and international, databases.'

'You think Anderson's killer was foreign?'

'No, sir. But I think the gun might be an import. And used before, perhaps by paramilitaries.'

Hetherington was being more open than I thought he would be, so I interjected.

'Let me handle that, sir. As you know, I had dinner with Professor De Lorenzo at the conference recently. I spoke to him about our Anderson case. He said he'd have an associate from Dublin give me a call.'

Hetherington's look of surprise pleased me. It reassured me that I had my fears in hand, that my defences were working.

'That's grand then. You, Kenneth, on the hair. You, Slevin, on the bullet and the gun. Let's see if we can make something stick.'

Hetherington gathered himself sufficiently to say,

'Sir, if you wouldn't mind, I could work on the gun. As well as on the hair. I've been making some progress.'

'Good. Lay it on me Kenneth.'

'Well, I … I've been cross-referencing the bullet with guns in the system and …'

'You've got a match?'

'No, sir. I've eliminated a large number of them.'

'Let me tell you about elimination, Kenneth. I eliminated a deal of urine and faecal matter earlier this morning. I wouldn't claim it added to the world's store of knowledge or to my understanding of the meaning of life. Or indeed increased our chances of solving the Anderson case, though that's what I was cogitating during that particular sitting.'

Hammy glanced at the clock on the wall behind us, stood up and reached for his jacket, thrown over a nearby chair. The 11 o'clock meeting upstairs put an end to his riff and he got to his main reason for calling us.

'Elimination? You find you've only got to do it again and again. Slevin has a personal connection, so he's on the gun. You're on the hair. Now, it pains me to say this …'

He began to gather papers together and put them into a folder. They looked like budgets and sheets of financial analysis. Meetings upstairs were mostly about money.

' … but you two desperadoes are the best out there in that room. Karolina and Josh are ace, but still young. Doherty and Goss are hitters but they'd wear the patience of the Prophet. The others can kick up the sand but they won't build us any castles. You two, now, you're cooking, so don't go off the boil on me. If you're pissing each other off, get over it. Do whatever it is you do nowadays. Get drunk. Kick the shite out of each other at five-a-side. Take each other away for a romantic weekend. Let me ask you directly, Slevin, as you're allegedly the senior desperado, do you want me to split you up? Get you someone else?'

I couldn't guess how Hetherington might react to such an offer. I feared he would continue going after the gun, even if he was taken off the Anderson case. I didn't want anybody going further on the gun, until I had finished my own enquiries.

'Thank you, sir. We're still very much on the boil, as you say. Sharon will be forwarding closed files to you today. Hetherington is due in court with another arrest he made. We remain resolved to close the Anderson case. No, I don't want you to split us up, sir. Hetherington's work is vital to the solving of the Anderson case. And to the others you have allocated to us.'

'Great. Hetherington, hair. Slevin, gun. Has a ring to it. Now, let me walk you back to your desks. I'll be smiling. I want you two smiling as well. The happy couple. I want you both beaming, in actual fact.'

We all left Hammy's office and processed across our floor. When we sat down, he surveyed the display I had arranged, then loudly said,

'Impressive, Slevin. Impressive. Feels like the foundations of an Empire. I'll be watching you. Sharon, short lease only. If there are no results soon, back to Maydown it goes. And Slevin along with it. Via the river, if necessary.'

He continued to the lifts at the end of our corridor. I kept on smiling. Hetherington hid behind his computer screen.

I stared at Dalzell's card, fixed to the plexi-glass display. The skeleton on the rock stared back at me. The caverns of his eyes held a vacancy that echoed in my stomach. The empty ribcage was as hollow as my own.

'I'm away out for something. You want a coffee? A sausage bap?'

Hetherington didn't take his eyes off his screen.

'Eh, naw. I need to get …'

'Yeh. The expenses. Want anything back?'

'Eh, I'll get something on me way up to court.'

I buttoned my jacket. The early morning radio forecast had said 'dry and chilly'. Hetherington, in summary. I was three steps passed his desk when he called to me and I went back towards him. It could have gone a couple of ways, depending on what he said next.

'I … thanks for speaking up for my work just now.'

'No bother, Kenneth. Your work's fine. Always was. Just, I don't know if it was the water you drank in Manchester or the company you kept there, but you're seeing evil spirits here, ever since you came back.'

'Jesus, Slevin, me seeing things? That's your trick. Fucking ravens in the trees.'

'The ravens saved your life, don't ever forget that.'

'And you brought me there. Don't ever forget that.'

'I won't, never you worry.'

I was standing over him and, though neither of us had raised our voices, colleagues began to look up from their desks. Goss shouted over.

'Go on, Kenneth, give him a kiss. Go on. Kiss and make up.'

I walked across to the desks shared by Goss and Doherty, keeping my eyes on Doherty, who stared at me with his mouth open and a 'what's up, brother?' grin on his face. That way, when I clouted his buddy under the chin, Goss was blindsided and didn't have a chance to come back. Then I strode to the lifts. I felt Sharon's eyes burning into my back and I welcomed them as a heat-salve for my weary heart.

EIGHTEEN

I took the lift and composed myself as it descended. I was licking the rawness on my right knuckles when I stepped out on the ground floor. The officer from Vice I'd almost shared a room with at the conference made to board, but stopped when he saw me.

'Detective Slevin, can I have a quick word, please?'

We moved away from the lift doors and the uniforms at the front desk, beside the exit.

'Something happened at the conference I wanted to tell you about.'

'Listen, about turfing you out of the room, sorry about that.'

'It's not that. You behaved like a prick every time I saw you, but that's okay. Jesus, you had IS and the CC on your case. Any wonder you were acting like a pig facing the bacon slicer. Naw, it's about that woman you had the wee runabout with. The shooter.'

'Christ, does everyone know my business?'

'Of course. We have to be good at something. We're the cops.'

I could like this fellow, I thought. Maybe I should transfer to Vice?

'You got sorted then? For a bed, I mean?'

'Never worry. Let's say, you weren't the only one running about.'

I remembered him laughing and finger-pointing with a woman at his table. He continued.

'It made for funny sights on the corridors and out in the

195

carpark when the fire alarm went off and we all had to get out. It wasn't a drill, so there we were, in various states of undress, in various unscheduled combinations, some of us a little under the weather, when the weather itself took a sleety turn. For your information, the CC and your other dinner mate looked well in matching dressing gowns.'

'The Professor had a dressing gown?'

'No. The woman. The Professor had an aul' surfing t-shirt and a pair of Bermuda shorts would have scared the sharks off the beach and out to sea. We were about to go back to the rooms, when the shooter came up to me, all guns blazing.'

'Amy Miller, she's with WART.'

We both smiled.

'Well, she's no wart, let me tell you,' he said. 'She's a dynamo. Nearly went through me for a short-cut. Eyes like lasers. "Where is he?" she demanded. "Haven't a fucking clue," I said. I knew she meant you.'

'Aye, we're the cops. We know everything.'

'Come on, fair game. I'm giving you a heads-up here. Think of my position. I'm standing in my boxers and overcoat, with my section head beside me in her camisole and my suit jacket.'

'I see it now. That's why ye call it Vice.'

'Don't get high and mighty with me, Detective Slevin. You're a bit of a lad yourself. Listen, be warned. Ms Miller is not one bit happy. She told me to tell you that you'd be hearing from her and that you mightn't like what you heard.'

'Grand. Thanks.'

'Listen, maybe I didn't make myself clear.'

'I get it. She's going to give me a bollocking. Or a grim message on my phone.'

'No, no. Here. Listen. She stood there, a bit of a Ninja thing on her ...'

'I'd like to have seen that.'

' … and she took a stance. A shooter's stance. Aimed squarely, I'm guessing, at you.'

'She threatened to shoot me?'

He stopped for the first time, then, as if he was going to withdraw something. Instead, he ploughed on.

'She pointed her finger at me and gave me the full lasers and said "when you see him, tell him to watch his back".'

'Ah, for fuck's sake, that's aul "Ninja pyjamas" talk. Hot air.'

'Didn't feel hot to me. Felt bloody cold in fact, with the sleet lashing around us.'

'And we're cops right? So you didn't say anything to her?'

'I'm telling you now, amn't I? What was I going to do? I'm out in the freezing night, half-dressed, beside my boss, in her underwear? Your shooter headed off back into her room. Or someone's room. I have no idea where she went.'

'Did anyone else hear her?'

'No.'

'So you're telling me that I should watch my back because a woman I had a … a runabout with is upset and threatening me?'

'She's no ordinary woman. If there is such a being. She's an ace shot and my section head knows her from working at the training college. She says Amy Miller used to eat recruits for breakfast.'

'And was your section head still wearing your suit jacket when she told you this?'

'Fuck off, Slevin. I'm doing you a favour.'

We both smiled again. I shook his hand.

'Sound. I'll keep you informed. Or you'll hear the news yourself. "Detective gunned down in drive-by shooting."'

He stopped smiling, shrugged and walked towards the lift.

I left the building and went out through the small pedestrian gate, onto the Strand Road. A City Council vehicle was half-mounted on the pavement opposite, as workers hooked strings of Christmas bulbs onto lamp-posts. I lit a cigarette and jogged across a junction, past the pizza place and the Chinese restaurant. I sprinted across the road, dodging traffic in both directions. I was still running when I reached the riverside railings, only their fixedness preventing me from plunging into the water.

I got over Christmas, by hiding under the duvet and covering shifts for colleagues with kids. The snow came with the new year. I watched its gentle benediction on the surface of the river from the open window of my apartment. It made more easeful viewing than the crime scene 8x10s I brought from the office.

Sharon gave me a hard look on her return from leave, so I packed away my boxes and my files. I took down the plexi-glass display board and put all the material from it, together with the crime scene photos, a memory stick of video images and the murder book, into one archive box. I wheeled the plexi-glass display panel back to the conference centre and parked it in a rack along with nine others, silently waiting for their call to display the grisly evidence of future crimes and our paltry efforts to solve them.

Hammy passed by as I worked.

'Good man, Slevin. New Year's resolution in action, I see. Take a break from the early Spring cleaning and give me ten minutes of your precious time.'

Sharon came up to me.

'I see The Sheik got to you before I did. Stack your boxes in that alcove near my desk. I'll get them back to Maydown.'

'Thanks, Sharon. Happy New Year.'

'Yeh. And thank you. For putting a pre-Christmas brick in that gob,' said Sharon, nodding in the direction of Goss and Doherty's empty desks.

Detective Inspector Omar Hamilton, my boss and our Sheik, according to Sharon, didn't offer me thanks when I sat before him.

'Ah, my man Slevin, the pugilist. You were lucky the Christmas intervened. Everyone goes a bit loolah at Christmas, though, Detective Slevin, I'm suspecting it's year round with you.'

'Sir?'

'Ah, yes. The innocence of the permanently guilty. Lovely, Slevin. Your unique talent for the ineffable, the unknowable and the unseeable. There's a squad room of detectives out there and not one of them saw you clout Goss. Not even Sharon's all-seeing eye caught it.'

'Sir, if no …'

'Slevin, spare me. I saw Goss' bake. More ravaged than normal and that's saying something. Even his sidekick, Doherty, seated opposite him, saw nothing, claiming he was engrossed in writing up the report on the snuff-film killers they had just brought down, fair play to them. I might be persuaded to put them back on the Todd Anderson case. They get results.'

'Sir, if I may, I don't think …'

'Perfectly true, Slevin. Maybe you actually don't think. Or what's worse, maybe you think too much. The old detective's curse, eh? I don't see what's in front of me. The victim is dead. Then who the fuck killed him?'

'Sir, myself and Hetherington …'

'Yes, yes. Hetherington, the hair. Slevin, the gun. That was last year's mantra. You and your buddy need a new *surah* for a new year.'

'Happy New Year, sir.'

'I'll ignore that. You haven't hit Hetherington, have you?'

'No, sir …!'

'That's not an accusation, mind you. It's an opinion. It is my opinion, however, that you did punch your colleague DS Goss, and that, in a room full of detectives, no one saw you do it, proof, if ever I needed it, that you are very much a shaman as well as a shamus. Okay. Let's move on, as no one, not even Gob Almighty Goss, is pressing charges. Allow me to offer you an astrological item. I predict that you will not punch DS Goss or any other detective in this coming year. Does that prediction seem sound to you, Slevin?'

'Perfectly, sir.'

'Now, what I can't predict is whether DS Goss or DS Doherty, or someone acting on their behalf, won't punch you. Even though Goss says he slipped on ice in his driveway and lost a tooth, which, he says, was already shaky, to the side of his car, I can't predict what may follow there. I do know that conditions remain icy. Goss and Doherty, ace detectives as they are, bear grudges. I've seen it over the years. They found each other in the old force, realised they had a vibe and have been playing on it ever since. It is my opinion that they have a list. And that you're right at the top of it.'

'Sir, are you telling me that I'm under threat?'

'If that's your opinion, Slevin, fair enough. We are the police, after all, so being under threat is part of the deal. And for what it's worth, I'd say your opinion was a fair one. One you could act upon, watching-your-back-wise. Let me give you a verse from one of my mother's favourite *surahs*. That's a chapter, for the non-Koranic among us.'

'I know what a *surah* is, sir.'

'Ah, Al-Quran is on the reading list at Maghaberry Prison. Of course. "O you who have believed, remember the favour of Allah upon you when armies came to attack you and we sent upon them a wind and armies of angels you did not see. And ever is Allah, of what you do, Seeing." Seeing, yes. Unlike the selectively blind that occupy this floor and further afield. My old friend Cossie Cosgrove gave me a tinkle. Said you took the soup with him at that conference.'

'No, sir. He had the soup. He slobbered a cascade of it down his suit and didn't bat an eye-lid'.

'Not likely. In my opinion. Cossie is fastidious. In the extreme. And he's as assiduous as a lioness gnawing off her lower leg to escape a trap.'

'May I ask a question, sir?'

'Ever the politesse, eh Slevin? And if I don't answer, will you thump me?'

'I don't thump the good guys. Sir.'

'Give us all a break, detective. Are you sure you even know who the good guys are? Ask your question.'

'Why is IS Officer Cosgrove interested in me?'

'Because you are who you are. Because the constable you killed, Edwin Norris, trained with him. Because his advice on the scheme to bring you and the other three desperadoes into the service was ignored. Because he is a political, "small p", policeman, who feels more should be thought of him.'

'And he's a friend of yours?'

'Don't lecture me about my friends. You're still seeing Dessie Crossan. No, don't object. I know. Or, let me say, that it is my firmly held opinion that you are still meeting Dessie Crossan, despite IS Officer Cosgrove's express order not to do so. That's another reason why he's interested in you.'

'Why doesn't he just pull me in, investigate me, charge me with something, then suspend me?'

'You're getting value for money here, Detective. Lots of questions. You had lunch with Cossie at that conference. Who'd you have the dinner with?'

'The Chief Constable, a Doctor Randolph … Rankin, I think, and a Yankee professor.'

'A cosy party, with the CC at the head of the table and yourself providing the whiff of cordite and sulphur to season the veg. As long as you're eating at the same trough as the CC, Cossie'll play you handy. Which takes us back to our business, murder cases that are open and unsolved, especially Todd Anderson's.'

'Todd Anderson is not special, sir. Todd Anderson is dead.'

'He's beginning to look like no more than a dead end. He's of interest to our CC and he's on our "to do" list. So do, Slevin, do.'

'Thank you, sir.'

'And, just before you go, you know how I said Cossie will be circumspect with you? Up to a point. Not everyone in IS is so sensitive. You may have encountered his two favoured buckos. Farm boys in waxed jackets, with fists as hard as dead-blow mallets.'

'Daffy Duck and Goosy Gander.'

'I'll ignore that too, even though it's good. Mind how you go, in the ice and snow. As the poet said. And with Cossie's farm boys.'

I shouldn't be talking to you.

The feeling is mutual.

You remember two boys we did time with?

Lots of boys, and women, did time.

Some of them, well, us, are out now and might be a bit confused.

I never thought you were confused. I thought you were stupid, which is mad, and the brains you're supposed to have.

You remember a boy I shared a cell with? Never shut up. And his handler, who worked his levers, with his hand up his back-passage?

I wondered when you might get to them.

Big Mouth and Pip Squeak, I called them.

Comrades all. You got the mouthy fella moved. They're both out this while. The main thing for fellas like us is to keep the head right.

You know where they are?

Listen, they're around, like the rest of us. And they're asking about you.

So you told them about me.

Didn't need to. You're in the papers. I heard their heads aren't right. How's yours?

They're asking about me. As in, 'how's the form?', like.

No. They're asking about you, as in, they remember.

NINETEEN

I packed the Todd Anderson murder book and one large archive box of files, evidence reports, photos and small artefacts. I brought the dead man home.

I bought a heavy-duty staple gun, staples, paint to create a white-board wall, a 4-inch and a 2-inch brush, markers and masking tape. I moved two bookshelves into the guest bedroom. I boxed up mythologies, anthologies, concordances of great texts, compendiums of fables, encyclopaedia of beliefs, religions, myths and tales.

I was scared. It was not a time for oracles. It was a time for facts.

Two empty walls joined one another at a sturdy right angle, opposite the windows, overlooking the river. I clustered the television, the mauve sofa and its companion chairs closer to each other, where they huddled in front of a view of trees that cast harsh shadows onto the sheen of the river. I left the music system in place, one speaker high on each newly-painted wall. I turned off Freddie Hubbard, on the jazz channel I usually played at night. I put on Turkish Sufi music, playing low. I entered a period of active meditation.

As the sufis chanted, the drums beat and the ouds thrilled and resonated, I stapled documents and scraps of papers onto the left wall: photos; timelines; the skeleton on the stone; forensic notes; my colleague's bullet points.

I cleared the low table of learned journals and I put them, along with the books, in the guest bedroom. I focused on the dead man, in the murder book, lying open as a wound on the low table.

I put my palm to the right, whiteboard-painted wall. The paint was dry, because I opened all the windows and freshened the room with the breath of the snow outside. The wall was as white as polar vastness.

I took a marker and began to write the key points of the Incident Report. The outline of the dead man's case built a column to support my meditations. Then I composed Venn diagrams, pert circles with names inscribed from the Murder Book. I searched for overlaps, crossings, connections, little spaces where the dead man's name and at least one other came together in a droplet of new information. I was convinced I was missing something.

The air in the room heated up. Outside the snow lay a gauze across my view of the river, which nonchalantly accepted the flakes as holy hosts dissolving on the tongue of a faithful communicant. I pored over the Chronological Log and I dabbed highlights from it onto the wall, breaking it down, name by name, time by time, once again searching for the moment when one instance slid across another.

I fidgeted through my colleague's profiles of suspects. They were thin and few. I stapled their meanness to the wall. I considered messaging the Gang Unit, then dismissed the thought. Whatever they were up to, I didn't want to draw the Gang Unit into my search. The drum beat and the rising thrill of the ney flute brought me back to the crime scene photographs, much-thumbed 8x10s I stapled to the wall. I stared ball-bearing eyes at them: the dead man sprawling; the blood on the red and white scarf, tacky enough to touch, even in black and white.

I pondered the murder method. A single gun-shot to the back of the head. I considered the gun. The gun, not found. I considered the missing gun. The gun I used? The room grew cold. I closed and locked the windows. I shivered. Ice formed round my heart in the shape of a chilling question I had dreaded to ask, even though I knew it could not be so: did I shoot the dead man?

I looked for myself in the Venn diagrams. I scanned the dead man's profile. I was not there. There was no DNA connection, because there was no DNA evidence. Every crime scene bears traces and I couldn't find a trace of myself. I was not in the Venn diagrams. I was not in the dead man's Murder Book.

I knew the murder method was universal. The projectile in the cranium. There was no purchase there for me. I recognised that the murder method was a dead end. The dead man's end.

The ouds thrummed. The sufis chanted. I went to the guest bedroom and scoured the boxes and the piles heaped on the guest bed. I lifted Rumi's verse in translation. I read 'We are born of love. Love is our Mother'.

I wondered why the dead man's mother didn't come to get him. My colleagues said the dead man's family were devastated and keen to move on. I questioned the chance of that.

I returned to the phone logs and the digital traces of the dead man's life. The word 'innocuous' rose up in my mind. I worked on, using the humility offered by the poetry and the music of the sufis to underscore my nightly investigations. I ate takeaway food: pizza and *chow mein* from nearby outlets. I piled the empty cartons and containers. I vowed to take them down to the waste bins outside, but instead, I constructed angled skyscrapers in futuristic urban models. I brewed my favourite coffee, a Yemeni blend from Amran.

I returned to the Murder Book, again and again. Patterns of words, images, lists and annotations rose up as I turned the pages in a slow rhythm to the thump of the hand drum and the breathy chants of the sufis. There were redactions, black as mascara tracks, across every page. They proliferated in the pages from my colleagues' reports of their visit to Manchester. I tried to peer under them. I tried to lift them, prising them with my nail. I got down on my hands and knees to peer beneath them. There was nothing to see. I was looking in the wrong place.

The phone logs offered no overlaps or crossings, no further details to add to the Venn diagrams. They whorled and spiralled across the right hand wall, like the trial pieces of the stone artists who carved Newgrange's monumental kerbstones. Whorls and spirals spun inside my head. The music played. Nights ran into nights. I spent short zombie-days at work, then returned to long nights at home. Still I looked, but did not find. I grew more afraid and confused, because if I could not find who killed the dead man, then I could not prove I didn't. My mind weakened at the thought. The phone logs blurred in front of my eyes. The strips of redaction darkened. The whorls on the wall spun. I drank more coffee. I piled food cartons higher, creating tilting and tottering edifices. I opened the windows and breathed the freezing air.

I unearthed the video files. I needed a grander view, a wider angle, greater perspective. I brought a projector from work. I got a king-sized white sheet from the linen cupboard. I stapled it to the wall, covering the Venn diagrams and the arcing lines that connected the dot-dash-dot of my chronologies. They peered through the sheet like ghosts.

I ran the video files. Bigger now on the screen, softened by the light cotton, the images were warmer and clearer. They heated me up. I drank coffee and chewed pizza. I had seen all the images before. The highlights of games; the goals scored; the dead man celebrating; the crowds; the CCTV footage from cameras in carparks, pubs, city streets, shopping centres and gyms; the personal videos uploaded on LifeShoot and other social media sites. The dead man laughing, blowing a kiss, enjoying a beach kick-about with other young men and women. Alone at the wheel of his car, then at the table-for-one in his favourite Italian restaurant, *La Toscana*.

I reviewed the compilation of images in the restaurant. His last night. A lone man quietly eating, waiting-staff coming and going, brief words and gestures exchanged. Diners at other tables, varied: couples; family groups, with teenagers busy on tablets; two business men; a quartet of women, easy and comfortable together; occasionally another lone man nearby. Then, in one startling image, the dead man rose from his seat and carried the tall, wooden pepper mill across to another solitary's table. They exchanged nods and words. When the dead man moved back to his own table I paused the projector and enhanced the image.

The chants of the sufis rose, the finger drums sped up. I searched once more and found the living man on another night, eating at the same table. He didn't speak to the dead man. Again I found him. I logged him four times in the space of three months before the dead man was found sprawled in a bloody mess across the penalty spot at the country end goal. Dates and times. Details. Did they exchange glances? Did they talk to each other?

I took down the sheet, switched off the projector and viewed the images on my laptop. I deftly clipped all the images from *La Toscana* into their own file, then I viewed them in sequence, running them as a slide show. I tagged sections, focusing on the living man. Again I clipped and pasted until I had a set of head-shots of this living man. Again I focused and enhanced. I drank more coffee. The sufis sang. The ouds raced. The Venn diagrams spiralled on the wall, Catherine wheels spinning on a fence dressed with fireworks. The lists oscillated and reverberated feverishly in front of my eyes, so that a darkening formed at their centre, a darkening that shaped into the two eyes of The Morrigan, louring under her wrathful brow. The darkening then took flight, hovered above me. The Morrigan's brow mantled me as she passed over me, dropping red spittle, rancid as a fruit bat's, before sweeping out the open window, where she hovered in the snow that choked the air above the river. I walked to the window. The Morrigan dissolved into the snow, the dark becoming light. As she faded, she pointed a gun at me and repeated, in a hiss,

'I am the shelter at your death.'

A ghost beam crossed the snow fall then, before vanishing into the white-flaked air. A woman running away, then diving headlong into the water. I shrieked.

'Ma!'

I wiped my hand across my brow. The fruit-bat spittle was my own sweat. I sat at the laptop. The head-shots of the living man beamed from the screen. The low chanting of the word 'Allah', the racing ney flute, the thrumming oud and the resonant tombak drum crescendoed around me. I stared. I saw. I stood. I raised one arm above my head, palm to the ceiling. I raised my other arm, palm to the windows, the snow and the river, fending off The Morrigan. I breathed with the sufis' chant. I stepped into the middle of the room. I know this living man. I saw the overlap and the crossing. I spun slowly, slowly. The music rose. I whirled slowly, in a trance of snow-blind seeing. I danced with the dervishes. I know this man.

I was hesitant to call what I had 'a lead'. I had no idea what I would learn when I spoke to the man who shared the pepper mill at *La Toscana* with Todd Anderson. I felt I was reaching for something just within my grasp, but so far beyond it, that my wrist strained and my fingers popped their joints, as I twisted myself to clasp a future, free of this case.

And everyday, there was more work to do, by following

Hammy's diktat that I do, do and do. I got lucky with the Laotian Bride Killing. Colleagues joked that I landed a classic Goss and Doherty closer and that those two would hate me even more now. I wasn't sure that was possible.

I checked the summary note on the front of the Laotian Bride Killing file.

The victim, Eric Whittle, was divorced by his first wife after three years of marriage. She sold him her portion of their house and moved to England. He was 35 years of age. He went to Laos, where he married a local woman, Kalam Savane, from the city of Vientiane. She was 14 years younger than Eric Whittle when they set up home in his house off the Culmore Road. She spoke no English at that time. They were married four years, when Kalama Savane killed Eric Whittle by stabbing him in the chest.

There was a pile of crime scene photographs, but more important to the case were the images taken by one of the uniformed officers who responded to a neighbour's call. Three calls from different neighbours were logged, all voicing concern at the noise coming from Eric Whittle's house, tucked into the apex of a small crescent of dormer bungalows, just on the northern side of the border.

The key image taken by one of the responding constables shows Kalama Savane standing in front of a cooker in the kitchen. She is wearing a thinly-strapped night-dress and pink fluffy slippers. There is a livid red weal across her left temple, shaped like the letter C in reverse. There is bruising on her right shoulder. Her eyes beam terror and anger straight into the lens of the officer's phone. In her right hand, Kalama Savane is holding a seven inch fish fillet knife, lacquered blood-red beyond the hilt. Her left palm is across her mouth. The colour quality of the images is poor, but the vivid red on her hands and on the knife blazed the truth of what happened. Another image elaborated the story: Eric Whittle, crumpled on his hunkers beside the worktop island, a blackened steel wok inches away from his right hand.

It was one of the easiest cases I had ever worked on, yet I drew no pleasure from it. I felt cheated. Why couldn't I have things this easy with the Todd Anderson case? Where was the murder weapon there? Where was the killer? Here, I gathered the victim, the murderer and the weapon in a deftly-staged tableau that left no doubt as to the tragic story of the death of Eric Whittle, even without Kalama Savane's plaintive murmur.

'I kill him. I kill him. I say "no more". He beat me hard. I say "no more".'

I did a final rewrite and edit of the Case Summary and put it together with materials I had gathered. Sharon would collate the medical, forensic, personal and immigration papers already to hand.

I had solved and closed another case, but that didn't settle me. The night-work on the Todd Anderson case left me exhausted. Even with something I could act upon, I grew more unnerved.

TWENTY

Despite having a lead on the Todd Anderson case and closing the Eric Whittle killing, I had no sense of a thaw. On a slow mid-morning, with the office full of surly, report-writing detectives, a miserly light came through the windows. Outside, grey clouds clustered and heaved, threatening more snow.

DI Omar Hamilton came out of his office and marched directly over to me.

'Where's Hetherington?'

'He's … I'm not sure …'

'Get him out of the bog. I saw him here five minutes ago. You and him are on. I'll follow with Karolina and Josh, when he turns up. She says he's away having his legs waxed. I'm not sure. Maybe Polish lads do that, but a muck savage like Josh, from the glen behind Broughshane, I doubt it. You heard me, Slevin. You're on. Now.'

'Yes, sir. On where? On what, sir?'

'The fire at Mobuoy Road. You must watch the news, even if you're not across police business.'

'I thought the fire team caught that.'

'Get up, Slevin. Get moving. 'Course they did. It's a fire. And the Gang Unit are on it too. Now they've found three corpses, they get to call us in, the real cops.'

'Three dead, sir?'

'No need for the echo, Slevin. Dead, with their hands tied behind their backs. Get Hetherington. Get out there. First response. And don't make any moves 'til I get there. You're boots on the ground, that's all. My boots. Move, for fuck sake.'

I got up and watched my boss trot back to his office. There's nothing he likes more than a spat over territory. He's a sparrow in a flight of sparrows. And that makes tits of the rest of us.

I walked down the corridor, past Sharon, who was in conference with a boss from Administration and Management Support.

'Excuse me,' I said. 'I'll be late with the Kalama Savane papers. Sorry. We're on the Mobuoy Road fire. Three murdered.'

I walked on and thumped on the door of the Gents.

'Button up, Kenneth. We're on. You're driving.'

We took a saloon from the pool. Hetherington needed no prompting to fire the lights and sound. I scanned my phone for updates from Hammy or from anyone else. Nothing but old news. The archipelago of dumps, landfills, toxic lakes and despoiled marshes on either side of the mouth of the river Faughan, where it enters the river Foyle, is a rancid blight surrounding the city's industrial hinterland. Efforts to cap, detoxify, divert, reclaim and recycle the material in the sodden dumps rise and fall like the tides that flush about them. Methane and other gases spew into the air and ignite by chance, by lightning and by human hands.

Me and Hetherington were pell-mell for a blaze in an old aircraft hangar that housed thousands of sacks of domestic waste that had bypassed the recycling process and ended up piled high in fetid bales that tottered and keeled over, like drunken pensioners. I looked at newly-arrived pictures of the fire-scene. The stacked bales reminded me of the take-away food containers in the corner of my apartment, stacked as my own personal megalopolis; Todd Anderson Towers.

'Who's in charge out there?' asked Hetherington.

'Hammy.'

'Hammy? He's not even out there.'

'That's why he's sending us. We're his John the Baptists.'

'For fuck sake, we haven't a clue …'

'Never said a truer work, Kenneth. Never said a truer word.'

Hetherington drove in silence, as the rising arc of the Foyle Bridge took us to its summit. Seaward, we could see venomous plumes of black smoke, their grey-purple fringes flaring with the most noxious gases. I turned my head and looked upriver, glad of the serene cityscape, smiling to note that the snow had ceased and that I had some respite from The Morrigan's accusing eyes.

Hetherington weaved in and out of the traffic as we descended the bridge to the east bank roundabout. He'd seen the plumes of smoke too.

'Looks like half the countryside has gone up,' he said.

'There's nothing new on the system. The fire, some photos, that's it. Hammy says they found three bodies, with hands tied behind their backs.'

'Any IDs on them?'

When we saw them we knew there would be no immediate identifications made of the bodies. Their charred remains lay desiccated as bog sculptures in parallel lines, hardly wider than three stripes on a football boot, on portable biers provided by the ambulance service. We were in a temporary tent five hundred metres upwind of the fire site, surrounded by medical and forensics vehicles. I didn't hear Karen Lavery come up behind us.

'The dogs found them, about an hour ago,' she said.

'The dogs?'

'Yes, Detective Slevin. The Fire Team bring in the hydrocarbon dogs as standard procedure in cases like this. WART handles them.'

No one laughed or even smiled.

'What do we know?' asked Hetherington.

'Let's wait until Hammy gets here for the initial forensics. Save Karen repeating herself, because he'll want it from the horse's mouth,' I said.

'Thanks for your consideration, Detective Slevin,' said Karen, grinning coldly. 'The bodies were retrieved at the north east end of the building. A gas pocket. Maybe cylinders, maybe methane rising from the rotting waste, blew up and took the wall away, sucking in air. The dogs went crazy when things settled. You'll see some of my crew working their way through the debris. They're wearing fireproof kit and breathing apparatus. You can approach, but not too close. And that's all you're going to get from this thoroughbred for now.'

She left the tent and Hetherington thumped his right forefinger into my chest.

'You're doing it again, Slevin. You're cutting across me. Every time I open my mouth, you jump in and push me back. Like you're afraid of what I might say.'

'Kenneth, untwist the old knickers there, as our boss might say.'

'You're a bullshitter, Slevin and I've had enough of your bullshit to do me a lifetime.'

'If you can't see how I'm trying to protect you from wading into something that will drown you, then God help you. Hammy said not to do anything until he landed and that's what we're here to do. Nothing.'

'Yeh, nothing. Nothing that will incriminate you.'

'For fuck sake, Hetherington, you're blaming me for this!'

The charcoal stick figures lay at our feet. I noticed for the first time that the ligatures behind their backs were not melted plastic or leather. Could they be metal?

A technician, in white scene-of-crime dungarees, came into the tent and reversed quickly when she heard our raised voices.

'Beresford was right. He said I shouldn't trust you,' said Hetherington.

'Worst thing you ever did that, going to Manchester. What did you come back with, only doubt and speculation, none of which helped us with the Anderson case? Your mate, Beresford, is filling your head with fog. You need to blow Beresford out of your nose and clear your brains.'

'I need to get rid of you. And the only way I'll do that is to get rid of the Anderson case. And that means getting the gun.'

'You're the hair man, remember? That's what Hammy said.'

'The hair'll come good, don't you worry. Have you actually done anything about the gun? Beresford asked me and I said I hadn't a clue. He said that only goes to show.'

I didn't tell him about not returning the call from the Dublin Forensics' lab.

'Only goes to show what exactly?'

'That you can't be trusted. You're not fully in. You're hanging on the edge, looking backwards.'

Hetherington's Beresford was my Dalzell, though Hetherington didn't know that. It suited me to keep it that way.

'So, your mate Beresford, what, you message him? Skype? Facetime him everyday? How'd you keep up?'

'I saw him last week.'

'You were in Manchester?'

'Here. He has other irons in the fire apart from the Anderson case.'

That stunned me. I didn't want that man anywhere in my vicinity, no matter what he called himself, Beresford or Dalzell. But I did need to know what he was pumping at Hetherington. And what he was sucking out of him.

'I thought you were going to introduce me to him next

time he was around.'

'He asks about you. And I'd say he knows more about you than he lets on. He says I should watch my back around you. I tell him I always do.'

'And I suppose you tell him all about our cases, all about our work, our jolly *badinage* and everything we get up to and everything we've got, though it's precious little enough when it comes to Todd Anderson.'

'He knows IS are investigating you. He knows you're the CC's pet. He knows you're not to be trusted.'

'And he is? Have you any idea who he is and who he works for?'

'He works for us, which is more than I can say about you.'

'Careful, Kenneth. You're beginning to sound like one of those conspiracy nuts we were warned about at the Training College. Or maybe you missed that module. So he works for IS then, your mate Be ...'

'I didn't say that.'

'And he doesn't work for the CC?'

'Look, Slevin, we're a big operation. Somehow, this Anderson case, there's more to it than just a bullet in the head and a dead man. And Beresford is helping me get it sorted.'

'Or he'll help you get a bullet in the head too.'

'No, Slevin. That's your style. Bullets in the head and the guns that fire them. Or is it just the one gun?'

'Beresford has put a bullet in your head already, the fucker, one that addled what little brain you have.'

'No need to worry about me, Slevin. I'll be alright. I can stand my ground. No one is after me. There's legions on your tail.'

Loud voices and footsteps sounded near the tent and the light changed around us as shadows massed outside. Hammy's voice rose loudest in the hubbub.

'I sent two go-boys ahead of me. Where the fuck are they?

We need to get a grip here.'

I saw Hetherington's eyes flicker towards the moving shadows as he tottered on his toes. The footsteps outside headed in the direction of the burning shed.

'Go on, Kenneth,' I said. 'Stand your ground and trot after the boss. Don't forget to tell him all about your mate, Beresford. See how our superior rates your judgement in making time to pass information to an uncredited nosey-parker.'

Hetherington moved past me to an exit flap, leaving just as my former Training College mate, Tony White, entered. He was dressed in crime-scene blue overalls, with his unit designation WART, printed on the back. I called as Hetherington's shadow passed within a few feet of me, outside the tent.

'Ask your mate Beresford if he wants to meet me for a sticky jam doughnut. I heard he likes them.'

Tony laughed and said, 'You getting your order in for break-time, Slevin? I saw your leader process by. How come you're not running after him?'

'There's a better class of corpse to commune with in here, Tony.'

We both looked down at the three charred remains, no more than seared strips of charcoal and beef biltong.

'Why is WART here, Tony?'

'We do the dog-handling for the arson crowd. Bit of a side-show from the main job. The hydrocarbon dogs are specialist and we all overlap in Lisburn, so my crew went in today and found these souls. First row of the day is heating up over there, about who ordered the bodies to be moved. Thankfully it was the Chief Fire Officer on site, and not one of us cops. He judged that something of their bodies had to be preserved and that was more important than preserving the crime scene.'

'A moot point,' I said.

'Lovely, Slevin. Lovely. Ever the uppity intellectual. I

haven't a clue what that means, but if it confirms that I told you there's a row, I'll let you off.'

'It does. How do you read it, Tony?'

'Me? The dog-handler?'

'The cop. The gunman. The lifer. And like me, the CC's pet.'

'Ah, now, Eddie, that's all you. I'm brawn, you're brains. I'm steroids and gyms. You're libraries and ideas.'

'Fuck off, Tony. This?'

'The usual. There used to be money in waste and doing nothing about it once you'd collected it, except piling it high, burying it deep or drowning it. Now there's money to be made, big money, in getting the contracts to clean up the waste. And doing nothing about it.'

'That's what this is. A contracts dispute?'

'My best guess, yes. Three males, all young, killed off-site, taken here for disposal. The fire is the cover. There's probably an acclerant used, but let the arson folks pick up on that. I just needed to see them, so I can write up my report.'

'Anymore in the shed?'

'Not according to the dogs and they're as infallible as the Pope and not nearly as pricey.'

'It's another gang thing then.'

'Another?'

'Like the woman blown up in the field.'

'I heard about that. Nearly took you and your young fella with her. Could be linked. You think they are?'

'I haven't a clue.'

'You okay, Slevin? You don't seem like your usual sparky self. Has the boss got you in front of the head-shrinkers?'

'Yeh, but I can talk to the wall in my own flat, if I need to.'

'I'd go back to the shrinks, if I was you. Boys like us Slevin, with the old anger and the guilt bubbling deep, we need the odd redd-out of the sump.'

We were still looking down at the three burnt corpses, not making eye contact. It didn't feel like a good idea to tell him that it wasn't anger or guilt I was carrying. Fear was the emotion that drove me and that lately threatened to overwhelm me, fear of the tides I sensed rising about me. Hetherington bringing up Dalzell, or Beresford as he called him, rattled me. Now talking to Tony White only added to my fears, yet I had to ask, given what the Vice man at the lift had told me.

'Amy Miller with you today?'

'Not just yet. We'll be changing shifts. Freshening up the dogs and coming back this afternoon, under lights maybe. She'll be along then. I thought maybe you'd be offering our Amy a pillow. I heard the two of ye lit up that conference before the Christmas.'

'Lit it up is right. Are your crowd always stoking fires?'

'Not us. Look, it's none of my business, I know that, but let me do the man-to-man thing. Our Amy is a star. A fairly incandescent star. If she wasn't a cop, she'd be a soldier, sniping somewhere south and east of Kurdistan, as we speak. If she wasn't a soldier, she'd be a hired assassin, in and out, clean kills, like you see in the spy flicks. She's a shooter and she likes killing things. Especially when she's angry. I like to keep that anger in check and give her an outlet every now and then. I'll be pointing her at the Olympic shooting team.'

'And you get paid for that?'

'You're a thick man, Slevin. Anger and guilt, like I said. That's what we're really about these days. And keeping the head right.'

'Speak for yourself, Tony. My head's grand,' I lied.

'Good. I'm just keeping an eye out for my Amy.'

'And so am I.'

'Not from 300 metres, at the wrong end of a telescopic

sight, you're not. And if you don't want to listen to me, you can fuck off. I have what I need for my report. Three dead? Poor fuckers. More? Wouldn't be at all surprised, the way you're going.'

Tony scribbled a note on a pad, gave me a mocking half-salute and left the tent. I was saturated in a sweat that had been rising up my back since the earlier exchange with Hetherington. I looked at the three corpses and shivered. How did I get here? And where could I go now?

The technician came in again and quietly said,

'Sorry, sir, are you finished here? We need …'

'Of course. No bother. Thanks. Nothing here but the dead.'

'Yes, sir.'

I stepped out of the tent. The heat from the burning shed rested on the air like a blanket. I felt its warm fleece on my head and on my cheeks. Two fire trucks began reversing, as they prepared to leave. Three more remained deployed, cascading water onto the blackened ruin.

Karen Lavery approached me, as I lit up a cigarette outside the tent. She looked so lithe and graceful in her crime scene blue, I almost fell at her feet, prostrate with desire.

'One of your team is inside,' I settled myself enough to say.

'Good. We need to close the first phase, then get the remains back to the lab. See if we can retrieve some DNA or something else to help with an ID.'

'The Chief Fire Officer moved them. You in on that?'

'No. Not me. One of the Higher Ups.'

'At least it wasn't a cop.'

'Tricky, I know, but if they weren't moved, maybe we'd have nothing to work on. I mean nothing. The fire people tell me the temperatures were at incinerator levels and higher in there. Then the gas explosion gobbled up the oxygen, so more of them survived than the killers intended.'

'You go along with the gang crime view?'

'Too organised to be passion. Too thorough to be random. Your old comrades are way past this game, though you had your day. I'd say gangs, yes, organised crime, money, drugs, contracts. Bad deals gone wrong. DI Hamilton is having it out with the fire people, the Gangs Unit and the Arson brigade. I'm surprised you're not over there, backing him up.'

We both looked in the direction of the fire scene, where, slightly above a cluster of vehicles, including Tony White's WART personnel carrier, I could see the head and shoulders of my boss, Omar Hamilton, with Kenneth Hetherington at his back. Hammy didn't need me.

'I'm going back. Might catch a lift with the fire brigade. See you, Karen.'

'Eddie, just … before you go. Could I come round to your place tonight? Get something to eat, whenever I finish up here? I don't know what time …'

'Sure. Yeh. Just message me, give me whatever notice you can, don't worry about it, and I'll get us a take-away.'

Karen smiled and went past me into the tent. I thought of all the boxes and cartons stacked in my flat and vowed to clear them before she arrived. I would get the place back into some kind of shape, make it less like a bachelor disaster zone. I had no idea what Karen might intend. Did we have a date? I was reasonably certain that she had no plans to shoot me.

I felt enlivened and glad, so I jogged gamely towards a departing fire engine. I flagged it down, showed my badge and asked for a lift back to the city. If the fire fighters thought that was odd, they didn't say and, as they had room for one more, they hauled me into a seat behind the driver and I listened to their speculations as to who lit the fire and who the three dead might be.

TWENTY ONE

After returning to the office to complete the paperwork on the Kalam Savane case, I had no time to clear up my apartment. When Karen messaged me, I dashed out for an Indian take-away. I was unpacking it on my kitchen worktop, as the door bell rang.

I let her in and relished her freshness as she passed me. She'd been home to shower and change, after being at the fire scene.

'You're redecorating, I see. Early 21st century student boho?'

'No slagging. That's all work. The Todd Anderson case.'

She stood in front of the wall of Venn diagrams, grids and timelines. Then she moved to the wall where'd I'd stapled documents, lists and artefacts. She ran her fingers down Hetherington's bullet points about the seated skeleton image. I watched her closely. She was wearing dressy leisure-wear; a light mauve fleece jacket, slacks that held the shape of her long legs and light ankle boots that would give her purchase on any obstacle she might care to scale. She had let her hair grow out again and now it rested on her shoulders and collar like the golden pelt of a rare cat, reflecting the fine mesh of her spectacle frames.

'Bringing work home now. I never saw you as a promotion-hunter, Eddie.'

Hearing her say my name in so ordinary a way made me melt inside. I was more rattled than I thought.

'I got an Indian. A few starters, a korma, a biryani. All chicken and veg. There's some nan as well as rice. We can buffet the lot together. You want a bottle of beer?'

I spread the food on the worktop and we perched on stools to eat from the packaging, sharing bread, passing cartons, plastic spoons and forks and kitchen roll. We let the music I'd put on – more from the oud players – be our dinner soundtrack. I hadn't felt so relaxed in weeks. Whatever way it went, it was a date.

I made coffee and we moved to the cluster of armchairs by the windows in the living room. There were two large panels, each with a more narrow panel beside it, which can open widely. Now, all were sealed tightly and the blackness outside held our reflections, high above the river. Low light from the three standard lamps ranged around, painted us into a simple, warm domestic scene.

'The Anderson case is getting to you, then?' Karen said.

'It was. A little. I think I've found a lead. Something we missed. I'll get at it when I've cleared my desk again. Hammy's on this fire thing. He'll have me weighing in there.'

'That'll play out in its own way. Here, take a bet?'

'Jesus, Karen, you're always gambling.'

'Never very high stakes. I'm like you, Eddie. Cautious as a thrush. And I only do it for the laugh. A fiver says Hammy gets a task force out of the fire thing.'

'A task force?'

'Whatever we call it now. A joint initiative. A combined venture. A Multi-Focus Group. I still favour Task Force. I bet you a fiver Hammy gets to head one up on this Mobuoy Road dump fire and murder.'

'You'll need a snappier title and, even though you're probably right and I always lose, I'll take your bet. A fiver says this'll go to the Gang Crime Unit and that Hammy'll be side-lined and he'll make the Serious Crime Team a bunker full of sore losers, sore heads and sore hearts.'

'Is that what you are, Eddie? A sore heart?'

'Me? What about you and farmer Bill?'

I had it said before I could stop myself. I thought she'd go quiet. Instead she came back gamely.

'Houl' that tongue there, lad. You're moving onto delicate ground.'

'Sorry, Karen. Sorry.'

'Might I be right in saying we're both a bit raw at the minute?'

'Well, I'm not long after being blown up in a field. And I have a big case going nowhere, so, yeh, you could say, I'm a bit raw. Yourself?'

Now she went quiet. And pinched her glasses back up her fine nose. And leaned back in her chair. And stretched her long legs in front of her. And let out a sigh so deep and searing, it burned into me with a flame more telling than the fires at Mobuoy Road.

I went quiet too. The music of the ouds hummed along, sonorous as warm breezes around us. I grew uneasy.

'You want more coffee, Karen? Another beer?'

'Can I ask you something, Eddie?'

'Of course, yes.'

'Can I stay tonight?'

My first thought was about the state of the guest bedroom. Almost immediately, I wondered if that might help get Karen into my own bed. She continued before I could speak.

'Just to sleep. Nothing else.'

'Right. Like an old married couple,' I said.

I was glad that made her smile.

'Yeh. Like a married couple. No need for the "old" there, Eddie.'

I smiled too, though I hadn't a clue how I'd manage to get through a night like that, without doing something stupid. I was as randy as a rutting ram in spring.

'What about your fella? That over?'

'It never really got going, if I'm honest. Not his fault. He's the classic case of the thoroughly good man I don't deserve.'

'Or wish for, maybe?'

'What do you wish for, Eddie?'

That stumped me. Is this how married couples go on? No telly. Low music. Food consumed. Appetites sated. I resorted to my book knowledge, as I often do when things get sticky.

'You know, being out at the fire today, reminded me of Prometheus.'

'Never heard of him.'

'Greek buck. Bit of a fire fiend. Stole it from the Gods. Tricked them in fact and, with fire, basically started what we call culture. Things made in heat and hearth.'

'Jesus, Eddie, I only want to stay over. I don't really want to get married.'

Now we were both laughing; laughing at ourselves, our aspirations and at what we couldn't say to each other, even in the warmth of food, music and hearth.

'You asked what I wished for? Right now, I wish I could sort this Todd Anderson case.'

'What's the problem with it? At the very end of this very exact day, as your boss might say, it's just police work and that's what you do.'

Now it was my turn to be quiet. When I looked at the windows I saw our heads in the blackness, hovering in the air, free-floating, like animated lanterns. Karen raised her coffee cup to her lips and I saw her reflection lean towards me.

'I'd better not drink too much of this or I'll not sleep. Though I'm so shattered, I don't think I'll have much bother. Can I help with this Anderson thing? Sounding board even?'

'Thanks. I don't … it's me. I … I usually get into cases

because I can make a story out of them. Questions. Answers. What happens next. Who, I wonder. That's it. I wonder. I speculate … I … then, I find something and I … this thing, it's like the fire. I'm afraid to get too close to it. Because I'll have to get into things I don't want to get into.'

'Jesus, Eddie, maybe I should book into a hotel. Or just go home.'

Again, we laughed and this time, when we made direct eye contact, I winked.

'Tell you what, we'll go to bed. I promise I won't snore. We'll be celibate as Buddhist monks and you'll not moan the price of hoggets in my ear and we'll rise in the morning as fresh as new-minted silage. I might even concoct some fried rice from the take-away leftovers.'

'Deal. Only don't worry about the snoring. That's asking too much.'

We tidied up and put away, working around each other in easy silence. I felt tension seep away from my shoulders and chest. I turned the music off, to hear us potter about.

Then we moved to the night rituals of toilet, bathroom and bedroom, all the time silent and at ease in our cloistered domesticity. I turned off the lights in the main room and watched my hieroglyphics, charts and diagrams lose their lustre. Maybe I could sleep without thoughts of Todd Anderson, my mother and The Morrigan raging in my mind?

I was in bed first, lying with my hands behind my head on the pillow. Karen came from the bathroom and turned off the last lights. I watched her step out of her clothes, an ebony silhouette in the night blackness. Her graceful movements as she bent, then unhooked, raised, dropped, lifted, folded and placed her clothes on a chair beside her, made my breathing deepen.

When she climbed under the duvet, wearing an undershirt and pants, she released a bottomless sigh, settled into a side-on crouch, facing me and whispered,

'Newtownstewart, 220 hoggets, 330 to 398 pence per kilo; Swatragh, 725 hoggets, 304 to 408 pence per kilo; Kilrea, 450 hoggets, 345 to 367 pence per kilo.'

'That's it,' I breathed. 'We're moving to Swatragh.'

'You asked about my farm man. To be fair, he liked me and I liked him. But not enough. And, well, we tried, but I was always trying too hard.'

'Try to get some sleep now.'

She turned away from me, reached back and took my arm, turning me to spoon with her. I grew hard as she rested her rear in my groin. It wasn't simply lust I felt. It was assurance. There was no urgency. I heard her breathing deepen and I let my palm rise and fall on her belly. My last thoughts were with Prometheus and fire, not as blaze and inferno, but as warmth, solace and closeness. I pulled closer to Karen and relished her warmth as we stole away together into dreams.

We woke, startled by the shattering of glass in the living room. Karen yelped.

'What's that?'

Did I register two small explosions, two thumps in close succession, the splintering glass? Karen sat up and I hissed.

'Get down.'

We climbed out and crouched on either side of the bed, as the night silence returned. I crawled to the bedroom door. When I pushed the door open, I heard wind rushing into the living room. I knew I hadn't left windows open. I pulled myself along on my belly until I made it to the nearest standard lamp and pushed down on the floor switch. The room lit up enough to see the shattered glass of the two main windows piled like snow particles on the carpet under the long ledge that fronts the apartment. Karen was on the floor beside me.

'A bomb?'

'Don't think so. And too neat to be stones or bricks. Anyway, the glass is too strong.'

'Gunshots then. Jesus, Eddie.'

'Another message.'

'What do you mean?'

'Nothing. I don't know. Could you make it back to the clothes chest? The bottom drawer has a gun and a torch.'

Karen shimmied backwards. I got up on my hands and knees and crawled across to push the floor switch on a second lamp. Now I could see two marks, at the same height and about metre apart, on the wall opposite. By an eyeline estimate, I put them dead centre of the two large panes that overlooked the river.

Karen was beside me again.

'Hold onto the gun. Shine the torch on the wall, there,' I said. 'And keep down.'

'Easy, Sergeant,' Karen said, as she ran the beam along the wall. 'Two shots. Neat as nipples.'

'Lovely, Karen. If there's going to be more, now's the time for them.'

I raised myself so I could see out of one of the unbroken side windows. The road was empty. There was nobody walking the riverside path. The river itself was as wide and flat as an asphalt airstrip. Sea gulls returned to sleep on the railings in random clusters, bowed heads facing the trees in the park opposite. I saw only hulking silhouettes and blackened backfill there.

'Two shots, then. Long range. Probably from the park,' I said.

'I should have gone home or stayed in a hotel.'

'No, you shouldn't. I'd never have slept. Are you okay?'

'Yeh, fine. I'm not hit or anything.'

'Me neither. It was all in here. Nothing in the bedroom. She didn't intend to hit us.'

'She?'

'They. He. Whoever did this.'

'You know who shot us.'

'Yes, I do.'

We were side by side on the floor. I could feel her breath on my cheek.

'Fair play to you, Eddie. My farm boy hasn't a hope when it comes to entertaining a cutty on a date.'

'See, I wasn't sure, but you're definite this is a date?'

'What else could it be? A thriller, and all. No sex, but what could be better, if not getting shot at?'

'Put the torch on your face.'

She did.

'I knew you'd be smiling. You have a great smile, Karen.'

'You're smiling too. What kind of buck eejits are we?'

We kissed warmly. It was familiar and exciting.

'You're not going to tell me who did this?'

'No. And you're not going to tell anyone it happened.'

'Hang on now. We don't report this?'

'No. Not yet. Give me a day.'

'It's someone from your old days. No. Not with a long range rifle and night-sight. Jesus, Eddie, it's the Army.'

'Look. Give me a day, will you?'

She took a while and then she said,

'Okay. Do you think it's safe now?'

'Yes, as far as I can judge. Stay down. Let's get dressed.'

We crawled and bummed back into the bedroom and got dressed on the floor. I saw Karen's legs scissors the air as she lay on her back, pulling up her slacks. Once again my heart bumped over a speed ramp and I remembered the solace at the back of her neck as I lay asleep, curled up behind her.

We crawled back into the living room. Karen kept the torch low. I turned off the floor switches on the standard lamps. Karen led off then, pushing the torch in front of her. I followed the soles of her shoes and bumped into her as she turned onto the ceramic tiles of the kitchen. We were well into the windowless room, before we got on hands and knees. I closed the kitchen door and turned on a light. We crouched behind the centre worktop and waited, but no shot ran out.

'What time is it?' Karen whispered.

'It's okay. I think we can talk. The shooters are in the park.'

'Now there's more than one!'

The fact that she didn't know it was Amy Miller was a relief, because it meant that she didn't know about me and Amy at the conference. That was important, if I wanted another date with Karen. And I did. Next time with sex and no shooting.

'You think we could do this again? I mean the food …'

'Aye, but let's eat out next time. In public.'

'Are you hungry?'

'Yeh, a little bit. Must be all the excitement. You promised me fried rice. What time is it?' she asked again.

The kitchen wall clock showed 6.10.

'Breakfast time.'

Karen cut peppers, an onion and some garlic, then fried them gently. She brewed coffee. I poured orange juice. I salvaged the leftover rice and mixed some oil through it. I beat two eggs together, added paprika and fried an omelette. The kitchen smelled like a freshly warmed samosa. Karen cut up a slice of ham. Again we worked in silence, though it was hard to rekindle the domestic peace of the night before.

I combined everything into the fried rice and, when it crackled in the pan, I whipped it off onto plates I'd set to warming in the grill oven. We ate the small portions in forkfuls loaded briskly into our mouths. The pop-pop of the percolator restarted as we stacked plates beside the sink.

'You've got a day,' Karen said. 'That means, you tell me something tonight. Basically, I want an assurance that it won't happen again. That whatever message this was about has been delivered and that the correspondence is closed.'

I raised my coffee cup in agreement.

'Did you sleep alright?'

'Great. Until I woke up in a shooting gallery. I took a while to nod off with that plank of yours nestled against my sacrum, but once it went away quietly, we both got over to a deep sleep.'

'Don't you worry. That plank never really goes away. It's always on call.'

'Good. It is over, isn't it? The shooting?'

'Yes. It's over.'

'You see, with the farm boy I started to feel old, well, not really old, just my age. And I don't want to die just yet. I've got things I want to do.'

'What are they, Karen?'

'Oh, you know, ordinary things. Like staying alive. I'll head into work a bit early. Get a head start on the three from the fire.'

'Let me know what you get, especially any IDs.'

'Will do. What are you at today? The Todd Anderson lead you mentioned?'

'If I can get to it, with other things, you know, the fire and the Kalame Savane report. I'll have Hammy and Sharon on my back. Maybe I'll go in early too.'

'Won't be that early. It's seven now. The clock's ticking everywhere.'

'Yep. I'll get this stuff. You head on.'

Karen lifted off her stool, stepped close to me, leaned in and kissed me on the cheek.

'Thanks, Eddie. What hope has a poor farmer got, no

matter what price he gets for his hoggets, when he's up against a desperado like Eddie Slevin?'

I couldn't resist. I grabbed both her arms and pulled her to me and kissed her paprika lips.

'Thank you, Karen,' I gasped, letting her go, half-wondering if I shouldn't, because she didn't immediately step away. That brief moment, me seated on a high kitchen stool, she standing between my thighs, lasted the eternity that is the greatest boon enjoyed by the living.

I spent two hours clearing the material off the walls, lightly scrubbing my Venn diagrams into soapy whorls and then drying the surfaces to pristine whiteness. I re-arranged the chairs, brought my bookcases, books, and journals out of the guest bedroom, which I left ready for any guests who might come, but not want to share my bed. As I worked through those pleasant hours, I was convinced that only Karen Lavery would ever do that.

I confirmed there were two bullets in the wall. I decided not to dig them out, but let the open-shelved bookcase cover them. I strategically placed Joseph Campbell's *The Hero with a Thousand Faces* and Ó hÓgáin's *Encyclopaedia of the Irish Folk Tradition* in front of them. I would always know where those bullets were.

Then I made two phone calls, one each on separate, disposable phones. First I called Dessie Crossan. He laughed at the notion that he would know anything about the shooting, but agreed to get his nephew, a glazier, to call me to do an emergency job. Then I phoned Tony White and we had a long conversation. He wasn't laughing. He said he would talk to Amy Miller. I said to tell her that I got the message and that I didn't need anymore. What I needed was assurance, just like anyone else.

TWENTY TWO

Tony White contacted me. He was brief and to the point.

'All clear. Messages passed. End of communications. No sweat.'

I wasn't sure about the 'no sweat', but I was glad I didn't have to worry about Amy Miller any more. I composed a brief message to Karen.

'Windows sorted. No repeats. Talk soon.'

I wanted to say more, but I was back in work mode and facing into the floods rising round me. I wanted to get moving on the Todd Anderson case.

I concluded the Kalame Savane papers and passed them to Sharon.

'I hope she gets off,' Sharon said.

'Me too. Out of our hands now anyway. Is Hammy at the fire scene?'

'No, he's upstairs. Rumblings and moves. Big wigs getting themselves all lined up. More dark suits than a Mafia funeral. Extra scones brought in. He told me to tell you to contact' – she scanned her laptop – 'Richard Arbuckle, from the Press Office.'

'Fuck that. I'm busy.'

'Watch your tongue, Detective. DI Hamilton says it's urgent and I've told you, so you can piss off back to your desk and act like a fucking underling. Richard Arbuckle, Press Office, awaits your call.'

Such was the radiance of her grin that I saluted her and smiled.

'Sharon, you're in danger of becoming the best thing

about this job.'

I phoned the Press Office and got Arbuckle. Despite my efforts to brush him off, he was more persistent than me. He clinched it by saying that the CC had pointedly directed that I be included in the TV package he was producing. He wanted two hours walkabout at midday. I agreed to half an hour at four, in Fiorentini's Café.

Dessie Crossan's nephew, the glazier, contacted me and I gave him the entry codes for my building and the alarm codes for my floor and apartment. I would have to change them later. He said he'd get the windows boarded up by the end of the day. He said that getting new panes might take time and he asked if I wanted bullet proof glass. I ignored that and told him the triple glazing would be fine. He knew he had me where he wanted me, by using him and not an official police-vetted glazier, so there was no point urging him to get on with it.

I printed off three head shots of the man in *La Toscana* I was keen to talk to about the Todd Anderson case. There was a note of his name, phone number and other contact details in the murder book, as Goss and Doherty had interviewed everyone in the restaurant on the last night that Todd Anderson had eaten there. There was nothing in their three terse lines. He was noted as 'not relevant – no follow-up.' I wasn't so sure, perhaps because I was looking for things way beyond the basics of the Todd Anderson case. I was looking for patterns and recurrences, echoes and ghosts. I was searching for sense. I put the details in my phone. Larry Mahon, 2b Craft Village.

There was a brief hiatus on the fire investigation while the Forensic people worked on the three bodies. I aimed to use it to get in contact with Larry Mahon. Now I had someone to ask, I could work on the questions I wanted answered. I decided the desk and the office hubbub were no help for that, so I headed out, telling Sharon I'd be back in ten minutes. She nodded without looking at me. She was used to my smoke breaks.

I sat on a bench in front of the city council offices and watched the river flowing to the sea, in the opposite direction to the clouds above, driven inland by an earnestly cold wind. I lit a cigarette, zipped my wind-cheater to my throat and looked at the photos of Larry Mahon. I remembered his brother Gerald, dead an age since. Gerald's attempted escape from a courthouse and the hail of bullets he died in were legendary. I was young enough then to have heroes and Gerald Mahon was one of them. He still is, in a more critical way. Thinking about him brought me to the time when I first joined up and did more than riot and cause street bother for the police. It was because of Gerald Mahon that I first handled the gun. Still, I wasn't sure what talking to his brother would tell me, except that it might take me closer to my own past and maybe to Todd Anderson. I had the two firmly locked together.

When I got back, there was still no word from Forensics on the fire-dead and no sign of Hetherington, so I gathered my photos, checked my gun and ID and prepared to go to *La Toscana* to ask about Larry Mahon, when Hammy's voice sounded from the door of his office.

'Slevin, before you slipe off for another fag, give me a minute of your priceless time.'

His tone was headmaster-stern. He continued in the same condemnatory way when I stood before him.

'Winds of change, Slevin. Winds of change. They don't often blow into these doldrum zones, but even we're experiencing a bit of a stir in the riggings and, as seems to be the case with most of the shite around here, you're in the middle of it. The Police Federation have storm-sails brimming, with gales blowing, since that bomb on the Braehead Road killed that misfortunate woman. Remember? And my pal Cossie tells me, unofficially of course, of your on-going dalliance with

Dessie Crossan, so the upshot is that your mentor, the CC, is getting some gyp, usual stuff, questioning her judgement and leadership and all that. I wouldn't be surprised if there was a push against her from the politicos inside and outside the service.'

'She wants me on a TV thing the Press Office are doing.'

'Aha! So, she's pushing back. Fair play to her. Make sure that goes well. Give them the full smile, the washed face, the convicted man so thoroughly rehabilitated he's now catching the baddies himself. Just don't go too near specifics, especially on the Todd Anderson case.'

'Will there be a Task Force sir? On this fire incident?'

'A Task Force?'

'Some kind of combined effort, across departments? Joined-up policing?'

'Way above your pay-scale, Slevin. I wouldn't worry your febrile head about that. But, for your information, there's a Focused Response Group set up since this morning. Us, the arson crowd and the gangers.'

'And you're at the head of it, sir?'

'Well, I am the senior officer, yes. And chair. What's your interest in this, Slevin?'

'Purely professional, sir. I'm glad we're – you're – at the helm.'

'Enough of the shite. I'm putting Hetherington as our lead in the field on ...'

'But, sir ...'

'... he's young, I know, but you've taken him as far as you can. It's time for him to shoulder some more responsibility. Winds of change, Slevin. Winds of change, they blow and blow.'

I felt the blow, but I stayed calm.

'Can I ask, sir, if you might know an operative, someone

called Dalzell?'

'Dalzell?'

'Or Beresford, perhaps?'

'Which is it, Slevin? Are we talking about the same man? You're febrile head's more fevered than even I thought.'

'He uses two names, sir. Maybe others. He's from Manchester, early-retired as a cop, maybe, now, a P.I. ...'

'Hold on, hold on. What's this all about?'

I almost blurted it all out then. It's about Todd Anderson. It's about me. It's about a gun. It's about where I am and where I'm going.

Hammy continued.

'Get on with your work and keep your nose out of things that don't concern you. If you don't attend the next psycho appointment, I'll suspend you. And, no, I don't know a Dalzell. Or a Beresford.'

I knew he was lying. He has a 'tell' I've seen before. He runs his left palm over the stubble on his head when he tells a lie. There, he did it right in front of me. I was confused and even more fearful than the night I crawled on shattered glass across my living room floor.

I messaged Karen.

'I owe you a fiver. It's a Focused Response Group. How smart are you!'

The wind blew me along the quay, all the way to the shadow of the shopping centres, then turned up Orchard Street, keeping close to the city walls. The mossy stones wept their winter glaze, as the early morning frost thawed. Straggly stems of buddleia poked out like aimless radio aerials and hardy tufts of ragged grass clung to crevices in the hope of Spring warmth.

At the junction with Carlisle Road, I thought about sitting

in a café, reading a newspaper and playing the role of the man who knows exactly where he is and what he's about. I didn't think I could pull that off, so I lit another cigarette, cupping it between my palms, trying to protect it from the biting winds of change and the late February chill, and I walked towards the disappointment I sensed awaited me at *La Toscana*.

Yes, the staff, busy with their preparations for the lunch service and the dinners planned for that evening, recognised Larry Mahon as a solitary diner, one who still came to the restaurant, unlike Todd Anderson, who they judged to have been a lovely man and a great loss to the city.

No, they couldn't say if the two men knew each other or if they socialised together.

No, they couldn't say if they left together on the night Todd Anderson was last seen alive, before he made his way, shot dead, to the penalty spot, via the old chiller, where he lost his shoe.

TWENTY THREE

I arrived for my press appointment at Fiorentini's at ten minutes to four, entering via the backdoor. I looked down the café and saw customers in twos and threes at tables, while a small TV crew set up in space cleared before the street-facing window.

Gino was stirring oil in the chip fryer.

'New cop drama for the telly? I never saw you as a screen idol, Eddie, but nowadays, telly's so crap, who knows? I'd say you'd be more suited to the horror meself.'

'Good afternoon, Gino. See when you get done stirring that oil and trying to get a stir out of me, would there be any chance of a cappuccino and a jam doughnut? And, see your man with the dodgy side-parting, down by the window, hasn't a clue what he's doing? He's one of ours. Tell him I'm up here, ready when he is.'

'Fair play to you, Eddie. I'll make sure there's a wee star on the frothy milk of your cappuccino.'

I took a seat in a corner, with my back in the angle of the walls, facing the back door exit and the toilets. I was scanning messages in my phone when Richard Arbuckle skipped up the short staircase from the lower level of the café. I stood and extended my hand as he arrived.

'Hello, Robert, is it? Very good to meet you. I'm ready, when you are. I'm on time too, which is great, so let's keep it rolling, as they say in your game.'

'Good, yes. Thank you. It's, eh … Richard. Can I ask you to come to the front area for the …'

'No. This will be safer, for all of us, if you don't mind me saying. The front window area is a bit exposed, even in these calm days, I don't need to tell a fellow police officer.'

He was unsure, but he left. Gino arrived with my cappuccino and jam doughnut.

'There's bit of handbags going on down there. You told them to move up here? Great. I didn't fancy losing the front for two hours.'

'You'll be back in business straight away below there and we'll be done here in half an hour.'

'One take wonder. Thank you, sir. I could ask one of the staff to put a bit of makeup on you if you liked.'

'I'm grand. The star looks great in the froth there. I don't expect it to last. Don't worry, I'll still be plain old Edmund Slevin, even after all this media attention.'

Two technicians, a man and a woman, came with their camera, lights and sound equipment. They were quiet and easy-going. I was civil to them and we worked out the set-up just as Madeleine, cheery and brisk as a confetti shower, arrived.

'Hello, I'm Madeleine. I'll be doing the interview and directing the film. I have to say you may be underwhelming this opportunity by hiding in the corner, but Richard explained your security concerns.'

Good man, I thought. After some final adjustments to lighting and the camera set-up, we were ready to go. I had no idea what Madeleine intended to ask me.

'We're a bit restricted here, because Richard told us we couldn't move you around, so we'll just get this interview and edit your voice over cutaways from the city. We're looking at an insert of about fifteen minutes spread across the piece, so we should be clear by six or so. It might take a bit longer. How's that?'

I nodded and smiled. I doubted she'd get two hours out

of me.

'Let's go way back, then. Rolling please. Did you want to be a policeman, when you were at school?'

'I didn't go to school much and I don't think I gave much thought to the future. I liked kicking football and running about with mates.'

'Then you got involved with paramilitary activity. Can you tell us about that?'

'I got involved in rioting, small, local stuff, on the edge of gang activity, beside the river. Giving the police bother. I suppose that was my first encounter with the police. I got to know quite a few of them.'

'But why did you start doing this?'

'Obvious reasons, really. I wasn't the only one who didn't think the police should have been around our streets. I was a growing boy, a bit wild at that time. Game for a laugh. I think sometimes the police enjoyed it too.'

Richard Arbuckle scribbled in his notebook. He seemed about to point his pen at me or to put it it to his lips, in an attempt to shut me up.

'Then you joined the paramilitaries. Why did you do that?'

'I suppose I grew up. The laughing was over and a bitterness had set in. A man I admired was shot dead. Not even the police were enjoying things then. And it was always about more than just the police on our streets.'

'You were involved in serious crime.'

'Yes.'

'Could you elaborate?'

'No.'

'Cut there. Thanks. Stop rolling. Thanks. Detective Slevin, I'm sorry, you're going to have to give us more than, well, "yes" and "no" answers.'

Richard Arbuckle joined her in her exhortations.

'And, if you wouldn't mind,' he said. 'Perhaps it would be best if you concentrated on yourself and what you did, rather than making general statements about the police, then or now.'

'You see,' said Madeleine, 'I want to just use your voice and your image. Me and my questions won't be in it, so please feel free to elaborate. I'll edit what you say to suit the images. You know, to give us your story. That okay? Roll please. Thank you. Can you tell us the serious criminal activity you were involved in?'

'I shot and killed a police constable, Edwin Norris. I was convicted of his murder and related charges. I served thirteen years of a life sentence and was released five years ago.'

Richard Arbuckle stopped writing in his notebook. The camerawoman pulled her eye back from the viewer and scrunched a knuckle there. The man working the sound mixer changed his footing. The oil spat in the fryer. I ate a mouthful of my jam doughnut and watched the jam ooze onto the plate when I laid it there. I drank the star from the foam of my cappuccino and used my handkerchief to wipe my lips.

'Though it might be better termed "war activity",' I continued, 'but I think you get what I mean.'

'Do you regret it?'

'At the basic, human level, yes. At the political and war level, no.'

'Why, then, did you join the police?'

Richard Arbuckle, even though he scribbled in his notebook, seemed to be on the point of running away. I continued.

'I joined the police because things changed. You could say the world took another growth spurt. An opportunity arose, courtesy of the foresight of Chief Constable Elaine Caldwell. I felt I might get answers to questions I still had, so I became a detective.'

'And did you? Get the answers?'

'No.'

There were two lamps shining at me, one from the side and the other upwards, towards the ceiling. I felt myself heat up and thought about taking off my jacket or asking for a break, but I didn't need to because, just then, a spectacular, natural break occurred.

Dalzell came up the short staircase and stood beside Richard Arbuckle, who almost saluted him. Dalzell spoke into Arbuckle's ear, tapped him on the shoulder, smirked at me, then went out the back door.

I pushed back the table, sending the jam doughnut sliding onto Madeleine's lap. I strode out of my seat, yanked off the lapel mike and tossed it to the sound man. I ploughed into a lamp, crashing it against the chip shop counter and onto the floor. I was past Madeleine before she could stop me and I made it outside just as Dalzell reached the end of the lane where it joined Clarendon Street.

I ran after him and, grabbing his shoulder, I spun him round. He went for his pocket, but I grabbed his wrist and forced my arm across his throat, pinning him against the wall. His eyes bulged, then relaxed when he recognised me. I eased up on his throat, but not on his gun hand.

'Have you cracked completely, Slevin?'

'No. But you have, thinking you can swan around here like a fucking pasha, spewing shite into Hetherington's ears and stirring muck wherever you go. Sticking a phone into that poor woman's mouth to tie me into it. Who the fuck are you and who are you working for?'

'You're further gone than I thought, Slevin. I gave you my card. Do you want me to give it to you again?'

'Which one is it this time? The one with Beresford on it? Keep giving them to me. I want the full set.'

I patted him down and lifted the pistol from his coat

pocket. I knew that he let me do that because he felt he was in control. I was shaking, spittle-covered and swearing. He was calm, focused and alert. I stepped back pocketing his gun.

'A handy wee Walther, eh. Personal protection weapon, is it? You wouldn't happen to have your licence on you at the minute, would you, sir?'

'That's good, Slevin. You're getting your form back. Banter away with me, while the world goes to pot around you.'

'Only when you're in it. Everything else is good.'

'That's what you think. You're swimming in the sump, Slevin. You'll never reach the shore. You could have. I gave you a chance, in there, months ago, when you did your Paddy-go-backwards routine with the sugar down your front and the waitress playing the paparazzi for you. You spurned your chance at really getting inside. Naw, you prefer to be the renegade. You're still fighting the war, Slevin. With the wrong side.'

'And you're not, you spook bastard.'

'I told you. I'm a private investigator hired by the Anderson family to mop up after you.'

'And Hetherington? Are you mopping up after him too?'

'Hetherington's a good lad and if he can hold his nerve he might do us some service.'

'"Us"? Who the fuck is this "us"?'

'Slevin, who did you think you were fighting? The cops on the beat? The loyal flag-wavers? The uniformed foot soldiers? Ask yourself who "us" is.'

I knew who he was talking about. I just wasn't sure where he fitted in.

'So, what have you actually got on this Anderson thing, then?' he asked.

'Fuck all that I'm going to tell you.'

'Or Hetherington. He says you're hot about a gun, an old

Magnum. Nothing as sophisticated as my shiny little PK. He tells me he's going to find that old gun and, with it, he's going to blow you away. If you only knew how much sweat I've expended, keeping him clear of it.'

'Now you're telling me you're protecting me.'

'I don't give a hoot about you, Slevin, an unreconstructed militant. In this case, you're collateral benefit. I may protect you and if you benefit, then lucky for you. My business is stability, in the midst of turmoil. I manage change, often using disruption and distraction, so things can stay the same.'

I pointed his gun at him.

'Would you be distracted if I shot you now?'

'You can't shoot me. You're one of the good guys. Like me.'

The anger that drove me from my seat began to drain away, just as Richard Arbuckle appeared at the back door of the café. When he saw me pointing the gun at Dalzell, he immediately went back inside.

'Listen, Slevin, you spurned me once. I understand that. Just don't do it again.'

'I want nothing to do with you or anyone or anything you touch. You're a poison.'

'You're right. In a way. But think of us as an inoculation. A kind of vaccine. A dose of us every now and then keeps the body politic in rude good health.'

'I'm thinking of arresting you, so …'

'You won't arrest me. You've already got plenty of jam doughnut all down your front and you don't want more. Your partner has gone sour on you; your boss is checking the winds and your angel-in-heaven, she's feeling the draughts too. Your old college mate, Tony White, when you're next talking to him, ask him about his plans.'

'None of my business. Or yours.'

'Have it your way. You just get on with your job, detective and, well, make sure that whatever happens, the good guys always win. If you want to join us, your call. It's not like you're not a "joiner". You've been sworn in more times than a dodgy witness.'

'Fuck off, Dalzell.'

There was an overflowing skip, full of builder's rubble and polystyrene sections behind me. I tossed his handgun into it. It bounced on one of the broken insulation panels and nestled there as if on a presentation platter. He stared at me, then walked round me, pulling his phone out of his pocket and sent a brief message. He reached into the skip, pushed aside the shattered window frames layered across the top of the rubble and retrieved his Walther. He wiped it down with a handkerchief and pointed it at me.

'This is how it ends, eh, Slevin? You're smart enough to know that there's more to the Anderson case than the killing of a footballer. But you're not smart enough to know what that is. Now you've pushed me away a second time, I know you're still not one of the good guys. You, Dessie Crossan and all the rest, all over this dump and dumps like it across the world.'

'You won't shoot me.'

'Don't bet on it. Now or ever.'

A black saloon, with an orange taxi sign on the roof, pulled up at the end of the lane. The driver buzzed down the window, then got out and stood by his door, his right hand in his pocket. He was as much a taxi driver as I was a dodgy witness, confirming the dead end I hit when I tried to trace the taxi Dalzell got into the first time I met him.

'Tell me,' I said. 'The folder on the train?'

'Part of the grand plan of the gods and, well, the gods move in mysterious ways.'

'If you plan to go near my Auntie Maisie again or my sister

Ruby, you'd better shoot me now, because I'll kill you if you do.'

'Fair enough. Let's add Ms Lavery to that list of the precious, shall we?'

Then he turned and walked to the taxi. Just as he reached it, he turned back to me.

'Oh, by the way. I hope it's not too draughty in your place.'

He smirked again and the boiling sensation I'd felt before rose up in me again.

'I can't help with windows, Slevin,' he called. 'You're on your own there. But I can help with other things. I'm a patient man and I like to keep everything on an even keel. So if I offer to help you again, or your Auntie Maisie, your sister Ruby or your darling forensics queen, let's agree it's the last time.'

If disdain could froth from his mouth his lower face would be covered, with more of it down his front. I hadn't been on the receiving end of such disregard since the early days inside. It took me years of daily punch-ups, book-learning and change outside to soften the sneers on the screws' faces. It might take a bullet to quench Dalzell's disdain and wipe the smirk off his face.

'I won't be taking anything you offer, Dalzell. Except an invitation to your funeral.'

Dalzell threw his head back and laughed out loud, as two police Land Rovers pulled up. Uniformed officers got out, weapons in hand. Whatever way things went, I had no plans to die in a farce, so I raised my hands from my sides and stood like a crucified man. Dalzell's dry laugh warmed into a smile. All the guns were pointed at me. None at him.

His driver opened the rear door. Dalzell saluted me, nodded at the uniforms and got in. By a sharp, three-point turn, the driver nosed out onto the road and Dalzell vanished up Clarendon Street, just as I'd seen him do before.

'It's okay. It's okay,' said Richard Arbuckle, arriving breathless behind me. 'Detective Slevin, please.'

He called to the uniforms.

'That's it, officers. Thank you. Everything's settled here.'

'Back to the interview then?' I asked, wearing a thinner version of Dalzell's smile. My phone sounded and Karen's name appeared on the screen.

'I need to take this, then I'll be with you.'

I stepped away from him, towards the skip where I'd tossed Dalzell's Walther. I should have held on to it, though I knew he'd never have let me. He could do anything he wanted with me, even with my arm across his throat and his pistol in my hand. He was playing with me, lecturing me about purposes well above my pay grade. I was calm by then, but an image of Dalzell standing over me, with a gun in his hand, persisted in my mind.

My voice sounded falsely upbeat. I had no doubt Karen heard this.

'I have your fiver spent already,' she said. 'Scratch cards. Seeing as me luck's in. Stick with me and all the power plays in your work will be revealed.'

'That's some promise. I'll hold you to it.'

I should have said what I really felt – 'I just want to hold you'.

'Listen, this fire thing's bogged down. We've no ID on the three dead. One thing, though. I saw a list on your Todd Anderson wall, with an image of a skeleton sitting on a stone. Is that something you're looking into?'

'Yes and no. I'm not sure what it means.'

'One of our eggheads said it's a talisman of some kind, a badge of honour or a reward. You know, like a tattoo, only more honorific.'

'Where did you find it?'

'It was part of a melted amulet on one of the dead. Haynes alloy 263, an American mix of nickel, cobalt and molybdenum. Very rare and expensive. Our egghead says it would survive a thermo-nuclear blast.'

'Could be just the job for my windows.'

I heard her laugh and the strain inside me eased.

'How about …', I continued, but she cut across me.

'Anyway, I've been told to hand off what I've got on the three dead. A forensic squad from the arson side is dealing with it now. And I'm off to Paris for four days of a conference, so I have to finish the paper I'm presenting, so …'

'Take me with you.'

'Jesus, Eddie, are you alright? I know, well, you had your windows shot out, but …'

'Okay, maybe not this time, but let's you and me go to Paris.'

'They won't let you.'

'They might. With you.'

'Aha, I'm your minder now. Keep giving me the easy fivers and we'll see. When I get back from Paris this time, you can show me your windows and things, right?'

'I have to go now, Karen. There's a boy staring at me and at his watch at the same time.'

'Hammy?'

'Not exactly, but I'd better go. Enjoy Paris and all its delights. Talk when you get back.'

A uniformed officer approached me. I recognised her.

'Detective Slevin, we need a word now,' the constable said.

'Bon voyage,' I said, closing down my phone.

'You certainly seem to be busy. And adventurous,' said the constable. 'Major traffic incident. Festival walkabout. And now you're up a back lane, acting like a gunslinger. Allegedly.'

'Good afternoon, Constable McLaren. Very nice to see you again.'

'Ah, you remembered.'

'And I read your name tag. We last met at Halloween.'

'Where you told me about throwing bangers off the walls at police officers. Now you're pulling guns on us.'

'Do you see gun in my hand, constable?'

'It would help if you handed it over to us now, sir.'

Richard Arbuckle approached us, with the officer-in-charge.

'This is all your idea then,' I said. 'A special for the press?'

'For God's sake, Slevin, catch yourself on. They told me you were bit rare, but I didn't expect a full-scale nut job.'

'Ah, that's how you're going to write it up. 'Strain too much for renegade cop. Lost the head and had to be put down'. The old 'rabid dog' defence.'

'Detective Slevin,' Constable McLaren said, in a calm voice. 'This is simply protocol. We received a call out to an officer bearing a gun, threatening a man. I'm asking you for that gun, so standard checks can be put in place, for when you're debriefed.'

'"Threatening a man." That's good. The man who got in the car and drove off? Do you know him, Constable?'

The officer-in-charge spoke.

'Not our business, Detective Slevin. Go on and give us the gun and we can all get back to our jobs.'

I held my hands up, then very gingerly reached inside my jacket, removed my PS(N) ID badge and my gun and offered them to Constable McLaren.

'All yours, Constable McLaren. Given in an act of trust, one police officer to another. You'll see I'm looked after properly. The man who left in the car has his own gun, a modern Walther pistol. When I inquired about his licence, he ignored me.'

'This is your only weapon?' she asked.

'Yes. I will submit to a body search here, if required.'

Constable McLaren exchanged glances with her officer in charge and with Arbuckle, then turned to me.

'That will not be necessary, sir. Please retain your ID badge.'

She smiled at me and stepped back, letting me know that as far as she was concerned this was finished. If her two colleagues wanted to take it further they could. Their silence told me they'd had more than enough.

'Now, Richard,' I breathed out heavily. 'As you seem to have called off the interview and this circus has run its course, I'll make my way back to the station and have a conversation with my superior officer about the fascinating afternoon the Press Office laid on.'

I walked onto Clarendon Street and headed for the Police HQ, on Strand Road. Whatever conversation I hoped to have with DI Hamilton didn't even get started. Hammy was in rant mode and tore into me immediately.

'… I mean, look at you. A dog wouldn't piss against you. You are unworthy. You'd try the patience of the Holy Prophet himself. You are a side-show and that's where I'll put you, to the one side. You have leave due. You are on it, one week, as of now, *in lieu* of suspension. There is a lifeline connecting you to the CC, but don't be depending on that. She's running out of rope herself. You've managed to get into a bust-up with the spooks and I have to pacify everyone, including the Police Federation. I tell you, it's easier to dampen down the flames on that blasted warehouse fire. While you're busy ploughing through your own trenches, full-scale gang-warfare is taking over the nightly news. One week to cool off. Stay away from here. Stay away from the spooks. Richard Arbuckle tells me I've a bill to cover for the kit you wrote off. He tells me the stuff you did to camera is unusable. The CC won't like that. I need you offside, until I figure out what the full damage is and how I can limit it. You'll return to desk duties. Hetherington will lead on the Anderson case. Give him everything you've got, meagre though it no doubt is. He can have Josh and Karolina. I'll sit on them until they get something, be it hair or gun. Hair or gun, I'll get something or I'll get nothing and that nothing will be something, enough, it will be enough to shut the whole thing down, for as the Holy Prophet says "Patience is at the first stroke of the calamity". And you're way past the first stroke, Slevin. Way past. You need to …'

When I came back after the enforced leave, Hammy returned my gun to me, without the rant.

'Bad and all as you are, we can't have you going around gelded. I'd say if you needed a gun, you'd be able to put your hands on one, but let's try to keep things vaguely official.'

If I thought getting my service weapon back meant life was returning to the way it had been, Hammy had other ideas.

'I'm chaining you to the desk, Slevin. Appearances, you know. The Higher Ups demand it and we're here to serve, after all.'

We were in a dark corner of the carpark below the main building. The weeping walls exhaled an odour of diesel and slimy rust. Police Land Rovers of dubious vintages, with little hope of redemption, sat comatose in moribund rows. Hammy had brought me there to explain the new order, out-of-sight of others. He staged us in a blind corner, deftly angled to the side of a lift shaft, beyond the view of the cameras.

'There's people want you drummed out, lad,' he continued. 'Not me. I prefer to have you inside, where we can keep an eye on you. But not too far inside, now.'

'Dalzell wants me out, then?'

'Dalzell? Never heard of him, except in your speculations. The suits in the Police Federation want rid of you. Never wanted you in the first place. I can't say I blame them, though they're not aware of your hidden charms, in the way I am. You see, Slevin, you've become a pawn in the old power play. For a while you had the run of the board as the CC's knight, pulling fancy moves left and right, dodging about where no one could see where you were going to or where you were coming from. But after this bout, you've been down-graded. From knight to pawn.'

Telling me my new position in the squalid bowels of the building was clear evidence of that. And the new desk arrangement Hetherington created while I was on leave confirmed it. He clustered three desks and two trestle tables into a tight phalanx, anchored his new team, Karolina and Josh, either side of him, and braced a ravelin of laptops, files, folders, boxes, tomes and stationery items to his front.

'While my colleague Hetherington is now upgraded to rook, castling about the place as the gay cavalier, laying siege to the dastardly criminals all across the board,' I said.

'Are you attempting to mock me, Slevin? Because if you are, it's in very bad taste, not least because it is a very poor attempt. Remember I am still the King, and the Queen, though she favoured you once, has her own woes to consider and she'll sacrifice you as sure as rivers flow into the sea and flesh climbs into the grave. Now, you'll be under Sharon's wing for a while – she's not your boss, more your care-worker – and listen well to what she tells you and do her bidding, for her bidding is mine. The King, right. It shouldn't be long before I get you back into active service and off my floor.'

'I don't want to leave Serious Crime, sir.'

'Oho, we're well past what you might want, Slevin. I'm saving your skin by an act of circumcision, if you'll permit me the image.'

'I wouldn't mock you, sir.'

'I know that. Not directly anyway. You may be buck-mad, but you're not stupid.'

I returned to my new half-desk, barely enough surface for my two elbows, well tucked into the alcove behind Sharon's desk. Did she pity me as she placed a list of administrative duties in front of me, ranging from filing to internal mail to watering her plants? I never lifted a watering can, but I complied with everything else. The board was reset.

Sniggering from Goss and Doherty's desks was the early soundtrack to my first days back from 'gardening leave'. They were ecstatic and pinned a sign to the edge of my desk. 'Nursery Corner'. It lasted three days, then Karolina spotted it, drew my attention to it and stuffed it in a bin. I thanked her with a nod and got on with my filing.

'No, you're not stupid, Slevin,' Hammy concluded, in the basement. 'But you are headstrong and foolish. And down-graded. So, expect to be elsewhere, in this building or maybe out at Maydown, in the next little while. *Insha'Allah.*'

TWENTY FOUR

I went in search of Ruby on St. Patrick's Day, because I felt alone, like the last survivor in a lifeboat. I was near the end of whatever strength I had. Once again, Karen and me had let work, indifference and fear fester embarrassment between us. An easy message to set up a relaxed meeting wasn't possible, so I sought out my sister. When the water is rising about you, you reach for blood.

A fresh spring day of squalls and bleary sunlight was coming to a tawdry end as I walked beside the river. A tricolour floated upriver in the black water, green band leading. The parade was long over. The floats and costumes were parked and stashed for another year. I'd allowed all that to go by. I had no need to wave my patriotism. I know who I am. Does anyone else know or care? Perhaps my sister.

Her phone was off. I tried a few pubs where I thought she might be. Finally, Jack, her ex, at the Castle Bar, said she had a new partner, a fella playing keyboards and trumpet. He said they had an early slot in the Anchor Bar.

I turned away from the river onto Water Street, walked across Newmarket Street and lit a fresh cigarette, as I climbed Market Street to the corner, where a clutch of smokers hugged the entrance to the Anchor.

I kept my head down as I shimmied through them, snibbing my cigarette, while inhaling the smoke around me. I felt a firm hand on my shoulder and a voice boomed in my ear.

'The very man. Look who it is. The last of the die-hards and the first of the traitors, all in one.'

The hand gripped my shoulder and spun me around so

that I stood in front of my former cell-mate, Big Mouth.

'You're here for the reunion, so. We didn't expect you, but seeing as it's the big day, why not? You're an Irishman too, even if you are a sour one. How's she cuttin' anyway, Slevin?'

'The best. The best,' I said, removing his hand from my shoulder. The men and the women around us moved away or re-entered the bar. All except for Big Mouth and Pip Squeak, who had been standing behind him, as if Big Mouth was indeed Pip Squeak's marionette. They'd both had a few drinks, but they weren't drunk.

Pip Squeak grinned and addressed me in his familiar high-pitched tone.

'The best, eh? Good to hear that, Edmund. Or is it Detective Edmund, I should be calling you now?'

Big Mouth moved to block my way to the entrance to the bar.

'A reunion? Nobody told me,' I said.

'Ah, you mightn't be on the list anymore. Let your membership lapse, ye see. Found another army to run with, leaving the old comrades behind,' Pip Squeak whined.

'You're a fukken traitor, Slevin, that's what you are.'

Big Mouth was more direct, though I knew from my time in jail with them that the two voices, the piping and the booming, both belonged to the small man.

Pip Squeak continued.

'Easy now, big man. Happy times and happy memories, that's what tonight is all about. You heard Dessie, in the bar.'

'Aye, that's for tonight, so. You might want everyone to forget, Slevin, but I don't forget, boy.'

"Course you don't, Big Mouth. You're an elephant, always was, and this wee shite is still pulling you round by the trunk. Now, if you don't mind, I'll go into the bar and listen to the music. I hear it's great.'

'Aye, if you like that blues shite. I'm more of a good ballad man meself.'

'You'll have to excuse me if I don't wait around to hear you murder "A Nation Once Again" once again, Pip Squeak. I heard you kill it often enough on the wings. And I heard that wasn't the only singing you did.'

I was ready for the lumbering, round-the-houses punch Big Mouth threw. I bobbed under it easily and stepped towards the bar, pushing the door closed behind me and lying against it, holding it fast against the humping bulk of Big Mouth.

Ruby saw me and gave me a small wave. She was standing on the banquette to my immediate left, a microphone in her hand. She then sat on the windowsill behind her, as her partner played a solo on his trumpet, tweaking a sink plunger mute, in and out of the bell, sounding just like Sweets Edison. Ruby gave me a hand signal and mouthed 'Five minutes'.

I moved away from the door as a party of four inched their way towards me. I slipped round them and they bamboozled Big Mouth back onto the street, oblivious to his ire. He could do nothing about their jollity and momentum. The packed bar reshuffled itself, with bodies moving left and right, changing seats, bumping round banquettes, swopping stools, exchanging positions on the stairs, allowing me to set myself against a slim pillar, from where I had a good view of the arc of seating occupied by Dessie Crossan and the reunion party. He pretended not to see me, but he knew exactly where I was.

The trumpet solo ended and Ruby stood on the banquette once more, feigning a wobble, before settling herself quickly, so she was framed by the window decorated with stained glass motifs of anchors, schooners and entwined hawsers, setting her firmly in a nineteen fifties gangster film on a quayside in the Caribbean.

'Billy Peoples, folks. Billy Peoples, on trumpet. Thank you,

Billy,' she breathed, then the backing track and Billy's deft keyboard chords picked up the main melody. People around me applauded. There were some jeers and whistles. Dessie Crossan clapped then stopped as Big Mouth and Pip Squeak bustled in and were reseated beside him. They scanned the crowd until they spotted me. Big Mouth began to get out of his seat, but Dessie stopped him and spoke firmly to Pip Squeak. I lip-read 'Not here, for fuck's sake'. I interpreted the words and the actions as 'not now', but not, 'never'. I checked the gun in my shoulder holster and looked towards the bar, estimating I could, if I had to, crash past people, get down the side of the bar and make it to the rear service-exit before Big Mouth could make it to the pillar I now held as vantage.

Ruby brought the song to a gentle close, reprising the verse with a moody skat over Billy's muted trumpet once more. The crowd clapped and called. There were a few cries of 'more', but the next act, two men and a woman with fiddles and a banjo, were already crowding into the corner space.

Ruby gestured to me to meet outside. I kept the crowd between me and Dessie Crossan's company, as I left the bar. I moved through another group of smokers at the porch and crossed the narrow street. I set my back against the rough stone of the city walls. I had as much open field-of-fire in front of me as I could hope to command. Anybody who came out of the bar looking for me would be well-lit from behind. And facing directly at me.

Only Ruby came out, immediately lighting up a cigarette. She crossed the street, pulled a light silver shawl around the open shoulders of her black party dress and offered me a cigarette from the box in her diamanté clutch purse. I took one, saying

'Sweets Edison. Straight out of Sweets Edison, your new man.'

'Yep. And he does Chet Baker, as well. And pretty much anything you like on the keyboard.'

'Can he sing?'

'Yep. Decent baritone. He'll take it down to a gravelly base, if he needs to.'

'Jesus, Ruby. And he looks half-right. The full package.'

'More than that. He's divorced. No kids. And he's not a bollocks.'

She took a pull on her cigarette and smiled.

'You're made,' I said.

'I'm thinking of giving up the clerical job. See how this goes. What about you? Any big plans?'

'It's good to see you, Ruby. I meant to, you know …'

'I know. Work. How's it going?'

'Shite, to tell you the truth. I've managed to get caught up in a mess of politics and spies.'

'I thought you were, like, crime, Eddie. Straight forward stuff.'

'So did I, but … it's like I'm swimming and making no headway, because I can't swim. How about you?'

'We'll see how things works out with Bill. It feels like time for a jump. No one's getting any younger.'

'How's Auntie Maisie?'

'Grand. Pains, like, but nothing serious. And her form's good. She always asks about you, but she, well …'

'She doesn't expect me to come round. Ruby, every time I see her, I see Ma and it rips the guts outta me. Even if Maisie says nothing about her, I hear her everywhere.'

'You still dreaming about her?'

'I am. What's worse, I'm dreaming about her in the daytime now.'

'I'm going to put a wee stone on the grave. A marker. She deserves that. It's been long enough. Jesus, we should a done it years ago.'

'Okay, Ruby. If you think that'll help …'

'I don't know if it'll help, but it feels like the right thing to do. Close the door. Walk away. Leave her rest. I'm saying that to you, Eddie. Leave our mother rest.'

We paused then, concentrating on our cigarettes. Two young fellas, wearing floppy green leprechaun hats, arrived at the pub, holding each other up and laughing.

'You still seeing that Karen Lavery?' Ruby asked.

'Aye, sort of. I'm seeing her. From a distance.'

'You need to do something about that. She's a good woman.'

'She is that. I'm not sure I'm a good man.'

'Get over yourself, Eddie. You're no more nor less good than any man.'

I didn't argue with her, but I could have asked 'Then why are there two fellas in the pub there who want to kick the shite out of me?' I couldn't put a simple stone on any of that. There was no way to close the cavern that was my past. Figures seeped out of the cavern to wound me, some I knew, many I couldn't even guess at. All of them malevolent as Medusa. Was my mother joining them?

'I see your old pal, Dessie Crossan, in there tonight,' said Ruby.

'Aye. Bit of a reunion. For the day that's in it.'

'Don't tell me you're still part of that set-up?'

'Look, Ruby, I don't know if I'm part of anything now. Did you ever feel the world was, I don't know, shrinking around you, closing in a bit. Old things you thought were buried, flourishing in the air.'

'Get out of the books, Eddie. Maybe not. Get out of the cops and go back to the books. You were better off when you were a professor.'

'Aye, director of the school of mythology in His Majesty's Prison.'

'You should know better than any of us, then. We don't ever get over the past. That's why you're still dreaming about Ma and I'm singing the blues. The past? All you can do is put a stone on it.'

'I'll send some money to your account. You do what you think is best.'

'You want to say anything on it?'

It wasn't a moment to be glib, cute or funny. It wasn't a moment to be humorous or to feign gravity. It wasn't a moment to quote or to compose on the hoof. It was a moment to be quiet, cocooned from the low traffic growl, the bantering hubbub of the smokers and the first strains of a jig coming from the fiddles, reaching us in chunks as the bar door banged open and slammed shut with all the coming and going at the end of a festive day.

'Keep it simple. Just put the marker on her grave. Maybe that'll stop her calling to me.'

'I'd better get back in. Give Bill a hand to finish up. You coming? The three of us could go for a drink or something.'

'Naw, thanks, Ruby. I'll head back, soon as I finish this. I only came out to stretch the legs.'

'I'm glad you caught us. What do you think?'

'Yeh, it works. Maybe not here on Paddy's Day, but somewhere.'

'That's it. There's always somewhere. I'll give you a shout when I get the stone sorted. I'll send you a photo, so you can see.'

When I transferred money, I added a message.

'Money for the stone and a dress, maybe.'

A few days later a message came back.

'Sorted. Me and Bill too. The money was put to good use.'

She attached two photos. The marker stone was small and round, plain granite, with basic details chiselled in a clear font. The other photo showed her and Bill standing before a young oak tree, a clutch of daffodils radiant against her full-length mauve dress, a cerise cravat lighting up his dark zoot suit.

Now, she touched my arm and crossed the street to re-enter the bar, as Dessie Crossan came out to a fanfare of banjo and crossed over to me.

I came out for a fag.

You don't smoke.

You think I don't know that?

What do you want?

Just checking you're happy with your new windows.

Delighted.

Only the young fella said you didn't go with the bullet-proof glass.

The triple glazing'll do.

Didn't work last time.

There won't be a next time.

No? You got that sorted then?

Yes.

You mightn't be able to sort everything.

I'll be fine.

Just because you think everyone's out to …

… I know. Doesn't mean they're not after you or that you're not paranoid.

You'd best head on now.

Are you threatening me?

I'm advising you. It's an old comrades' reunion, right?

I didn't renew my membership.
We're not like the cops, who dump you when you're down.
No, we kick the shite out of you and say we love you.
You haven't lost it. Yet.

TWENTY FIVE

I judged when Hammy and Sharon were comfortable, in their different ways, with my compliance. Then I went to see the man from *La Toscana,* on a bright morning, during a gap between April showers.

I took a long way round, sweeping along the riverside walk as far as the double-decker bridge and then up Carlisle Road, so that I entered the old city by Ferryquay Gate. My destination was the Craft Village, a partially-successful attempt at retail and residential development with artisan shops, upstairs flats and a covered square. Flat 2b was above a café and reached by wooden steps fixed to a wall sprouting buddleia. I knocked crisply on the red door and it opened immediately. I was expected.

The man who opened it was taller and older than me, with a tanned face, lined and etched in a way that should have been handsome, but, in his case, only made him seem lived-in. It was his eyes. Green, but so far back in his head as to be no more than black holes.

'The detective, yes?'

'Eddie Slevin, yes, that's me.'

I showed him my ID, but he barely glanced at it.

'Come on in. Am I a suspect?'

And so we were straight into it. I was the detective on the case, but he was the one asking the questions.

'I have the kettle on. Tea or coffee? Or something herbal? Soft drink? Juice? Tea all right?'

More questions from the chatterbox I judged to be a shy man, unsure of how to behave in company. Or perhaps he was simply edgy.

The flat was tiny, a basic two room bedsit. He pointed me at a table and two chairs, then promptly joined me with a large teapot and cups on an ebony tray. There were framed photos of great trees and extensive tropical forests on the walls. A large, modern globe sat on a pedestal in the corner and, just like in my own flat, though smaller and tidier, there was a shelf of books, in this case mainly engineering, conservation and travel titles. There was a stack of large-format photographic books. Again, like my own flat, there were no obvious personal or family photos or mementos.

'You're investigating that footballer was killed? That's what you said, right? Ages ago now, wasn't it?'

'Coming on a year, yeh.'

'Do you take sugar?'

We were both on tea. It was strong, dark and reassuring. With a good splash of milk, mine looked bronze. There were chocolate-covered biscuits in a packet. I dunked one and said,

'You were the last person to speak to him, Todd Anderson, before he went missing.'

'You still haven't found anybody for it then?'

'No.'

'I suppose it does take time. Yes, I was the last to see him. Your detectives told me that, when they talked to me. Was that a year ago? Can you believe how the days go? Yes, Todd Anderson. A lovely fella, I'd say. I heard he was a good footballer, but I couldn't tell. Was he?'

I stored the line about 'my detectives', smiling to myself that he thought I was Goss and Doherty's boss and continued drinking tea and dunking biscuits with a man who made asking questions the rhythm of his life.

'I went to a couple of games at the Brandywell Stadium, with my father, years ago. Then he died. I never got into it,' he said. 'Are you a football man? No? Probably no time. Police work, isn't it? Full-time I'd say, that line. I pick and chose really, work, you know. Lucky to be able to do that. Freedom, you see. Everyone values their freedom, even though they're scared of it. Freedom and taking it away. That's your business, isn't it, detective?'

'I read the notes of your interview. They interviewed you and everyone at *La Toscana* that night. A number of people said you and Todd Anderson left together.'

'And they're right, but only in a meaningless, matter-of-fact way, the way two people step off a train together or walk out of queues at the pictures having bought tickets. More like we left at the same time, you know? We both finished, final dab of the cheek with the linen napkin – don't want to be with walking about with *pesto di ruculo* across your bake, do you? – headed for the coat racks, had a bit of banter with Lucia and Amelio and out the door.'

'You weren't sitting with him?'

'Ah, no. We never sat together. Did we? No, I'm pretty certain we never did. He was a good bit younger than me, enjoying the food and the solitude, yeh solitude. I usually go there on a quiet night, early enough. Still do. You can get into a bit of habit, right? Of course the food's very good, for a local restaurant, you know what I mean? Do you like Italian food, detective? Eddie? You can get Italian food everywhere now, but I expect you know that. I had very good *Spaghetti alla Gricia* recently. You ever have it? No? And not in Rome, as you might expect but in Douala. I was on a forest conservation job in south west Cameroon. Do you like Italian food? I imagine you do. What's not to like?'

I had no sense that he was trying to bamboozle or distract me. He simply rattled along as the only way he could manage being opposite me, across a tiny table he usually occupied on his own, under a framed hi-gloss image of a river curving through a rainforest, as a fisherman cuts chevrons into the still surface with a paddle.

I changed tack.

'Lovely tea. Thanks. I knew your brother, Gerald.'

He poured us both refills of tea, then without speaking, he signalled his intention to freshen up the teapot. He returned promptly and tasted his own mug before adding a dribble from the milk carton.

'I taught him to swim, Gerald,' he said. 'Do you have any skills? Swimming, like? Attributes? Capacities you're proud of? Yes, swimming. I gave Gerald that. I swim near enough everyday myself, when I'm here. That's why I asked you to come early. I'll be in the pool at eleven, unless, of course, you detain me. You have no plans to detain me, have you?'

He wasn't joking and yet I felt he wasn't really worried.

'No. No plans to detain you.'

'Yes. Our Gerald.'

'I was at his funeral.'

'I was … away. I was away a lot that time. In the rainforests. With Searwood and other logging companies. I still am, away, only on the other side now. Funny that, isn't it? You could say I crossed over. Am I a traitor, Detective Slevin? A turncoat? I often ask myself that. My father never said, but I know it hurt him that I didn't come home for Gerald. Or my mother. Did you go to your mother's funeral?'

'I don't think so. I don't remember. I was young.'

'Yes, memories. A blur. Not mine. Mine are vivid as a meteor shower, racing out of the dark. Intermittent, yes, but vivid when they come. Have you ever seen a meteor shower?'

'Did you talk to Todd Anderson about them? Memories?'

'No, not about memories. Or meteor showers. We didn't talk, you know, beyond "lovely weather", "aye go on, I'm finished with the parmesan". That night, we walked out together, almost in step. It was a warm night. I had a jacket on, a light jacket, a bit like the one you're wearing, sort of a Harrington, a mod thing I have for years. He was wearing a suit, I think. And good shoes, yes, great shoes. Yes, we walked out onto Carlisle Road. I turned right and climbed towards the Walls and the Diamond. He turned left, down towards the bridge, well, I don't know where he went. He went to his death, didn't he? I wonder did he know that was his direction of travel? Did he? Anymore than any of us know.'

'And how did he seem to you, that night, as you walked out with him?'

'Who can tell? The same? A quiet young man. Athletic. Well, why not, that was his job, right? He was paid to be athletic, wasn't he? Calm. Yes, calm. You know, and free. I always thought of him as a free man.'

'Did you ever see him with other people?'

'Oh, yes. Quite a few times. I mean, he was a young man, so, as you'd expect, he dined with other young people, like himself. You know, fit and healthy people, jolly, but not rowdy, women and men, sometimes in groups, four or six. Occasionally with just one woman, but he seemed to like his own company the best. Yes, women and men, but mostly he'd be on his own, civil to the staff, to Lucia and Amelio, who he liked to talk to about football, Italian football. And shoes. I suppose your detectives talked to all his friends. What did they say about him? How did they think he seemed?'

'Pretty much as you said. Calm.'

'Yes, calm. That's what I'd say about him. I would love to be so calm, wouldn't you, detective? I guess he would just love to be alive. Do you believe in the after-life?'

The sudden lurch wasn't really a surprise.

'As much as I believe in the before-life.'

'Good answer, yes. Good answer. I'd be a bit the same. Two great black holes, either side of a flickering candle flame, more or less short, but short, no matter what. Short for Todd Anderson. Very short. And for our Gerald.'

'I was one of the party who fired the volley over his coffin.'

This time there was no tea to freshen up or mugs to refill, so the silence rested between us, until he stared directly at me and said,

'You joined the following wave, then. There's always something to be angry about, isn't there? Something unfair and unjust. Something violent that breeds violence. Like in Gerald. I mean, he was my brother. I taught him to swim and all that, like, we grew up together. He was younger than me. You were younger than him and you followed on. I didn't. Couldn't. I mightn't be a traitor, Detective Slevin, but could I be a coward? You joined the police. I thought you came round to tell me you'd made an arrest or that there was some other development in the Todd Anderson case. There isn't, is there? Any developments?'

'No, there isn't. At least nothing very, I don't know, nothing very hot.'

'You thought I might be. Hot, in the way you mean for clues and leads, like the cops on the telly. I'm sorry, detective. I'm like the teapot. Fairly lukewarm, by now.'

'Did Anderson ever mention anyone special? Anyone he might have been wary of? Anything he was worried about?'

'You haven't a clue, really, so you haven't? It's okay. Don't mind me. I don't either. Have a clue, I mean, so how could you? I didn't really know him. We hardly spoke. Why would he tell me anything, especially something he was worried about? I didn't know you were in Gerald's firing party. I knew the other two. One's Dessie Crossan, you probably know him. You must know him. He's still around. You see him some times, don't you? Todd Anderson was a free man, in the modern way of being free. He was guiltless, if you know what I mean?'

'I thought you said you didn't know him. That you didn't speak.'

'I knew this much. He was good-looking, fit and healthy, well-paid, well-liked, well-regarded, drove a fine car – I'm guessing – some kind of sporty saloon, used good hair products, knew his Italian shoes from his country clogs and never gave the slightest thought to how he could have all these things and be all these things and never once wonder how things could be just so, when millions of people are starving and the ocean levels keep rising and the global temperature climbs and bubbles like a cheap alcohol thermometer left in a sun-lounge on a scalding day in July. Do you think he ever worried about that? No. So he was calm. And free. Do you think Gerald was ever calm? Or free?'

'No. Not in the way I think you mean.'

'Well, he's free now. Has been for some years. People think you get over things, but you don't. Things get under you, which sounds like it should be the same thing, but it's not. Under your skin. Under your eyelids. Under your fingernails. Under the layers of your brain you use to cover as much as you can, but under there it goes, then leaks and seeps out, like river water rising in the bilge of a small craft down there on the Foyle, bobbing on the tide, one surge short of submersion. Can you swim, Detective Slevin?'

'No.'

'You'd best learn. The floods are coming. They're about our ankles already. Can you feel them?'

'You were away, when Todd Anderson's body was found. When did you leave exactly?'

'I told the detectives all this, the first time. I showed them itineraries, boarding passes, hotel bills.'

I'd seen all that in the file. He'd been away for ten days, so he couldn't have killed Todd Anderson, but I wanted to rule out the possibility that he could have set it up, paid for it and planned for it to happen when he was away.

'I was back in Borneo,' he continued. 'First time in ages. Not logging, like before. Conserving. Finger in the dyke stuff, really. The big trees are almost gone. Meranti. Keruing. Seraya. Patches of them still under state control, as a form of museum. The past itself is a commodity, detective, called heritage. And the rain-forests are now heritage sites, what's left of them. I advise on roads, access, the historical accuracy of the lay-out of representations of the logging camps. I consult and I advise on how we might keep the past in the past and even make some money from it, certainly how we might salve the anger of the local people, the forest dwellers, by giving them jobs as tour and museum guides, waiters and cooks in the food franchises, cleaners in the hotels and resorts. Sell them modernity and call it progress, even though we doubt it ourselves. You believe in progress, don't you detective?'

'Are you an angry man, Mr. Mahon?'

'What a surprising question! Yes. I am angry. More confused than angry, which at my age, probably amounts to the same thing. You're a bit younger than me, so you're probably still fairly clear about your anger. And you're probably comfortable with it, am I right?'

'Did you and Todd Anderson have a relationship? Did you fall out?'

He stood up then and went to the bookshelves. He pulled a slim, large format book of black and white photographs towards him and returned to stand over me. I braced myself, expecting him to hit me with it.

'You're neither confused nor angry, detective. You're lost. And you know it, which makes it very hard for you. Page 28, the two-page spread.'

I opened the book and saw a younger Larry Mahon, in shorts and bush shirt, enclosed by the buttress of a giant rain-forest tree, a spray of red and white survey markers under his right arm and his left palm raised towards me, saying 'back off'.

'That was some time ago. Me, caught red-handed in an act of deforestation. When Todd Anderson was killed, I was back there, about 15 kilometres from that exact spot, engineering roads for a children's camp and hill resort. Passing through KL, I caught the retrospective exhibition of the photographer, who took that image all those years before. She's a smart woman. Yeh, she caught me rightly. Trousers down, you might say. All that confusion and anger. See the forest enclosing me? And my survey sticks? All those trees are gone. My handiwork. No, I didn't have a relationship with Todd Anderson. I am sporadically heterosexual. No, I did not organise to have him killed, while I gave myself an alibi by being away. You'll have to do better than that, detective. Would you like to see another photograph? One I now know has you in it.'

He led me toward the window that overlooked the walk-way towards the central square of the Craft Village, but instead of taking in a view of the sturdy beams and buddleia be-decked walls outside his flat, he pointed me at a framed photograph beside the window, warmly illuminated by a fine spotlight. A thin black frame held a copy of a newspaper photo, slightly blurred by enlargement, but it had not been retouched, so it presented reality in all its spare staginess. A wooden bier. A coffin, draped in a tricolour. Three figures in combat jackets and balaclavas, in spread-legged stances, small arms held above them in resolute two-handed grips, facing the camera and now facing me.

'The big man, on the left, died a few years ago. In his bed. I went to his wake. The other two are still alive. You're the small lad in the middle. That's Dessie Crossan to your right, yes?'

I neither confirmed nor denied that.

'And my brother Gerald is in the box. See the crowd, behind you? They're close, obviously, but also far removed. Miles away. I wasn't even there.'

'It was the first time I used that gun.'

'But not the last?'

'No.'

'You would use it again? That, or one like it?'

'Yes.'

'That's why I have the photo on the wall. I wouldn't. Use that gun. Or any other.'

'No one can say that.'

'A gun put Gerald where he is now. In the box, there. In the ground, up in the cemetery, now. In the after-life, a pool of darkness on the other side of light, bookended by the before-life we never know. A short life story.'

I thought about my mother. All that river talk. The body in the box. The water rising. I wasn't looking for Todd Anderson's killer. I was looking for the dead.

'And a long, long death story,' I said.

That made Larry Mahon laugh.

'The detective, as philosopher, eh?' he said.

'Mythologist.'

'More tea?'

'No.'

'More questions?'

'No. And yes. But not here and now.'

TWENTY SIX

Hetherington grew impatient. With me. With the Todd Anderson case. He had more questions. He wanted more and better answers. Hammy gave him the platform from which to ask them, though Hetherington was clear he had no desire to share any platform with me.

'I offered my opinion, sir, as to why I thought it was inappropriate that DS Slevin should join us at this time, but given that he is here, it allows us to put some questions to him. If I may, sir?'

It was no surprise that Hetherington didn't want me there. The surprise came earlier, when Sharon prompted me with a pointed finger and a clear message. I thought I had been fully set adrift.

'MR9. Hammy wants you. Now.'

Five adults is just about the limit of the small meeting room Hammy had allocated. He was pacing. Karolina and Josh were in chairs by the window, where a broken blind limped across a view of the side wall of the Technical College next door. Hetherington, by means of his recent moves up the ladder and the boost that gave to his self-esteem, managed to capture the focus of the room by sitting on a high-stool he'd lifted from the coffee nest beside MR9. All the other furniture was stacked against a wall as if the decorators were expected any minute. I stood by the door, not planning to stay very long.

'You may certainly put some questions. But not before you give me some answers. Have you got that gun?'

'No, I ...'

'Have you connected the hair tissue with the victim?'

'I was …'

'That's another "no". Do you have at least one suspect?'

'No.'

'Any motives?'

'No.'

'Any leads?'

'No, but if …'

'Let's keep with the "call and response", though the odd "yes" would make a nice change.'

'Yes, sir.'

'Nice try, Hetherington. Nice try. But not the full pakora,' said Hammy.

I hugged the door-frame, ready to reach for the handle and be the first out of the room when the boss cleared it. Hammy began pacing again, more briskly now, five steps to the left, swivel on the heel, five to the right, pause, turn, five left once more, then repeat. Each time he came towards Josh and Karolina they lifted their feet further and further off the floor. If his pacing continued much longer, their knees would be at their chins.

'I gathered us here this morning, because I need to crunch down on this Todd Anderson case. It's been eleven months or so now, up in the air like some kind of birthday balloon no one loves anymore. We need to bust it or let it fly off to the outer edges of our universe with all the other flyaway balloons we can't tether. So, Hetherington, with your full team gathered around you, give me the three-line pitch for the successful closing of this case.'

There was a pause, as Hetherington scanned his tablet. Josh made to open a window above him, but Hammy strode towards him and he folded himself into Karolina and brought his knees up to his ears. I bowed my head and smiled to think how good the job could be at times.

'Now would you please be so kind, DC Hetherington, before these two climb on top of each other and we have to separate them with a pail of boiling water, like me Da used to do when the dogs in the street got too amorous.'

Karolina and Josh extricated themselves from each other, replanted their feet on the ground and blushed like harbour beacons in a fog.

Hetherington was resolute.

'This is a complex and intractable case, sir. Despite strenuous efforts by numerous officers and teams – and I've only had oversight of the Todd Anderson case for a short period – no untrammelled leads have been found.'

'"Untrammelled". That's good. Too "Oxford Shorter" for Josh and Karolina here, but straight out of Slevin's primer on obfuscation. Eh, Slevin? Whadya think? You taught him well, eh?'

'Sir.'

'*Homo Monosyllabus*, it is then. Could you do something for me, DC Hetherington? Would you mind unravelling some of that trammelling, like a good man?'

'Sir, perhaps … certain matters I have before me …'

'Spit it out, boy. You're not on Crime Hour, where you have to build a false sense of suspense. We're the cops, remember. We only do the answers, not the drama.'

'As I said, sir, I'm unhappy that DS Slevin is attending, as some of these matters relate to him.'

'Not at all a surprise to me, Hetherington. Not at all a surprise. Josh, get up there and open a couple of windows, will you? I was round at me Ma's last night and enjoyed one of her finest wazwans – pungent qeema, a splendid rogan josh, rista, kofta, piles of biryani, delicately tuned yoghurt. I expect it will find expression low down in the digestive tract anytime now.'

Right on cue, DI Omar Hamilton farted loudly and ar-

omatically. Karolina bound out of her seat to open two windows. Josh bent over laughing and said,

'Grade A, sir. Best silage this side of the Glenshane Pass.'

I held my breadth and Hetherington breathed steadily and
held my gaze. Furiously.

Hammy was smiling, fully in control of his material and
of us. He knew where he wanted to go with this meeting. He
was prepared to let Hetherington decide the packaging, but
not the content.

'Now, that we've managed to clear the air – thank you for
your alert action, Karolina – please put your questions to DS
Slevin.'

'Perhaps it would be best if, well, some of this material is sensitive and, I feel ... junior officers, such as Josh and Karolina ...'

If Hetherington kept going like this, I would have nothing
to fear. He'd already alienated himself from his boss and now
he was insulting his colleagues by openly admitting he was
keeping things from them. Josh and Karolina made no move
to leave and Hammy didn't want to take any of the pressure
out of the room. I added my own ginger to the spicy mix by
opening the door slightly and stepping aside.

'Good man, Slevin. Ever helpful to your old pal,
Hetherington here. But, no, we won't be letting any more
wind out of the room and neither will we be letting our
highly-esteemed new cadre exit either. We're all in this together,
as the bankers keep telling us when the economy collapses at
their instigation. Shut the door, Edmund. The air in here is too
refined for the bloodless ghouls around the corner there.'

Hammy smiled when I recognised his 'round the corner'
reference. Just past MR9, at the start of the abutting corridor
were ML1 to ML5, where representatives from Internal
Security had their labyrinth.

'Now, Hetherington, your questions. And no hesitations.

Let's keep the old TV thing going. Courtroom drama, please. Ask the questions directly. And, Slevin, straight answers, if you can possibly manage that. And you two, no notes, no tittle-tattle afterwards. This is the grown-up version of the game. We're way past the watershed. Proceed.'

Hetherington was still unsure, but couldn't back out now. He took a moment and then spoke directly to me, keeping his eyes fixed on mine.

'Do you know the crime scene technician Mervyn Campbell?'

'Yes,' I played along.

'Did you meet him at the canteen in Maydown?'

'Yes. He supported my work when I solved the case of the drunk murdered behind the electricity sub-station.'

'Bravo!' said Hammy. 'Bravo! See that, you two? Let us not speculate about what DS Goss might say about who solved that case. Continue.'

'You didn't meet with him on any other matter?'

'No.'

'You didn't discuss the Todd Anderson case?'

'Of course we did. In general terms. "What are are you working on now?" sort of thing.'

'Exemplary. Top of the class, Slevin,' said Hammy, with a brief round of applause. Nothing was real anymore. He was taking us into the fantasy of a role-playing exercise at the training college. It was Hammy's play, an exercise in theatre, looking and sounding good, but as empty as an irrigation ditch in a drought.

Hetherington consulted his tablet.

'And when you met Mervyn Campbell, in January, did you meet with anyone else at Maydown?'

'No.'

'Why did you take Sharon's car and not one of the pool

vehicles?'

Karolina and Josh leaned forward at this. Another layer of office politics seemed to be growing across this cesspit, a skein of illicit romance, perhaps. They liked the smell of it. Hetherington ploughed on.

'And why would you be meeting Mervyn Campbell when the case you worked with DS Goss was well and truly solved and closed by then?'

I took some pleasure in how much more confident Hetherington had become. He now had three questions running with me and no matter in which order I took them he could still feint a cross question onto the one I'd ducked.

'Yes. The case was solved. I found the key clue, the blood-soaked towel, the item that closed the case …'

'Don't lay it on on too thick,' Hammy warned.

'… and I had some final follow-up, some administrative notes to go over with Campbell.'

'I am looking at footage here,' said Hetherington, browsing his tablet, 'which shows you in the canteen with Mervyn Campbell …'

'I had the lobster. Mervyn had the surf and turf. Prawns on a bed of carrigeen moss, adorning his sirloin.'

Josh enjoyed that one, coming in with 'Good man, Mervyn' and Karolina mouthed a protective warning at him.

'Then I have footage of you climbing into the small red car you came in, some forty-five minutes later. It can't have taken you three quarters of an hour to get from the canteen to the car-park.'

'Toilet run, I imagine. The lobster was dodgy. I should have known. It looked more cerise than pink.'

'So, you went to Maydown, in a civilian car, not your own, and you met a technician allegedly to discuss a case already closed and then went missing for almost an hour. Why do I think all of this points to you being at Maydown for some reason other than the reason stated?'

'I don't know why you think what you think. I'm good, but I'm not that good. I had lunch with Mervyn, went to the loo, had a laugh with others, admired the scenery and left as planned. Mission accomplished. Oh, and the mystery car. Sharon's. I was having trouble getting a vehicle from the pool and she kindly offered me the use of her personal vehicle. I was grateful to her, of course, and bought her a pineapple the next day, in thanks.'

Hammy stopped pacing and moved to stand beside Hetherington. Putting a hand on his shoulder, he said,

'You have to understand what you're dealing with here, Kenneth. Slevin is well used to being interrogated. He can bat away with you like this for hours in a tiresome game of Pac-Man. Remember that? Too young? Computer game. Two paddles. Pock pock. Back. Forward. You see, he knows he's going nowhere and so he'll sit tight. He throws you information, stuff you already have and is of no real use to you, and all the while you're wondering where you want to get to and what you and your paramour might have for the tea.'

'I'm trying to assist DC Hetherington as best I can, sir,' I said. 'However, I'm glad Josh and Karolina are present to hear your remarks, as they give a succinct description of the to and fro of an interrogation. This really is a very good, role-play training event. You should perhaps have made that clear at the start, though it adds to the depth of the training, letting it emerge as it goes along.'

'This is no game, Slevin and you know it,' said Hetherington. 'This is you covering your tracks, just when the truth is about to come out.'

'Put it to him, Kenneth,' said Hammy. 'If you've got something – is it the hair or is it the gun? – put it to him.'

'I … I know what you were doing in Maydown. Yes, you met Mervyn Campbell, but it wasn't solely on the case of the drunk behind the electricity sub-station. You talked about the Todd Anderson case …'

'Of course we did. Mervyn asked, as you would expect, if we were making any progress. I asked him if he had any thoughts on it. That makes sense. He's a very experienced police technical officer. He regretted he couldn't offer me anything, beyond saying that his steak was excellent. His prawns did look a lot better than my lobster, on reflection.'

We all knew the bill of fare at the Maydown canteen did not extend to that level of fine dining. Josh couldn't hold himself any longer.

'Between your Ma's vindaloo, sir and DS Slevin's lobster, we're certainly getting great training in international cuisine.'

'Stick to the chips, peas and gravy, you,' admonished Hammy. 'Now Hetherington, unless you have any more questions you'd like to ask, perhaps we could get back to some real police work?'

'One more, sir. Thank you, sir. DS Slevin, when did you remove the murder weapon from the archive of the case of the murder of Police Constable Edwin Norris?'

'I did not remove …'

'I put it to you that you went to Maydown, that day in January, intending to return the gun to the Norris case archive, but failed to do so. Is that not what happened, DS Slevin?'

I let that sit in the air between us for as long as possible. This was good news for me and added the rich aroma of flounder to the spicy digestive and fetid perspiration smells already filling the small room.

'You've lost me, Hetherington. You're saying I took a gun into Maydown, to put it back into an archive box, then, for some reason, I didn't, so I took it out again.'

'And where do you think the gun is now, DC Hetherington?' asked Hammy.

'DS Slevin has it.'

Right on cue, Karolina spoke up.

'Sir, I am so sorry, is this a training exercise or a, eh … real interrogation? This gun and Police Constable … Norris. Are we connecting this with the killing of Todd Anderson?'

I kept my eyes lowered, because if she caught my gaze she might see me signalling 'thank you' and thus know that I was guilty, even if neither of us could be sure guilty of what.

'Well,' added Hammy. 'Is that what we're saying, Kenneth? Is that what you want to put to DS Slevin?'

All eyes were on Hetherington. He was under investigation, not me. If I had almost admired him earlier, I didn't pity him now. I now knew he hadn't a clue about the gun involved. The fact that I didn't know either was worrying, so I decided to give things one last twist.

'DC Hetherington has made similar wild assertions before, sir. I fear the stress of handling major criminal investigations, such as the Todd Anderson killing, may be too much for him, at this stage in his career, and I suggest, sir, with respect, that you and I were ill-advised to have placed so much responsibility on such young shoulders, as we did in this …'

'Spare me the offal, Slevin. Don't you think the room smells rank enough at present without adding your sanctimonious shite to the affluent?'

'… and I feel that DC Hetherington may be under the influence of elements of the security services, who are pursuing a political agenda, aimed at discrediting the work of this unit and of PS(N)'s current leadership.'

Josh and Karolina exchanged glances. If they were any younger they would have hi-fived each other. They had enough material now to enliven after-work beers with their colleagues for weeks to come.

Hammy returned to pacing. Hetherington sat bolt upright on his high stool. I pinched my nose and gently swung the door open and closed. Karolina smiled. Josh stifled a laugh.

'Thank you, DS Slevin. For managing to both clear the air and foul the air at the same time. "And they fall upon their faces, and the Quran increases them in humble submissions", as we say. Here's the drill from now on. In regard to these matters, I will take the Todd Anderson case back onto my desk. Slevin, you will continue on your current work assignments, pending a full resolution of your situation. Josh and Karolina, revise your case loads and bring me short notes this afternoon at 4. Hetherington, use the rest of today and all of tomorrow to draw the Todd Anderson material together. Write me a one page summary and another one page of your best thinking for the front of the Murder Book. Have all of that on my desk no later than 9.00am Friday. You will need to re-organise that corral of desks in the main office to reflect the disbandment of this team.'

'But sir,' Hetherington pleaded, 'Slevin was not part of the team. There is no need to disband it. In fact, we're just beginning to make progress, so now is not the right time …'

Hammy jumped in.

'There is never a right time, Kenneth. There is only now.'

He had got us where he wanted us. He was back in charge and quoted another surah from Al-Quran to conclude.

'"By the Time! Man is surely in loss, except those who believed and did good works, and exhorted one another to Truth, and exhorted one another to patience." Don't worry, Kenneth. You'll get over this. Unsolved cases are what defines us as police officers, especially in this neck of the woods. And the Todd Anderson case, whatever else it may be, is a defining case. If we solved every crime, there'd be no need for us, would there? So, do as I say. Now. The only time there is. All this talk of food has put me in the form for an early lunch. Feel free to join me in the canteen. We're all in this together, though some of us are less clear on what it is we're in than others, and that includes me. Soup, I think. I'll avoid the salad. The last one I had, the lettuce was singed and charred at the edges. And peppermint tea. Yes, peppermint tea, to settle the inner man.'

He rubbed his tummy, tapped Hetherington on the shoulder again and strode towards me. I opened the door fully to let him out and promptly followed him, pulling the door behind me, to let Hetherington stew in the questions I knew Josh and Karolina were bursting to ask him.

Hammy took my arm and steered me to the door of his office.

'Now, Eddie, whatever shenanigans you and your spook friends are up to is your business. I won't let it pollute our good work anymore. You'll be off this floor quicker than shite off a slate. In the meantime, sit at that desk yonder, do whatever the fuck Sharon tells you to do, and no more. I haven't a clue how all this is going to blow up, but blow up it will and I guarantee that, when it does, it won't be on this floor. Now, fuck off.'

He squeezed my forearm and pulled me close, so I could smell the full range of his mother's wazwan on his breath. Then he pushed me away and hissed.

'I mean it. Fuck off.'

TWENTY SEVEN

Sharon kept me busy and days passed, each one growing lighter, into Spring. Better than any of us, she knew how the ball broke when players contested for it in the middle of the field. The strong jumped high to field it. Then others scrambled about to pick up the pieces. She was full of sporting sageness, from her own kick-boxing career.

'What you don't want is to suffer a knock-out. Take a couple of clouts, yeh. A few flakes to the kidneys. What's a bit of bruising? Get the lovely Karen to rub on the arnica. Ah, don't tell me you and Ms Lavery are not sparring any more.'

'We're between rounds. What happened your eye?'

'I'm coaching one of our young ones for the nationals. I got a bit too involved and well, I'm not as quick as I was, so she caught me. Don't worry. She's alright and, well, it's useful, sometimes, to get knocked out, when you're young. It'll stand to her in competitions.'

Sharon touched the bright green dressing on her left cheek bone with her black lacquered fingernails and continued,

'She bent in too low, after clocking me under the eye. Everyday's a school-day, Eddie. Just like here. And the lesson you're learning is that Sheik Hamilton is not your opponent. He's the owner. You're not fighting him. You're fighting for him. He owns you. And me, in a different way.'

'I'd say he's scared you'd kick him in the balls, so he stands well back.'

'Listen, one good side to all of this is that the floor is getting back to normal. Hetherington's attempt to build Fortress Kenneth is stalled. Josh and Karolina can go back to playing at being detectives again. You're stuck with me for a while, so just keep your head down, duck and weave, duck and weave and watch out for Sheik Hamilton's long left leg, because it's coming and you'll feel it from your kidneys right down the sciatic nerve, through your heel and over you'll go unless you have yourself well and truly rooted.'

'What about a move to Vice? I could work there.'

'No chance. That's a prime location for folks on the rise. Go-ahead folks like Josh and Karolina. Hetherington may have missed his chance, but, we'll see. Redemption is possible. One shot only. You've used yours a dozen times over. Here, take a mouthful of these. Chewing'll take the glum look off your bake.'

She held a plastic tub of nuts, dried beans and seeds before me. I pinched some between my fingers and tried them. They tasted like perfumed grit from the bottom of last Spring's potpourri.

'Saffron. You getting it? That's the buzz in it.'

As well as filling me full of wisdom and roughage, Sharon had confirmed what my only contact in Vice, Joseph Dickson, told me when I travelled with him in the lift to his floor.

'Your man, Hamilton and our top madam, DI Quigley, had a fine do-dah up here last week,' he said. 'Where are you going now?'

'I'm hanging out with you is all.'

'Jesus, Slevin, do me a favour and volunteer with The Samaritans if you want to do some befriending. I'm good for mates just now, online and face-to-face.'

'I have to collect some papers up at Vice. Some depositions.'

'Like fuck you do. You're up leering about, seeing if you can imagine yourself on our floor. You can forget it. The two bigwigs did the finger pointing and the pouting behind closed doors most of the time, but she sent your man packing with "and if you think I'm going to take your cast-offs, just to save your skin", which she delivered full-throated from her office door, held open to usher him through. The word is you're the cast-off and you can forget Vice. We're not having you.'

I stayed in the lift as he got out on his floor.

'What about the depositions?'

'I got what I wanted,' I said, as gamely as I could. My form plummeted as surely as the lift. Sharon simply confirmed what Joseph Dickson had told me and my morale plunged to the basement.

'Options won't be great, Eddie, but we're a big concern, the police, so some cubbyhole or other will be found for you. And you know what, I'll miss you. You're the first assistant I ever had,' Sharon said.

'I'm not your assistant, Sharon.'

'No. You're too old and too well-qualified to be my intern. So what are you?'

'I'm your corner-man. Do ye have them in kick-boxing? I'm doing your cuts, your ice. I'll throw in the towel, if you need it.'

'You won't need to do that. Not for me. Not for yourself, neither. Stay in the game. Root yourself. Guard up. Kidneys covered. Go on. Do something.'

'What?'

'What? Jesus. Go out and buy yourself an Easter egg, like a good lad.'

It had to happen someday, even with me taken off front-line activity, so, when I got into a lift with Karen Lavery, I wasn't surprised. She'd come up from the basement carpark. I was delivering papers to Sharon, who was on the top floor, staffing Hammy at a Joint Case Conference.

'Hello, Eddie,' Karen said. There was no hint that the last

time we'd met had been under gunfire at my flat.

'Karen. You here for the conference?'

'Yes. You going?'

'No. Not exactly. I'm sort of a runner.'

'Ah. They're coming down hard on you.'

'You could say that. Paris good?'

Two men got on at the third floor and we both went silent, but stood closer together. I liked the fact that we were the same height. When we turned towards each other, our eyes met directly. I felt such a rush of desire, that I had to look away, which I immediately regretted. The lift stopped and the other two got off. Being alone again felt more charged and intense.

'Paris, yes. Ages ago. The conference was very good. Got out and about a wee bit too. You know how we say the French are standoffish and cool? I didn't find that. The hosts were really, you know, sound. And the work was fascinating, like, so much new stuff going on. We get lost in ourselves, here, Eddie, you know, sometimes.'

'You'll go back out then. Follow-up?'

'There's … we'll see. And what about you? Lighter case-load?'

'Nil case load. I'm desk-bound. Glorified office-boy, under Sharon's thumb.'

'Jayus, Eddie. Mind she doesn't hit you a belt.'

'Naw, she won't. Up to a point, she's the only one on my side.'

Eddie, I … I mean …'

'Hammy wants me out, so I'll be out. Where, I have no idea, but something back-office, no doubt.'

We reached the top floor and I let her step in front of me. She was wearing a royal blue trousers suit, with a fitted jacket that held her slim figure so gently it seemed to shimmer on her. When she turned back to me, her thinly-framed spectacles glinted. She smiled. If beauty is in the eye of the beholder, I was beholding. If love is something you fall into, I was in a headlong tumble. I managed to say,

'You look gorgeous, Karen. The suit? Paris?'

'Yes. Thanks, Eddie.'

'I'm guessing you're in the main conference room, along there,' I pointed. 'I'm dropping these to Sharon, then getting back to my filing. Oh, that fiver I owe you.'

'Eddie, Jesus. I don't like seeing you so down-beat. Keep the fiver, so I'm in credit.'

'Always, Karen. I'm not that down-beat. You mind that plank you noticed against your back the last time we were together? I'm doing my best to keep it trousered at the minute, pressing these files across my front and not saying too much.'

Karen laughed wonderfully. Her timing was perfect, because Officer Cosgrove and his two henchmen, Daffy Duck and Goosy Gander, approached. They had shed their great winter coats, but kept their morticians' suits and dark ties.

'Hello, Ms Lavery. Are you planning to bring DS Slevin to the conference as your "plus one"?', said Officer Cosgrove.

'Good morning. DS Slevin has other duties and won't be able to bring his insights to bear on our work this morning. Which is unfortunate.'

Cosgrove ignored that and turned to me.

'I haven't had time to see the footage, limited though it was, of your latest cock-up, Slevin. Something too strong in your espresso, was it? Something about a gun and you a danger to the public, not to mention costing us a pile of money in ruined broadcast equipment and causing my old friend DI Hamilton all sorts of bother. Not nice. Oh, and by the way, your police-college mate, Tony White? He's away. Took a package and headed off. Probably in a caravan in Millisle, as we speak, counting raindrops on the windowpane. You're the last one, Slevin. The last idiot in the CC's idiotic scheme. She'll be here today and I'll take the opportunity to bring her up to date. Go, Slevin. Let's make it a clean sweep. Say I can tell her you're for the hills too, where you and your likes belong.'

'Have a good conference, sir. You'd better get in fast, before all the scones are gone. Your two care-workers look like they could do with getting fed.'

'Ms Lavery, could I have a word, before we go on in? Walk with me a moment, please.'

Cosgrove took Karen by the elbow, turned her and led her to a two-seater bench at the end of the corridor. Goosy Gander and Daffy Duck moved either side of me and launched their double-act.

'No scones for you, Slevin.'

'No hot, hot, hot Ms Lavery neither.'

'Lovely girl. Karen, is it? She'll have a farm a' land, no doubt.'

'A good catch, right enough.'

'I might give her a go.'

'Ah, you'd crush her, big lad. She has no more meat on her than a pigeon.'

The thought of either of those two with their hands on Karen blew the fuse that had been fizzing in my head for weeks and I kicked Daffy Duck squarely in the balls, then moved quickly to the other end of the corridor, where support staff for the conference was stationed in a long, narrow office and storeroom filled with tables, copiers, a phone bank, spare tablets of various sizes, display boards and stacked chairs and desks. I put my papers on a table next to Sharon.

'Good man, Eddie ...' she began, but I cut her off and blazed past.

'Two big lads coming, Sharon. I'm not here.'

I kept going, left the room by the far end door, ran to the

end of another corridor and dashed down the service stairs, taking them in bounds of three and four, swinging off the newel posts and laughing like a teenager, thinking about Daffy Duck's gasping and bent figure.

The story became Sharon's stand-off with Cosgrove's duo. I was written out of it. The version I heard from a constable I shared a cigarette with in the basement later had it that two big men burst into the room, one of them limping slightly, shouting my name and Sharon calmed them by saying her aide was on an errand and could she be of any assistance. The constable said he thought the two fellas would explode, then the fella with the limp got a message on his phone and they went back out the way they came. Sharon returned to her work, picked up a stack of papers and made for the conference room. The constable said she was smiling.

I laid low for a couple of days and then slipped in early one morning. I was alone with Sharon, long enough for her to give a post-fight analysis.

'Kidneys, was it?'

'More central,' I replied.

'Balls. Illegal. But not if you're a cage-fighter, which is what you are, Slevin. A bloody cage-fighter. I don't blame you. Big bastards, those two lads, which seems to be a requirement for IS. You're either a measly wee shite or a shire-horse. You got two shire-horses and gelded one of them.'

'I had no choice.'

'Don't give me that crap. You sound like a bad politician and you're better than that. Your old flame, Karen Lavery, asked about you and I told her you were grand. She knew something had happened, but not the details. Nobody knew them at that point.'

'Anybody come looking for me since?'

'No. Eddie, listen, they know where you are. And they haven't been idle.'

Sharon pushed a single sheet of paper towards me. Key words and phrases beamed out at me, as I scanned the classic PS(N) memo layout.

'Reassignment', 'annexe NW14', 'necessary redeployment', 'six months' review'.

It was signed by Hammy, my boss, above the telling line

'On the authority of Chief Constable Elaine Caldwell.'

'You see, Eddie, you're the bargaining chip that broke the logjam.'

'Where the fuck is annexe NW14? London?'

'Maydown.'

'Jesus.'

'I know. And you're too young for a bus-pass.'

'You live out that way, Sharon. I could move in with you.'

'Last thing I need is a lodger. A man under my feet? I had one of them. Tolerable father. Useless husband, especially when his "rod of destiny" – what he called it – began to lose its gleam. Me and the two girls are grand as we are and Daddy can do the weekend thing and clap himself on the back for it.'

'And this, what is this Heritage Crime Strand of the Legacy Unit? Should I bring swim wear?'

'It's muddy trenches, not sandy beaches, the strand you're headed for. You'll be wading through blood. Don't quote me on it, but as far as I know Heritage Crime is the new thing. You know, really big crimes you can't blame on anyone and that ones are still suffering from, you know, like slavery. You'll love it. It'll be just like your college days, in jail. Reading books, then writing books nobody'll read. And cops instead of screws to keep an eye on you. Maydown in May. A new start.'

I read 'redeployment to commence on 1st May, at current grade. DS Slevin will report to the Strand Leader, DI Williams' and asked,

'Williams? Do you know him?'

'Never heard of him. Likely a dud, coasting to retirement in a few months.'

The office began to fill up around us. Karolina waved, as she shrugged off her coat. Josh gave me a 'thumbs up' and continued to munch on a breakfast roll, which dripped red sauce like a punctured jugular. Hetherington ignored me and sat with his back to the room, which was fine by everyone else, but meant that he was vulnerable to the sort of japes that only Goss and Doherty could get up to. They nudged each other in delight as they went past me, singing softly.

'They seek him here, they seek him there.'

'They seek him everywhere.'

I envisioned a further pair of balls I could usefully kick. Sharon read my mind.

'Don't even think of it, Rocky. You've already been over that ground and won't get away with it again.'

'You reckon I've come to the end of the road, Sharon?'

'More of a fork to a side-road.'

'Aye, down a dead-end track.'

'I'd say they could put you in a convent with silent monks and nuns and you'd get them talking. Maybe more. Ms Lavery seems to have a notion of you. Did she get a bang on the head or what?'

'She's perfectly sane, Sharon. She's up there with yourself, when it comes to suss.'

'Thank you, kind sir. You're still not moving in. May in Maydown. A new start, eh? I'll go easy on you for the next wee while, so you can properly clear your desk. You won't have to water my plants anymore …'

'I never water …'

'Exactly. So carry on and keep your head down. No more

kicking. Balls. Kidneys. Or anywhere else.'

More people came into the office. Hammy breezed through, all efficiency and command, no words of greeting or incitement to his staff.

'Action man has entered the building,' said Sharon. 'Expect a flurry of documents and memos. You'll have plenty of filing and paper-carrying until May Day at Maydown.'

I got up, saying,

'I need to talk to him about this.'

Sharon snapped loudly enough for heads to turn in our direction.

'Sit down, Eddie.'

I heard Goss' aside to Doherty.

'Mammy's not happy. The wee lad's after wetting his pants again.'

And Doherty's reply.

'Ah, poor Mammy. And all the training she done on him. I heard she's getting fed up. Shur, it'll be a relief to her when they put him in a home and cut the little thing off altogether.'

'Sit down, Slevin,' Sharon repeated, in a hiss. 'Hammy won't see you. When he handed me that paper, he said "Sharon, make sure he doesn't cross my threshold between now and May. If he fucks about 'til then, we're fine with that."'

'What "we" is that then?'

'Every "we" that matters. The entire Focused Response Group. A side-deal at the conference.'

'They can't do that, Sharon …'

'Eddie, I was there. In and out, ears wide open. Eyes taking it all in. Hammy at the head of the table. The crowd from Gang Crime looking like the leftovers from a bank holiday weekend. A suit from Fraud. Your pal, Cosgrove. The CC herself at Hammy's side, but she might as well have been in New Zealand. Two pin heads from Spooksville. And

Hetherington. He had the phone traffic. Columns of figures, with luminous green strips shining across each, collating the calls and the people. Joining the dots between the woman in the field and the three fellas in the shed. They were both fires. So the Arson crowd insisted. They were there too, a man and a woman.'

'Bullshit. She was blown up. Hetherington was at the big conference?'

'He had the gold bars, see. He got the lead from your old mate, the good looking Traveller.'

'Mick.'

'Yeh, film-star Mick, your buddy.'

'Haven't seen him in ages. Months.'

'He came round to talk to you. Must have been when you were still on leave, recovering from the woman thing.'

Was Sharon referring to the bomb blast or to my relationship with Karen? She continued.

'He spoke to Hetherington. He was back at his desk, patched up, being talked about for a medal. Talk that faded, once the deals were done.'

'The crawling wee shite.'

'Now, now. Whatever he got from the Traveller, he took to Hammy and, hey presto, they banged a few names and logs of intercepted phone calls together, thereby exciting the boys and girls in the Gangs' Unit, who raided a couple of apartments in Belfast, got the Spaniards to do the same to a villa outside Fuengirola, which led to the main man, a Dub based in Amsterdam. They've been after him for five years.'

'Hetherington cracked all that? With Mick's info?'

'Slevin, I'm giving you the edited highlights. Basically, it has moved on. The gangs will shuffle the decks, shoot each other for a season, go quiet, then go back to business, hard.'

'Sharon,' I said. 'How ... let me rephrase it. When did you

become so cynical?'

She looked at me for a long moment. Her brow furrowed and her eyebrows rose like two cormorants taking off above her crystalline eyes. I never noticed it before, but my own eyes were drawn to an amulet wrapped in three stands round her left wrist, tipped in a snake's head, tailed in a silver point, an asp's rear. She bounced the end of her ebony bob and replied,

'Who said you get to ask the big questions? Still, it tops anything Hammy comes up with. "Sharon, can you get me that quarterly thing, the budget thing, you know, projections?" or that oaf, Doherty, "Hey, Sharon, line-dancing tonight, is it? A bit a' threshing with an aul' farmer, eh?" Karolina tries her best. "Can I buy you lunch, Sharon, you know and be friends?" God love her, she's trying so hard.'

'The immigrant's burden. And you, Sharon, you have a future on the telly. Impressions. On one of those obscure, niche channels, nothing mainstream, mind. Or maybe voice overs on the radio? I think I got them all. Do you do Josh? Hetherington?'

'I got cynical the day you joined us. I thought to meself, full of shite and badness and all as it was, at least the cops held the balance over the politicians. Now the politicians think they run the show and all that happened was the balance was tipped and the spooks grabbed the keys of the whole fairground.'

'You don't want me around the place, Sharon.'

'No. You know what? You don't like this place and you don't want to be around here anyway.'

'You're not cynical, Sharon. I apologise. You're smart. I don't have long, do I?'

'End of the month. Fresh start in May. Blossoms on the bough. Longer days. Sunshine in feeble dollops and rain in great plumps. Just take it handy 'til then. Keep the head down.'

It was good advice, so I immediately ignored it, re-read the redeployment memo, stuffed it into my pocket and went over to Hetherington, who, because his back was to the room didn't register my presence until I clipped him on the side of the head and leaned over him.

'That's for being a sly boy and not telling me Mick was looking for me.'

Sharon was beside me instantly and took a stance which told me that if I wanted to continue with two kidneys I should think carefully about my next move. Goss and Doherty were on their feet, prospects of a fight avid on their faces. Josh called 'Ah, come on, Eddie' and Karolina reached under her desk for her night-stick.

'Ye can all calm down. I just need a wee word with my former partner, young Kenneth here. And, heh, don't put Goss and Doherty there in charge of the whip-round for my leaving present. They'll only rob you, the thieving bastards.'

'I have nothing to say to you, Slevin,' Hetherington said, as Goss boomed,

'Leaving present? We're paying Sharon to drop-kick your arse to Rockall.'

I almost laughed at that. Karolina leaned over to Josh, who explained that Rockall is a contested rock in the North Atlantic. The room settled and I pulled up a chair beside Hetherington. Sharon hovered around me a little longer, until I convinced her with a 'calm down' palm press gesture and she went back to her seat. In any case, Hetherington was now turned towards me and fully alert.

A sickly slime of bile rose up in my chest, as I wondered how I had ended up like this, hitting people and acting like a shit. It was time to get out, memo or no memo.

'What do you want, Slevin?' Hetherington began.

'A quiet word.'

'Then keep your hands to yourself.'

'Sorry. I preferred you when you were a docile young apprentice, not the high-flying cop you are now. It's the company you've been keeping. Both of them. Dalzell. And Beresford.'

'You know more about him than I do. All that stuff is right up your dark alley. The whole service is talking about your set-to in the street. They're calling it the Clash of the Ice-Cream Cones.'

'Good one, Kenneth. Good one. I don't expect you'll be minded to help a colleague of yours, one who has assisted your rise …'

'Assisted my rise? Yeh, right. You practically blew me into the clouds.'

'Not my fault. Could have been anyone working with me. Happened to be your privilege at the time. Remember Hammy put you with me.'

'I told you we should wait. I told you to get back-up, but you ploughed on and nearly got us killed.'

'You've seen the reports. What happened wasn't personal to you…'

'It was personal to you, Slevin.'

'… or to that poor woman. She was the worst of all collateral. It was a broadcast to gangland. With a calling card left for me, maybe. A broadcast, yes, heard far and wide, which led to the incineration of the three messenger boys in the shed behind Campsie. But, you're well across that, seeing as you solved the whole thing, with information that was meant for me.'

'I didn't solve it. I passed on a lead. The Gangs Unit took what I had, shut me out in the yard, made the arrests and got the bonuses.'

'Ah. Hence, no medal for you. But you were at the big conference last week?'

'For ten minutes. Like a party piece. I sang my songs as a warm up act for the Gangs Unit, then Hammy asked me to leave and everyone smirked. You're all the same, Slevin. You don't give a shit about anything, except your own backs. So, don't blame me, if I start acting like that myself.'

'Ah, Kenneth. Not the cynicism of the old timer. Please. I thought you'd never succumb to that. Listen, clear your conscience. Where's the gun used to kill Anderson?'

If I thought a sudden lurch might bounce him into an answer, I was completely wrong. He swivelled his chair, so he faced his desk once more and spoke out of the side of his mouth.

'Not my case anymore. Ask Hammy.'

'He's not talking to me. What about Dalzell? Or Beresford?'

I could see a sneer edge across his face, as he continued to talk sideways to me.

'He's another one. Treats me like a toy. You're all users, Slevin. And I'm done being used. Last I heard, he was back in Manchester. When he wants you, he'll come for you. Be ready, is all I can say.'

I stood up and pushed my chair away. I managed to say 'Thank you and good luck, Kenneth', because I was genuinely saddened by Hetherington's bitterness. Whatever Dalzell had done had left him hurt and alone. Worse than me. I didn't pity him. I needed all my emotional reserves for myself.

Goss mimed a violinist playing a lament, as Doherty intoned, like a broadcaster at the funeral of a politician.

'Now the reconciliation is complete and the warring tribes commit to a peaceful future. Together? Doubtful. This is a solemn, yet happy hour – cocktails at half-price – as Slevin, the great bollocks of the West, parts from Kenneth, the half-man of the East, and peace returns to the office. Hallelujah!'

Josh began to applaud slowly, but I stared him down.

Karolina stashed her night stick.

I walked back to my desk, in the alcove behind Sharon. She didn't raise her head from the case papers she was collating, bundling and packing into files and then into an archive box.

Dalzell's card sat pristine and prominent as a newly minted first-class stamp on a brown envelope, in the right-hand corner of my desk. I reached for it, as I sat down and pulled out my phone. Then I remembered what Hetherington had said,

'When he wants you, he'll come for you.'

And I decided to wait to see what May might bring.

TWENTY EIGHT

As the first of May approached, I grew vaguely optimistic. Hammy had a victory to celebrate. He'd won ground and could pass his success to the Gang Crime Unit and let them do the dirty work. He wouldn't mind not getting his photo in the papers on this one. There was something unclean about the war between the gangs. And though Hetherington was wounded, he would recover. Hammy had put him in a box. I knew he wouldn't go after the gun. All the bullet points, skeletons, fancy Italian shoes, marks on the neck, and who knew what about them, came to nothing. I expected Hetherington would leave Serious Crime as soon as he could. Maybe transfer out altogether.

Cosgrove and his goons at IS had me where they wanted me. Behind a desk in a back-office. I knew they weren't finished with me, but I didn't have any idea of what they might do next. And Dalzell? If he had the gun, he'd come for me. So, full of the daredevil sap of May, I didn't care.

For my last day at the Serious Crime Team, Karolina and Josh organised buns and coffee from Fiorentini's. I thanked them. Karolina passed me an envelope, with an apologetic smile. I pocketed it, thanked her and later passed a clothes shop voucher under the door of my next door flat. My neighbour had just lost his job.

The only hand I shook was Sharon's.

'Good man, Eddie. If you ever need a reference, you know, just to say how good an intern you were, all you have to do is ask.'

'Thanks, Sharon. I mean that. Thanks, Sharon.'

'Josh is on about us all going for a drink after work. I don't …'

'Never worry, Sharon. That won't happen.'

'I always said you were the smartest. Too smart, maybe.'

'Where's Goss and Doherty?'

'On that rape case. Victim No. 3 overnight.'

'I hope they get the bastard.'

'Amen to that. Here, enjoy the weekend. Bank holiday and all. You might catch a bit of the jazz festival, eh?'

'Yeh. Then Maydown, first thing Tuesday.'

'All new-fangled.'

'Yeh. That desk is cleared. Do you want me to move it?'

'No. No, don't move it. I'll be pushing Hammy for a replacement for you. Not likely to be as qualified, but I've gotten used to having an assistant. Someone in my corner, like you said.'

'Good luck with that. And with everything.'

I put out my hand and surprised her, but she recovered and clasped mine firmly in both of hers, the way a cleric does. Then I walked out of the office, without looking back, brushing crumbs from my jacket, as I took the flight of stairs down to the exit, for the last time. Karolina had asked what I planned to do for the weekend and I said 'sleep'. If she had any ideas of getting me out to jazz gigs, the rebuff put her off.

I went straight round to the riverside walk, found an empty bench and lit a cigarette. Two young mothers, one with a set of twins, pushed buggies and chatted as they passed. A man, with a dog as pointy-snouted as himself, limped in the other direction, his gaze angled to the river at all times. He reminded me of myself, never taking his eyes off the water.

When I went to the flat, I stood in front of the window and stared at the river. The new glazing gleamed. It cost me a lot less than I expected. Maybe Dessie Crossan got me a discount.

I made one final meal out of the lamb stew I'd been eating for the past two days, by thinning it into a soup, using vegetable stock fortified with soy sauce. I defrosted two granary rolls and broke them into a large ceramic basin of the soupy stew and set myself up at a window.

The last morsels of tender lamb surprised me each time one of them found its way onto my spoon. I sucked soggy bread chunks, getting all the soy and the seeds out of them before swallowing the warming mush. It was the best of comfort food.

I crossed my ankles and placed them on the sill, putting the empty bowl away from me. I was asleep in seconds and a familiar dream came:

I run beside the river, barefoot on the grass, wearing shorts and no shirt. I laugh. I am seven or eight, skinny as an ash-plant. A woman runs after me, barefoot too, her hair streaming behind her. She wears jeans and a white t-shirt. She is not chasing me. We are running round each other, the way lambs do in Spring. I laugh and laugh. My mother, I feel it is my mother, though I don't really know who she is, laughs too. She has a silver bough in her hand, not silver, a bough of hawthorn, rich with white blossoms swinging above her head. She comes close. I whimper and she swerves away again, trailing the hawthorn bough behind her. I run in the opposite direction, then, breathless, I stop to see where she is. I look around, but she isn't there. There is a trail of white blossoms on the grass and I follow them to the river's edge. More blossoms float on the water, but there is no sign of the bough or of the woman. I pick up some petals from the mud squelching around my toes. Fine, white porcelain they are, with the blood-colour of life showing in the red tints at their edges. I squeeze them in my hand, then toss them into the water. I look at my palm, as bloody now as a stigmata. I begin to cry.

My phone sounding woke me up. It took me a scramble

to locate it, in a pocket in my dark suede jacket, thrown over the sofa I was sprawled across. My sister, Ruby, sussed me immediately.

'You still in your bed? You sound groggy. Bit of a leaving do last night was it, though you're not really "leaving"? Or are you at work?'

'Jesus, Ruby. I'm on me lunch. Having a doze and I just woke up.'

'Ah, that's right, no crimes get committed during lunch-hour.'

'Not my game anymore. Filing clerk from now on.'

'You alright about that?'

'Not really. No choice.'

'Have you been up to the grave?'

'What?'

'Mother's grave. Have you seen the stone?'

'I seen the picture you sent. It looks great. Thanks.'

'You haven't been up. Right. I'm taking Maisie up tomorrow. It's the anniversary.'

I knew that. Not the exact date, more the season. The blood blemish on the hawthorn told me. Ruby continued.

'I could pick you up and we …'

'Ah, no, Ruby, I don't think I …'

'You haven't the excuse of work anymore. Filing clerks don't work on a Saturday, especially on a Bank Holiday weekend.'

'No, Ruby. You and Maisie go.'

'Right. Me, Maisie and Bill'll go. Fair play to him. And I've booked a table for four at Turmeric, for six o'clock.'

'Maisie eats Indian food?'

'It's the jazz weekend. It was the only half-decent place I could get us in. They'll have chips and she can pick off our plates.'

'Bill is on for all this? He's even more of a catch than I

thought.'

'He's my husband. It'd be good if you and Auntie Maisie met him.'

Auntie Maisie had chips and wedges. The rest of us had a range of curries. Maisie tried each one, dipping her chips cautiously, then pronouncing on their qualities.

'There's too much cream in that. You'd get heartburn, if you ate all that. Chicken, is it? Nice white flesh anyway.'

'Spinach? You wouldn't get me eating that. I didn't know you were vegetarian, Ruby. You're not. Then tell me why are ye ateing the spinach then. Here, just a wee dip. I must be mad.'

'There's gunpowder in that one. Or coal. Something black anyway. You'd have to have that one, Edmund. Look at the colour of the bowl. There, let me just mop up that last bit. Lamb, is it? No, no meat, just the juice.'

Ruby defended me from Maisie's abuse for not visiting the grave.

'God knows, Edmund, it wouldn't have killed you to go to see your mother's grave and it the anniversary and all. Bill was up there, fair play to him. And the lovely stone Ruby put on it.'

'Edmund gave me money for it, Maisie,' said Ruby. 'He done his bit. Would you like the Black Forest Gateaux?'

'Is it Indian? Long as there's no rice with it.'

'No, Maisie. Or the Banoffee, maybe? Shur, we'll get the two and we can share them.'

'Banoffee, yeh. And the Black Forest. Trem ...? What's that? Get it anyway. Three, aye.'

We shared the desserts, Bill and Maisie enjoying the lion's shares. I took to Bill the moment I met him. He managed to look like an eccentric jazz musician, while exuding the steadiness of an actuary, his clothes riffing on swing trousers, spats and Hawaiian shirts.

I knew the evening was orchestrated by Ruby and I enjoyed it. I didn't object when she announced that I would accompany Auntie Maisie home, as she and Bill had to dash for an eight o'clock spot they had at The City Hotel, as warm-up for the big band coming on at half nine.

'Unless you want to come with us, Maisie?'

'On these feet? Ye must be joking. No, I'll head back. I'll get a taxi. I'll be no bother. You know me.'

Ruby raised her eyebrows at me and I said,

'Shur, I'll go with you, Maisie. We might call into Docs for one on the way home.'

'Docs! If they saw me coming in there now, they'd send for an exorcist. No ghosts allowed.'

Bill returned to the table, nodding at Ruby, as he sat down. I realised he'd paid the bill and I felt a sharp surge of resentment rise through me. The phrase 'not his place' trailed across my brain, until I realised that, contrary to my first reaction, this was 'his place'. He was part of my family now. I looked around the table. My sister and her husband dressed and made up in show clothes, musician-clowns decades out-of and right-bang-up-to date; my aunt, in a fine cotton long-sleeved summer dress, navy blue with white blossoms, tinged with red, dappled across them. She could have passed for a singer in a nostalgia outfit, a special guest for the festival; me, in a new corduroy jacket, summer chinos and deck shoes, no socks. I could be a musicians' manager and part-time jazz academic. This is my family, I thought and the depth of the notion pleased me, so I smiled hard and Ruby asked 'You alright, Edmund?' in a voice that echoed out of days past. I was a boy, sitting on the wall of the factory opposite where we lived, my aunt crossing to me, her arms folded across her small breasts, asking me the same question.

'You alright, Edmund?'

Would I have cried if Bill Peoples, my new brother-in-law, who made our family fuller, had not been there?

'I'll get us a hack, Maisie,' I said.

'Aye, one of the perks of being a cop, I suppose,' Maisie said. 'Town's mad today with all the jazz.'

On our way out, Maisie stopped by a table and spoke to a woman her own age, on the edge of a large group.

'I never thought Indians could do chips right, but they were lovely, right enough. Aye, the Tramashooee was tasty.'

Outside, the evening was clear and warm. Late blueness, dotted with fluffy, white clouds slowly migrating to night, swept above the rooftops. Bill left to get the van.

'He's a grand fella, Ruby. I see he paid up.'

Ruby nipped whatever resentment that lingered very firmly in the bud.

'We all did. 'Cept Maisie. You can send me something. I'm glad you joined us. It meant a lot to Maisie. We're all she has.'

'What does she think of Bill?'

'She's grand with him. She never gave much thought to men. "Long as you're happy" is all she says to me.'

'And you are. Jesus, Ruby, you're radiant.'

'Curry and hot-flushes. You set for the new job?'

'Yes and no. I'm worried it'll be a back-water. It will be a back-water, what am I saying?'

'You heard Maisie, inside, when you told us about it. She reckons you'd be better off back at the books.'

'She might be right. I have a few things to finalise. Then, we'll see.'

'Don't wait around, Eddie. Christ, where's Maisie? She didn't want to go out, now we can't get her home.'

Bill pulled up in the van, keeping the engine running.

'Go on, will ye,' I said. 'I'll tell Maisie ye had to dive, to get set up and all. Go on, on.'

Ruby danced on the balls of her feet, then settled. The patient look never left Bill's face, gazing at us from behind the front-windscreen of the van.

'Look, when you get her fixed up, why don't you come and join us? We'll have a drink. You and Bill can do a bit of bonding and all that.'

'Yeh, right. The cop and the jazz musician. Not a common combo.'

'Wise up, Eddie. You need to get over yourself. It'd do you good to get drunk.'

She kissed me on the cheek, a benediction that warmed me. She climbed into the van and Bill waved as he pulled off. I waved after them and felt tears well up in my eyes.

'They away?' Maisie asked, when she came out. 'That Ruby never has a minute now she has her Bugler Bill. No stopping her now. What are you crying for, you big wean?'

She pulled a handkerchief out of her bag and passed it to me.

'Christ, you'd better come back with me, so. Get yourself settled. Was there something in your curry? Too hot, was it? Imagine, Josie Donnelly out eating curry with a gang. It's her book club, she says. You never know, do you. She was a right dunce and we at school. Still, she did capture Fisher Sweeney and held on to him for forty years, 'til the smoking and the drinking caught up with him.'

The taxi came and we headed to Maisie's house. The plan had been for me to look after her. The roles reversed, as smoothly as two tango dancers move round each other.

I composed myself in the taxi. Maisie made tea, less formally than usual. Two plain mugs, two tea bags, milk from a carton. No scones, biscuits or treats. We sat upright in straight-backed chairs, my aunt opposite me, lifting the tea-bag out of her mug and tossing it from the spoon over her shoulder, directly on to the stainless steel draining board. I'd prepared myself for a dressing down, a pep talk, an evaluation, a heart-to-heart, an exhortation, a captain's half-time speech, whatever Maisie planned to deliver. None of the above came. She gave me a bollocking. Both barrels.

'Look at the state of you. Give me back me hankie there. Time you got hankies of your own. Look at your sister. Finally making a life for herself, though I hope he's not a go-boy. Some kind of showbiz fly-by-night. Plenty a' them out there, you don't have to tell me.'

'Was Fisher Sweeney one a' yours?'

Maisie didn't bite.

'You going to let that tay bag stew in your mug? Go on, then. Poison yourself.'

'It's grand,' I managed.

'That's right. It's grand. Let me tell you, young fella. "Grand" will not do it, not at your age. You had a good job.'

'Thought you didn't like me being in the cops?'

'What's it to you if I like it or not? It's a job, isn't it?'

'I still have a job. Same money. Same grade.'

'How long do you think they'll pay detective wages to a filing clerk?'

'I'm not a filing clerk. I'm investigating historical cases, for a research team in the legacy unit.'

'The past. You spent a pile a' time going into your own past and all it got you was grief. Standing outside the restaurant there, like the boy didn't get the ice-cream. Can you not be a bit happy for your sister, not to be always pulling her down and holding her back?'

'Jesus, Maisie, I never did that.'

I was shocked that Maisie had that view of how I got on with my sister.

'Well, what is it, then? Stress at work? Christ, you're lucky to have work.'

I sat there, stunned and took it all in. Strangely, I enjoyed it as much as I hated it. Who else could cut me with such love? Maisie continued.

'Don't give me that aul "stress at work" stuff. Boy like you could have any job he wants.'

'Maisie, with my record?'

'I'd say there's TV programmes would love to have you presenting them. Universities mad to get a gunman working for them. I'd say the Yanks'd love you. You'd be a novelty, God pity them. And you're smart too.'

Her slagging washed over me like a balm. I was now fully under her wing, safe and secure, as she castigated, cajoled, berated and encouraged me at one and the same time.

'How many a' dem fools in the cops can you call "doctor"? I know what I used to call them, but I suppose like everything else, even the cops got smarter, or else they think they have, because they have all them computers. You can do the computers, can't you? Isn't there loads a' jobs wi' computers these days?'

'Maisie, hold up. I have a job. There's been a bit of a reshuffle is all.'

'A reshuffle? A wholesale kick-over-the-bed, if you ask me. You'll go off your head stuck behind a desk, up to your oxters in books and folders and computers blinking nonsense at you.'

'Maisie. Wait. Didn't I do that for years and I studying for the degree and the doctorate you're so fond of?'

'So you did. So you did. But only because they had you locked up and you couldn't go anywhere. Some pair, I had. Ruby never left the house. She was like a fledgling never fledged. And you were never in the house. I shoulda locked you up then.'

A memory rose in me, bright as a whin-bush.

'Mind the day the seagull fell in to the yard? Mind?'

'A seagull? When …'

'I was only wee. Well, not wee. Like a teenager. I came back over the wall.'

'Aye. Your scamp days. Running and telling no one. You and that boyo Dessie Crossan and yeer pals, the cops.'

'Yeh, I was about twelve, maybe. Running, right enough. And over the wall I came. I musta been hungry. There it was. A right thing. Grey, black, mottled as a brindle cow and half as big.'

'It was big, right enough. More of a small dog, only with wings and black pearls for eyes.'

'It fell off the roof. Mind, up by the chimney.'

'Fell? Pushed. The Ma got fed up of it hanging around and said 'shove off' and gave it the elbow, the wing, like, and it plonked down by the coal bunker. Next to the monbretia, coming out of the cracks in the concrete, just starting to get a bit a' colour.'

'I nearly stepped on it. That was my way back. Over the wall, onto the bunker, into the yard in two clean jumps. I never trampled the monbretia.'

'So you never.'

Maisie was right. Fell or pushed? At least the seagull survived, as far as we knew.

'What did you do with it?' I asked.

'Me? Nothing. I was knackered them days. On me own, with you and Ruby. She was useless. You were worse. You'd have battered it. Or ate it.'

'Ah. Jesus, Maisie, I wouldna.'

'You et everything else. Then vanished again, until some scowling cop tossed you at the front door, rang the bell and sped off as fast as he could. She flew, the seagull. In her own time. She just flew off. The other ones cajoled her, swooping down and squawking, coaxing her and threatening her, 'til she flew.'

'And now Ruby's after flying too. No need to worry about her. She looked great tonight.'

'Aye, she did. Leading Joe the Blow along with his horn, God forgive me. You look good too, on the face of it. Only you never fully fledged. One scratch and you peel away blubbing like an infant. My sister got the best of you.'

A film crossed Maisie's face, as if an invisible hand had covered her with a veil. Her features darkened and sharpened, as if clipped and shaped into a wooden face-mask worn by an actor on an ancient Greek stage. Her eyes hallowed out and her mouth rounded and formed a wide portal of her vivid lips. The instant this transformation took sufficed to relocate me to a between-time, when my mother left and my Auntie Maisie emerged as the most important person in my life.

And with that her face clamped contemporary again, her features loosened and wrinkles repossessed her visage. She became my aunt, who dipped her chips in our curries; who worked all the hours of the day to put food on the table her sister cooked for Ruby and me; who took us on, when her sister fled this world for watery oblivion.

'Look here,' she said brusquely, charging on once more. She got up and went to the dresser, where she lifted down two display dinner plates of her fine, parian china. She placed them side-by-side on the dresser shelf, then retrieved a small package, brown as the tea we were drinking and tied parcel-wise with a slim green ribbon. She placed it on the table between us, and when she nodded permission, I opened the ribbon and folded out the paper to reveal an old photograph. The colours were almost as dun as the wrapping paper, but I could make out four people: a boy, a girl and two women.

'There's your mother,' said Maisie, not pointing or being

clear, so I wasn't sure who she meant, the woman I could see as the younger Maisie or the woman at the farther end of Ruby and me, separated from me by a strip of sellotape, yellowed as fly-trap sticky paper.

'The one at the end got ripped off,' I said.

'My sister, aye. I was going to give it to you, but I didn't know ... anyway. I'm going to give it to you now.'

'Who tore it up, Maisie?'

'You did, Eddie. You did. Just ... well, not long after. You know. It was a bad time. You were young.'

'And you stuck her on again?'

'I found it. After. Yeh. Torn, like. One piece, up in the room above. The other piece, the small piece, out in the yard. You must a' thrown it out the window. I stuck 'em together.'

'You just got on with it, Maisie.'

And she laughed, relieved to have shown me the photo, to have presented our severed foursome: her sister, me, Ruby; blood relatives, bonded by mysteries not even my detective training could resolve. I knew the people to ask, but I didn't have the questions.

'Go you on,' said Maisie, 'I'm grand now. Do you not have a girl or anything? Jesus, maybe you're gay, though I'd probably've known that. Do you have a fella?'

'Maisie, I have you. And I have Ruby.'

'And she has Bill. God love her. He's another boy never grew up. Thinks he's going to win a talent show on the telly. Did you see the suit on him tonight? The lapels were as broad as Shipquay Street and twice as steep.'

'I'd say he's not as gormless as you think. I might meet them, after. If you're okay?'

'When was I never okay?'

'Keep you the photo, Maisie. If I want to see it again, I know where it is.'

'If you're sure. I do take it down sometimes, for a wee look, just, I don't know, to prove it all happened.'

'What happened, Maisie?'

'You know something, Edmund, I haven't really got a clue. There was me and me sister, Alice, and our parents died and then ye came, gifts and a turmoil, all in a storm of winters. There was work and Alice and she heart-broken so hard she went into the river and I had no choice, with ye to look after. Until ye got big enough to go yeer own mad ways, 'til now. Jesus, I'm so glad Ruby's finally off me hands. I said it to Alice, up in the cemetery, before the dinner. "Alice," I said, "Isn't it great to see Ruby settled. Now I only have the one to sort out."'

'Meaning me. Listen, Maisie, I can sort meself out. What did she say back to you? Alice?'

'Feck off you. She didn't talk to me and we up at the grave.'

Alice. She talks to me. In my dreams. Alice. Saying her name unsettled me.

'Ruby done alright with the stone,' Maisie continued. 'You, too. It's fitting. I said to Ruby, I'll go down with her. There's no sense in buying another plot. Do you mind?'

'Of course not. Jesus, she's your sister, isn't she?'

'Only well …'

'Listen, Maisie. Some day, maybe, we'll have another chat, like tonight. You, me, Ruby. Bill even.'

'I seen Ruby getting him to pay for the dinner and all. Fair play to her. Start as you mean to go on with them fellas and don't get caught out. She's right there.'

I didn't tell her how Ruby saw the dinner getting covered. I was more interested in Maisie's reference to 'them fellas' and to 'getting caught out'. Another whole investigation had opened up in front of me, one that might lead me to my mother's story.

'You'll have to tell me about my father.'

'Ah, shur …'

'I'll know him only when I get his armour to wear. And his weapons. His *claíomh* and spear and shield. I might forgo the chariot.'

'That's another one of your stories. The boy again. Setanta.'

'The man he became. The nearly-man by then. *Cú Chulainn*. All the armour they gave him, he threw off him and it broke or he bent it sideways and useless.'

'Dechtire's his Ma, am I right?'

'You are. As far as I can say. And who's his father?'

'The long-armed fella? Or another fella?'

'We'll never know, but the lad never fully fledged until he put on the king's armour and broke the king's spear across his thigh. That's the kit that fitted and he needed.'

'The king, eh? The randy bastard, eh? You haven't a hope, you don't. Don't blame your father. Or me. Or Alice. It's only an aul' story. Get on with it.'

She stared right through me then, full lasers at 600 watts pulsing at 30 to 35 metres per second, sufficient to burn the eyebrows off my face and to leave my cheeks reddened as if by a slap.

'You know what you're like, you and my … you and Alice? You're not one woman or even two women. You're just women, like in a story, yeh. There's a chorus of ye. Or a host. Yes, you two are a host.'

'How much wine'd you have with the curry?'

'Ye're like Danu, the Goddess, the Presence, one and all.'

'Go you on now and have that ice-cream you never got. Dry your eyes, wee man. Dry your eyes now, there's a good boy.'

TWENTY NINE

I didn't get an ice-cream, but Bill Peoples handed me a pint of stout, when I arrived at the City Hotel.

'Get that into you. We're a couple ahead of you. Maisie settled?'

It was twice the number of words he'd spoken to me during the meal. A message from Ruby located them, all set for the finale of the Jazz Festival weekend. As participants, they were on the guest list, with perks.

'We're upstairs in the ballroom, but it's easier to meet you here and get you in. Ruby said you'd like a pint. We're on the complimentary wine upstairs. Plentiful, for a while, and drinkable.'

'So I'm a jazz musician now,' I said.

'From what Ruby says, you could be anything and anybody.'

That intrigued me. What lines had Ruby fed Bill Peoples about her family? We climbed the stairs, easing our way through the ascending and descending crowds, glee and merriment travelling in both directions, sampling music from nooks, corners, daises and stages throughout the building.

'Well, do I pass?' Bill asked.

'What do you mean?'

'You know, the Slevins. The brother; the big cop and the gun-man. The Aunty, so staunch even the republicans are scared of her. And Ruby, the most sought-after woman in the town, among people of a certain age, more broken hearts behind her than Billy Holiday.'

I smiled. The more he talked, the more I liked him. I laughed, as we reached the door of the ballroom.

'You're grand, Bill. You married me sister. You're not my boss. Here, sorry I didn't make …'

'Never you worry. It wasn't a big thing. Just a few musicians of a Sunday, round the back of a mate's house. We had rings and vows, speeches, food and all that, sure enough. A mate even pronounced us man and wife.'

'So you're not formally married?'

'But we are "husband and wife". I wanted to do it the whole way. I'm mad about her and I know I'm the luckiest middle-aged pot-bellied trumpeter in these islands, but she wasn't having any of it. She said "we sing together and that'll do us".'

'So, no certificate, no registration, no licence, no priest, minister or registrar?'

'No. Just Bell End Bennigan and his trombone in a Bishop's Halloween outfit saying "You may now kiss the bride and, if you don't, me and everyone else here will". I'm all clear, after the divorce and all, legal and friendly enough. Ruby said my family might be happier that way, you know, less formal. Thing is, my nieces love her, like a big sister. Swopping clothes with her and everything.'

We went into the ballroom. When I saw Ruby I knew there was no point mentioning the conversation I had with Maisie. She was holding a large glass of red wine, slurring and giggling like a child coming off happy gas, following the successful extraction of something very painful.

'Ach, Eddie, great. Thanks, Bill. Shur, aren't you the best? Over here, over here. 'Mon.'

Ruby and her party, mainly musicians, were in a corner, strewn like battleground wounded across three circular tables, amid a slew of chairs and instrument cases. There were glasses and bottles of red wine, scattered like skittles in disarray and bottles of white wine in buckets, dripping condensation. The remains of sandwiches and sausage rolls lay scattered among the bottles, waiting to be swept into black bin bags.

'Sit you there. Sit you there, aye. You can start on the wine, when you finish the pint. What do you think of Bill?'

The hushed whisper on the last question underlined the pressure Ruby felt. The visit to the grave to see the stone and the meal in Turmeric were very important to her. Did she do right by her mother? Did she do right bringing Bill into the family, even if she only half-married him? Were her actions approved? How often, even in our adult lives, do we weary ourselves offering proofs to our families, people, who if they really do love us, do not need such proofs? Ruby used the happy gas of the curry and now the happy juice of the wine to seek the reassurance that all was well and that she was okay. It did me good to offer her some of that assurance, though I doubt she took in much of it.

'Aye, great Ruby. The whole thing. Bill and the stone, some job, and getting Maisie out. She's grand now. Settled. She's delighted for you. And so am I. Delighted.'

Ruby beamed and pushed my pint glass to my lips, until I supped up. Then she took it from me and planked it on the table beside us. She dragged me out of my seat and led me onto the dance-floor, where we soon buffeted and danced in a throng of people, as a fourteen piece big band belted out 'In the Mood'.

'They're from Glasgow,' Ruby roared.

But it didn't matter, for Glasgow was here and here was everywhere and we were everyone and the confusions opened up by Maisie's answers to my questions were submerged in the joy of being with my sister, as if I was indeed at her wedding or even at my own; as if all we ever wanted was to be settled and if not yet settled, then dancing in a throng, carefree as children chasing blossoms.

Back and forward between the tables and the dance-floor we ran. Bill filled my glass of red wine each time I landed back at our base. The complimentary stuff ran out, so people kittied up and more bottles appeared. The band blasted on, a mix of jazz standards played at a breakneck speed and popular hits that kept bodies sweating, jiving, swinging and laughing. On we danced, in pairs, foursomes, raggedy circles, unwieldy groups, swirling chains and slewing congas. I jigged about on my own to Cab Calloway's 'Minnie the Moocher', calling out hi di hi di hi di oh, hi di hi di hi di hi, surrounded by a dozen fellow dancers, who laughed and clapped along. I'm sure they nudged each other, saying 'you'd never think he was a cop, Jesus'.

After that I decided I'd better leave. Last thing I needed was to fall flat on my face, at a public event. I was just about to move off quietly when the band launched into the big brass opening of Jackie Wilson's 'Reet Petite'. One of Ruby's friends, petite herself and brimming with the pleasure of the music, grabbed me by the wrist and dragged me right across the dance floor, well away from our tables, patently intent on making me hers alone.

I had just enough red wine, so that when she pulled me in close, options other than going off quietly, readily emerged. Then, as the kilt-clad bass player spun his upright electric bass, sending spangles of light across our faces and onto the faces of people at tables near us, a delicate golden glint, a mere fibre of early dawn light glimpsed peeping between clouds, drew my eyes to a group of four women, seated in a row, laughing and swaying in unison, as if strapped together into a fairground ride. The gleam that caught my eye came from the far end of the row and with each sway and smile my attention fixed deeper and deeper onto the woman at the end of the row, so that I disengaged from my dance partner with a muttered 'Sorry' and strode across to the four seated women, who continued laughing and swaying, until Karen Lavery bellowed,

'Good man, Slevin.'

When the music stopped, Karen stood right in front of me. I felt the heat of her breath on my lips.

'You live near here, don't you?' she said.

'I do.'

'And you got your windows fixed?'

'I did.'

'There'll be no more shooting.'

I hesitated, then said,

'Not at the new windows anyway.'

Karen paused. I feared I'd lost her, but she turned to her friends and said,

'I'm away.'

One of the women called,

'Ah, you got your own ride. Better be a right, good one.'

The others laughed and hi-fived her.

Karen lifted her clutch purse and faced me once more.

'You heard the woman.'

She took my hand and we moved into the crowd. Ruby's friend stood in a clearing on the dance floor, her hands on her hips and thunder on her face. I mouthed 'sorry' again and she glared at me, gave me the finger, burst out laughing and jogged back to her table, where she'd no doubt confirm to Ruby that her brother was gone and a complete bastard anyway.

The crowd heaved before us. Karen led me round the edges of the dance floor towards the exit. We easily negotiated the heave surrounding the bar and glided past the first floor lifts, as they opened to disgorge late comers we slalomed through, en route to the stairs. Two lads, intent on their phones, shimmied aside as we approached. At the turn of the stairs, Karen squeezed my hand and I squeezed hers in return. A bouncer I knew from the old days held the front door open for us as we exited.

'Goodnight, Mr. Slevin. Miss. Go safely now.'

We skipped down the hotel front steps, turned left, crossed at a red pedestrian light and raced to the riverside railing, where we paused to catch our breaths.

'Is the glass cleaned up off the floor?' Karen asked.

'Yes. Everything is exactly as it should be. And as it will be from now on.'

'I heard you had a new job.'

'Aye, a handy number. I might have to think about, you know, settling down.'

Karen grinned and bit her lip.

'Good man, Eddie. Not far now.'

Then she began to run, her cerise party frock flying behind her like the tell tales on a racing yacht, as if along, not beside, the river.

I ran too, laughing, my crepe-soled feet slapping on the tarmac, as I chased in her wake, keeping the river to my starboard and catching up with her, when she pulled up opposite my building. Two seagulls stood sentry along the railings, eyeing the dark surge of the water, brimming upon itself.

We strode hand-in-hand across the road. A car horn blared. The entry codes worked without fluffing. Our feet barely touched the two flights of stairs to my floor. Through charmed minutes of breathless, ardent and exhilarating undressing and embracing, we cajoled each other into the full-press hold we both sought, while the revellers at the hotel, long behind us now, applauded the final chant of the great Jackie Wilson song. Higher and higher and higher.

My phone sounded. I scrabbled for it. The room was dark

as a tomb. The back-light from the message-screen illuminated my face.

'If you want the gun, be at the broken bridge in ten minutes.'

It registered as 'number unknown', but I knew who it was. I had been waiting for this, as the seed pod waits out the winter and responds to the first heat of Spring.

The bed creaked as I rose up. I dressed as briskly, but not as passionately as I had undressed two hours previously. I was cold and quiet, urgent and singular. I armed myself. Springs clicked into place, the breech engaged. I was ready.

Karen stirred behind me.

'Where are you ... Eddie ...'

I leaned over her. I kissed the nape of her neck. Her breathing settled and she returned to her dreams.

I exited the building by the rear door, onto the lane behind the Chinese restaurant. I crouched at a dumpster, wreaking of discarded cartons, stale rice and evaporating soy sauce. Lights from street lamps and a flat above me showed the lane was clear. I checked my phone and timed a three minute wait. I tuned my ears to the night sounds. A rat rummaging in the dumpster. Pigeons, unsettled by my presence, grumbled, but remained on their night perches. Wood lice scurried, not knowing day from night. They sensed my heat and grew alert to opportunity and to danger. My phone vibrated on three minutes and I moved off, at a crouch, turning and reversing until I reached the junction with Clarendon Street, where I hugged the wall of my building, then, judging I was as clear as I could possibly be, I dashed across the empty street to the river-side railings. There were no seagulls watching for me. I ran beside the river again, this time against the direction of the ebbing tide, now emptying swiftly to the sea.

On and on I ran. Stragglers stumbled from the City Hotel,

corralling the last of the taxis. The Guildhall clock eyed me, as I passed. A drunk lay in a heap at the entrance of the Peace Bridge. Another urged him to get up, pulling at his arm, then letting it flop down, where it rested across his lap, limp as a clubbed baby-seal. I gave them a second look. They were the same lads I'd seen at the top of the hotel stairs, scanning their phones.

I ran on. My breath blew constant and regular. My legs pumped strong and vital. My gun bumped gently on my hip. I would use it when it came to it. I would get answers to my Todd Anderson questions.

I ducked my head, though there was no need, as I went under the top deck of Craigavon Bridge. I planted my feet carefully as I approached the old railway sheds, all disused and shuttered, then I minced across the rusted rail tracks and crouched fully once more.

Ahead I could see the truncated bridge, the muted blue metal arcing in aspiration over the water. The river itself lapped high on the other side of the wall. I was close to where my mother went in. Confusion unsettled me once more. One set of questions at a time. The gun. Todd Anderson. The file. The past. The case unsolved. The dead end.

Footsteps? Is that a squeaking shoe? A squeaking voice? Hulking figures? There? Sudden as an embolism racing down an artery. Two figures? Four? A blow and lift. A rush and toss. A high-flying toss. Air. Air. Height. The wall below. Air. Air. Too late. To reach. Water. Splash. The phone. More splashes. Gun, wallet, keys, over the wall. Topsy turvy. The cold douse of the water and now, in the slap of the tide, the chill of the liquid, the Ophelia-embracing water, on the surface the coloured lights dancing and reaching from one broken bridge to another, reaching, ever reaching.

Under, into ink as cold as glacier melt and twice as cutting. Darkness, total. Morrigan? Medusa? No. The last light of Dechtire, Danu, sister, mother, aunt, lover. A hand? A promise of the heart, leading further on.

Gone. Gone.

Lung-filled. Tide-swept.

Gone.

About the author

Dave Duggan is a novelist and playwright born in London, raised in Waterford, and living in Derry. He is the author of the novels *The Greening of Larry Mahon* (Guildhall Press, 1996), *A Sudden Sun* (Guildhall Press, 2012), and *Makaronik* (Cló Iar Chonnacht, 2018). His film work includes the Oscar nominated *Dance Lexie Dance* (Raw Nerve Productions, 1996).

Dave's theatre work has played throughout Ireland and in Edinburgh, Liverpool, New York and Afghanistan. He won the Stewart Parker Trust Award in 2007 for *Gruagairí* and has published a collection of plays written between 1994 and 2007 entitled *Plays in a Peace Process* (Guildhall Press, 2008). Dave has also written an imagined memoir, *Related Lives* (Guildhall Press, 2016), based on a set of family anecdotes.

Oak and Stone is Dave's fourth novel and his first with Merdog Books.

About the publisher

Merdog Books is an independent publisher based in Donegal, on the northwest coast of Ireland. The mythical merdog is a symbol of what excites us about literature. The raw power, beauty and danger of the sea are combined with the boundless curiosity of a dog unleashed along the shore.

Merdog Books publishes fiction and nonfiction titles that reflect our love for powerful and affecting storytelling, and probing, persistent investigation of important issues.

Merdog Books is proud to offer *Oak and Stone* by Dave Duggan as its first fiction title.

merdogbooks.com